THE UNICORN'S GIFT

Shara sang her Gypsy song, then raised her grey-green eyes in mid-chorus to see the warm eyes of the Unicorn peering out from between the rose bushes. Thorns did not pierce his skin. She fell in love at once, as was his magic, yet continued her song because this love, pure as she was, as he was, was not a demanding passion. Rather, the Unicorn's love was a giving sacrifice. He quietly stepped from the roses, foregoing his invisibility for the sake of allowing her to see him. Shara made her fingers dance along the mandolin strings, for the pleasure of his ears.

The Unicorn knelt before her, laid his horn across her lap . . .

Ace Books by Robert C. Fleet

WHITE HORSE, DARK DRAGON
LAST MOUNTAIN

LAST MOUNTAIN

ROBERT C. FLEET

ACE BOOKS, NEW YORK

This book is an Ace original edition,
and has never been previously published.

LAST MOUNTAIN

An Ace Book / published by arrangement with
the author

PRINTING HISTORY
Ace edition / June 1994

ISBN: 0-441-00062-2

ACE®
Ace Books are published by The Berkley Publishing Group,
200 Madison Avenue, New York, NY 10016.
ACE and the "A" design are trademarks
belonging to Charter Communications, Inc.

PRINTED IN THE UNITED STATES OF AMERICA

10 9 8 7 6 5 4 3 2 1

for
Alina
moje serce
and
the memory of
Mara

CONTENTS

PROLOGUE 1

NANCY 7

PASAJEROS 43

ANNUNCIATA 59

KARUS 95

AVENIDA DOLOROSA 135

FORTUNE 167

CABALLOS 201

SACRIFICE 207

PLACE 241

PICHILINGIS 283

ACKNOWLEDGMENTS 289

"If the true history of the world were ever told
—and it never will be—
it would be told through myths and legends."

DJUNA BARNES, *NIGHTWOOD*
OR "D-MINUS" OWENS, PH.D. LIT.,
LECTURING AT SYRACUSE UNIVERSITY, 1973,
"AMERICAN LITERATURE, 1920–PRESENT"
(A REQUIREMENT)

DISCLAIMER

It is considered proper to state that "all characters, situations, etc., are fictional, and any resemblance to persons, living or dead, is purely coincidental"—or words to that effect. However, such is not entirely the case here: several real locations and people who I like are presented in their own names because, quite frankly, they deserve a little recognition. And I like the Southland—a lot—even if I do see the warts.

LAST MOUNTAIN

PROLOGUE

How long it was since sunset he did not know. It was twilight, the sun below the horizon, and colors were turning to grey. There was a close, comfortable feeling to the evening: he could see clearly, the shadows posed no threats. There *were* no more shadows, it was too dark, greys blended with greens now.

Somehow, at this time of evening, sounds seemed clearer as well. Most certainly this was not true: in the dark his ears would have to be more perceptive of noises by necessity. Still, reassuringly, the rustling branches and soft crunching of his own footsteps murmured with familiar clarity.

Mulholland Drive stretched out before him, its ribbon of paved road scratched across the top ridge of the eastern Santa Monica Mountains. The sun had set behind his back: he was headed east, compelled, to face each morning's rising sun. He left the small stand of fir trees and crossed the asphalt. The click of his hard nails on the road's surface was almost impossible to hear.

Too loud, though, he thought, *too loud—I could have crossed in total silence once. Before.* But he was out of sight again without incident, so self-recriminations were unnecessary.

He knew these mountains intimately. The only real challenge was in keeping track of the changes that the developers wrought unexpectedly. A house sprung suddenly on matchstick stilts propped against the steep slope of Benedict Canyon, cutting off a path the deer had walked clear a hundred years earlier. Of course there was a way around the obstacle; the coyote had been doing their job even as the City of Los Angeles road crews pursued theirs. This new path was very faint still, smelling of scavenger dog, but it was acceptably functional. The green arms of the trees thrust their way before his white chest and were brushed aside accordingly. His scent would encourage the deer to follow, knowing now that more than predators had passed this way. Within a year, he knew, even hikers would discover this path, beat it down with their heavy-soled boots.

But no hunters—Los Angeles was lucky at that: with the press of humanity came the restrictions of civilization. Guns had not been removed from the city, but hunters had. At least hunters after animal game. Along this same spine of mountain ridge surrounded by the great city, only a memory ago, a group of people had descended into Laurel Canyon and massacred their like kind. He had not seen it, only heard the cries, arriving too late to help—and that had surprised him. Not the tragedy of delay, but the desire to help. He had not wanted to do that for such a long time. Not so actively.

A car horn honked in the distance. Without conscious decision, he stepped away from the path and into a stand of eucalyptus trees. Their thin bark peeled in dense strips, like skin being tortured. *They had tortured Cuauhtémoc*—he brushed away that short memory brusquely: if you remembered everything there would be no time to live forward. He could see the beautiful spread of city lights twinkling in the Los Angeles basin below his vantage point. The city's reflected lights killed most of the stars in the sky—only to replace them with stars on the ground. He admired them as he slid between the eucalyptus.

The low-slung Corvette slid up to Mulholland without effort; its shifting gears were almost a part of the background clamor of city noises drifting up to the ridge crest. In point of fact, inside the fire-red sports job, the driver and his passenger heard nothing of the city outside their windows: this was a warm October night, the air conditioning was cranked to full and the digitalized, CD, Dolby-perfect sound system was pumping out enough decibels to keep smiles intact and reality at bay. The tinted windows looked bitchin', too, all view out, nothing in. Insular security on an L.A. night.

The driver was vaguely familiar with Mulholland Drive, where sharp turns and blind curves were the stuff of dragracing and city legend. The Corvette took the corners with a vector-defying sense of balance. The driver was aided in this task by the strategic placement of road mirrors along the shoulder. He watched the next one carefully as his headlight beams struck its reflective surface, revealing the unseen road around the bend. Hot light flashed back in his eyes a second—the mirror had been knocked out of alignment—and then illuminated a stand of eucalyptus trees—

The Unicorn reared up on his hind legs, striking at the light with his sharp hooves.

"What the—!"

The driver's foot slammed down on the brake pedal with a force he did not control, jarring his passenger with a jerk that almost joined teeth to dashboard.

"Why'd ya stop?!?" the passenger screamed in panic, looking about frantically for the oncoming vehicle he expected to plow into them any second.

There was nothing reflected in the mirror. The driver swallowed breath after breath of conditioned air.

"It . . . a . . ."

The Unicorn knew that he was safest close to the car. He watched from behind a neglected hedge that had overgrown its mandate. The human's voice was clear.

". . . Unicorn!" The man behind the wheel was all of twenty-seven, his passenger twenty-five. The driver had been racking his brain for the past thirty seconds to remember the word for what he had seen, a classical education not being a requisite of study in the practical world the young professional inhabited. His passenger thought him a dipshit.

"If it was anything, it was a deer," the passenger said with heartfelt annoyance, sitting back in his seat and wondering vaguely if the stiffness in his neck was the beginnings of whiplash. "Get your mind back on the road before someone plows into our rear."

The road mirror was truly out of alignment: the image reflected now was that of the Corvette itself, bathed in the dimming glare of its own headlights. Of course it had stalled out with the sudden stop. The driver looked at the road mirror insistently, hoping to catch another glimpse of the horned white horse that had been so clearly caught in the glass circle.

To the Unicorn, the tinted windows and two bright "eyes" beaming through the gathering darkness reminded him of the Dragons that had once roamed Spain five hundred, no, eight hundred years earlier. Gone now, replaced by new monsters. There were humans inside that motorized "Dragon," the Unicorn knew, but he could not see them and, anyway, did it matter? This was not his Place, certainly not the Last Mountain, so all these were were annoyances or obstacles or simply things to be bypassed on his way to the Last Mountain.

He heard the little red Corvette Dragon sputter to life again, saw the headlight eyes glow brighter with the new surge of energy. Then the human-driven monster carefully rounded the corner where he stood hidden—alert and invisible—watching the threat wind its way along Mulholland Drive until its twin-eyed red tails gleamed down into a dip and disappeared.

The Unicorn began to walk east again.

NANCY

October in Los Angeles, properly named *El Pueblo de Nuestra Señora la Reina de los Angeles de Porciuncula*, aka L.A. ("El-Lay" to Angelenos), rarely comes close to approximating the fall season the rest of the country enjoys. This year was no exception: two weeks into autumn and the mercury refused to dip below ninety degrees until nightfall. Then a sudden rush of ocean breezes fogged over the seacoast area, while a gushing mountain draft swept down upon the eastern city borders—fighting it out in a mass of orange smog above the No-Man's-Land of Downtown L.A., where the powers that be continually conspire to join every transportation link in the Southland into a circle of auto-clogged freeways.

Not that everyone minds the L.A. October. There is always something smugly satisfying about watching the rest of the nation begin to chill its collective butt off with freezing rains and sudden snow flurries (always Montana)—while wearing a T-shirt and shorts, feeling the hot air curl around your naked feet. It is untrue that all Southern Californians do not wear socks—but it is safe to say that bared arms and legs are intimate parts of the Los Angeles lifestyle for eight months of the year.

With the price to pay.

This Saturday the price to pay was a city baking and heat-waved in the midafternoon sun. Downtown Los Angeles is essentially deserted on weekends, the towering office buildings erected in a storm of development in the 1980s having driven out the Skid Row living quarters and small businesses that were heavy in street traffic but low in prestige. Now you can drive down clean, barren streets, into the dark, cool caverns of a high-rise parking entrance, follow a short, security-guarded tunnel to a transparent-walled elevator, then ascend above the empty streets to a hidden floor of comfortable, undistracted shopping pleasure.

Only an occasional earthquake disturbs this Downtown serenity: although these new skyscrapers are cushioned upon shock-absorbing rubber pylons, no one can persuasively dispute the feeling of terror that invades your heart when floors eleven on up begin to swing in twenty-foot arcs. To date, though, only a few windows have popped out during the recent earthquakes, shattering with miraculous harmlessness on the streets below. So—the clouds continue to be pricked by new erections; offices and condominiums fill with nouveau tenants; everyone from the Mayor on down tries valiantly to ignore the fact that a heat wave in October is followed by an earthquake in California three years out of five.

Of course, outside the freeway-enclosing circle of Downtown Los Angeles the sky is rarely scraped and the streets take on more of the appearance of a city. The area embraced by Los Angeles is huge, especially if one includes the County borders—which almost everyone who lives here does, heart-, mind- and I.D. -wise. "I live in L.A." does not necessarily mean that the speaker resides in the city proper, particularly if he or she is addressing an outsider from, say, Boston, who does not recognize Los Angeles as being a "true" city anyway. Names like *Glendale, Burbank, Westwood, Venice, Playa del Rey* and so forth spring up in conversations between Angelenos—all are within the L.A. County border and id—but it is almost impossible for the outsider to know which ones are truly a part of the *city* per se. Many residents would be hard pressed to tell the difference. It should be noted that Los Angeles County extends from the Pacific Ocean east, north and south to cover an area roughly the size of Belgium. Within the "country" of L.A., several mountain ranges thrust their rough fists up into the horizon, creating a "hill" and "valley" division of neighborhoods; further subdivided into "canyon" folk and "beach dwellers," "THE Valley," "The Basin," "San Gabriel Valley"; fifty miles east to nibble at the edges of the ominous-sounding "Inland Empire."

Or you could live just outside the magic circle of Downtown, in any one of three hundred sixty degrees direction, to the neighborhoods fighting the slow descent that decades of neglect and economic decline have inflicted on them. Poverty in L.A. is not like it is elsewhere: once upon a time this was a land-rich area, where a person could be poor and still have a small house and a yard and even a tree (lemon or orange—the smell of fresh fruit fallen on the ground is also a distinct part of Los Angeles). Fear of earthquakes, recently

forgotten Downtown, kept the older parts of the city's buildings low-slung, rarely topping four stories. As a consequence,
even where apartment buildings push together in the poor sec-
tions of L.A., there is less of the oppressive crowding of brick
and concrete that characterize poverty elsewhere. In some sec-
tions, terraced hills look positively picturesque, dotted as they
are with wood-framed and stucco structures.

There is a greater sense of life here than on the Downtown
streets, especially on a Saturday afternoon. Certainly the three
thousand people sitting around the muddy pond at MacArthur
Park could be taken for happy weekenders. This is not the
crowded sensation of New York. People and cars circle, move
and hum with vitality, space. It looks a lot more habitable than
most urban centers of less-than-middle-level economic status.

Still, these were streets where Nancy del Rio was beginning
to feel defeated by it all.

She was almost thirteen years old. Still a child inside and
out, with not much time left to be one. Nancy's long dark hair,
eyes and complexion told of a Spanish origin—which was not
surprising since practically everyone she passed on the street
was Latino. Even the old woman calling to her from the second floor of the fifty-year-old apartment building held a look
of Old Spain in her eyes.

"Annunciata!" she called.

Nancy's attention was on the crack in the sidewalk, her eyes
focussed on a thought five thousand miles deeper.

"Annunciata!" the old woman repeated, not raising her voice.

"Nancy," Gloria Esposito said, nudging her friend and pointing up toward the apartment window. Gloria had been trying
to convince Nancy to cut her bangs and tease the front of her
hair straight up just like a certain popular singer who Gloria
was pretty certain she herself resembled, give or take thirty
pounds and talent. "Your grandmother's calling," she added
in a twangy Spanish that sang of her family's native Sonora.

"Abuela?" Nancy brought her eyes up. They were hazel
eyes, sometimes dark, sometimes a deep green. Her grandmother's.

"What do you want, Abalita?" she called, rising to her feet
and walking the few short yards over to stand beneath the
window.

Gloria watched her friend and lost interest in the conversation when thoughts of what would be the best eye makeup

to wear tonight drove away concerns for Nancy's bangs. *Let Nancy continue to be a* girl, Gloria thought with easy dismissal, *we got only two, three years left now to be a* woman. She turned her attention to the conversation between the three junior high cholo hopefuls on the corner behind her: Bato was describing the best way to tune up an eight-cylinder gas eater; Jimmy told him he was a fool; and Damian was looking glassy-eyed, so he probably was high on something. Bato saw that Gloria was watching them. Gloria quickly turned her head away—having already decided that either Bato or Jimmy looked good to her—to look at Nancy and her grandmother talking again. The junior-league cholos returned to their argument.

"I don't care: I'm gonna get a timin' *light*!" Jimmy declared.

"You gotta do it by feel, loco, by *feel*, like Lope y Los Barracudas!"

Gloria heard the name of Nancy's cousin, Lope, uttered with proper reverence by the three wanna-bes, even as she saw Nancy's grandmother, whom Nancy called with familiar reverence "her Abalita," toss down a small cloth coin pouch to the dark-haired girl. Gloria felt a momentary pang of jealousy at the long, loose hair that billowed away from Nancy's back as she leapt forward to snatch the pouch in midair. Then she remembered the difference between her own mature designs—and her girlfriend's childishness—and smiled a generous smile at the sight of Nancy chasing after the second item dropped from the upper-story window: a piece of paper fluttering through the air in open defiance of Nancy's waiting grasp. The page of notebook paper curled and dived, rose, then slid onto the ground with the definite intention of evading the girl's fingers. In the end, in fact, the paper came to a halt at Gloria's feet.

"Shopping list?" she asked Nancy, having scooped up the fugitive note and handed it over to her breathless friend.

"Abalita is cooking from a cookbook again," Nancy sighed.

"What's a cookbook?" Gloria smiled. "Your grandmother don't know how to cook?"

"She doesn't like only Mexican food," Nancy smiled back grimly. "We're eating Korean tonight. I've got to get her something called 'kim chee.' "

"Oh, I understand." Gloria didn't, but she figured Nancy's abuela was crazy, so why rub it in.

Neither one noticed the white van passing behind the three cholos, a panel truck, actually, like an old-style UPS delivery van. Without markings. Well, maybe stoned-out Damian did: he saw an old beard-face staring out at the streets from behind the windshield, sitting high on his seat and handling the steering wheel with the casual grace of the *vaquero*. Even the panel truck seemed to have an old-style personality, like a horse coach. Damian thought things like this when he was out of it. He liked drifting into these thoughts.

Bato and Jimmy both made rude remarks to Nancy as she passed, indicating that they considered her worthy of their fourteen-year-old attentions. Damian woke up from his stupor enough to ask her to say hi to her cousin Lope for him—a request Bato and Jimmy both immediately copied—then Gloria stepped between them and hurried Nancy along her way: these two busters were supposed to have attention only for *her*.

The problem of finding "kim chee," or any Korean food, near Nancy's neighborhood was not one of availability. Rather, it involved a matter of *access*. Vermont Avenue was only a short bus hop west, a central artery in the lifeline of that amorphous entity known as "Koreatown." Koreatown this year extended south along Vermont to Olympic Boulevard, from where it branched out east-west, a long string of small stores and mini-malls devoted to the buying, selling and ownership of Korean items—from Koreans, to Koreans, by Koreans. Abalita had never been to Koreatown. A chance invitation from an old friend found Abalita eating something called Korean Barbecue—"Meat! Meat! Meat!" Abalita had cried with glorious delight—and a growing obsession in sharing this discovery with her progeny.

Her first rude discovery was the price. When her old friend paid the bill, Abalita learned that the exquisite Korean Barbecue cost an arm and a leg. This dinner invitation, in fact, was the bonus side of being a winner of the California State Lottery. It would have been nice to report that Abalita's old friend had been a multimillion-dollar winner, but he wasn't. A winner nevertheless, "Mr. Will" took his modest winnings and ate out at a different restaurant for the next seven straight months—before dying of a heart attack in his sleep thirty happy pounds overweight for his sixty-year-old, divorced, single man's frame. Abalita burned a candle for him at the church, set out a bottle of wine on the windowsill for a certain other

Señor, and determined to recreate "Mr. Will's Korean Barbecue" on her own.

That decision made, with an admirable ignorance of the details of Korean cuisine, Abalita set about quartermastering the supplies necessary to transform a Mexican-American kitchen into an Asia-friendly environment.

At Nancy's insistence Abalita went to the public library and stumbled among the pages of inappropriate reference books until, somewhere between Jewish and Portuguese, she found a single, lone, Korean listing.

For Barbecue.

Korean Barbecue!

It could be said that Nancy's stock rose considerably in her family's eyes for having taken her grandmother in hand and putting her on the proper road to fulfilling her dream. Truth to tell, Nancy (or "Annunciata" as Abalita persisted in calling her) already stood rather tall in her grandmother's eyes. Her mother and father had been dead for eleven years. Aunt Victoria and her children, living in the apartment across the hall, respected Abalita as head of the family—even cousin Lope, he of Los Barracudas, would think highly of whatever Abuela thought well, and Abalita thought well of Nancy, and so—

But Koreans in Koreatown did not think so well of young Latino girls carrying a small change purse and showing little prospect of major purchase. It was not Nancy's fault that shoplifting and worse crimes were regularly perpetrated upon the Korean shopkeepers by the residents of their surrounding neighborhoods. It was not the Koreans' fault that the U.S. government required them to set up business in "depressed areas" if they wished to immigrate to America. It was not the United States government's fault that the typical shop owner from Korea and the average worker from Mexico and the everyday black kid from South Central Los Angeles did not have much more in common than fear, distrust and envy. But that's how it is, and it did not make going into a Korean store to buy kim chee any easier for Nancy.

Rather, it made it next to impossible—despite the fact that the first store Nancy entered appeared to display a picture of grocery goods in the front window.

The lettering on the display, however, was completely in Korean characters; meaningless. Interior shelves were filled with canned goods; there were pictures on the cans—the problem was that Nancy had not the slightest idea of what a kim chee was (or were?), let alone how it looked.

The glaring woman at the register counter did not encourage the Latino girl to ask questions.

Nancy backed out of the shop without a purchase.

The next shop, halfway down the block, looked more promising—here there were fresh vegetables and foods you could touch. Inside, though, the line of Korean customers come into the city to do their weekly shopping had three clerks hopping in several directions simultaneously. No one was overtly rude, but Nancy felt like an intruder at a family dinner. She retreated from here as well.

From this point her prospects fell sharply: the next three shopkeepers were openly hostile to the young Latina—or so their expressions appeared. They might have been saying "Welcome! What can we get you?"—Nancy did not speak Korean, so she would never know. She did manage to utter "kim chee" twice, which roused a shaking of the head "no" from one hurried owner and a cock-headed look of inquiry from the third storekeeper.

The Korean man sighed, reached under his counter and pulled up a small jar. Then he opened the jar and extracted wide hunks of red-tinged Chinese cabbage; a slight, pungent odor filled the room, making Nancy's mouth water pleasantly.

"Kim chee," he said. "Lunch."

He held up a slice for Nancy. She pointed at the peppery Chinese cabbage. "Kim chee?"

"Sí," the Korean smiled.

And then his wife walked in, and the smile left the store owner's face with a sad twitch. She asked him something, he tried to explain, then she turned to Nancy and said aggressively:

"No kim chee, no food. Lunch. Good-bye." Her husband did not smile at Nancy as she left the store.

Blond Annie was standing on the corner.

Nancy liked Blond Annie, which wasn't easy, considering. Blond Annie was Lope's girl, but she was also an Anglo. Blond Annie had masses of bleached hair piled around her face, skin-tight jeans and hang-loose double-layered T-shirts that practically spilled out one or both of her boobs at any given moment. She usually wore a bee-sting pucker of red paint on her lips, disguised her English-pale eyes behind an Oriental almond of mascara and possessed a set of (natural) long fingernails that had manicurists on Alvarado Street fighting to take credit for them. She was also deaf as a doornail and spoke like her mouth was full of food—when she spoke at all. Instead, flashing her hands like a manic magician and clicking her three-inch nails with the rapidity of castanets, Blond Annie spoke in something Lope called "Sign." Nancy tried her own version of it now, thrusting her hands in front of the surprised Annie as a way of grabbing her attention.

"H—I." Nancy wiggled her fingers into the appropriate contortions.

"Nancy!" Blond Annie cried in her cottonmouth slur. Her nails tapped a rapid tattoo. "How are you today?"

Oddly, from the very beginning of knowing Blond Annie, Nancy had found it easy to understand the deaf woman's hand gestures, even though her own efforts were primitive and slow. Annie read lips, too. Nancy moved hers slowly:

"I am trying to find kim chee."

Blond Annie shook her white mane, confused. "I don't know Spanish, remember?" she clicked, touching a long green nail first to her lips, then Nancy's, to add: "Speak to me slowly, again, and I will learn it well." Blond Annie's language always seemed so formal when she signed, much like Abalita's Spanish did when she spoke at home. Nancy liked that. She held up a cautionary, non-signing, finger to Blond Annie.

"No," she mouthed the words, not even bothering to add voice to them, "this is not Spanish. It is a Korean food, see—" She showed Blond Annie her grandmother's shopping note. "I need to find a Korean store where they speak English."

"Maybe in Korea!" Blond Annie laughed out loud, drawing a few stares at the unexpected voice—along with the usual leers aimed at her narrow waist and tight rear end. Her fingers and hands danced: "Will you want to wait for Lope? He is coming for me and he may take you to this store."

"He wants to be with you, not me."

"He is always with me."

"That's because he wants to."

"You are to thank," Blond Annie signed, "for the compliment and the pleasure. I would kiss you but my lipstick is fresh." She put a fingertip to her bee-sting lips and drew it away: it was wet red with fresh paint. She tapped Nancy's forehead smartly, leaving a dot.

"Here: now you are a Hindu. Go find your King Cheese."

With that she turned away from Nancy, who understood that Blond Annie did so from necessity rather than rudeness: she had to *see* the traffic to know when Lope arrived; she could not trust to a timely honk of the horn or other nonvisual signal. Nancy crossed Vermont Avenue in the opposite direction and guided her footsteps toward what appeared to be the entrance to a large Korean shopping mall. Some place in there had to sell kim chee.

Some place in there, possibly, but not through this entrance: the door was locked from the inside. A permanent sign said something in Korean, with an arrow indicating "around the corner." Following the arrow, Nancy saw that *all* of the entrance doors were locked, with the same sign pointing to some unseen entrance around the corner. Curious now as well as determined, Nancy followed the route of the arrow to its end: at a parking garage entrance. Nancy shook her head with the same curious expression Blond Annie had employed a few moments earlier—to the same effect, as her hair billowed annoyingly around her face. She pulled it back with both hands and tied a loose braid, watching a half-dozen cars, each loaded with Koreans, enter the parking garage. This, she determined, must be the mall entrance. Nancy started to walk down the ramp into the parking garage.

"Where's your parking ticket, girl?"

A smartly dressed security guard stepped out of the pay booth. "Only cars can come down here. You gotta go back."

"I want to buy something Korean," Nancy said, sticking out her lower jaw in the way that Abalita said would make her look ugly when she grew old.

The security guard stepped over to Nancy quickly; he was a white guy, possibly Anglo or maybe not. He left a handsome-looking Korean partner in the pay booth answering a question from one of the arriving drivers. "C'mon," he groaned sarcastically, "you can buy something Korean anywhere up and down this street. People in here, they don't want street traffic buying in here, meaning they don't want locals, meaning they don't want you. Get a car, drive in if you want: they won't like you, but I won't stop you." He tried to give her a clandestine wink, but the result was a disappointing grimace; he grew annoyed with his failure to convince the pretty little girl that he was an OK guy. "But I'm not gonna let you get hit by a car walking down this ramp!" the security guard growled with a sudden vehemence. "We got insurance rules, too!" He made it clear to Nancy that turning her away was one of the easier tasks of his day. She took the unsubtle hint.

The only consolation was hearing the security guard mutter to her back under his breath, "We got so *many* damn rules!" before returning to his companion in the pay booth. Abalita would have disapproved of the man's language, but Nancy appreciated the sincerity of his unintended apology.

Nancy heard Lope coming before she saw him on the busy street: the shock waves of the bass booming from his car stereo speakers drove through her body in a rhythmic assault. Lope said that even Blond Annie could hear it—through her feet. Nancy half-believed her cousin. Meanwhile, she had yet to locate his car: although she knew the jefe leader of Los Barracudas was somewhere around her, it was impossible to pick out a single car in the rush of hundreds that streamed across Vermont Avenue at that moment. The sound of the bass was enveloping, pushing in on her without direction—when Nancy realized that Lope and Annie were parked on the side street behind her. Lope wore his professional mask of indifference, eyes hidden behind sunglasses and face an Aztec blank.

And he drove his Barracuda.

A 1964 Plymouth Barracuda: cream white, fastback ugly, with a four-hundred-plus engine that drank gasoline by the bellyful and purred—even now—with hunger and power. In the six years since Aunt Victoria had brought her family to live near Abalita, Nancy had seen her cousin take apart every single piece of that car, rebuilding it with patient care each time: the interior of the brake drum, she knew, held no more than two weeks' grime and filings from the brake linings. The speedometer went up to two hundred forty-five miles. There was a rumor, Nancy heard it from one of the Los Barracudas cliqua members, that Lope had gone up to the Mojave Desert and found his speed with the wind there, touching the needle to the top *without making his engine groan*. The five cholos who followed Lope each had a Barracuda engine carefully rebuilt under Lope's inexpressive eye. Jorge said they called themselves "the only real Low Riders left in L.A.," although he did not say this in front of Lope—just like nobody called Lope's woman "Blond Annie" in front of their jefe, either. Lope's blank face was too scary to risk finding out if he was pleased or insulted. Only his eyes gave him away.

Which was why Lope wore sunglasses.

Except at night, behind the wheel.

Or with Blond Annie, alone.

Or with his abuela, Nancy's Abalita, at home.

His eyes were always sad.

"Hey, li'l one, Nancita! C'mere!" Lope called in Spanish with the thick village accent his father, brothers and sisters used. Only Aunt Victoria spoke Spanish with the purity of Abalita, but she had brought her family to live near her mother too late to counter the dialect of the village. Lope's English was just as bad, and Nancy was employed regularly in trans-lating car specs for him. "C'mere, Nancita: Annie say you need some wheel!" Nancy barely heard what he was saying over the boom of the music, but Blond Annie was waving her to come closer and she saw Lope push open his door to let his younger cousin slide in behind the driver's seat.

"No luck insid'?" Lope yelled over his shoulder as Nancy crouched her way into the cramped back seat of the two-door sports coupe. "Abalita gonna get her King Cheese?"

Nancy leaned forward and punched off the stereo: she was not afraid of Lope, even if he was Indian-cruel handsome.

"I can't get in," she explained in English so that Annie could read her lips. She told Lope about what the security guard had said. The eyelids behind the sunglasses crinkled wolfishly at the story.

"You wanna go in, li'l one?" he asked; the smile of the clever *mestizo claro* cracked his stoic Aztec face.

Blond Annie reached across the front seat to scratch him gently on the shoulder with a long fingernail. "Say it again," her fingers commanded: she could hardly read Lope's lips to understand his heavily accented, cholo English. Lope began to spin his hands in the air in response.

Surprisingly, although Lope spoke only primitive Spanish and street-heavy English, he Signed in Annie's "language" with an odd fluency. In a moment of grudging confession, he had said to Abalita once: "I do things with my hand, tha's all," and maybe that was it. Or maybe it was because, if Lope *wanted* something, he could do it. So far he wanted only his

Barracuda and Annie. He spoke to her now in a trill of quick-moving hand gestures, summarizing Nancy's exclusion from the Korean mall with a succinct formality that put the insult in its true light.

"Do you want to drive her in, then?" Annie asked, prepared to steel herself for the encounter.

Lope looked at himself with disapproval: he was wearing the polyester blues and dirty sleeves of his work clothes.

"No," he signed slowly, "they would win today. If Nancy goes in, she must win."

"I just want to get the kim chee for Abalita, that's all," Nancy chimed in, albeit with voice, not fingers.

"I take you to the supermarket," Lope answered, snapping the stereo back up to full crank, sending the Barracuda into a minor shiver of ecstasy as he goosed the gas pedal. He slid the car effortlessly out of the side street, across a seemingly solid wall of oncoming traffic, and turned left into the southbound lanes of Vermont. As usual, Blond Annie did not notice the thousand angry drivers honking their car horns hysterically, while Nancy swallowed her tongue with fear. Lope was wearing his mask of impassivity again and did not respond to anything except the solid feel of the Barracuda steering wheel in his hands. You could have turned off the music for all he cared: it was a sideshow to the display of his car and driving skills.

Even after the initial shock of near-collision, Nancy had to admit that the metal-heavy car her cousin piloted moved with a smooth grace. The shock absorbers alone reduced Vermont Avenue's pockmarked surface to a tiny, massaging ripple along her spine, not unpleasant. They glided south with the wave of Saturday shoppers down Vermont, the thousands of expatriate Koreans who lived in the outlands of Los Angeles descending on Koreatown to do their week's shopping among faces and accents they could talk to without effort. Nancy never understood this kind of lost feeling: reared in L.A., she had always felt the vaguely disorienting and familiar mix of the polyglot city to be an everyday part of life.

Lope did. He never wanted to return to his father's village, but he was frequently sick of the loneliness that seemed so much a part of this place. Only Annie helped a little . . .

"I love you," he let his fingers trace in the air, hidden from his cousin in the back seat, perhaps too subtle even for Annie to see.

A long green fingernail scraped gently along the denim seam of his pants leg: she had "heard."

"Ole," Lope said without flair, waving a laconic left hand out the window as he guided the Barracuda into a deft parallel-parking spot with the right. "Here's your King Cheese, Nancita pampita."

Across the street stood Plucky's, its huge "Super Value" supermarket mass tucked deeply into a vast parking field crowded with vehicles. Nancy was offended.

"It's just a grocery store, Lope! I didn't come all the way to Koreatown just to go to a Plucky's. They probably won't even *have* kim chee!"

"Gonna have *gringo* King Cheese in here, li'l one: better go get it quick or Abalita's gonna shoot you for bein' late."

"Moo' it!" Blond Annie laughed as she leaned forward in her seat to let Nancy out on the sidewalk-side door: her teased blond hair filled the air from seat top to roof, and the combination of hair spray and perfume added to that, forcing Nancy to puff her cheeks in little blasts of breath in order to escape the car without either a mouthful of hair or asphyxiation. Lope pulled the Barracuda away from the curb at once, leaving Nancy to hurry over to the corner and push the crosswalk button.

The pedestrian crosswalk signal, as par for the course in L.A., lasted about long enough for an Olympic sprinter to make it across Vermont Avenue safely—barring a sideswipe by those perceptive drivers who considered the rule "turn right at a red light after stopping" to actually mean "turn right and don't even *consider* slowing down!" Nancy reached the other side of the street in one piece—no mean accomplishment, but she was a city girl after all—then negotiated the next quarter-mile of parking lot with the selfsame look of alertness characteristic of deer crossing a crocodile-infested river. Hurried shoppers pulled out of their parking spaces with an impervious disregard for blind-side obstructions such as twelve-year-old girls. Perhaps if Nancy had been a grocery cart with metal edges capable of scraping a foot-long strip of paint from a fender she might have been given more respect.

"Good afternoon, shoppers! For today only we have a special on Plucky's tenderloin cuts: only—" The face belonged to a commercial-familiar redhead, ensconced in a television monitor that greeted entrants to the World of Plucky's: the omnipresent voice wafting overhead began to describe yet another Plucky's wonder. Nancy stepped deeper into the cold, overly air-conditioned bioclimate, pushing through a shiny turnstile.

"So what did you think of the waves?"

It was a sleek haircut talking to a muscled tan.

"Powerful. Powerful."

Both decked out in Plucky's aprons.

"Yeah." The sleek haircut effortlessly hoisted a heavy box onto his shoulders. "I was gonna go again tonight, but the car needs waxing—Lori likes that."

The muscled tan applied the final polish to a display of brandy bottles.

"You get the sheepskin covers?"

"Last week."

Twenty-three rows of handsome-packed shelves. Nancy lost track of where she was. She glanced down at Abalita's note.

Kim chee.

She felt hungry—maybe something else, too?

The coins jangled with solitary clinks: Abalita had put aside her spare change for a week for the mysterious "kim chee," no room for extras, no matter how hungry.

Lope was right; the supermarket had a huge Oriental food section. Apparently the Anglos had already figured out what it had taken Nancy all afternoon to learn: in Koreatown, it was not easy to buy Korean food. The kim chee was available in small, medium and large jars: expensive, a small fortune, and a large fortune, respectively. Nancy had no doubt that across the street, if she only knew how to ask—and they how to listen—the same kim chee could be bought for less. She selected the smallest jar and hoped that it would be enough for Abalita's "Korean Barbecue."

A small bell tone rang through the airwaves above Nancy's head. The redhead appeared on a television monitor at every corner of the store.

"Good afternoon, shoppers!—"

◆◆◆◆◆◆◆◆◆◆◆◆◆

M**onday morning bright sun-
shine. California autumn light and fine. Inside the window-

less walls the fluorescent lights made it just as easy to see as outside, but without the cheer or optimism of daylight.

Or the warning.

"Migración! LA MIGRA!"

The two doors—front and back—burst open with a violent rapidity. Inside the factory, forty-three men and women rushed for the emergency exit.

The Dreambreaker let them open it for him.

He was waiting there outside the factory, his Immigration and Naturalization Service Border Patrol uniform clean and— if not well pressed—fitting well. Los Angeles was well above the border with Mexico, but N. D. Charny, The Dreambreaker, had extended the reach of the Border Patrol investigation teams he commanded to include the logical destination of seventy per cent of the illegals who crossed into California. He even recognized a few of the faces that appeared at the emergency exit, disappointment now filling their faces.

"I thought you qualified for the Amnesty, compadre?" he asked the round-faced Mexican of Indian descent who lingered behind the others as they retreated back into the factory.

"I don't know," was the muttered reply. Charny held the door open for him with a courtesy expected of The Dreambreaker.

Inside the twenty-five-hundred-square-foot rectangle of space, a lamp assembly factory servicing a nationwide distribution to building contractors, Charny could see the plant manager making the usual protestations and disavowals of responsibility. "I asked 'em if they had working papers, they said 'yeah,' or 'sí,' you know they don't speak English too good. I asked 'em, they showed me: they're legal as far as I know. So why're you hassling me? This is harassment, y'know—" Or words to that effect.

Except that Charny already knew there was no paperwork to back up the manager's claims. The immigration Amnesty had been over a couple of years now; no more excuses.

No more excuses. The Dreambreaker advised the workers to return to their work stations and gather their belongings; they would probably not be coming back. It was time now for The Check. Charny allowed the plant manager to continue berating the other Border Patrol officers—they were subordinates, let the man waste his breath.

The Dreambreaker began the business quickly, pacing up and down the three rows of workers, past an occasional Resident Alien "green" card laid out on the workbench, past the more frequent, totally beside-the-point Social Security cards. Midway, he picked up a Social Security card and held it next to the face of its "owner": the name said "Ella Leiber," the face said "born in Chihuahua."

Despite the process, many of the workers looked at the man determining their immediate futures with a curious interest: they had heard of The Dreambreaker, it was important to know his face. N. D. Charny was a man in his late forties, clean-cut, athletic, of slight stature. But not threatening: in his uniform and bearing, Charny looked not so much like an American military man as a French Foreign Legionnaire—there was a dash to his movements, an "edge." A relaxed, dangerous quality. His movement among the Mexican workers was not oppressive. In some ways, in fact, it was reassuring—the inevitable had finally happened to these people, and it did not wear an angry or ugly face.

The Dreambreaker passed the last of the workers and nodded an OK to his men. The Border Patrol began to lead the dispirited men and women out of the building to the waiting transport vans, to be driven south for processing and a return to Mexico the next day. Three women had green cards; they stayed behind.

Charny stopped the man he had spoken to earlier at the emergency exit.

"Not you, compadre, you stay, too: your Amnesty application is still in process. Why did you run?"

The man shook his head slightly.

"I was scared."

The Dreambreaker smiled gently.

"Don't be, amigo: if they turn you down, I will find you. Until then you are legal."

❖❖❖❖❖❖❖❖❖❖❖❖❖❖

A small sound. Almost a tinkling of glass, but deeper (just as fragile, though).

A neglected network of canals and "reinforced" rivers runs

through the city. When there is not drought, in the spring the melting snowcaps on mountains five hundred miles away flush these waterways wild and full. But it was October, the dry harvest season (or, *once* it was the harvest season, when Los Angeles was still a pueblo servicing lazy ranches and groves): only a small stream coursed down the concrete bed of the near-empty canal called the Los Angeles "River." It was dead nighttime, the bright bold harvest moon long since reduced to a pale circle clinging to a mountaintop above a township in Los Angeles County called Altadena. Down here in the river, surrounded by a "Glendale," only the occasional passing sound of a car crossing the bridge ruffled the soothing spell of the running water trickling past the Unicorn's sharp hooves.

He let his feet shuffle slowly through the inches-deep stream.

The Glendale was east of the Santa Monica Mountains, the Altadena east of the Glendale: he should be near that pale circle moon by morning if he followed his impulse to the Place. The Altadena mountaintop was not his Last Mountain, but the Unicorn knew it was in that direction.

And safer, now that he could no longer count on the power to remain invisible with such consistent ease. Was that the power of the Last Mountain, to sap his strength? The Unicorn did not feel weaker, but had the others before their time ended? How many ever lived to pass away anyway? Certainly there were no more Dragons. Or Griffins . . . The Altadena mountain held a promise of safety—

Which promise had never persuaded the Unicorn before— as it failed to do so now. His compulsion to go eastward to the Place was strong; the urge to turn south stronger. This river, he knew from experience, would take him toward those towers of glittering lights in the center of the city's vast territory: it was the right general direction for his whim, if not perfect. He would have to backtrack some. Maybe not tonight, it was too late. A day—

Two days—

There was time still.

It wouldn't matter if he made it to the Last Mountain without finding her. That was a Rider's obligation, not a Unicorn's.

An elaborate graffiti portrait of a cat disguised the concrete tunnel opening into the cement retaining wall that had replaced the riverbank two decades earlier. The Unicorn raised his head, letting his horn emerge from shadow long enough to catch the moonlight, then retreated into the tunnel to rest. Perhaps it was too early to rest, but he felt tired and, besides, he had always liked the Cat's Head since discovering it years ago.

✦✦✦✦✦✦✦✦✦✦✦✦✦✦✦✦

"There is still one minute before the final bell and I *will* finish the announcements—"

It was called a "Magnet" School—a center for like-inclined students of exceptional talent in a particular discipline, also a lingering remnant of the forced-busing issue which had torn apart the Los Angeles Unified School District—until government budget crises forced educational cutbacks to such an extent that Angelenos no longer had breath left to face the problem of institutional segregation.

"—The school newspaper meeting is cancelled today,—"

Nancy qualified for the Magnet School as part of her identification as a post-elementary school GATE student: the "Gifted And Talented Educational" Program devised by administrators as a desperate means to pry some additional Fed funding from twelve years of reluctant administrations in Washington, D.C. The powers that be liked the concept of an elite, educational or otherwise.

"—there will be no late bus passes for this activity. The— Shut UP!" Three seconds of angelic faces. "As I was saying, the—"

Which was why, two years after elementary school, Nancy found herself riding a daily seventy-minute semicircle through the L.A. Basin on a bus rounding up economically deprived students like herself and depositing them in one of Encino's tony junior highs. Ignore the fact that she had no way of competing with the local students' lifestyle: this was an educational opportunity. Nancy tried to remember that idea as she felt the usual embarrassment of pulling out her multi-hand-me-down rucksack and filling it with textbooks.

"—those of you living—" The final dismissal bell gratefully

cut off the teacher in mid-notice. She stuck it onto the bulletin board with a thumbtack and a hurried "Read this if you're interested," rushing out of the classroom to cover her assigned watchplace in the halls.

Valley Junior High School was a large facility, well kept and clean, as befitted the upper-middle-class residents who dwelled around it. Nancy could have been unlucky in the selection of Mag Schools: even the prestigious University of Southern California experimental school was surrounded by a zone of gang-dominated, near-poverty neighborhoods. The trade-off was one of personal self-consciousness; it was hard for Nancy to watch her classmates being picked up by new, well-kept Mercedes, BMWs, Hondas and Toyotas. Once Lope had tooled by to save her the long bus trip back to Alvarado Street: the Low Rider's sleek Barracuda had seemed foreign among the bland and expensive cars; Lope himself looked poor, low-caste.

Nancy knew it was not a question of race or culture: there were Latinos in her school, many Iranians, many more Asians—but Anglo ideals ruled Valley JHS. Nancy did not know if she agreed with those ideals or rejected them. Surely she understood them academically. And she felt ashamed of Lope when he had appeared in his car.

But he was her cousin!

She would like it, maybe, if everyone did not see her and the other Mag students getting on the same bus together, the bus that said, "We are poor little minorities and you gotta take care of us." Nancy certainly did not want to go to the junior high school on Alvarado Street, where cholos would try to sweet-talk drag her just 'cause she was a good-looking freak and Lope's cousin and could drive with him in a gleaming Barracuda instead of a sun-bleached dirty hooptie junk car. Not to mention the busters, those wanna-be cholos who— No!

Nancy shook her head with the distaste of her thoughts: just to *think* of home was to fall into the caló slang of the gangs. This is not me, this is not Lope, Nancy's thoughts raced angrily, this is not my *family*!

"Hey, chica, c'mon to the bus!"

It was Maria Beltran, standing next to a different bus than normal. Dopey-looking Roberto was standing next to her.

"They changed the bus," Maria explained, "an' a new driver!"

I hope he knows the way—it's long enough goin' home without getting lost."

"Hey, you want to get lost with me?" Roberto asked in Spanish.

"You get lost by yourself and see who comes to find you!" Maria spat back in a rapid kick of words.

Three pimpled fourteen-year-old faces popped out of bus windows to taunt Roberto:

"Dogged you, pachuco! Man, she dogged you good!"

The dopey-faced Roberto gave Maria's left bun a squeeze, received a sharp wrist-slap for his efforts, and entered the bus behind her in unrepentant triumph.

"What you watchin' on TV tonight?"

"I don't know." Nancy looked thoughtfully out the window. "Lope might be riding tonight."

The bus started with a jolt, followed by the usual "OOHH!" from the crowd of excited teenagers.

"He take you with him?" Maria asked, impressed: she lived near enough to Nancy to know of Los Barracudas.

"Not at night—he's got Blond Annie, you know."

"He's loco! What's he want with that Angla maniqua?" Maria imitated Blond Annie's speech with a vicious precision.

"I . . . like her."

Maria gave her friend a condescending look, then felt her eyes widen with interest as Mano popped a tape in his boom box and filled the rear of the bus with Latino street pop. The words had an easy, sing-song quality that lent themselves to duplication by a chorus of eager junior highers. Maria jumped in on the first verse, while the boy in front of her used the back of a seat to duplicate the wham-crash! of the drums. Mano very seriously played the air guitar.

Roberto stuck his head out of the window and screamed "Hessians" at a bunch of blond rockers outside as the bus pulled away from the Valley campus, its Latin rhythm rocking in defiance of the neighborhood. The rockers debated sticking Roberto's head in a toilet the next day, decided against it, but enjoyed the idea. As it turned out, somebody else did it a week later and the action met with universal approval from the student body: Roberto was a jerk of truly cross-cultural proportions.

The mood of song and afterschool freedom was so infectious that even Nancy joined in on the chorus. She liked better maybe the música de salsa of Ruben Blades with his rhythmic politics and heartfelt questions—he was not even Mexican, the betrayal!—but this hot afternoon the street pop was strong and seductive.

Until they reached the Sepulveda Pass.

To return to the Basin, every day, the Magnet students' bus crossed south along the San Diego Freeway through a passage carved into the mountains. On the way up the Pass, ascending above the layer of smog, the sides of the mountains were dotted with Italianate villas, encircled by long rows of cypress stretching their fingers toward the sky. From there the mountains appeared almost wild, the steep hills kept green by heavy watering to protect the extremely expensive homes perched on top from the Southland's pervasive autumnal brush fires, when months of dry summer weather combined with hot Santa Ana winds to make every blade of grass a potential match.

Nancy, as always, remembered her history lessons when she went through the Pass. The houses were impossible to see in any detail from the moving bus, but Nancy felt that they gleamed in the descending afternoon sunlight as the Parthenon must have stood atop the Acropolis once, perched there impregnable, distant. From another world.

She had lost track of the new song the others were singing; Nancy twisted her neck painfully around to look past her friends, through the side windows, barely catching a parting glimpse of the place. She began to hear a new music in her thoughts, separate from the bus, so much a part of the place she was travelling through. She would have to wait, though, for the next crescendo.

The bus descended the freeway into the city: it was the beginning of rush hour; the San Diego Freeway had become a mass of automobiles standing still. The western horizon, where the falling sun signalled the shortening days, was cast in an orange pallor not altogether unattractive.

Within the bus everyone was tired now: some a little irritable, some a little "blanked out," listening to Mano's boom box with minimal attention. Only Nancy watched the outside world with any interest, a small flicker behind her eyes betraying a curiosity in what she saw.

Which was nothing extraordinary, but in its own way very graceful: the curving lines and shadows where the San Diego Freeway dipped beneath the bridge leading to the Santa Monica Freeway—

> Pull onto that bridge
> Soar
> Past the flat-streeted city below
> Off the new highway
> Past
> Always past
> Los Angeles is a city where you always drive past
> Even in a bus.
> Past an industrial area
> Up a road—
> La Cienega
> (Even the ugly names, "The Swamp," carry a romance
>   in Spanish)
> Up a new pass into a small set of mountains:
> Stark, almost wild,
> Dotted with oil wells.

The Los Angeles Unified School District routing of buses led its drivers a merry chase around the Basin, looping a wide area, depositing its Magnet students everywhichwhere and here— through the small swelling of hills that La Cienega Boulevard pushed aside, smaller and uglier than the Santa Monica Mountains, but a wilderness of coyote and deer and oil wells in the middle of the urban landscape as well—Nancy's bus reached the halfway mark on her journey home. Her song reasserted itself here, as Nancy's hazel-dark eyes hungrily devoured the sheer "differentness" of the hills. It was an idle hunger by now, of course; still avid, but dulled somewhat by familiarity.

Until her attention was caught by the figure of the Man on the Hillside.

It was not the man, actually, that caught her attention at first. Rather, it was her perception, against the vastness of a large expanse of empty slope, that something was *human* about it today. Then Nancy's eyes focused in. She saw, for a brief moment, the figure of the man standing alone and dark in the middle of those hills: he wore a beard, sprinkled with grey, and his face had a squint from the sun. It was impossible from the moving bus to tell if he was a large man or not, pitted in size against the hillside as he was. He looked strong and, vaguely, wild. Just as Nancy was looking at him, the man was watching the bus as it went by—

His glance met Nancy's.

The setting sun struck the pane of glass in front of her, causing the man to turn his eyes away in sudden reflex to the glare obscuring the girl's face. Nancy, too, turned her head away as the sun blinded her eyes.

The bus had pulled too far away from the slope for Nancy to find the man again against the silhouette of hill and sun. His song, though, filled her memory as the bus left the wildness behind.

❖❖❖❖❖❖❖❖❖❖❖❖❖❖❖❖

In the sunset hour you could always remember your places: where to go, where you have been. The last hour of daylight. The last days of life, after— how many years? The Last Mountain loomed ahead, distant, unseen as yet. It was there, the Unicorn knew that, without doubt. Behind him was the millennium: there, too, without doubt.

Although sometimes it seemed to start only five hundred years earlier . . .

It was not important to know, exactly, when a memory became a dream—or the reverse—but the Unicorn had a curiosity about his thoughts that sometimes made him question their reality.

When he could.

Instinct and thought were all the same to the Unicorn: a flash of meaning came into his mind, and he acted accordingly. There was no analysis: it was all impulse. Sudden, irretrievable, nonreflective. Some things he *knew*, without tutoring— there would be a situation, then a response. The knowledge, the response, could be shallow, could be deep: there was no animal with instincts sharper, no man that could reason so thoroughly. Yet the Unicorn's actions were not animallike, nor were the reasons characterized by human logic.

Every thought was simply *there*, from the moment he had been born nearly five hundred years ago—half his lifespan's millennium—to the chase of this Iberian morning.

Not that there was no room for experience in the Unicorn's mind: centuries of living, surviving traps, seducing virgins were never forgotten. Even the Moorish princess yesterday . . .

No, not *remembered* (to use the human concept for contemplated nostalgia), but it was *there*, in his instinct-thought, to be used—

—when necessary.

Of course, shaking his mane and lowering his horn to charge through a refreshing shroud of morning haze, the Unicorn never thought out when or what "necessary" was. Dreams, memories, instinct, thought—these came to him as the Creator saw fit. If sometimes from the outside it looked as though the Unicorn was lost in pure contemplation, well, it was an observation from the *outside*, wasn't it? Unicorns, Griffins, Phoenix, Satyr—no, no more Satyrs—each had his, her, *its* own being, separate from any outside criteria save the Creator's. And *this* Unicorn liked the smell of dew hanging onto the short hairs around his muzzle! Whew! It had been close, the chase this morning—but who would have thought that Moors would take up the Christian stratagem of staking out a virgin just to lure him? Truly, you could not trust a dark-skinned beauty anymore. Was it time to move back into the mountains?

The Unicorn could see the onion-domed minarets of Granada rising above the castle walls up there against the foothills and let a shiver of rejection ride down the surface of his skin. In this reaction he resembled the horses, those slow-brained cousins who constantly sought him out at the streams and rivers late at night, trying in their feeble-minded way to think of a request from the great relative who could outwit the humans who dominated them. The Unicorn, although impatient with their *animal*ness, let the horses try: they could hardly create a cogent thought, let alone a request.

And he did not forget that the men rode horses when they chased a Unicorn. Swifter, faster, more clever a Unicorn may be, but numbers could sometimes win; the humans these distant family let ride on their backs *were* clever. How else the staked virgin as a lure? How else the traps that killed so many? How else—his anger rose—

And then fell. The Unicorn could not stay angry long enough to hate the horses, nor even the humans. Hate was anger petrified—that would require the "reasoning" of men, not the instinct-thought of the Unicorn. If anything, tolerance and love continually reflooded his heart. He loved the women— Ah!—he loved the Moorish virgin yesterday, so chaste, innocent, beautiful inside (where it counted). If she was a lure, it was unwitting: you could not remain pure with conscious betrayal gnawing at your heart.

She had sat in the garden—built outside the castle walls by her great-grandfather a hundred years earlier, did she know?— happily strumming a mandolin.

A small thought of appreciation at the Moors' cleverness: the Unicorn remembered how many of the Christian traps had featured a *mournfully* singing maiden. But, of course, usually that was the maiden's choice; slow and reflective music was supposed to convince him of her virginity, make him overlook the duplicity in her heart. Foolish. Weren't Christians supposed to think of the soul first and then the body? A virgin was someone of pure intention, be she a whore in Madrid— how *did* he end up in a city that time?—or a noble-born lady of twelve scarcely touched by womanhood. True, the latter tended to be a more reliable bellwether of innocence (if you could not sense virginity like the Unicorn), but why were Christian virgins often so doleful?! The Unicorn admired the laughing eyes and modest smile of the Moorish princess, who sang with the mandolin a Gypsy air that danced through the garden's roses and tingled his own sense of humor. Oh, her Allah must be displeased with the princess' levity at Evening Prayer time! *That* was the moment the Unicorn chose to arrive, tripping in lightly so that no one would hear—save the virgin, of course—and letting her know that the music pleased him.

The seduction after that was easy: the princess, Shara, would do anything to keep the Unicorn by her, his golden horn once laid in her lap filling the young woman with such pleasure . . . !

All thoughts of instruction the men had given her were driven away.

Shara sang her Gypsy song, then raised her grey-green eyes in mid-chorus to see the warm eyes of the Unicorn peering out from between the rose bushes. Thorns did not pierce his skin. She fell in love at once, as was his magic, yet continued her song because this love, pure as she was, as he was, was not a demanding passion. Rather, the Unicorn's love was a giving sacrifice. He quietly stepped from the roses, foregoing his invisibility for the sake of allowing her to see him. Shara made her fingers dance along the mandolin strings, for the pleasure of his ears. The Unicorn knelt before her, laid his horn across her lap, to let some of his magic power surge into her. She continued to sing, dropping her hand onto his neck, to return his magic with a caress.

The men and women prayed to their Allah in the mosque behind the garden. Unvigilant for this brief half-hour, they were content to believe that the Unicorn had not yet come if the Princess Shara was still singing so beautifully. After all, had she not been instructed to strike a discord in the harmony should the Unicorn arrive? (So that, they lied to her, "We all may see this wondrous beast escaped from Paradise.") They did not—*could* not—imagine that, having once seen the Unicorn, Shara could not have sung false without a tremendous exertion of evil will (or thoughtless caprice, there was always that threat to the Unicorn's safety: the Creator did not rule out the randomness of chance and free will from The Design).

As luck held out, there was no caprice on the Princess' side—only that of Chance itself: a Christian hidalgo in the hire of the Moors wandered from the King's retinue at the royal mosque, bored with the Muslims' Evening Prayer. His responsibility to stay near his liege vied with an attraction to Shara's beautiful song. The attraction won out—halfway.

The hidalgo, Don Honorio de la Verdad de Madrid, saw through the mosque doors that the King was head to the ground in obeisance to his Allah. Don Honorio then judged the distance to the nearby gardens; he was able to skip quietly across the small plaza to the flower-perfumed low wall in mere seconds. A quick glance back—he could still see the King, the Evening Prayer was yet in full progress. At the garden wall, Honorio peered into the thicket for a glimpse of the Princess. No luck: her voice was clear—did she always quaver so with emotion?—one hand could be heard plucking the mandolin strings—wasn't there a harmony on this Gypsy melody, where was her second hand?—but it was impossible to see the King's beautiful daughter.

The Gypsy song was familiar, even to the knight:

"Good night, Magdalena, I fear I must go:
The sun is arising, the moon's sinking low.
The shadows are shrinking, there's no place to hide:
I've stayed far too long, Magdalena, good-bye."

Magdalena—a Christian name! Honorio laughed gently at the irony of the Muslim princess singing a Christian song to entice a Unicorn. Ah, the influence of a Spanish night! he sighed with content, retreating from the garden wall for a reluctant return to duty.

"Good night, Magdalena, I'm wondering why
Your tears stain my pillow, your tears fade the dye.
I've told you I'll return with the next setting sun:
I've stayed far too long, dear, and now I must run."

And why return so soon? Honorio demanded of himself: I can see the King through the doors, he is surrounded by loyal blackamoors. Does he need a Christian hidalgo even at his prayers? The song is too beautiful to leave behind.

"Good night, Magdalena, your jewels shine so bright.
Did you wear them before or was this the first night?
They would cost you as much as the price on my life:
When I come back tomorrow I'll make you my wife.

"Good night, Magdalena, you've held me too long:
The sun is now shining, the birds sing their songs.
I am certain of capture, but I cannot leave here:
I love you too much, Magdalena, my dear."

The hidalgo leapt the low garden wall without effort, leaving his King to the protection of his non-mercenary officers. Honorio did not want to disturb the Princess' song; he crept roundabout toward the center of the garden, where—as everyone who laid the trap knew—Shara would be sitting in her mother, the Queen's, comfortable wooden chair, padded with

cushions of down and made (so the merchant swore) of sturdy
oak preserved from Noah's Ark.

"Good night, Magdalena, will you whisper a prayer?
Will you wish me the luck to leave safely from here?
Someone has betrayed me, someone's sold my life:
I've stayed far too long, Magdalena, good-bye."

There were tears, then, in Shara's eyes when the Christian knight in her father's retinue raised the alarm at
seeing the Unicorn with his golden horn placed gently
across her lap, her hand grazing quietly against his nose.

Don Honorio shouted in uncontrolled delight at the first,
unexpected, sight of the magic animal—followed by a more
considered call to the mosque, where twenty archers chosen
for the trap knelt behind their King in prayer instead of pointing their arrows at the dark night's prey. He himself rushed
forward to grab at the beast—

To be gored for his efforts and cast aside with a fling of the
Unicorn's muscular neck.

The Unicorn looked quickly back at the Princess, sitting in
shock upon the cushioned chair: there was dismay in her eyes,
no sign of betrayal. *Good!* The Unicorn tossed his mane with
something of a conceited manner. *I did not want to be wrong
about her!* He made certain that he brushed her leg as he rushed
past, a parting gift to the virgin he would never see again. An
arrow whizzed harmlessly through the air across the garden,
telling the Unicorn clearer than words the direction from which
his pursuers would come.

Honorio gasped in utter pain, the Unicorn's golden tusk having opened a mortal hole in his lungs. A lesser man might have
fallen unconscious at once, dying in the immediate moments
after: Honorio fought for thought, sight, hearing—the memory
of the wonder he had just witnessed was too glorious to end
so quickly. The Christian knight needed to hear if they would
catch the Unicorn, to know that he had died for a reason.
Through force of will alone Honorio fought off the Shadow
of Death a long hour of agony.

And, because he did not die at once, Honorio did not die at
all, for—given the time to experience its miracle—the Christian knight learned what alchemists had long surmised: that the
Unicorn's horn could cure anything short of Death itself! The

hidalgo must surely have been mightily wounded—deeply, in many places—because an hour is an almost impossibly long delay for a Unicorn's horn to work its magic. Indeed, after the first goring thrust, the glowing ivory had already begun to heal the immediate places on the body where contact had been direct. That is why the Shadow of Death appeared so quickly, to grab at Honorio's life before it was too late: "If only the heart had stopped!" he later complained to the Creator. "Or, if the hidalgo had only closed his eyes to find respite from the pain in sleep, he would have been mine!" The Creator only nodded, without commitment, looking to the Son, who smiled, and the Shadow turned to one of the Evil Ones to commiserate: Lucifer was angry, too, for the mercenary's soul would have been his if captured this night.

The Creator's Son let it lightly drop that there would be a new Saint to join him in the future: He knew—He always knew and Lucifer did not—that this once-mercenary Don Honorio would now become a friar in the Son's service—Or maybe in His Mother's service; the Son had not looked too closely into the matter. (It was better not to look too closely into the activities of the Virgin Mother's pets: wondrous miracles and glorious beauty aside, they had created several scandals in the millennium and a half since the Creator had given the Son more or less reign over the Kingdom.)

That had been yesterday, when the Unicorn's garden adventure and all-night-to-morning flight had drained him of much-needed strength.

No, it had been half a millenium's yesterdays ago.

He stood away from Granada now, across the long plain of five hundred years that spread out from the foothills where the castle was lodged. Still, for all the distance, the Unicorn could hear the baying of the hounds' retreat behind the thick walls, dejected at having lost the scent of their prey. The plodding clack of the horses' hooves leaving the dirt road for the cobblestone streets of the castle city echoed less clearly to the Unicorn's ears. The sound of defeat.

Then another sound drifted through the centuries to alarm the Unicorn's sensitive ears—from the empty plain itself this time: the clatter of many horses. An army. Two armies—

The armies of Fernando II of Aragon and his wife, Isabel of Castilla, the land of castles.

The Unicorn shook his head and discharged the past in favor

of the future: the Last Mountain beckoned; a Lady Fair was needed. And a Rider. Would they find one another in time?

He did not consider for a moment that his Lady Fair already knew a part of his memory-dreams from her history books. The Moorish princess and the Christian hidalgo were lost in the story, only the next morning's war remained—that was the difference between a human's and a Unicorn's memory: love and hate. To the humans, in the Lady Fair's history books, this would be recorded in Isabel and Fernando's chronicles as the final crushing of their Moorish adversaries in the battle for control of Spain. An important conquest, it was not built around a major siege, nor a single, decisive battle—only a series of heavy skirmishes before surrender to a force of greater number. The Moors, despite ranks complemented by an alliance of Christian hidalgos, seemed dispirited and unprepared this morning, with no chance to rebuild their will in the following weeks of conflict.

It was apparent, King Fernando's advisors agreed, that the sudden appearance of their most Holy Roman Catholic majesties had been a shock to the Muslims.

Good, Queen Isabel's wise men concurred: This was Anno Domini 1492; time now to consolidate their kingdom and look beyond the Iberian peninsula.

◆◆◆◆◆◆◆◆◆◆◆◆◆◆◆◆

Lope, too, liked the música de salsa of Ruben Blades—he had played it first for his young cousin, Nancy—but the music tonight was motors.

Eight-cylinder, sports-formula motors. Six: Los Barracudas.

You did not race a motor such as this. It was unnecessary. From the moment the powerful ignition sparked the engine, a careful, controlled roar would fill the chest pleasantly. There was strength here, in one's hands, dangerous, cultivated strength, much as one must have felt as a *caballero* holding the reins of a Spanish stallion: speed was possible, or distance, exhilaration—or the sudden loss of control which preceded disaster and catastrophe.

All of which no one imagined, much less put into words:

all Los Barracudas knew was that Lope had guided them in rebuilding these magnificent motors, restoring their sleek, old-style metal bodies. And Lope would not let them screw up their cars with Low Rider tricks like peeling out at lights and knocking off the muffler to get a better crash of sound from the motor. He would not let them drive borracho on tequila or beer or touch a bud when behind the wheel: "Use grass I smash your ass," Lope warned. These were *his* cars, for all practical purposes, even if it wasn't his money that paid for the parts. Don't try to disrespect Lope's cars—or it end up like Victor's wreck. Victor sold off his remade Barracuda before getting into one of the violent cliquas—sold it to one of the hopped-up veteranos of the cliqua: it *disintegrated*, man, *died* on the road before a week was up! Nobody could point at Lope, but you knew, you knew.

The pale moon knew. It was time for the ancient pageant.

The fastback windows had been carefully washed: a gleaming, slanting curve of glass.

A second ignition fired life into a motor—even with the hood up, the rumble was one of *quiet* power. Tomas let his hand slide carefully along the fender, feeling the tremble of energy in the metal, before lowering the hood to click it down into locked security.

Lope supervised Bato's handiwork on his car—he was letting the wanna-be touch the jefe's own car!—watching closely as the thin knife blade ran along the edge of the chrome stripping, cutting away any excess metal adhesive that Lope's earlier attentions may have missed. There had been no earlier sloppiness, but Lope let Bato take the long stroke—for feel rather than for reason. He told the buster to hop into Tomas' car: over at the sidewalk, Gloria Esposito felt the thrill of having chosen correctly the weekend before, her Bato now inside with Los Barracudas.

There were three black Barracudas, each with a Latino face behind the wheel.

Before them, two red Barracudas idled impatiently, a different song blaring from the customized stereo of each vehicle. They were illuminated from the rear by the headlights of the Blacks: the slant-backed racing form of the Barracuda clearly highlighted. The silhouette of yet another such car, Lope's White, stood before them all. Six engines humming in the too-warm October dark.

Lope rested his hands on the roof of his White, noting that the others were now ready. Blond Annie was already sitting in his Barracuda, a new mask of face paint applied for the night run, her lips needing a touch from his. Lope smiled wickedly with happiness. He jumped in through the rolled-down window: it was big and wide enough to do so easily. The sparkle of polish and line was heightened by the assembly behind him. He punched on his stereo and added another Latin song to the street.

Six cars. Six songs—falling together with the balanced disharmony of a mariachi. Nancy stepped off the sidewalk to face the headlights. This Lope would allow her—and only her.

The "parade" of Low Riders began its stately exit from their side street, their engines in unison a powerful rumble of emotion, watched now not only by Nancy but by others on the streets:

Gloria, of course, hoping that Bato would open his door and invite her to join him, knowing that he could not, on this, his first trip with Los Barracudas.

A small boy and his even younger sister stopped playing in their front yard to watch.

The older Mexicanos, heavier with age and work, wearing their straw cowboy hats—

Dopey Roberto from the school bus—

Maria, come to gossip with Nancy, maybe do homework—

Abalita, grandmother to the girl and the driver, leaning from her window—

All looking with some admiration, probably some envy.

Victor—he now of the violent cliqua—watched with the jealousy of the lost lover—but who would take on Lope? Locos Barracudas y Lope y his pendeja Angla!

Some pride—

And Nancy.

She stood in the middle of the street, watching the parade come toward her, lit first by the white lead of Lope and Blond Annie. The White slid past Nancy: only inches from her face, Lope allowed a faint smile to break his mask of Aztec indifference; Blond Annie's long nails, now purple-and-glitter, drew a Sign of greeting in the air. The White leader was followed by the two Reds, the three Blacks. The twelve-year-old girl, still standing in the middle of the street, turned to see Los Barracudas speed up and disappear into the night, taking their music of motor and mariachi with them.

A single guitar—Jimmy practicing some hard-found notes in his family's fourth-floor apartment—crossed the street to Nancy's ears: it was a deflating simplicity after the brief pageant of color and sound. The illusion was gone. All that remained of the fantasy was the head-aching reality of the lingering exhaust fumes.

Nancy left the street and crossed up to her apartment building, closing the entrance door behind her, remembering to lock the iron grill that was so necessary to keep the hallway from being vandalized.

PASAJEROS

Anno Domini 1520. The words meant nothing to the Unicorn; he only noticed that the carving in the stone was fresh. Every year a new Christian dedication to the Son, or the Virgin, or Santiago Matamoros—displacing a mosque, or whatever other Moorish shrine had stood there before. The horned beast looked at the smoothly sanded letters one more time, forgot them, and continued on his wanderings.

The Unicorn did not leave the safety of the Sierra Nevada Mountains behind easily. Granada, nestled in the foothills, had always been one of his favorite cities. But now, with the Moors gone these three decades, the magic beast followed a whim and the streams up into the mountains and back down again. South.

To the Port of Cadiz.

Well, maybe not such a surprising whim: he saw the Lady passing along a road below and followed her. Her coach with curtains drawn against the cold mountain air had been driven by servants wearing fine leather boots and soft cotton cloaks. The wind caught at the curtains and fluttered them back—to reveal her face and innocence to the Unicorn's incurious eye.

Then his heart had stopped—losing a beat in surprise—and his whim took over and sent him cantering after the coach. There was no hurry—at least for the Unicorn—and he took advantage of the humans' leisurely pace to enjoy the new smells that drifted up from the south. He felt he had never been so far south before, ignoring his birthing century in Greece, where Mediterranean breezes wound through the Thracian ruins of his childhood. That was at the beginning of the millennium, so easy to forget anyway.

The second hundred years in Italy had brought the Unicorn no further south than Roma (who would want to go further south than Roma?) with the tweaking Cherubs constantly begging him for rides (as if they couldn't fly with their stubby wings!). The Cherubs quickly tired of Unicorn adventures and decided to stay around the churches and cathedrals, playing in humans' dreams, so that the artisans would carve their figures in stone, paint their faces on wood. They were so vain!

Many, so many, beautiful virgins in Italy, though—the young Unicorn galloped about Firenze for decades gliding among the cypresses, hearing their songs, touching them with his horn. Some of them, to his disappointment, became nuns: dedicating their chastity to his memory, trying to explain the emotions they had shared together as if innocence and celibacy were the same thing. Ha! Where did they think the *Centaurs* came from, then?

For some reason, though, the Unicorn had always been drawn west—across a France that was mainly sad while he was there—down to a Spain, that had been very exciting on his arrival. Oh, the Moors and Gypsies, Christians and Jews! The Unicorn skirted their little wars when a conflict was flaring and listened to their contrasting songs with pleasure. This new Lady now—he had heard her called the "Doña Aline"—she was surely a bit of all of them. When the humans camped for the night at a rough mountain cottage, the Unicorn slipped close to the road to see her face again as she emerged from the carriage.

Dark eyes and blonde hair—a sharp tongue when she spoke to a young man (her brother?), but not cruel—strong chin and characteristic nose. Another human emerged from the carriage, to whom she spoke with kind, seductive respect. They were all so cloaked against the cold, the Unicorn could not see the details of this man—Ach! A friar! Something about the old man familiar, but still a rather useless religious to the Unicorn. Better to look at the Lady Aline.

Which was only a short glimpse, as it turned out. She, her brother and the friar hurried into the cottage, where a satisfying fire must have been shortly set to burning, to judge from the billows of dark smoke that coughed from the primitive chimney a few moments later. The smoke itself was hard to discern against the darkening sky, although a few sparks flew up with it to twinkle above the thatched roof. The travellers were careless and lucky with their fire at once: the sparks would have been deadly had not a fresh fall of snow drenched the matchlike straw roofing. The coach horses were led into the cottage by the two servants—obviously experienced in the ways of mountain banditry—a heavy chest following to the accompaniment of cursed (and ignored) suggestions to

"Let the thieves break their backs, not us."

When all that could fit inside the cottage was within, the door was closed and secured by a log bolt. There were no windows in the cottage. The Unicorn stepped up to the very door itself to listen.

"*I* am to look out for Father's interests in the New World, Aline! *You* are not necessary," the young man's voice complained, a resigned whine.

"They are *our* interests, too, Miguelito. And perhaps, if you had bothered learning to read, I would not *be* necessary: but there you have it, there it is, here I am, *there* we are going!"

"I could take Fra Benedicto to read for me."

"He is not family."

"I would not betray you," the older voice said.

"But you would not have the power to defend us, either," the Lady answered with quiet reassurance. "Miguel—and I—will have many decisions to make—for our family. You are with God's family, my confessor, you cannot do this for us."

"Others do."

The Lady Aline looked into the old friar's eyes and he felt his love push against his vows. "You are no longer Don Honorio, but my beloved confessor, Fra Benedicto: that is not like others."

The Unicorn raised his head with a start. The thought that was memory that was instinct that was dream heard the cry in the Moorish princess' garden—"Don Honorio is killed!"—and knew at once that this was the same man. An insane happiness filled the Unicorn's spirit, for though he would defend himself to the death, he did not like to kill. The knight had not died! And he was with the Unicorn's new Lady! The Creator had an excellent sense of humor.

So— The Unicorn pawed the ground with an impish glee. *Here* was a triangle to be dealt with: he needed only to separate the old hidalgo-turned-friar from the Lady . . .

It was full dark now, a nighttime deceived by the glowing white of the snow everywhere around. The voices inside the cottage echoed the laughter of warm food and a game of cards: Miguel had made his daily protest at Aline's accompanying him to Cuba, she had dismissed it, Fra Benedicto played peacemaker. The ex-knight even cheated at cards to keep young Don Miguel from feeling stifled by too close association with religion and learning.

The Unicorn's attention wandered: he was not cold—he never was—but it would be good to find a comfortable spot to sleep the night. Caves were always best.

It was while he was away from the cottage that the Lady Aline decided to step outside for air. A servant accompanied her for protection. He was a very good servant, a very poor protector.

The figures jumping down from the trees did not even bother clamping a hand over Aline's mouth: her scream curdled the crisp mountain air and broke through the cottage door with the same force that it penetrated the Unicorn's cave. The servant was knocked senseless immediately with a hairy-fisted blow to the skull. Miguel, Fra Benedicto and the second servant burst from the cottage an instant later, losing precious seconds when they mistakenly assumed that Doña Aline's assailants would be trying to steal the carriage. They also expected resistance, and skirted the carriage gingerly in case a second ambush was planned. Those wasted moments proved costly: Aline was dragged into the deep forest before they could rescue her.

The Unicorn was not so slow—but his code of noninterference in the battles of humans prevented him from helping the Lady. A code at war with his immediate interest in her. The Unicorn saw the dark silhouettes of men drag Aline into the woods. He decided to follow.

But first to watch and see what her brother and the old knight-friar would do: perhaps they were strong enough to help the Lady.

Miguel, poor Miguelito, was at once enraged and frightened. The first rush out of the cottage to save Aline had taken him unawares, leaving his discretion lagging behind inside. Now, facing the reality of his sister's kidnapping by brigands, fear seized him with the tardy power of a lover once brushed away and now able to wreak revenge. It was a reasonable fear: of the dark, unknown mountains; of the dark, unknown men; of his own dark, unknown emotions. At the same time, shame and simple boyish anger filled Miguel's eyes with a passion that cried, "This is my *sister*, damn you! Give her back!"

Then, of course, there was the inexperience of youth, which sided with his fear to paralyze Miguel with indecisiveness.

Fra Benedicto, née Don Honorio de la Verdad de Madrid: only an hour earlier Doña Aline had chastised him gently for having no blood connection, no chivalric allegiance to her family and, hence, no drive to help her or her brother. In this she was unfair: the "help" she referred to was that of the Design, the Ambition, the Game of Power—Fra Benedicto had no allegiance to those drives, it was true—but in all other respects the old friar would die for the Lady Aline. Where Miguel stood frozen in soul and limb, the ex-knight pushed aside his religious vows and thrust a sword in each hand. He assessed the young nobleman with the objectivity of a fighting hidalgo used to protecting his own back.

"Miguelito," he said quietly, "your first duty is to preserve at least one of your father's children for the mission to the New World: gather the two servants near you—see, Juan is already on his feet again—and do not separate. Reload the carriage, harness the horses. Have them ready to flee at a moment's notice. I will follow the bandits' tracks; it is easy in this snow."

Miguel did not object to the usurping of command or the command itself. But he was not without concern, either: the friar was old.

"You will recapture Aline yourself, Fra Benedicto? I think that is impossible!"

Fra Benedicto tried to judge the young hidalgo's promise, found it impossible: no one could foretell what a man would do in battle, run or fight, triumph or fall.

"I will find where they camp, Don Miguel," he nodded with respect, deciding to give his Lady's brother the benefit of doubt. "They will not travel far in this snow—it is possible, even, that this cottage is their hideout of a normal evening. I will follow them, confirm that Doña Aline is safe, and then return"—he looked at the two servants, seeing the desire for revenge growing in the beaten Juan's eyes—"for your help."

He turned away from the grateful Miguel at these words, feeling both the thrill of adventure and the damp wetness of the snow entering his bones. Fra Benedicto would have liked to disappear into the forest with brave strides, but the drag of the snow on his friar's robes (combined with an arthritic knee) made him appear more like an overgrown badger shrugging through the drifts. He stumbled more than once on buried roots. His muscles began to tremble.

The Unicorn decided to relieve the old man's shame.

Fra Benedicto's vows forbade boasting, but the thrill of seeing the golden-horned beast approaching *him* through the dense tree pillars was a source of pride that strengthened his weak limbs immediately. Perhaps he should have been surprised: but the old man was too enervated by excitement and concern for Aline to have room for any more emotion. One moment he was struggling into the forest, leaving sight of the cottage behind—the next moment the Unicorn stood before him, stepping silently toward the ex-knight with a singleness of purpose that left no doubt as to its intent.

And then there was the fact that one "spoke" with the Unicorn without words. Thoughts, ideas, words flashed between the two of them—the Creator had not endowed Unicorns with speech as given other creatures (not only humans could talk!); speech was unnecessary when communication could be direct and pure. The weakened hidalgo-friar knew what he was to do: he threw down one sword, tucked the other in his rope cincture, and hauled himself onto the Unicorn's back with a deft grasp of mane in one hand and a flopping leap that plopped his belly across the magic animal's back. From this awkward position the old knight settled himself upright and grasped the Unicorn's mane loosely in both hands. They rode together with ease, not so much a tribute to the Unicorn's gentleness as an example of the hidalgo's comfort on horseback. They had no trouble following the snow-revealed tracks.

This would be an odd situation, the Unicorn realized almost at once. His code did not reconcile interference in human intercourse—but the tracks told clearly that the Lady's captors were the Wild People, and were they really *human*? The Unicorn did not know.

He did know that the Wild People were as unpredictable as humans, with an animal impetuosity instinctively naive and innocently violent. They look like humans, except covered by hair (not unbecomingly so). The Wild People did not have speech.

They were somewhat cursed with thought above the animal level, though, which created in them an anguish of failed communication again and again.

Which was why they turned to their bacchanal music and Unicorns for understanding.

The Unicorn snorted with anticipation of displeasure as he followed their trampled snow trail. The Wild People were as rare as Unicorns, more so in Iberia. They had been numerous in France, where, he recalled, rumor had it that Unicorns were

tamed by Wild People and *ridden like steeds*! This was enough
to inspire a Unicorn to a frenzy of goring anger, were they
creatures so inclined. What pompous religious ascetic, dried
out by decades in a monastery and hiding from the world, had
misread ancient texts and come up with *this* blasphemy? Unicorns rarely crossed paths after their youths, but the magical
creature recalled in flashes his years passing through France:
in a chance meeting with another of his kind, the two golden-
horned beasts came to the conclusion that one of the Wild People had been captured by French peasants when young, trained
like a monkey, and had probably nodded in agreement to the
stupid human postulations about relations between Unicorns
and Wild People in the hope of obtaining favours from his
masters.

Tamed—ridden like steeds— Pah!

The old knight had been wrong in his estimate that Aline's
captors would not stray far from the mountain cottage. The
Wild People had no use for such humans shelters and romped
freely through the forests with much speed and little regard
to distance. In one sense only were they held back this night:
the Lady they had abducted was not one of them, nor was she
dressed for long foot travel through snow. The Wild People
were forced to take turns carrying her on their backs. Strong
though they were, the Wild People had no discipline. After
the first round of enthusiasm wore off, they halted in mid-
mountain to squabble with their usual wordless passion over
whose turn it was to carry the load next and "Wasn't this a
pretty prize?" fingering of Aline's skirts and, as all gath-
erings of the Wild People end, to find resolution in the evening's enterprise in the solace and exhilaration of music and
dance. So, far away from the cottage as they were by human
standards, the Wild People's flight with the Lady Aline was
still very close by Unicorn reckoning.

Doña Aline, naturally, viewed the hurried journey with a
less dispassionate eye: her dress was shredded to tatters by
the clawing tree branches that her scampering captors failed
to notice were striking her while she was carried on their
backs, even as they ducked their bodies to avoid such collisions. Her face was somewhat spared—but only because her
now-bloodied right hand had been left free, and she used it
as a shield. Aline's ribs carried the bruises a piece of luggage
might show at the end of a trip's bouncing.

For all that, Aline was not as frightened as she was made curious by her plight. It had all happened too quickly, this dropping from the trees—capture—flight. Perhaps later fear would set in, when there was time to worry about the situation. For now, the Lady had her thoughts full concentrating upon the tricks and techniques of moment-to-moment existence.

And perhaps she would never be afraid: the daughter of Conde Rodrigo inherited his discerning eye for situation—which gave the battered captive solace now as she evaluated the hairy creatures who spoke not a word and fought, first over possession of her, then over rejection of her. When finally a strangely shaped flute was produced—it reminded her of a painting of the Greek demigod Pan's flute (she did not know these were his cousin descendants)—Aline was not surprised, but pleased, to hear the lively notes disrupt her captors' argument with cheer-producing melody.

The Wild People burst into a fit of dance then: wild, anarchic dance, befitting their name. A second flute appeared, deeper-toned than the first, then a third, hitting an harmonic counterpoint. They were all three carved of wood, not reed: Aline might have been excused for mistaking them for sticks and thinking the musicians to be comical giant woodchucks gnawing on their supper, for so they looked, instruments and players. The dancers appeared hardly more human, bouncing from rock to tree to fallen log with the skill and speed of squirrels. Their bewildered captive could hardly distinguish male from female. She might have thought them demons, but for their eyes.

But for their eyes . . .

It was there, in the eyes, that the Lady Aline saw their humanity—and her hope. At whatever point the Wild People left off being human, whenever music was played it recaptured their souls from the netherworld of Purgatory and gave them grace again. A more severe Creator might have been offended by the Wild People's mad cavorting, their lewd display of breast and loin. The Creator's Son did not care, knowing they were a leftover from the earlier gods he had replaced, a bit too raucous to be His Virgin Mother's pets, but holding a place in her heart nevertheless. Aline, like the Virgin Mother, felt her face go flush at the sight of the Wild People dancing—then felt the flush enter her own heart and loins. She was truly sorry for the Wild People that they could not sing, and rushed into their midst with a loud burst of incomprehensible song, trying to leap from hand to hand in dance as they did.

The Unicorn heard the flutes long before Fra Benedicto, but as soon as the old knight recognized the sounds he knew as the magic animal did that they were on the trail of the Wild People. Man and beast let wariness fight off the music's seduction as they approached the dance circle: the Wild People could be thoughtlessly violent. Most definitely they were stubborn. And the Doña Aline was, after all, *theirs*. Communication with the Unicorn was one thing—the Wild People would be grateful to be able to "talk" *to* him, with one another *through* him— still, it would not be unimaginable for the Wild People to turn on the Lady's rescuers in frenzied defense of their prize.

Fra Benedicto fingered the sword's hilt: it was Miguel's weapon—the grip was decorative, hardly made for use. *No matter, really,* he reflected. *The Wild People will not have swords, technique will not come into play.*

Numbers will, the Unicorn commented.

Do they you use wood for clubs? Or sticks for missiles? the ex-soldier wondered.

Only their hands.

Oh . . . You will carry her away swiftly if it is necessary, then? While I hold them back?

We are here for her.

The friar-hidalgo was reassured of the Unicorn's honor. Fra Benedicto was supposed to make a short prayer of peace with God now, but forgot. The music sounded very close, wicked flutes and pumping rhythms, as the Wild People clapped their hands and stamped their feet against hollow logs. After a moment's uncertainty, both the Unicorn and the man suddenly understood what they had been listening to for the past quarter-hour—the Lady Aline was singing!

The Wild People did not use fire—Uncle Pan had promised Zeus never to pull a Prometheus trick with the Olympian Gods' power, so the gift remained only a possession of humans and Dragons; the rescuers' approach to the dance circle was guided only by their ears. No bright circle of bonfire beckoned. No springing silhouettes danced around the musicians, hand in hand with the captive Singer. Fortunately, the moon was full, reflecting off the snow with a bright glow. The Wild People had chosen a treeless meadow for their revels: as the unicorn and Fra Benedicto drew close, the scene was as clear as dream.

"Ah-yiiii!" Aline cried in pristine song, whirling from fur-thick hand to arm; the Wild People could make no sound from their mouths, but the flutes repeated the cry, the "drum" logs pounded the pulse. Aline danced as fast as the fastest dancer, a lean monster of fiery hair and stone-blue eyes. "Ah-yiiii!" she called again, spinning her shredded skirts to a flying circle, her feet scarcely touching ground. "Ah—"

She collapsed, unconscious.

The Wild People, if they are callous in so-called "human" considerations, more than make up for it with a sensitivity to their music. Aline's voice had become part of the Wild People's song: its sudden absence cut the music in half, dragging their dance to its knees. The Wild People were shocked. Even the sudden rush into their midst of the human on the Unicorn's back did not affect them half so much as the loss of their Singer.

Fra Benedicto slid off the Unicorn's back and fell to his knees at Aline's side without thought to the danger that might surround him. His sword, in fact, was in the way. He threw it aside without hesitation. The Unicorn, too, knelt at the Lady's side immediately, pushing his muzzle under her arm to smell the state of her health. She was a virgin—he had suspected as much! How badly was she hurt?

The Unicorn shifted to his feet, angling to lower his healing horn to touch her breast if need be, her forehead, wherever necessary.

The Wild People melted away into the mountain forest, the musicians deserting the meadow last, the player of the harmonious flute laying his stick instrument at the Singer's feet in tribute: tomorrow he would carve a new flute to capture her beautiful "Ah-yiiii." For now, knowing nothing of healing or human (or even their own) ills, the hairy player joined the other Wild People in leaving this mystery behind. In an hour they had forgotten her—although a replacement flute was carved with, for some reason, a new hole added to make a particularly attractive sound to please the Wild People's dancing hearts. But that would be the next day, and knowing the future was the realm of Witches, not Unicorns, humans or Wild People.

The Unicorn was ready to heal the Lady; she was little more than a girl, really, scarcely sixteen in years (though in Court her friends were all married and several with child), but the old friar bending over her stood in the way. The Unicorn grew impatient with worry—until he listened to Fra Benedicto's words and understood once again the human frailty:

"Ah, mi Doña Aline, you dance too hard! Remember to breathe: I told you this so many times: Remember—to—breathe. And singing, too! I have heard the nuns tell you that, when you sing, *remember to breathe*. No wonder you faint! And, of course, you have to be the best, don't you, mi Aline? The best dancer, the best singer—'The Lady Who Out-Danced The Wild People!'—Do we tell the world of your triumph? (Or better to keep it a secret between a Lady and her confessor, lest the asinine brains of the Inquisition confuse the Wild People with Devils and try to warm your feet over a fire. Eh? I think a secret is best, yes.)"

"Fra Benedicto—?" The dark eyes began to flutter open.

"No, sleep, my Lady: I know you are safe—the scratches will sting tomorrow and the bruises will ache, but nothing is broken and you are safe. Only, remember to breathe, my little stupid, when you live with the magic ones. Remember to breathe now, when you see—"

"Oh!"

Her eyes caught the Unicorn's and they smiled together. This was not the time or place for a seduction, but the Unicorn was not hurried: his Lady was exhausted, the old knight perhaps too close and too jealous for his vows. Besides, there was time. Almost five hundred years of time to go, in fact. The Unicorn was in his prime.

Miguelito was more than a little jealous to see the old friar carrying his sister out of the forest, alone. (The Unicorn had no inclination to let himself be seen by other humans.) It was, perhaps, fortunate that Fra Benedicto began to stagger rather quickly under the load—allowing Don Miguel the opportunity to rush forward, lift the weakened Aline from the ex-knight's back, and responsibly order his servants to carry her "At once, do you hear, at once!" to the carriage. As for the rescue itself, Miguelito was curiously incurious, once the story Aline and Fra Benedicto had devised was told: that the bandits were nothing more than poor peasants who, successfully stealing the Lady's necklace and bracelets, abandoned her in the forest with vague directions back to the roadside cottage. Fra Benedicto found her halfway, the story went, and when the delicate stitches of her carriage shoes dissolved, Doña Aline's confessor became her pack mule. Unromantic, tedious—a story without true adventure—serving only to illustrate Miguelito's oft-repeated point that Aline had no business accompanying him on this important mission to the New World on behalf of their father.

The Unicorn was intrigued by his desire to follow the Lady and, unlike Aline and Fra Benedicto, had not the opportunity to recuperate from the night's adventures by sleeping through the next day's journey. There were a dozen branches of road descending the mountain toward the sea; the Unicorn could not know which one their carriage would take unless he followed. Their speed was easy to match, only weariness made it difficult. It cost him little in strength, but perhaps—no, probably—dulled his brain a fraction too drastically. That was the only explanation he could imagine in the centuries to follow to justify what happened.

The carriage made good its descent to Cadiz in record time: they arrived at a convenient hostel outside the city by nightfall. The Unicorn stayed near—and taxed his powers even more by remaining invisible in order to follow the carriage at close range when it exchanged mountain road for grove-lined highway and then, finally, for the edges of the port town itself.

It was in the hostel that Miguel, Aline and Fra Benedicto learned the news both good and bad: a ship for the Hispanic Indies carried room for passengers—and that ship was leaving at first dawn. The next ship would be . . . whenever. This was important: Conde Rodrigo was counting on the speed and discretion of his children to secure an investment in the freebooter Hernando Cortés' rumored "Meshica Gold," while he remained at Court and protected their position with King Carlos, son of the late Fernando and Isabel. The fabled mainland of Asia had finally been breached!—But not, fortunately, to the general knowledge of the Court as yet. Conde Rodrigo had made his own fortune by growing sugar cane in Cuba and playing politics in Spain, but his lessons had been learned in the saddle of a knight in battle: the spoils of victory go to the quick!

And now there was a panicked hurry. Places were secured on the ship, but provisions had to be located, purchased and stowed aboard before first light. Despite sleeping most of the day's trip, none of the travellers could lay claim to feeling refreshed and clear-minded as they rushed about Cadiz, waking merchants with midnight demands to open warehouses and accept good Castilian currency in exchange for decent merchandise.

It was this last hour that betrayed the Unicorn. A ship before departure is a busy, hectic place, but the sailing vessels of these early days were small, the crews smaller. Six men up in the rigging unfurled sails in the dark, working by feel and experience, unable to see the deck below them in this late medieval world where city lights had not yet grown so bright as to blot out the stars. The captain was in his cabin, carefully demanding of the port navigator the latest information on tides and shifting shoals that could beach his ship prematurely on its voyage, were he so careless as to ignore the local waters' dangers. Other crew were below deck, shifting cargo and securing it as it arrived—it was almost all there by now—lashing the water casks securely so that two weeks out to sea they would not belatedly discover that their precious sources of drinkable liquid had rolled and cracked and leaked and left them dying of thirst in the middle of the desert ocean.

In fact, for long minutes, only the Lady Aline stood on deck, under the pale light of a small lantern, carefully checking casks of grain and salted meat against a hastily written list of supplies purchased. The Unicorn saw her clearly under that light. His wearied, trembling legs began to prance with anticipation even as he knew that he was too tired to meet with her again this fast departing night. He was very tired, and hungry, and when the seven horses were led aboard by a sleepy groom, tied tail to nose harness, the Unicorn understood at once where he could find food and rest and be near the Lady altogether. Staying invisible was not difficult. There was even no need to tread lightly: his footsteps drummed along the wooden gangplank in unison with the horses' plodding hooves as they crossed onto the ship.

Aline felt a warm glow pass by her shoulder, a moment of unexplained enjoyment fill her breast, briefly, before leaving her to look up from the list, catching at her breath: she had forgotten to breathe. Just then Miguelito and Fra Benedicto appeared at the wharf, riding a cart filled with new provisions. Doña Aline deftly stepped across the gangplank to them and explained that, with only two dishonest exceptions, the food merchants had fulfilled their obligations.

On board ship the horses were installed above deck, feet hobbled and harnesses tied to a food trough filled with rough millet. The Unicorn was used to eating better—fresh, dew-sweetened grass—much better. Still, he thanked his cousins for their sharing and wandered down the hold to the bottom of the ship, where he could be certain of sleep among the hemp ropes and extra masts without bother from the crew, who were busy on the top deck now bringing the late-arriving provisions aboard amid complaints by the captain. The Unicorn did not care to listen to human grumblings. He would rest this day, see his Lady tonight, and be off to the mountains before morrow. He could understand why she would like to sleep here: the gentle rocking of the ship was a pleasant narcotic.

ANNUNCIATA

5:45 A.M.

The line stretched out from the locked entrance, around the corner, down the side of the Federal Building, to the back. Nancy found the tail end of the line first, arriving there five minutes before her slower-moving grandmother could search it out.

8:00 A.M.

Time for the entrance doors to open. A little push on the line—not much; the immigrants were too close to Authority to risk attracting Official Attention: too often Official Attention meant "Detain and Imprison" in their native countries.

9:10 A.M.

"Those here for Information only: go to Line Two or ask for a red ticket, I repeat, red ticket. Those here for green cards need blue tickets, repeat, blue."

The clerk from the Immigration and Naturalization Service—INS—voiced the rote instructions with all the enthusiasm of a school secretary, Nancy observed. Anyway, at least they were *finally* close enough to the entrance to hear the clerk's instructions.

10:50 A.M.

"—tickets. There are no more white tickets today; you will have to come tomorrow."

Sylvia del Rio, Nancy's abuela, was growing feisty.

"This already *is* tomorrow. I hope they don't run out of tickets *today!*"

"What color do you need, señora?" a tired-looking Salvadoran asked politely. Everyone on the line looked tired.

"Blue," the Mexican woman answered. "Green card problem."

"I thought you immigrated years ago, Abalita?" Nancy asked by way of (also politely) informing the Salvadoran that her grandmother was not another wetback.

"They lost my records again." A patient sigh: this was not the first time, probably not the last.

11:59 A.M.

The INS clerk reappeared at the door.

"The office will be closed one hour for lunch. There are no more orange tickets."

"Ohhh!" Nancy groaned wearily, leaning against the glass wall of the Federal Building and sliding to the ground. Abalita bent down and whispered in her granddaughter's ear: "Stand up, Annunciata."

"I'm tired, Abuelita," the almost-teenager complained. "We have an hour: let's sit."

A flash of anger: with the proud stiffening of her spine that had earned Señora del Rio the somewhat fearful nickname "*Doña* Sylvia" from her late husband, the abuela bent her knees and knelt to speak closely with her granddaughter:

"We are not campesino peasants who squat on the earth: stand up like a lady!"

"I'm only being practical, Abue—"

"Up!"

In none of this had the grandmother's voice risen louder than for the girl's ears.

"Why do I gotta come?" Nancy grumbled, letting her embarrassment goad her into insulting her abuela. Doña Sylvia, having won the point of honor, could afford to be gracious now.

"Because you are loyal to me." Abalita smiled gratefully. "To me!"

And then a moment of sad reflection:

"And because your father, my son, and your mother, my heart, did not finish the naturalization process to this country when they bothered to die in that foolish car—and now I will tell them here, officially, that you are mine."

The tired and restless girl was not so easily placated. "They already know I am here!" Nancy said testily.

"That's right. And they know I am here for twenty years—until they notice they cannot find anything about me in their records. Do you know you are not 'real' until they have a record on you?"

"I'm real!" Faced with this new consideration, Nancy began to feel a little unsure of herself.

Abalita saw the look of uncertainty cross the hazel-eyed girl's smooth-skinned features. She played a very old and stupid family joke, running her wrinkled hand down her granddaughter's face.

"Hey, little one: why does my hand go down your face so

easily—and get stuck going back up?" She caught her hand on Nancy's nose. The two of them began to giggle.

"Do you need an orange ticket?" The short-sleeved man spoke directly to Abuelita in English, making his way back along the line, away from the door.

"They ran out of orange tickets," Abuelita informed the man, adding: "Besides, I need a blue ticket."

The short-sleeved man looked at Sylvia del Rio and Nancy with an appraiser's eye. "Oh," he said, unimpressed. "Green card, eh? I thought you might be an orange ticket. Well"—he turned his eyes to the Salvadoran, who looked away—"they might run out of blue tickets before you get there. If you need one, just go here—" He handed Abalita a flyer. "Do you read English?" He pointed to a specific paragraph. "To get a blue ticket—(I mean, for them to fill out your application)—it's only sixty dollars."

"How do they get these tickets?" Sylvia del Rio asked the man severely. "There is no charge for these tickets: it is for the first to come, the first to be served!"

The short-sleeved man was already seven people further away from the door, handing a flyer to a Thai couple who, indeed, needed one of the impossible-to-get-today orange tickets but had remained in line on the vague premises of hope and "maybe": maybe there would be *just one* extra by the time they arrived at the counter where the precious tickets were doled out, maybe someone would cancel, or, maybe, get sick . . .

1:30 P.M.

"There are no more blue tickets today, you will have to come back tomorrow."

But Sylvia del Rio had her ticket, the last blue ticket of the day. The old woman and her pretty granddaughter followed the blue line painted on the floor, clutching their ticket in hand, to disappear through a security-guarded door.

Past the door, they found themselves in a huge, cafeteria-like room. Lined on two sides by INS clerks behind boothed counters, the third wall was a blank, while the fourth wall was a ceiling-high series of window panels looking out on the sidewalk line Nancy and Abalita had just left. Tinted windows, impossible to see in. Looking out, however, Nancy could see that the line was still discouragingly long.

"Please go to the appropriate section—Blue, White, Red or Orange—and be seated. Wait until your number is called.

Green tickets proceed to Room Two-Twenty." The loudspeaker voice was clear and impersonal; Nancy marvelled at how the same lack of human expression could be conveyed in the three foreign-language translations that followed. Especially in Spanish, which was so warm!

Lines. Everywhere lines.

Signs. Everywhere signs. Cardboard signs with Magic Marker instructions.

—Please have your I-30 ready.

—Identification required.

—H-3 and H-2 on Wednesdays and Thursdays only.

Nancy and Abalita found two empty plastic seats near where their blue line ended at one of the booth counters and settled in for the afternoon's wait gratefully: they were inside, they were tired, there was air conditioning, and they would see someone from Immigration to clear this matter up—today.

Behind them a small glass door exited to the sidewalk: opening only from the inside, it disposed of "done business"; that is, those applicants who had filed their papers, paid the cashier the necessary fees (one did not enter the United States of America for free) and had not been ushered any deeper into the bowels of the Los Angeles office of the Department of Justice, Immigration and Naturalization Service. Needless to say, a uniformed security guard stood by that door to make certain that those completing their transactions did not loiter.

Shortly after Nancy and her abuela sat down, a group of three tried exactly that. One man opened the Exit door to leave while his two companions "discovered a friend" still within the room. They wandered away from the Exit door; the security guard was forced to follow them at a close skip and explain politely that they had to leave *now*. The first man, meanwhile, remained at the Exit—accepting the handshake and ten-dollar bill extended to him by a bearded man waiting on the sidewalk—before ducking outside as quickly as the bearded man disappeared among the crowd *inside* the room. The security guard, bringing the two wanderers back, was ticked off to find the Exit door ajar: he read off the small Chinese woman who was attempting to enter through it in no uncertain terms of authority. "See?" he explained to the two men he was escorting out. "*You* waited all day—and these late-comers just try to jump the line on in!"

2:30 P.M.

"Blue Two Eighty-Three!"

Nancy did not hear the quick command, but Blue Ticket 283, Sylvia del Rio, did: without hesitation she deserted her grand-daughter to join a small line of four people. Almost there.

Nancy gathered up the scattered knitting, book, food wrap-pers and purse contents that Abalita had left behind—it was easy to be fast when you had someone else to pick up after you—rejoining her grandmother at the short line. They were separated from an array of three booth counters by only ten feet of linoleum and a strip of white tape across the floor. A handwritten sign was pinned above each booth: Do Not Cross White Line Until Called. Ahead of them a nervous Senegalese man in suit and tie was listening carefully to a Nigerian dressed in the long, loose robes of his national costume translate yet another improvised cardboard notice:

"Signature of full consular authority is required."

The caftan-clad Nigerian thought about the words a moment, then rapidly translated his interpretation of the regulation into French for the benefit of the more "American"-looking Senegalese. An expression of alarm crossed the listener's jet-black face.

"Non, non, non! C'est impossible!" he shook his head, before starting to ruffle through the handful of documents clutched in his hands, muttering in his native African dialect with panic.

The English-speaking Nigerian, whose name Nancy caught somewhere in-between the French and African as "William," turned to the two ladies behind him to explain with the shared sympathy of cattle on the same railroad car:

"He is very worried: they want a consul's signature, but his country gives only this type of document." William spoke with a sing-song grace, lamenting, "This is his last chance—no papers, no job."

"Next."

It was impossible to tell which INS clerk had spoken: more than one counter was free, but all of the clerks had their heads turned down to the counters. The Senegalese chose the booth manned by a black woman. William winked to Nancy's abuela: "Ah, maybe he gets a chance, at least."

He noticed that Nancy was more than a little intrigued by his clothing: with the nod of a born showman, William aban-doned concern for his African acquaintance in favor of entertaining the ladies. "A chance," the Nigerian repeated mock-portentously.

"But," he continued, pulling a deck of playing cards from a fold in his gown, "if it was only a question of chance, then I could have no luck: I am the thirteenth son of a thirteenth son; I was born on the thirteenth." He began to shuffle the cards nonchalantly in front of Nancy's nose, indifferent to her wonder: she hardly spoke to black people on the street—it just was not done—and this man was blacker than black.

"So I cannot believe in luck, can I? Maybe if I was born on the seventh I would have a different perspective." He dealt right hand to left four cards in quick succession, fanning them out for public view: all sevens. The cards disappeared into the middle of the deck with a deft tap of fingers. "But I wasn't, so I have to make my own luck, yes?"

Another quick deal—four sevens again!

"Next."

A red-haired female clerk stared baldly across her counter to fix on the Nigerian's back. William was oblivious to her voice as he reshuffled the deck.

"Or, maybe, thirteen *can* be lucky—"

"NEXT!"

"Ow!" William winced. "A voice like a rat!" He spoke rapidly to Abalita while holding out a playing card facedown toward Nancy. "What is her name?"

"Annunciata Cymbelina de las Flores del Rio," Abalita answered at once, adding to her granddaughter sternly: "That *is* your name."

"Annunciata Cymbelina de las Flores del Rio," William repeated, pointing his black eyes into her hazel green. "Let's see if thirteen can be lucky." He flipped the card over and dropped it into her hand, spinning on his heel to face the flame-haired woman behind the counter. "Yes? I was translating for the ladies, they only speak Spanish, you understand, and . . ." His voice was lost in a rush of intimacy as he leaned quietly across the counter.

Nancy—Annunciata—looked closely at the playing card William had given her: in the top right-hand corner was printed a "6"—in the bottom left corner a "7."

"Next."

"Our turn, Annunciata." Once more Abalita deserted the almost-teenager in answer to an Immigration command. She

proceeded to a third booth, where a woman clerk of indeter-
minate middle age took her papers dully. Despite the near-
insulting blandness of the transaction, Sylvia del Rio was
faring better than the Senegalese next door. Nancy joined
her grandmother at the booth to see the black woman thrust
his documents back across the counter separating them.

"These no good," she said derisively. "You go away."

"But . . ." The African groped for the words in English. "I
do not understand you. My consulate said—"

The Immigration clerk had no time for the foreigner's expla-
nations, threatening: "You better get outta here before I call the
guard!"

"But, I—" The Senegalese stopped, speechless: he could
not find the words to plead his case. Almost in tears, he
turned away from the counter and rushed out of the building—brushing aside the bearded man who had only recently
slid in the Exit door and was still trying to look invisible. The
man looked considerably more "average" than he had the evening before, sitting on the hillside along the La Cienega Pass.
Yesterday he had not cared who saw him, lost in the search
as he was. Today he wanted only to watch, unobserved.

Nancy and her abuela were encountering a different kind of
rejection.

"I'll take these, and these—" The dull Immigration clerk
sorted through the DEL RIO, SYLVIA documents, bored.
"You keep the I-Thirty and come back with the I-Seventy."

Visions of the day's ordeal pounded on Abalita's imagination.

"But this is *everything*, here, now! I have the I-Seventy, see?
Can't we do this now?!"

The clerk tried to stifle a yawn, failed. "No, we can't,"
she decided with a tired finality. "Go to the cashier, pay for
these, and come back when the appointment says to." She
turned from the counter and began speaking with another
tired woman at a desk a few steps behind the array of booths.
Nancy and Abalita stared at the woman's back an ineffective
quarter-minute, then walked away from the counter as well.

The man from the hillside tried to make sense of the scenes
unfolding around him, found that he couldn't.

He searched the room for the two Latino women again. He
found them at one of the small cashier's windows—where the
Feds were still winning:

"Can't take this check," the cashier said brusquely, her voice muffled through the pane of thick, clear plastic separating her from the public. She slid the check back to the disconcerted Abalita through a small hole cut in the bottom of the window. Her scalp itched; the cashier scratched it with the eraser end of her pencil.

"Wh-why not?" the old woman asked, stunned by the rejection of her payment.

"No telephone number. Next, please."

"But you took her check two weeks ago?" Nancy protested, sliding the rectangle of paper back through the window slot. The cashier shoved it out again.

"Internal policy. Please let the next person through."

"I believe you should take the check, ma'am."

Nancy, Abalita and the cashier all looked up with surprise at the intrusion of this new, male, voice: the bearded man spoke with a slight twang to his words. He nodded first to Sylvia del Rio, then to her granddaughter:

"I couldn't help but think I might be of assistance." He smiled politely to them before turning back to add to the cashier: "You took the check two weeks ago—policy doesn't change that fast. Why don't you just write down their telephone number on the check: some people have unlisted numbers, you know."

The cashier sized up the man at once—he was on the other side of the window—that was all *she* needed to know. "I don't have to explain nothing to you!" she smiled in thin-lipped superiority.

The smile changed to a grimace of anger as the bearded man pulled *her own* handwritten cardboard sign from the wall and held it flat against her window.

"Read," she heard the man quietly growl. "It's all written here, isn't it? 'CHECK PO-LI-CY: Must be—One: Local bank. Two: Have address. Three: Must have I.D.' " He slid the sign down to reveal his grizzled face practically pressed against the plastic pane. "See? Policy. Nothing about telephone numbers."

It was almost time to close down the cash drawer for the day—in fact, she already had: the cashier had *no* time for this fool nonsense!

"You better get outta here or we'll take away your green card!" she trumpeted oppressively, using the INS's Ultimate

Weapon. She was rewarded with an unexpected explosion of anger.

"You can't do that!" the bearded man burst out, his drawl now a pronounced accent of indignation. "You *can't*! I may be from Texas—and God knows we should have stayed an independent country—but we're part of America now and you—can't—do—that! You can't even *say* that!"

Despite the man's vehemence, the cashier knew Power was on her side. "Here comes my manager," she said smugly, stepping aside to let the heavyset (but not fat!) woman in INS uniform grey step up commandingly to the window.

"Get away from the window so the other people can go through," the manager coolly ordered.

The man on the hillside—Nancy began to recognize the grey-bearded stranger: he took a gulp of air, lost the anger from his voice (if not his eyes), and turned politely to Abalita, asking:

"I'm sorry, it is your decision: do you want to come back tomorrow and pay cash?"

Nancy saw that her grandmother's eyes, too, were filled with anger. "No," Doña Sylvia said simply.

The man from the hillside turned back to the cashier's window to ask the impatient manager: "Will you accept their check?"

"Get out of this building." There was no question of entertaining discussion in her tone.

"Then we will not move until you prove that the policy has been changed."

The manager's eyes now joined Abalita's and the bearded man's in being charged with anger. She was about to bark an order to the cashier to call Security when a voice from the line called out:

"C'mon! Let the rest of us get through!"

It was a delicately perspiring, well-dressed man carrying a leather briefcase, so obviously an immigration lawyer that people came up to him and asked for his business card on their own. He was surrounded, front and back, by a line of frightened aliens, all waiting to pay at the cashier's window the bearded man was blocking on behalf of Nancy and her grandmother. The man from the hillside looked over this new entrant to the argument objectively: the lawyer did not wear the same tired, harried expression of the others on line.

"How long have you been in this building?" he asked the immigration law specialist.

"Twenty minutes!" the attorney answered, annoyed: this was taking too long! "Now move, please!" he demanded with a reasonable sense of urgency.

The man from the hillside dismissed the immigration lawyer from sympathetic consideration: "Most of these people have been here all day," he noted, the anger rising in his voice again. "How come *you* get through so fast?!"

The manager disappeared from the cashier's window. "I'm calling Security."

The bearded man jammed his mouth down to the payment slot and shouted: "While you're at it, call the police—I want to report that someone is selling your admission tickets!"

The manager froze.

The man from the hillside, his jibe obviously striking a nerve, turned to face the immigration lawyer—and the line of scared foreigners who stared at him in awe.

"I'm sorry—" he began, his voice half an octave higher than intended. He directed his eyes to the frightened brown and yellow faces standing behind the lawyer and tried again: "I'm sorry this slows you down. But you have to stand up for your rights! If you want to be citizens of this country, you can't let them take away your freedom, you can't let them become small dictators. You have rights!"

He directed his next comment directly at the immigration lawyer. "I've been here all day: I didn't see you standing in line. Did anybody here see him standing in line? How did you get your admission ticket?"

Another suit-with-briefcase-with-unharried-expression was picked out from further back in the cashier's line: "You, sir—you weren't in line today. How did you get in without a ticket? Everybody needs a ticket to get in here." He paused for breath, then announced in a voice loud enough for the entire waiting room to hear:

"Who in the Immigration Bureau is selling the tickets?!"

Up and down the line of booth counters, INS clerks froze in their activities, listening hard, waiting with dread to see where the finger of accusation would point.

The manager saw their growing panic. "How much is the check for!!?" she shouted through the cashier's window.

"A stupid ten dollars!" the man from the hillside shouted back.

"TAKE THE CHECK!!" the manager screamed at the cashier.

"Thank you," the man from the hillside sang heartily to the furious cashier, taking the receipt for DEL RIO, SYLVIA's payment.

"Go—away!" the cashier spat at her personal antagonist; she was rewarded by the immediate departure of the bearded man and the two Latinas.

"Gracias," Abalita said with sincere gratitude to the bearded man handing over her payment receipt: it was not all over with the Immigration Service, but she would not have to spend the next day in line just to give them ten dollars.

Nancy stared up at the man from the hillside. "I saw you—" she started to say.

"Yes," he smiled, cutting her off. "Adiós." He turned and walked away into the street crowd.

Sylvia del Rio muttered a Spanish proverb about rudeness.

"Probably," Nancy agreed. There was a disappointment to the girl's voice the grandmother had not expected to hear.

"He was a nice man," Abalita said by way of feeling out her granddaughter's emotion, "but a little without control at the corners."

It is perhaps possible, if Nancy and her abuela had not stood outside the Federal Building discussing the man from the hillside, visible through the tinted window-wall panels for all inside to see, that Immigration and Naturalization Service Border Patrol agent N. D. Charny, a.k.a. The Dreambreaker, might not have noticed them. Probably it was impossible for him to ignore their existence: Dawn Boulfat, the Division Manager, raged up and down the back hallways, informing everyone (willing to listen or not) that the concepts of "respect" and "proper order" might as well be thrown out the window when the integrity of *her* floor staff was questioned. Charny had no interest in the floor staff, their integrity or lack thereof. "Proper order," however, was a matter for INS concern.

Plus, he was a good investigator.

Routine and bureaucracy can bog down the best of minds. Nathan Daniel Charny had avoided that trap so far in his career: a lead was no more than a scrap of information that paid off, information took many forms. He walked over to the source of some possible new information and asked to see the file containing the recent "problem." Flush-faced Mrs. Boulfat wasted no time putting the manila folder into his hands. She was also quick to point out two of the three miscreants—the third didn't even have any *papers*!—those two Mexicans were standing outside on the sidewalk just now, you could see them, right there through the window—

Charny leaned down and looked through the cashier's window at the two Hispanics pointed out: a handsome old woman and a young girl. Just a quick glance, enough to confirm the photos paperclipped into the file. The file was incomplete: there was no documentation to cover the teenager.

Absence of documentation alone was not enough to attract The Dreambreaker's interest in a couple of probable illegals. He'd need to dig a little further. Information. *Scraps* of information. These were what built into a reasonable case. It did not take much to build a case: N. D. Charny was knowledgeable in immigration law. While the rest of the American system was based upon British tradition and the philosophy that "the accused is innocent until proven guilty," the Immigration and Naturalization Service, like the Internal Revenue Service, operated under a federal mandate founded on the Napoleonic Code—the accused is *guilty* until proven *innocent*.

Charny went through the file, idly reviewing its contents as he headed toward the Investigation Division, deeper, much deeper and floors higher, inside the Federal Building: he had only been down this low on the totem pole of process and responsibility to return a few files from the Week's Catch.

"Congrats, congrats!" the File Supervisor beamed, proud to have a hand in the kudo-attracting aspects of the Service. "The Silicon Valley people were really getting ticked off by that wetback electronics firm you guys busted." He took the returned files personally—noting the one held back: "Whatcha got there?"

"Another lead—not even in process yet, hardly."

"That's all?"

"Part." Charny smiled dreamily, his mind working on the scraps picked up so far. "Then I've got to know 'Why?' "

If Charny had not been lost in his own deductive thoughts—about connections between an elderly Resident Alien and her (probably) faked-up "grandchild"—he might have noticed that his thought processes were miles above the File Supervisor's in terms of perceptive power. But the people he investigated intrigued him: the Border Patrol agent could even see a line of them through the open door at the end of the hall, crowded into the waiting room still at this late hour of the afternoon.

"You have to ask yourself," he said aloud, although not specifically caring whether the File Supervisor listened or not, "just exactly *what* do they think? Why are they here? They're going to a crappy place to live, stumble around in a language they don't know, do work that no one else wants to do—live, work, starve, fight, die—what for? They should stay where they are. There's no chance for them here. No chance. Don't waste their time. Don't waste their lives." He remembered to include the File Supervisor in his musings; he needed the man's cooperation. "Do you think about that?" he asked pro forma.

"No," the File Supervisor answered without hesitation: *people* weren't his business.

"What *do* you think about?" Charny queried, mildly intrigued by the personality profile of his allies.

"Baseball. Sometimes football."

Not much in common, Charny thought. Still, diplomacy required tact:

"Yeah," he smiled after a moment, "so do I."

⬥⬥⬥⬥⬥⬥⬥⬥⬥⬥

The Unicorn was agitated and could not tell why. It had been stupid to come out of the concrete tunnel in daylight, even though experience told him that here, at the other end of the mountain water runoff system, here was a heavily wooded park with plenty of cover. He could always decide to remain invisible, too, if he chose. . . .

But that was becoming difficult, a draining effort. The Unicorn would have to begin holding something in reserve for when it was important, not squander his diminishing powers on these moments of whim.

Still, Unicorns are incapable of self-recrimination for sus-

tained periods: the park was empty of people, the sun a hot
orb ready to fall on the horizon's edge within the hour, and
the Unicorn's springing muscles flooded him with a sense of
well-being at this freedom of movement, even as anticipation
flirted about the edges of his consciousness. The "park" was a
mile-long canyon scratched into the foothills by the incessant
grinding of a stream pounding down from on high. Even here,
only short miles from the center of the city, the Unicorn could
find a wilderness where few people ventured except with heavy
shoes, packs of provisions and hours to spare—and not at sun-
down, when the swift-falling mountain darkness would bring
disorientation and an autumnal chill. It might be in the mid-
eighties at noon, but nightfall would see this canyon shivering
under snow-tinged breezes carried over mountaintops from the
northern desert. Other canyons might be hot tonight with a
Santa Ana "Red Wind" curling across the city from warmer
southeastern deserts. You had to know which would be which
by personal experience and an instinct for the weather; the Unicorn had both.

The Unicorn needed to run. Despite his thousand-year age,
the end of the millennium did not diminish his physical strength,
only his magic. The concrete tunnel had led to a stream higher up
the mountain—it was a heart-pounding pleasure for the Unicorn
to run down the canyon to the very bottom itself, hopping over
the stream, through it, as the need fit, as the moment felt right.

Then back up again—not all the way—to the waterfall spilling a twenty-foot curtain of spray, catching the last glints of the
day's sunlight in a thousand tiny rainbows, a glow to the magic
beast's golden horn for the instant before he was to disappear
into the dark shroud of the woods' evening shadows again.

Refreshed, he turned his eyes toward the looming glass pillars of the downtown city once more: where he needed to go
was just outside the perimeter of their cold glory.

❖❖❖❖❖❖❖❖❖❖❖❖

"It was beautiful, that wom-
an's face!" Sylvia del Rio laughed, and her daughter, Victoria Reynaga, laughed louder.

"She was yelling 'Take the check! Take the check!' " Nancy stood in the middle of the small kitchen, imitating the furiously shaking, wide-bodied stance of the INS Division Manager at the cashier's window. Her aunt Vicky screamed a little louder with laughter.

"I don' even have to *guess* what that fat lady was thinking!" she cried with delight. "Ohhh! I'm laughing so much I'm gonna hafta piddle, Mama!"

Nancy saw her grandmother flash a brief admonitory look at her daughter—Abalita did not approve of foul language—before breaking into a grin again. The teapot on the stove that dominated the tiny kitchen began to hiss its readiness (the whistle had long since passed away). Abalita started to rise from her seat for it.

"No, Mama, my job." Victoria sprang to her feet with the paced energy of a woman in her early forties with a family of five. "But they still didn' take all your papers?" she added with a shake of her head while pulling down a handful of cups from a warped metal cabinet. Despite the obvious run-down character of the place, Sylvia del Rio had never let the poverty of the apartment's construction stop her from painting the walls a buoyant color yearly. She sewed her own curtains and placed a value on the needlepoint in her tablecloths. Her daughter wished that she could do the same with *her* apartment across the hall, but so many kids, so little time, no talent . . . The telephone began to ring.

"My turn, Victoria," her mother insisted. "You make the coffee." Abalita took the two short steps from the kitchen to the living room (which also doubled as Nancy's bedroom) to pick up the ringing telephone. Nancy joined her aunt at the minuscule counter.

"I like coffee, too," she whispered conspiratorially.

"Yeah, an' Mama don' like you gettin' caffeine. Back to business: I heard right? They didn' take all the papers?"

"Nope. We had them, but—"

"Pain in the ass."

In the moment of silence that followed—while Nancy debated whether to tell her aunt about the man from the hillside, and Victoria nervously wondered about her own family's status as Amnesty applicants with the INS—Sylvia del Rio stopped listening to the hysterical crying that travelled across the telephone lines and began to speak herself in low, strong tones of reassurance:

"I will be there, then, and do not cry. I will be there."

Victoria's eyes widened at hearing the half-English/half-Spanish phrases: Mama was talking to a child—and the only child she would talk to like that was Ramon's son, Benny, in El Paso, Texas.

"I will leave tonight, mi Benito, do not cry. I love you. Stop crying!" Doña Sylvia's voice grew proud. "Small hombres del Rio do not cry"—her voice softened again—"because I will be there. Tell your mother that I love her . . ." Gentler still: "You are not crying? Good. I will be there. Do not cry tonight. I love you." She then spoke a rapid string of instructions to someone obviously older on the other end of the line. Victoria and Nancy stood behind her as she hung up the telephone.

Her Spanish was flawless as she commanded her daughter: "You will take care of Annunciata, then? I must leave tonight."

"Sí."

"I hate cars. I hate them!"

"Abalita?" Nancy looked at her grandmother in helpless concern. Sylvia del Rio was still too furious at an unknown source to answer.

"Tell your Lope"—she turned on Victoria—"tell your son that these automobiles are *death*! First my son and his wife— Do you hear that, Annunciata? Your mother and father did not have to drive their own car, they did not have to die on the highway!—And now mi Maria is in the hospital, dying from the wounds of a car!"

"Aunt Maria!" Nancy cried: she had thought it was Uncle Ramon who was sick or something—it hurt more somehow to think it was Benny's mom in the hospital.

Her burst of anger vented, Sylvia del Rio returned to calmer tones of instruction:

"I will go to El Paso to help them," she explained. "You know men are no good with children." She bent down and began pulling a small suitcase from beneath the sofa Nancy slept on.

"But what happened to Aunt Maria?" the girl cried, anxious for details to cling to.

"I'll go an' make arrangements for you, Mama," Victoria

said, already halfway out of the apartment. "What time you wanna go?"

"I can be ready in an hour. Lope will drive me?"

Nancy stood in the middle of the crowded living room, ignored.

"Of course. I'll call the bus company an' see when the next bus is. When you wanna come back? What about the apar'ment?"

"I don't know: let Annunciata stay in the apartment."

Victoria was gone. Nancy watched her grandmother place the small suitcase on top of the sofa and unzip its cover. Suddenly Abalita turned to her granddaughter:

"Little one, this is fast, yes? I am a little scared for my daughter. Are you okay?" The look in her eyes pleaded for understanding. Nancy could not refuse.

"Oh, sure . . ." she shrugged, feeling the scare deep between her shoulder blades, "I'm okay."

◆◆◆◆◆◆◆◆◆◆◆◆◆◆◆◆

Not everything that feels right is right, but why is it that so much of what feels wrong is *called* "right"?

The Unicorn moved toward the spired silhouette of the city, knowing all the while that it was a mistake to come so close. Lady Fair, ha! If experience was to mean anything, he would have to remember the lesson of the *real* Spanish Lady—

The Unicorn hated the Lady Aline, that much he knew with certain clarity from the sulking perspective of his hideaway in the ship's hold: it was *her* fault that he was trapped here in the middle of the Atlantic on the tiny Spanish ship. It was a caravel, built to withstand the fearsome waves of the unknown ocean wilderness, not for speed; the gentle rocking motion that had lulled the Unicorn to sleep so easily that first night in port became a plunging, climbing seesaw once the ship hit open sea.

After his first shock wore off, the Unicorn understood that the ship was not a human trap; his Lady and the old knight-turned-friar were not betraying him: they did not even realize he was aboard.

The Unicorn could not decide if he would let them know. His smoldering resentment at this unexpected predicament made him want to punish someone. Aside from defending himself in the heat of chase, the only punishment the Unicorn had ever inflicted was that of denying his magical presence to a desirous human. But, for that desire to hurt, the Lady would have to know that he was not lost to her already. He would have to reveal himself again then withdraw—which was impossible: the Unicorn knew that she was innocent. He could not inflict a cruelty upon the innocent. Resolving such conundrums was not in the realm of Unicorns, and he brooded in the dark hold, frustrated, for a week.

It was not uncomfortable, this self-imposed seclusion. On the contrary, the Unicorn's powers of purification made the voyage a pleasure cruise for the usual vermin residing in the dank recesses of the hold. From boredom—or kindheartedness, the Unicorn did not bother to distinguish—he befriended the lowly creatures, treating them as vassals to bring him food from the horses' troughs above (the mice ferried this admirably) and linen cloth from the cargo bundles for a passable bedding (the rats were competent scroungers). A truce was negotiated with the ship's cat; the scarred, clever feline brought down various human articles from the captain's quarters for the Unicorn's perusal. In return, he touched his golden horn into the sour bilge water and purified it to a taste of sweetest spring freshness. The vermin brought him their own food scraps— shavings of rock-hard cheese, worm-ridden biscuits—to which the Unicorn's magic touch gave qualities of gourmet excellence. Gradually, the Unicorn's sulk resolved itself into a reign of gracious indolence: there was nothing he could do anyway. The question of whether to reveal himself to the Lady would resolve itself when the opportunity arose.

And then, in response to a lazily phrased curiosity about his sea-locked habitat, the Unicorn learned from the filthy bilge rats that the caravel was christened *Santiago Matamoros*— Saint James the Apostle the Moor-Slayer. Coming to know the original Santiago intimately, the Unicorn disliked the voyage even more.

For Santiago Matamoros was on board the ship that bore his name.

Santiago Matamoros.

Apostle Saints were that odd invention of the Creator's Son that seemed to live past their own millennium. Of course they were *His* friends, so some favoritism was expected. And the pain they had endured in giving up their human lives was respected, revered among the humans (although Prometheus had played them one better in the sacrifice game and yet, when the millennium set by the Creator reached its natural end, the Bringer of Fire faded away just as surely as the Unicorn probably would at *his* thousand-year mark). The Apostle Saints, by standard reasoning, should have been gone by the human-reckoned year Anno Domini One Thousand.

But the Creator was nothing if not fickle: just as a Titan or two had been allowed to slip forward centuries into the new millennium, the Creator granted the Apostle Saints, *en masse*, a new millennium altogether. But the Virgin Mother's pet Unicorns rarely played with the Son's friends. Through no design or intent (although with the Creator, who could tell?), their paths rarely crossed.

Which did not mean that the Unicorn had not seen St. James the Apostle before. The extension of existence into a new millennium meant that the Apostle Saints needed to expand their purpose. One joined with the Archangel Michael (another favorite) and became patron of the Dragon Slayers, a rather cruel irony given that Dragons had never challenged the Creator. Saint James—*Santiago*—became the champion of the *Moor* slayers: Matamoros.

Allah-at-One-with-the-Creator-as-God was not happy with this, finding fault with the Son's explanation that—as the Creator had divinely ordained Free Choice among humans—the inherent flaws in human character created a situation where both sides of the Christian/Moor argument could sincerely believe they were right: was it unfair to deny the solace of an Apostle Saint to His side? The Allah-Will of the Creator did not believe in the efficacy of Saints to begin with—let the humans talk to Me directly!—and so this favoritism of the Son was allowed to stand.

(About the Dragons, it was rumored, the Creator was less ambivalent: while they had never actually sided with the Evil Ones, Dragons were a too . . . independent . . . being. The Creator had not created a system of rewards and punishments yet when Nature slipped these intelligent beings into her world.

Valuing intelligence—the Creator did not like fawning respect, as Evil Ones did—some said that the Creator patterned humans on the Dragons. But the Creator had given humans a Choice of reward or punishment: the Dragons had none; Nature was not so prescient. Not even Fear inhabited their beings. Dragons were without a proper soul, as were so many of the things Nature produced without the Creator's express direction, and their intelligence struggled against this void. The Creator appreciated their struggle, but knew there was nothing better to come of it. It did not bother the Creator, then, that Saint Michael the Archangel would use Dragons as the symbol for Evil and set humans to slaying them, just as the Creator could not be upset about water wearing down a mountain into sand.)

The Unicorn first saw Santiago at the corners of a battlefield in northern Spain. The Apostle Saint listened to the prayers of the Christian knights and carried them to the Son. The Unicorn rarely attended human battles—his interests detested those affairs—but, as the Christian ring closed around the Moorish kingdoms, the Iberian peninsula seemed to grow smaller; Santiago Matamoros and the Unicorn encountered one another more than once. The Apostle Saint himself was little interested in the Unicorn's doings: his mission was to give solace to Christian warriors, not converse with magical beasts. Besides, he was a spirit, the Unicorn flesh, their reasons for existence in different orbit around the Creator.

Still, once the Unicorn recognized the Apostle Saint's residence aboard his namesake ship, respects between Special Creations must be made. A week into the voyage the Unicorn made his presence known to Don Santiago Matamoros.

The Apostle Saint was cool and proper.

—*Blessings, creature of the Beloved Mother.*

The Unicorn bowed accordingly.

—*Her Son is well served*, he answered. The deck swayed under their feet: it was the darkest hour of morning, the caravel as quiet as it would ever be. —*How come you here?* the Unicorn asked by way of acknowledging Santiago Matamoros' power to travel through the barriers of space.

—*They have asked me, through their prayers, for protection against new enemies of the Son.*

—*The Moors have retreated to Africa. We are headed . . . ?*

—*To replace different Gods.*

This was the first the Unicorn learned of the *Meseta* Gods—
The Hummingbird, Cloud Snake, Plumed Serpent—the annoying pichilingis, others: he did not even know their names then.

—*Where . . . are they, these different Gods?*

The Unicorn knew that he would have come across them
somehow in his travels.

—*Across the world,* Santiago answered with the superior
smile so common among those privy to the knowledge of the
Son.

And then, because Unicorns must have instinctual knowledge of the world in which they live, the Virgin Mother flooded
her straying pet with the necessary insight for existing in the
"new" world.

The Apostle Saint saw at once that his own exalted knowledge was now equalled by the Unicorn's intuition. He drew
back into the propriety of his position:

—*I am to accompany my Living Brothers on their mission;
they will be sorely tried. If I can aid thee, please come to me,
but my priority may keep me fully occupied.*

Don Santiago Matamoros waved a deprecatory blessing over
the Unicorn's head and disappeared into the captain's cabin.

The Unicorn breathed a sigh of relief that the pompous Saint
had not chosen the Lady's cramped quarters for his sanctuary.

Still, with an Apostle Saint nearby, the Unicorn knew that
a visitation with the Lady would be unfulfilling. Even to reveal
himself to the ex-hidalgo Fra Benedicto would be a mistake
at this point: their eyes opened to the mystery of the Unicorn,
the humans could not fail to notice the presence of Santiago
Matamoros as well. Purity was one thing, devout piety and
knee-bending abnegation of the flesh another: the Unicorn did
not want to push the Lady into a nunnery, or the friar into a
bout of confessional ablutions. It was better to remain con-
cealed. At least until landfall.

Which did not mean that the Unicorn returned to full-time
residence in his secluded refuge below. Curiosity is not a
major character trait of Unicorns—whim and impulse take
that honor—but he had never been in such lengthy proxim-
ity to humans before. Now, thrown into the opportunity, the
Unicorn spent hours walking among the crew, listening to
their talk, comparing their words to their thoughts, smelling
their hopes and fears.

He took this opportunity to look in on the Lady as well. Doña Aline was faring poorly when he found her, not so much from the violent seasickness that raged through her brother and the old friar as from an intense malaise that mirrored the Unicorn's own sense of loss at something irretrievably left behind. Time quickly cured the Unicorn's pain, memory being so small a part of his soul: he saw that the Lady's hurt would last much longer. (With more than a shade of conceit, the Unicorn convinced himself that a large portion of her nostalgia was for *him*.) He did not explore the Lady's thoughts for the source of her discomfort, though. Rather, the magical beast countered Aline's heart pain with a reassuring touch of horn to her shoulder while she slept.

He saw Santiago Matamoros frequently, to the mutual discomfort of both. Truth to tell, the Unicorn had never spent so much close time with the Above Plane, either—save when running with the Cherubs. (He could not picture the dour Apostle Saint wearing tiny wings and showing a pink butt to the wind!) Respects dutifully paid to one another, the Saint and the Unicorn had little cause to commingle. The Unicorn suspected Santiago's disapproval, as well.

As it happened, Santiago Matamoros—far from giving solace to the crew as a whole—confined his attention to the ship's ambitious captain, Guzman, and the Lady's young brother, Don Miguel. Standing invisible among the "uninteresting" crew, the Unicorn often saw the Apostle Saint hover behind the two as they discussed the ultimate objective of this voyage, listening to their prayers for speed and success and dutifully passing them on to the Son. The name "Cortés" sometimes drifted across the deck, to make no impression on the sensitive ears of the Unicorn, who had by now taken to eating at least one meal daily with the horses. Touching horn to water and millet, he rid their sour seagoing fare of taint and vermin; the animals grew fat and healthy, the opposite of common travel example. Santiago, despite knowing better, allowed the reverents calling upon his name to take this as a Sign of the Son's Favour. The Unicorn took it as a sign of gluttony on the part of his primitive cousins; they would become butter-muscled by the time the caravel reached its destination if the voyage took much longer than a mouth.

It took longer than a month, although first landfall was reached after only three weeks: there were two stops, important ports of call, made before the caravel *Santiago Matamoros* reached its final destination. The first landing was at an obscure island in a warm sea—to renew provisions of water and grain.

The second stop was off the coast of Cuba, for provisions also: armed men.

✦✦✦✦✦✦✦✦✦✦✦✦✦✦✦

The scratchy quality of the loudspeaker system made the Announcer's voice impossible to understand unless you had already looked at a schedule:

"... Seven-ten to AlbuquerqueSantaFeElPasoDallasHouston now boarding. Passengers to Denver change at Santa Fe."

More words were said, but the loudspeaker confirmed what they could already see with their eyes: Sylvia del Rio's bus was almost ready to leave Los Angeles.

"You should have gone home with Lope," Abalita said for the third time. Nancy gave the same answer for the third time:

"It's not very far home—the only reason he drove us was because of the suitcase." She added a lie and a faked shrug: "It's not dark dark anyway."

The lie was a failure: it only caused them both to consider how dark it was—and the danger of city streets in this part of L.A. at night. An awkward silence followed for a moment, broken by Abalita:

"I like your face, little one, only tell me: Why does my hand go down your face so easily"—Nancy felt the smooth, old wrinkles of her grandmother's touch—"and get stuck going back up?"

She "caught" her index finger on Nancy's nose, held it there a moment, then pressured the girl to tilt her head back and look up at her abuela. Nancy's hazel eyes reflected a darker color than their customary dancing green. "I'm sorry," Abalita apologized with a self-mocking smile. "It is a very old and stupid joke, but it is better to laugh than to cry—and, besides, I *am* very old!"

Nancy found herself hugging her grandmother, filled with

a sense of emotion she did not know she possessed. Abalita pressed her cheek next to Nancy's—it was easy; they were practically the same height—speaking quietly in her grand-daughter's ear:

"I will be back, Annunciata, I *will*, only it is so hard now, so very hard, and it will get worse. Enjoy your friends and school, Aunt Victoria, Lope . . . they are here."

Doña Sylvia straightened her back, moving away from the young girl preparatory to stepping onto the waiting bus. Almost as an afterthought, she ran her hand down Nancy's face.

"When I come back, we'll see if it still gets stuck!" She pinched the chin sternly: "Go straight home!" Then Abalita was inside the bus.

"I will!" Nancy promised the departing back.

"I will," she reminded the closed doors.

Abalita had given Nancy the money to take a city bus home—sarcastically called "Rapid Transit"—and had the girl so chosen, she might have been back at the apartment within fifteen minutes.

Nancy did not feel like being home so soon. Without con-sciously deciding the matter, she wandered past the bus stop just outside the terminal, shuffling along the rough street in the direction of the next stop toward home. This was in def-erence to Abalita: with the instinctual hair-splitting legal mind of youth, Nancy *was* obeying her grandmother's command to "go straight home." Not *fast*, that's all.

She felt crappy.

Nancy was used to feeling confused or distant from what was going on around her. When Maria or Gloria—or even Aunt Vicky, for that matter—started talking about cars or shopping or who was going with who, Nancy often felt so apart from the shared camaraderie of everyone else at the moment that it seemed she was more lonely then than when she actually *was* alone by herself. Once, at a party for Aunt Vicky's husband, Uncle Tino, when a dozen cousins and two dozen neighbors crowded into the two apartments (they opened Abalita's apart-ment across the hall to catch the overflow), Nancy had been hit by such an overwhelming sense of loneliness that she was forced to retreat to the bathroom, close the door, and stare at herself in the mirror for a full minute trying to figure out just exactly *who* this girl was. She never learned that day—but stopped worrying about the feeling when she found Abalita in the same bathroom an hour later, staring into the mirror the same way. Abalita tried to make a joke, saying she was proud to have found a pimple on her nose—at her age! Nancy laughed at Abalita's lame joke as was expected and nothing more was said directly. A lot of things you never said directly. A few weeks later, having the feeling again while visiting Aunt Victoria across the hall, Nancy was surprised by Abalita's gentle, laughing suggestion that "You look like you feel a pimple on your nose—go look in a mirror."

But that was not the same feeling of—crappy—that Nancy experienced now. It was like she was—something!? She saw the Coke bottle and it focussed her feelings, whatever they were.

It was a classic. An old-fashioned, been-here-forever-style Coca Cola bottle that was not just a remake, but a true original itself. The street people who collected bottles for the redemption change would have recognized its value immediately: the glistening curves and swirls of the glass fetched a pretty penny at the mid-scale antique shops, no five-cent-deposit chump change this! Even the design fulfilled a classic intention: whosoever beheld this Coca Cola receptacle would thereafter desire to hold it in hand. The bottle fit into one's palm perfectly.

Nancy felt that perfection immediately, causing her to hesitate once she had bent down and scooped it up from the curb. She gave pause to consideration of the bottle, looked up and down the street in thought—there were no pedestrians on this block of closed industrial shops.

With a smile of satisfaction, she hurled the bottle against a brick wall with a strong, smashing throw!

Nancy held back a sudden urge to cry, turning and walking with fast, long-paced strides toward home. She felt crappy—exhilarated!—crappy.

Behind her a white Barracuda sat motionless across the street, indistinguishable in the dark twilight from the line of cars parked before and after it along the curb. Lope had promised Abalita to see that Nancy made it home safely. Or maybe he had not promised her—they did not talk too good together—but she expected it of him. Now he watched, to make sure the chica didn' get herself hurt: this wasn't gangland right here—too industrial, too much Polices guardin' the money behind the barbed-wire walls, relatively safe territory despite the look a' the dopers 'n drinkers sleepin' on streets. Still, up the road was Colors territory: if Nancy didn' get on a bus soon, Lope knew he'd hafta play jefe 'n pick her up.

Blond Annie sat beside him: that was her place. She traced a heart of love across the back of his right hand while they waited for the little Nancita to emerge from the bus station. He didn't turn the tunes on, too tired of noise to want to listen to anything. He was real tired, and still had to hit a midnight start time on the job tonight. Midnight—shit! Still, it was a job. Nancy came out of the terminal and they started to watch her.

She didn't go to the first bus stop, she was walkin' kinda sad, Lope figured he knew why. She picked up a bottle and destroyed it against a wall. Lope figured he knew why for that, too. A look of helpless disappointment crossed Annie's face.

****

There was no disguising the fact that the apartment building was old and run-down. Nancy had never seen the landlord in her ten years there, but it was rumored that ownership had changed hands three times. The only decent thing about the changeovers was that each time the building was about to be sold a superficial coat of paint was slapped on the walls, the linoleum floors were patched (in the halls only, of course), and the plumbing had a quick rootering so that prospective buyers would not come across the common sight of an overworked toilet coughing back its recent deposits.

Someone in the building had read that the current owner was maybe a Hindu dentist or a Beverly Hills doctor, a big supporter of the Mayor's Cultural Preservation Committee, who lived over by the Pacific Ocean in Malibu in a walled-off compound. This security-consciousness of the absentee landlord was probably the reason why the strongest things in the seventy-year-plus building were the iron grill gates at the front and back entrance. Nancy used her key to slide the heavy bolt back with effort, then let the gate clang shut behind her from the contraction of the retaining springs. The tenants by the entrances hated the noise of the gates crashing shut. Usually

Nancy was careful to close them firmly behind. Nobody came out to complain this time, however; she knew that her regular consideration was the exception rather than the rule.

It made her jump a little, though, the unexpected clang of metal hitting metal just behind her back: it woke Nancy slightly from her malaise. She was home. This was home.

The hall doors between Abalita's apartment and Aunt Vicky's were open: Victoria stood in her mother's living room, talking on the telephone in Spanish.

"Sí!" she shouted, using that tone of voice people do when speaking long distance. "Tomorrow night, bus number—" She must have seen Nancy enter the room out of the corner of her eye, for she called out over her shoulder: "Nancy, what was Mama's bus number?"

"I don't remember."

Victoria nodded. "It doesn't matter," she told the telephone, "and how many buses come from L.A. at night? Kiss Maria for me. Vaya con Dios!"

"Tío Ramon?" the girl asked.

"Um-hmm." The telephone receiver returned to its cradle. Victoria began to calculate numbers in her head, saying aloud: "Rent's paid for four weeks—Lucky this happened at the beginning of the month, eh, Nancita?" She flashed a tense smile at her niece. "We can cheat it the next two . . . yeah."

Victoria let her thoughts find their way to the present moment—where a long-faced almost-teenager was standing in front of her. "You feel lonely tonight, Nancy? You want to sleep in our apartment?" A loud scream of play monsters screeched across the hall. "I know some little wolves would like to have you with us tonight."

Nancy felt more than a bit bewildered: she did not want to be alone, but the idea of staying with the little kids was less appealing, and she did not know how to refuse the offer. Luckily, her aunt picked up on the indecision and made a new suggestion after only the briefest of pauses:

"Or—you could move into Mama's bed until she comes back. I can't let you stay here alone, so we'll draw straws to see who gets your bed on the couch here for a few weeks." There was one more perceptive suggestion, made as the aunt stepped past the niece to return to her own children:

"But maybe tonight you can have your own house. I'm going to put the wolves to sleep, Nancita, then I will come back and

tell you about Maria. We'll straighten up the place tomorrow."
She shut Abalita's door as she left.

Tía Maria was hurt—Abalita was gone. Nancy listlessly
picked up the scattered rejects of her grandmother's clothing
that had not made it into the tiny suitcase, hooked an arm
through a strap of her school knapsack, and opened the door
to Abalita's bedroom.

She stopped in the doorway, seeing the room very differ-
ently now that her abuela was not sitting on the bed, or on the
windowsill, talking or reading or—living—there. Nancy was
not expected to enter the bedroom when Abalita went out shopping; she was trusted not to. She had been invited in a million
times, had slept in the bed with her grandmother often as a little
girl. She did not remember sleeping with Abalita when she first
moved in, after her mother and father died in the car accident,
but Nancy knew she must have: the sofa bed she slept on was
not purchased until she was four, when Abalita complained
that "the little one's wiggling is like a fish with legs."

"A fish with legs!" Nancy laughed at the torn simile. "Fish
don't got legs," the little girl scolded her grandmother.

"They don't sleep in bed, either," Abalita agreed. "Or at
least I didn't think they did until *you* got into bed with me:
now I believe that 'Fish got legs,' like you say with no gram-
mar!" Abalita was very boring about Nancy speaking English
correctly; she saw how hard Tino and Vicky's children were
having it, especially the talented, inarticulate Lope; she wanted
nothing stupid like language hurting the grandchild she was
bringing up as her own daughter.

Standing almost as big as her grandmother—and Nancy's
abuela was a tall woman by Mexican standards—the girl realized just how small the bedroom was now that Abalita was not
there to make it feel larger with her presence. The room was,
in fact, only just large enough to hold the single bed and a
black, head-high standing closet that Abalita called her "Black
Maria." A three-quarter-length mirror was built into the
Black Maria; in its age-smoked glass Nancy saw reflected the
alleyway through the open window at the foot of Abalita's
bed. There were no bars on the window: this was a second-
floor apartment, the landlord's security concerns ended at the
ten-foot mark. Nancy flopped across the bed on her stomach
and looked over the footboard out the window.

She was not aware of falling asleep. Nor did Nancy notice

when Aunt Victoria entered the apartment, then the bedroom, roused her niece, dressed the standing-in-her-sleep girl in a full-length sleeping shift, and tucked her under the sheets. It was going to be a stuffy night; the window was left open. Victoria locked the apartment door from inside and closed it behind her: Nancy could get out, nobody could enter.

It was after midnight when Nancy woke with a start.

There was no reason for her to wake up so suddenly. No reason. A quick glance out the window told the girl's darkness-adjusted eyes that it was very deep into the night. The city noises coming off Alvarado Street were considerably reduced from those of the day. Nancy lied back down and closed her eyes. She felt an odd rush of excitement, crazed, almost breathless. Yet calming, too. *It must have been a beautiful dream,* she decided. *Too bad I woke up from it. If only I could capture it again, even just remember it for just a minute.*

Odd sounds drifted in through the open window: a faint, almost tinkling chime; a mockingbird sarcastically imitated a pigeon; you could almost imagine hearing the waves rush onto the beach at Santa Monica; a faint clapping of hooves on the pavement below . . .

◆◆◆◆◆◆◆◆◆◆◆◆◆◆◆◆

Orson was homeless.

Not to put too delicate a spin on it, Orson was a homeless *wino*. This was not a matter of shame to Orson; rather, it was a point of pride. Orson thought of himself as carrying on a tradition in these modern, troubled times. He was a wino because he drank to forget. What he needed to forget Orson had long ago forgot, but he knew that if he stopped drinking he would remember and it would be terrible. He took pride in having a terrible experience to forget. He was not like the homeless drug addicts or the homeless mentally ill. Or especially the homeless working stiffs who somehow found themselves without a place to live even though they had been doing everything right except for being in an industry that left L.A. to go someplace else—usually across the border to Mexico, which was a hoot in the barrio, since most everybody here had done everything they could to get *north* of the border to find work. Orson wasn't like any of *those* poor homeless, and, although he felt sorry for them all, he also felt superior, knowing that *he* carried on the honored tradition of the self-made derelict, rather than the hapless defeat of the circumstantial lost soul.

Orson was old. If he tried to remember hard enough, he was sometimes able to recall that he had been sort of old when he first became a wino. That was twenty or more years ago, according to a faded, expired welfare registration card Orson used in place of a driver's license for identification. This made Orson truly old now. When he had first become a wino, Orson expected to die soon in alcoholic bliss. Obviously, the circumstance of still being alive told him, his life before becoming a wino had been a healthy-lived one. Or Orson had been fortunate enough to be born of solid peasant stock with enough genetic resilience to defy practically every degenerative practice known to humans and still emerge with arteries unhardened and liver unscathed. His kidneys ached occasionally, but Orson attributed that to hard water and limited his liquid intake to straight drinks only, not taking chances with what came out of the public drinking fountains and rest room faucets. He had a few hidden stockpiles, a couple of regular sources. In fact, tonight being Tuesday—or Wednesday (hard to tell once it got dark, might even be *Thurs*day?)—Orson was here to make his weekly visit to "Donna" Sylvia's window.

Donna Sylvia was old, just like Orson. She told him, once, that he had known her dead husband Arturo or something. It didn't matter to Orson (as long as she didn't remind him of the past, of course!): the important thing was that once a week, for as long as the wino could remember, Donna Sylvia left a bottle of wine on her second-story windowsill for Orson. The bottle was always almost-full, recorked, and tied around the neck with a thread that hung down to the ground below. It was impossible to see that thread unless you knew it should be there. Orson had to wave his hand back and forth beneath the window until he felt its thin tickle. Once found, a gentle, steady tug would tilt the bottle off the sill—and down into Orson's outstretched shirt, waiting to catch the gift with the delicacy of accepting a newborn baby. Orson wasn't certain who thought up this strategy for protecting the wine until his arrival, but he was pretty sure that *he* did. He must have been a smart gringo once. Donna Sylvia thought of the signal, though: the lamp on her nightstand was left on whenever the gift was ready for Orson. Sometimes overnight even, or for two days, when the old drunk forgot or was too far away to walk the distance in one spell.

There was no lamp on tonight.

Orson was astounded. Donna Sylvia *never* forgot! What's more, even though Orson began to realize that maybe it was much later than he'd realized—there being a faint, pinkish glow to the sky over by downtown—he could actually *see* a bottle on the windowsill. . . . But was it his? Without the lamp as a signal, Orson could not know. He did not want to take *Donna Sylvia*'s wine. The thought failed to enter his head that, even without the lamp signal, if there was a pull-thread attached to the bottle then the nice Mexican lady had left her regular tribute to the wino. And of course Orson was incapable of believing that fine ladies like Donna Sylvia could have troubles like him. There was a sky and an earth and drinking to forget—these were certainties—and the bottle in the window, yes . . . but no signal. Something was screwed up in the universe.

The white panel truck must have been tuned up recently: its engine rumbled only a comforting purr as it slid by Orson to park nose-in to the building the wino stood beside. It stopped exactly under Donna Sylvia's window, in fact. A man not much taller than Orson (who was not small but still only of average height) stepped from behind the driver's window and began to quietly climb on top of the panel truck. Halfway up, the man—whose close-cut, full beard was sprinkled with grey—noticed Orson: instead of reacting with surprise, the bearded man smiled conspiratorially, holding a finger to his lips for the wino's silence. He was standing upright on the top of the truck now—a mattress was tied across it?—his head even with Donna Sylvia's windowsill.

The bearded man looked at the window a moment, lost in thought. Then he noticed the wine bottle sitting on the edge of the sill. He plucked it up and tossed it down to Orson, again holding his finger to his lips. By the time Orson had finished catching the bottle in his shirt and gave consideration to looking up again, the bearded man had grasped the brick sill in both hands and was hoisting himself up into the open window. He looked down at Orson one more time—a friendly face, full of energy—before turning to explore the dark room inside.

"I—know you—" Orson could hear the girl's voice gasp from just within.

The old wino strained to hear what they were saying—the sounds were audible—but it was just beyond reach of his understanding of the words.

"Yes, you're the one!" the bearded man nodded enthusiastically. "Come on!" He stretched out his hand to the dark interior. Out on the lawn, the black-haired girl could barely be seen over the bearded man's shoulder: a shadowy outline, standing to face the intruder, unafraid.

"Who are you?!"

"My name is Karus—and yours?"

"Nancy."

Orson watched as the girl—Donna Sylvia's granddaughter, he remembered—took two steps nearer the bearded man.

"Karus."

The pink dawn light bathed her face in its livid glow. "Where are we going?" she asked, reaching forward to grasp his outstretched hand.

Karus' high spirits dived into a serious plea: Orson did not believe he heard the words right.

"To find the Unicorn before he dies," the bearded man said. Immediately his enthusiasm returned: "Come on!"

And with that Karus pulled Nancy out the window after him.

Afterwards Orson told everyone that they fell in slow motion. Yes, he was sure of that; they fell in slow motion: the bearded man backwards from the window, the girl flipping in her mid-air flight down—to land on the mattress that was strapped to the roof of the white panel truck. It was a long, glorious fall, Orson said, a long, glorious, *slow* fall—to a bouncing flight back up in the air again (at least for the girl), then down again—to be caught in the bearded man's arms.

"Little one, I need you!" Karus shouted, setting a mutt with the spirit of a lion trapped in an apartment nearby to barking furiously.

The bearded man scrambled with his load down the side of the truck, popped himself and her through a door, and started up the engine. The real miracle began here, in Orson's story, when the white panel truck took off with a roar and a shine down the streets, a swirling rainbow of colors trailing in the air behind. Or, maybe it was the effect of the sunrise on his eyes, seen through the filter of Donna Sylvia's wine bottle Orson was tilting to his lips at the moment.

To Nancy's eyes, however, Los Angeles had never looked more golden as the dawn sun finally broke the mountain horizon, topping the high downtown buildings with its glow, while where she was on the highway below twilight still sat. The white panel truck pulled onto the half-empty highway that would lead them past Downtown—to the Harbor Freeway. Nancy had never seen the harbor, living near one of the largest ports in the world. But the bearded man guided his truck north, away from the harbor, and Nancy missed seeing the port again.

She scarcely noticed. Caught up in the moment, Nancy looked at the passing buildings as if for the first time: a large, mirror-walled tower reflected the image of the building opposite it as if that reflected building were moving on its own. To her left the low-lying Basin neighborhoods began to shine under the sunstruck haze of morning. On the Harbor Freeway, passing beneath a mural-decorated bridge, the white panel truck pulled even with a delivery truck about to exit.

"Lope!" Nancy cried in recognition of the sleepy-looking man sitting behind the steering wheel of the delivery truck, sipping at cup of coffee. She began to wave to her cousin.

Lope shivered at the chill of morning air hitting his tired body. Automatically he steered the delivery truck onto the Third Street exit ramp, his peripheral vision checking the extended side mirrors to make sure no suicidal toy cars were hugging his blind spots. Some kid was hanging out the window of a panel truck, waving happily, hair pushed by the wind all over her face. Without thinking much about it, Lope noted they were in the East/Pasadena Freeway lane.

Nancy pulled her windblown head in from the window and turned to Karus. "That was Lope!"

"Good for him," was the good-natured reply.

"He's my cousin!" she said proudly.

"Better for him! But—question: what did you say your name was again, little one?"

"Nancy."

"Ah, 'Annunciata'—a beautiful name!"

And Downtown became an El Dorado fading behind them, further and further away, as the white panel truck passed out of the City of Angels and through the craggy hillsides.

KARUS

It is easy to act on a moment of impulse, very difficult to continue doing something after that moment has passed.

"No! Of course the Unicorn didn't just appear from nowhere: he's been living there for years!" Karus' Texas twang grew more pronounced with each emphatic answer to Annunciata's increasingly skeptical questions. She was beginning to feel like a fool.

"Well, I didn't hear about unicorns being in L.A. before!" she countered with equal emphasis, her own Mexican flavor creeping in with the emotion.

"That's because"—Karus searched for quick, convincing words: the waitress was coming and he did not want to be overheard—"because," he whispered, "first of all, he can be invisible when he wants to—here!" Their waitress, a handsome woman clad in knee-length Pakistani qameez and blossomy shalwar pantaloons, set down a pile of plates between Karus and Annunciata: fried eggs, hash brown potatoes, link sausages, toast, pancakes, syrup—

"I will be back with the coffee and juice," the woman promised with a singsong lilt to her voice, the jewel in her left nostril sparkling from the full morning daylight that rushed in through the floor-to-ceiling windows at the front entrance. "Aftab, please—" She turned and rattled a gentle request in Urdu to her husband, the concentrated man in front of the huge grill creating the delicious-smelling feast. Annùnciata stared at the plates before her.

"You hungry?" Karus asked matter-of-factly, nipping a finger of sausage between his teeth.

"Yeah," Annunciata nodded, hesitating. In fact, she was famished. The El Paso emergency had killed all appetite last night; it was almost thirty-six hours since she had eaten a regular meal. But this whole situation was weird, and now this: *supposedly* they were in a Greek diner in some town called Montclair, but the food was mainly American and the people who ran it Pakistani. Okay, this was maybe normal, but it seemed weird anyway.

"Take what you want to." The bearded man waved magnanimously at the full plates between bites of toast.

Annunciata took another look around the place (a sign declared "THEO'S Greek Restaurant—*GYRO* Explosion!") before giving in to the lure of the smells. "Thanks!" she mumbled, her eyes downcast, adding: "I'm afraid, you know."

"You should be."

Annunciata had not expected that answer—yet there was no menace to the man's voice, more the concern of a parent. Abalita had not been afraid of him, even when she hadn't known his name. *Karus*. The name did not make Annunciata feel any more confident.

"Maybe I should . . . go back—you don't have to take me back: I can call!" Despite (or maybe because of) her nervousness, Annunciata began to nibble hungrily at the sausage and bacon.

Karus leaned forward to rest his elbows on the table.

"First let me tell you why you're here." He pointed at the knife and fork laid across a paper napkin at Annunciata's elbow. "Eat properly while I talk." Rebuked, the girl brushed her long hair back behind her shoulders, picked up the eating utensils, and began to attack the huge breakfast with civilized intensity.

"You're here because the Unicorn has lived in the hills a long time," Karus began. "Five hundred years. You say you didn't know it, but I guess you did, because you found me."

"I didn't find—!"

"Call it 'mutual finding,' then, 'cause I was looking hard and getting nowhere until we saw each other over on the hill a coupla days ago. Which was about the last minute, too: now it's time for the Unicorn to die. They do that, too."

Annunciata looked up from her plate to see that the sun-browned, bearded man was looking at some faraway memory.

". . . Before . . . he could wander wherever he liked, invisible, safe from anyone. Now he's dying, and he hasn't got the strength to waste on being invisible. He can be seen. He has to find his Place to die now."

Karus brought his focus back to the girl.

"He can be seen, and we have to help him find his Place to die."

"But . . . what'll happen when I'm gone . . . from home?"

"I don't care an awful lot."

"Wh—?" Again Annunciata was disconcerted by Karus' unexpected, dismissive answer.

He added in softer tones: "It's a *different* problem: a Unicorn—a beautiful, magical beast—is about to die—and he needs a Rider to help him do it right, something I never thought could be possible and real for . . . me. And I need a Lady Fair to help me find his Place, his Last Mountain where all this is going to happen. Is there anyone who needs you back there?"

Anyone who needs you? Annunciata repeated to herself. The answer was unpleasant for her to say out loud: "N . . . no."

"You see?" Karus held his hands in open supplication. "*I* need a Lady Fair to find the Unicorn."

"Why?" Annunciata found herself back at the central doubt to this weirdness—a doubt addressed by Karus with an exaggerated, matter-of-fact shrug:

"That's just the way it happens!"

"Oh."

No! The Doubt:

"But I don't even believe in unicorns!?"

The bearded man did not answer. For a brief moment Annunciata held her breath, hoping that he *would* say something, hoping there were words to convince her of this loco, beautiful-dreaming stranger.

There were no words to do that.

Only a gesture.

Karus pointed down toward the floor, where Annunciata's bare ankle peeked out from beneath the hem of her full-length night shift.

There was a hoofprint on the cloth.

"Here," Karus said, sliding a handful of coins across the table. "Call whoever it is you left back there: I don't know if they'll understand, but you can try."

Annunciata's eyes searched the small restaurant.

"Where's a pay telephone?"

"This is California: I think they've got more car phones than they do public ones. Try the gas station across the parking lot there." Yet again the sun-darkened man dismissed Annunciata, turning in his seat to accept from the Pakistani woman a small cup of steaming black sludge that he euphemistically called "coffee." Greek coffee. Karus let the savory bitterness surround his tongue, his back still to the girl, until he was certain she had left the diner. Then he gulped the cup's contents, paid the bill, and hurried out to his truck. As he crossed the short distance from restaurant to parking spot, Annunciata was nowhere to be seen: she wouldn't be if, indeed, the public telephone was around the corner at the nearby gas station— or if she had run away. Karus did not have time for concern over either thought; at this late date trust had to take first place ahead of second thoughts.

The white panel truck had been a parcel delivery vehicle once. There was only one seat originally, the driver's stool, but Karus had bolted a passenger seat behind the right front window. He let a bit of whimsy affect his judgement there, fitting in a living-room armchair on a swivel stand, colored in a green-based tartan.

The rest of the truck's interior may have reflected an eclectic bent, but was chosen for practicality: where the original truck had a hollowed-out twenty-by-ten-foot rectangle of cargo space behind the driver, Karus built a small home, separated from the front by a makeshift curtain. A low cot was bolted into one corner, running lengthwise with the truck and covered by a thick down sleeping bag which was, in turn, covered by a thin square of paisley-printed cotton material. A heavy mirror, cast off from a vanity table, was screwed onto another wall. There was a darkwood chest of drawers, and a heavy trunk reminiscent of the attic in which Karus had found it. The final effect, for all the disparity of styles, shared the comfort of a Victorian dream. The bearded man briefly checked himself out in the mirror for obvious signs of the sleepless night he had spent, found few at this hour of the morning, and addressed his attention to the trunk.

First step: remove the pile of *New Yorker* magazines on top of the trunk. This took longer than intended, since Karus caved into his major addiction: reading. He began leafing through an issue he had apparently missed. The cartoons were great—*New Yorker* cartoons always were—and even though the bearded man could never make it through the magazine's short stories and poetry, he would sit for hours parked on the side of a road poring over long articles that always were titled "Letter From." Letter From *Washington*. Letter From *Madrid*. Letter From . . . *Los Angeles*. He had been to every city there was a

Letter From. That was how he had become a Rider. That was
how he had come to decide on Los Angeles.

With a sudden shudder of his shoulders, throwing off relaxa-
tion as a dog shakes off rain, Karus put down the magazines
and readdressed his interest to the trunk. Opening the iron-
cornered lid, he looked down on the several different styles
of clothing revealed within—another bounty of shopping at
garage sales.

"There's got to be something for the Lady here," Karus
nodded in agreement with himself, beginning to sift through
clothes that ranged in age from two to twenty years. His own
few belongings were on top. A woman's blouse was a man's
shirt with buttons reversed. A skirt, however . . . Karus did not
think to offer the Lady Fair a pair of *man's* pants.

Annunciata, the Lady Fair, was still undecided on her choice
of staying with the man who spoke crazy but seemed to have
the proof of his eyes on his side, or returning home. Again
Karus' apparent indifference confused her: Annunciata was no
campesino ingenuo up from a village where you knew everybody and called every man (probably with reason) "uncle"—
L.A. was full of perverts—but this man *trusted* her? There was
nothing to stop the girl from running into the gas station and
asking for help. Or even—over by the McDonald's on the corner—calling out to the policemen sitting in their patrol car . . .

Except for the hoofprint.

"Eighty-five cents, please . . . Deposit eighty-five cents,
please . . ." The computerized voice repeated its avaricious
mantra patiently in Annunciata's ear. She dropped the coins—
Karus' coins—down the appropriate slots in the pay phone.
". . . Thank you . . ." The gratitude seemed feigned.

Two rings. Annunciata hoped that her aunt answered the
telephone and not one of the kids. As soon as she heard the
receiver picked up, the girl spoke excitedly:

"Hello, Aunt Vicky!?"

She was surprised to hear the answer in hushed tones.
"Nancy? Is that you?" Annunciata could hardly hear her aunt.

"Aunt Vicky, I've got a—" the girl began, then stopped
abruptly: she realized that her aunt had pressed the receiver
to her body to muffle the sound and was talking to someone
else in the room—in English.

". . . friend of Nancy's . . ." Annunciata could barely
make out the muted words resonating through her aunt's chest.

" . . . don't know . . . El Paso with my mom . . ." The next words were clear as Victoria spoke directly into the receiver again:

"Hello?"

Annunciata was too excited by her own situation to consider what was happening on the other end of the line: Karus had asked, "Does anybody need you there?" The answer was "No."

"Aunt Victoria—" She took a deep breath and made her decision: "I-have-to-go-find-this-unicorn-I-don't-think-it'll-be-very-long-but-he's-going-to-die-and-I-have-to-help-find-him-he-left-a-footprint-on-my-dress-and-I'm-okay-that-man-who-helped-Abalita-and-me-yesterday-at-Immigration-needs-my-help-so-don't-worry-okay?-Don't-worry."

◆◆◆◆◆◆◆◆◆◆◆◆◆◆◆◆

Annunciata hung up the phone before her aunt could speak: the answer might not be one she wanted to hear.

Victoria, however, had barely understood her niece's jumbled explanation. Only the words at the end—"don't worry"—made their way past Victoria's immediate concerns to nudge a response.

"I won't worry . . ." she said into the dead telephone; if Nancy was safe somewhere else for the moment, that was better than being *here*.

The Dreambreaker was here.

"It was pretty sudden, then, this everybody leaving L.A.?" N. D. Charny said when Victoria returned to her mother's apartment across the narrow hallway, where he waited . . . patiently. He idly examined an unopened newspaper, *La Opinión*, noted odds and ends of Abalita's scattered belongings that Nancy had overlooked the night before when picking up. "Gone so fast that no one knows," he said to a kitchen still holding the dirty cups from yesterday afternoon.

Victoria was afraid to answer The Dreambreaker: Tino had paid all the immigration fees, filed the Amnesty documents; everything was legal and supposed to be all right—but they did not have their final Resident Alien classifications—the precious "green cards"—yet.

Charny stepped over to the closed bedroom door, looked to the Latino woman for permission—she gave it with a hesitant nod—then entered. The bed was slept in last night, still unmade this morning. The window was open. There were footprints on the sill. Information. Scraps of information.

"Hard to get to El Paso this way," he commented dryly, secretly pleased that his intuition about these people was being confirmed.

"Here'ss paperss."

The accent made the words a harsh guttural: Lope.

"These're my fam'ly's paperss. Whole fam'ly legal," he said sullenly to the INS investigator, displaying a handful of the documents the Amnesty advisors had cautioned his father to hold onto. Lope could hardly read the English gobbledygook. His father, Tino, out at work, could not even make a claim on the "hardly." Lope did not let his ignorance stop him from making an aggressive defense. "We're legalss. You see these: we're legalss."

"For now."

The Dreambreaker glanced over the documents briefly. He knew the Amnesty laws better than the people in the room here: prove that you (and *every* one of your dependents) had been in the country *continuously* for the ten years before the start date of the immigration Amnesty—fulfill those simple conditions with proper documentation—and you would be granted Resident Alien status. No matter that most illegal aliens had spent their time in America *covering up* documentation of their presence in the country. Ignore the fact that a simple trip across the border to Tijuana disqualified the applicant's Continuity of Residence claim. Or that the law granted no leniency for families that might be split apart when one member's claim was accepted and the other's denied.

"You're still 'in process' is what I read here," Charny said without a hint of threat to his voice, handing the documents back to the Indian-looking Mexican, a mestizo probably, standing next to the frightened woman. Information. Scraps: Charny made a mental note to check the originals back at the INS office for forgeries. Aloud he explained: "I'm not interested in your family. I am interested in the family of Sylvia del Rio—"

"She is my abuela," Lope answered, unable to remember the proper word for his mother's mother in English.

"—and her dependents: Annunciata del Rio . . . and any others also undocumented."

"Mama's been here over twenty years!" Victoria cried, seeing where The Dreambreaker's line of reasoning was leading.

"I'm only asking questions right now," Charny replied with his patient, professional smile. "It would have been easier, if they were here, to ask your mother why—if she is legal—*you* didn't apply for immigration as a relative instead of under the Amnesty?"

"You know the answer to tha'!" Lope snarled, angry for the humiliating fright of his mother. " 'Cause they applied fi'teen yearss ago 'n waited 'n waited 'n woulda hadda wait 'nother ten yearss!"

"But you would be here *legal* now—instead of 'in process,' " Charny smoothly noted, shifting the focus back to the footprints on the windowsill by stepping over to it. "They left rather abruptly, didn't they?"

"They're both on the way to El Paso." Victoria repeated the lie lamely. "Why do you want them?"

"I'm only asking questions. Only asking—not answering." Charny placed a card with his name and office number on it into Victoria's hand and left the apartment. Lope followed the INS agent out into the hall, trailing The Dreambreaker down the flight of stairs to the ground floor: let the Anglo know he was not wanted in their homes. Charny surprised him by stopping at the bottom of the landing and saying in perfect Spanish:

"You probably think this is unfair, that there is no justice in what I am doing."

Lope was unprepared to answer so bald a statement. And his Spanish was too poor: just as his English had failed the jefe of Los Barracudas up in the apartment, he was unable to use his mother tongue here. His fingers twitched in articulate expression—Blond Annie would have understood—but Lope could only blurt out the usual street angers:

"You know iss no justice! You put us in jail firs', you shoot out on th' street wi' us firs', you gonna execute us firs'! Yeah, you right, I think iss unfair 'n no justice!"

"That's because it is."

The Dreambreaker looked up at the young Latino—Lope was still standing a half-flight up the stairs—and let his words fall into the space between.

"You might as well accept the fact that the word 'justice' doesn't belong in any discussion of what we do here." There was no sense of superiority to his words, no threat. If anything, The Dreambreaker sounded to Lope as if he were sharing a sad discovery about his family. "And when I say 'we,' you get to be a part of the picture, too, compadre: 'justice' just doesn't apply to what we do—me and you, us and them, all of us. Take it for what it is."

"Those jus' words you sayin'," Lope said down on the man aggressively. "Don' excuse killin' us."

"Who said we need an excuse? You want to hear excuses? Hey, listen to arguments about capital punishment and how we need to 'protect society' and see how those get wrapped up in the word 'justice.' *That's* an excuse, cholo: what we're really supposed to call it all is 'revenge.' You understand *revenge*, don't you, cholo?"

"I unnerstand revenge."

"Good, 'cause when we—you, me, us—talk about capital punishment, a.k.a. killing the killers, we sure don't mean 'justice.' 'Justice' comes from the word 'just'—it means things balance out: but none of us seriously believes that one stinking criminal murderer's life is equal to the one—two—more!—innocent lives he took. You think that?"

"I don'—"

"You think that?"

"I—"

"You think that?"

"I don' think no killer'ss life worth a innocent life!"

"Neither do I, so when somebody says executing a killer is justice, fair is fair, and all that crap, I keep thinking, *I value those dead people a lot more than the life of one piece of shit.* So now we get to 'protecting society' . . ." The Dreambreaker's eyes were so far from focussing on Lope that the younger man had to comment:

"OK, Mister Migra, you make you point. Why you talkin' so much?"

The Dreambreaker did not refocus his eyes, although a wan smile crossed his face. "Because I need *you* to understand," he said evenly. "I need you to realize what you're up against."

He focussed in on Lope again and began speaking in a lecturer's tone of voice:

"About 'protecting society,' you see, justice is again beside the point if we talk about execution: the convicted murder is already in prison, off the street. We are protected. . . . But we do not feel satisfied. We need revenge.

"And execution—capital punishment—Killing The Beast That Hurt Us—is revenge at its purest. Did the killer have a disadvantaged childhood? It doesn't matter: revenge does not require an exact balance. Revenge benefits from the simple act of striking back, free from guilt—*because I have been hurt and I want to hurt back*. There is no hypocrisy in this, no 'Let he who is without sin cast the first stone' fence-straddling. I do not need to be a judge holier than thou because *thou* hast struck me first and now it's my turn."

Lope was lost—because the man was making sense and sounding loco at the same time. He wished Nancy was here to listen to The Dreambreaker: the little chica was young, but she heard good and understood. He wouldn't talk to her, no, but Annie would. And Annie would "talk" to him, with her fingers, on the highway. Maybe it would make sense then. Or wouldn't. But he would not be alone hearing it.

"Okay, there'ss no justice. You got your point to me." He wanted the Migración man to leave.

The Dreambreaker did not move. "I haven't even started on the 'point' yet, compadre: I want you to understand it *all*." His smile was broad and directed inside. "We take it pretty straight that capital punishment is about revenge and not justice, once you look at it head-on. But *we*—and now I'm going to use a word called 'society,' I hope you know what it means—*Society* is very uncomfortable with a word like 'revenge,' smacking as it does of the ol' personal pronoun 'I': *I* am not interested in justice or protecting society, *I* want my child's killer legally murdered by the state because it satisfies *me*. You see, cholo, 'society' is somehow seen as having a higher purpose than the individuals within it. The philosophy of our civilization—do you know what the word 'civilization' is?—is somewhat grounded in a belief that *society must transcend the individual's prejudices and emotions.*

"And now we run head-on into the contradiction of arguing the 'justice' of killing our killers: is this the triumph of individual self-interest over the collective aspirations of the whole?

"Or do we already recognize that fact: isn't the whole enchilada just a cover-up? We're afraid to admit our own primal truth and try to hide it behind a carefully constructed facade misnamed 'justice.' "

He stopped talking. The Dreambreaker stared up at Lope with an expression that pleaded "please understand," gave up the effort as a failure, turned away and exited the apartment building. Lope remained on the stairs.

He lingered a full five minutes there before returning to his mother to ask:

"Where'd Nancy say she wass?"

Victoria was moving on automatic pilot, too nervous to do anything else, systematically cleaning up her mother's apartment, making the bed, washing the dirty coffee cups. She tried to recall her conversation with Nancy.

"She didn' say where she was . . . She said she was okay—and something crazy."

Lope looked at the dirty windowsill: the footprints included that of a horse and a man.

"Everything's loco," he said.

"The lead pans out?"

Charny concentrated upon the information scrolling down his computer screen, hardly acknowledging his supervisor's question.

"I think so."

"Nothing solid?"

"No one is going to openly confess to me, Tom."

"I just thought—"

"I need a name for the man!"

Charny's sudden burst of impatient self-demand was followed at once by a series of stabbed-in commands on the computer keyboard. His supervisor, Tom Nethers, watched with a mixture of admiration, bewilderment, and boredom: Charny always produced; getting there was what was tedious.

There was nothing of apparent use coming up on the terminal screen; Charny turned away from it and sprang across the room to point at a map of the region.

"Okay, the guy from yesterday doesn't pan out yet—even though the old drunk puts him at the apartment with a truck. The telephone call came from *here* this morning—"

"What guy? What truck?" Tom asked, more as a matter of form than from interest: as Charny's supervisor he needed to have a general idea of the status quo in the Border Patrol's ongoing investigations.

Charny himself was aware of the administrative indifference: a mediocre job ranked with them the same as a good job—volume and result stats were what Tom Nethers and his ilk thrived on. Charny worshipped nothing.

He liked explaining his thoughts as they crystallized into realities, though:

"Unidentified man—possibly Anglo—helping two Latinas push their docs through the process—"

"Normal," Tom commented.

"Until someone here objects—then he creates a diversion, makes a lot of noise, bullies the papers through, beats a hasty retreat."

Tom saw the implication: "Ordinary immigration business would have turned to the client, demanded more money, and told them to come up with more documents."

Charny liked to be understood.

"Unless *he*—my guy from yesterday—supplied the documents in the first place along with his fee, and the documents are dirty: then he's got a reason to be nervous. And a reason to want them to beat it away from the city in a hurry."

"You know that for certain?"

"I place him downstairs with the women yesterday; got a drunk on the street who saw the guy this morning taking the girl out through the window."

"What about the old lady?"

"My bet is she's legal—probably fronting a fake relationship with La Latina for a fee. Anyway, my old drunk didn't see her. Maybe she went to El Paso after all."

"You keep talking about a 'drunk' witness: he reliable?"

Charny thought about the mixed-up story Orson had told him—was trying to tell everybody, in fact—weaving unsteadily on his feet that morning on a corner of Alvarado. Cutting out the wino's embellishments about rainbows and floating, the man and the girl, Annunciata "del Rio," fit into the right descriptions. Plus—

"There was a telephone call from the girl from area code nine-oh-nine," he said by way of answer to his supervisor's doubts, pointing to an area east of downtown along the foothills of the San Gabriel Mountains. "We'll circulate photographs of the girl and the old lady in this direction." He turned away from the map to smile at Tom Nethers: "And no, Tom, I am not positive about that—or any of this yet—so we'll hold up until I can get a little 'street' confirmation." Information. Scraps of information.

"How soon?"

"Today."

A surveillance is not an easy operation to arrange. It was a trib-ute to Charny's track record that so many young Border Patrol hotshots wanted to be in on one of his stings. By noon there were two plainclothes agents in place, watching the abandoned apartment and the goings-on of the "family" around it. One stayed with the apartment while the other tailed the one called "Lope" as he contacted his Low Rider associates throughout the afternoon. Charny himself stayed in the office, setting up shifts, directing the ferrying out of equipment to the stalkers. He wanted information.

Information could be had through photographs and video-tapes; the telephone was tapped, but conversation over the phone was minimal: the "aunt" put in a call to El Paso, the "cousin" called in sick to the graveyard shift at work. Outside on the street was where the cliqua jefe did his talking—and the Border Patrol surveillance equipment was not designed to break the sound barrier of boom boxes cranked to "kill."

Blond Annie stood beside her man, her long fingernails unpolished, glowing only with the dull reflection of the orange air that characterized a sundowning day in the center of L.A. It had taken Lope all morning to figure out what to do, all afternoon to assemble Los Barracudas.

"I saw her goin' nort'east on Five, but headin' towarda One-Ten Pasadena," he explained in Spanish with the same primi-tive accent that he had in English. "I know the truck. Anybody can't go?"

No one said anything. Two girls got to go along this time, like Lope's Angla, in expectation of their being overnight somewhere.

"I don' wan' trouble ri' now, so no formation on th' free-way. No colors."

"That's not dope, Lope, no good!" Bato protested: Lope was letting the young wanna-be ride with the Reds.

"I don' trouble!" said Lope intensely, cutting off further dis-cussion by adding: "Bato, if you need colors, go play violent wi' Victor!"

He stared down the teenage buster, then let his eyes fry into the other cholos. It was a lost cause, Lope knew: we too much half-Indian, half-not—nobody ever wanted us mestizos even in Mexico, 'cept on the outside of whatever's *in*side, 'n what's the outside *here* 'cept bein' jacked by the Blueshirts and La Migra? All that was left to a Mestizo with any pride was the cliqua. Los Barracudas wadn' no proper cliqua, only a buncha cholos followin' Lope 'n his car dreams—'n Lope's dreams were gettin' tired.

"Which don't mean we go slow," he said to Los Barracudas with a flash of smile. It was enough to send the Low Riders back to their heavy Reds and Blacks, where the cranked-up music threatened to deafen the passengers as much as Blond Annie already was. Watching their backs running happily away from him, Lope allowed his smile to disintegrate into a more fatalistic expression. He climbed into his White Barracuda, to find Blond Annie already waiting there.

"Jefe, what's the number?!" Bato called out from the passenger side of the Black Barracuda three cars behind. Lope shouted out the number of the Spanish radio station blaring from his radio, which was quickly copied up and down the line: no "colors" tonight, only a unity of music. Even as that unison was established, however, Lope felt a sudden disgust for all sound and switched off his own stereo. He fired on the engine, then turned to Annie to explain where they were going to try to find Nancy.

Annie was not paying attention to him: she was looking out her window at the other Los Barracudas getting into the line of cars behind. They were beginning to sway and nod to the music bouncing from their radios, waiting with happy anticipation for Lope to begin this half-conceived chase. Lope felt a slight chill spring into the wind; it would be cold near the foothills once the sun was fully set. He rolled up his own window, then Annie's. The music from the other stereos hardly penetrated the metal body of his heavy sports car. Annie turned to Lope and began to bounce and sway to the music she imagined was playing on their own radio, in imitation of the others.

"I can feel the rhythms." She smiled to Lope, looking for acceptance to his world. "I like music."

Lope flashed a smile and grabbed her hand for a quick moment—then dropped his hand to the stick shift between them and put the car into gear.

Click!

It was too dark for the video camera to capture much with distinction, but the INS plainclothesman handling the still camera had sufficient light to record the White Barracuda's license plate.

Click!—The next car, a Red, had a personalized plate easy to remember.

"They're moving out: do you want us to pick them up?" the Border Patrol agent handling the unused video camera asked over the selected radio frequency.

"No," The Dreambreaker replied, "we'll follow."

Click!—The next car, another Red.

Click!—The next car, a Black.

Click!—A Black.

Click!

****

The Unicorn picked his way among the rocks, sure-footed, alert: it was not hunting season, but humans with guns were known to fire them into the mountainside at any sight of a wild and free living creature. The white beast did not look like a deer, but that would not stop the stupid. He could waste energy on staying invisible, of course. Too much effort. To save his strength was why he chose to scramble through the cragged mountains, leaving the sharp-edged city behind. The Rider and his Lady Fair had met up, that was good. The Unicorn knew from experience that it was no guarantee they would succeed, though. Experience? Hard-won disappointment . . .

Fra Benedicto tried to caution Miguelito, but the young Don had fallen under the spell of Captain Guzman.

"Guzman notes"—Miguel's eyes shifted haughtily over the friar's rough fabric robes, comparing them unfavorably with the fine shirt of the ship's captain—"that there is much to be gained by being present when this swineherd Cortés divides the conquest—in the King's Name. Our grant . . ." Here he unfurled the parchment that Fra Benedicto himself had assured the young Don's illiterate eyes was signed in King Carlos' own hand. ". . . is very specific: we will supply one hundred soldiers to the Conquest, we will receive land accordingly."

"You could simply send the men. The Conquest is supposed to be over, my lord. The King's grant will still apply."

"Yes, well, Guzman does not trust this Cortés to honor the King's writ. Neither do I."

Miguel was parroting, of course, the words of the ambitious ship's captain—to whom, Fra Benedicto noted with alarm, the inexperienced Don offered commission as commander of the troops to be picked up in Cuba. The old friar appealed to Doña Aline:

"Your brother has no experience with these sort of men: he—and you—would be better off remaining in Cuba on your family's estates there."

"La famille est—tellement importante," she replied ruefully, "so important," repeating her mother's oft-uttered reason for joining her Parisian family's fortunes to that of the Conde Rodrigo's—even if it required an exile from France for the noble daughter whose marriage would forge the bond.

Still, the Lady Aline did not disagree with the final reasoning of her confessor-cum-advisor: Miguelito had no business attempting to "lead" a command of mercenary soldiers, even if it was only to back up the family's claim to Encomienda estates in the new Conquest. No, her father had been clear: the children were to arrange the forceful presentation of the Count's claim—then, only when affairs of the Conquest were settled, should they themselves desert the estates in Cuba for the new Encomienda in . . . wherever this Meshico was. Doña Aline presented this position to her brother privately, in keeping with the respect Don Miguel deserved in front of Captain Guzman and the confidence they shared as family.

Miguel, in return, lied to his sister.

He denied any part of "Benedicto's old-woman worries about my riding with the soldiers," although admitting that he *had* engaged Captain Guzman to command the private troops.

"I have had the opportunity to watch him these several weeks, Aline. We will not have such leisure in Cuba, only a day or two, a week at most, to find, judge and select a man to trust." Guzman's brief tutelage of the young Don proved more effective than Fra Benedicto's years of wasted effort: Miguelito repeated his mentor's persuasive speeches almost word for word. Even Aline was impressed; not familiar with Guzman's easy tongue, she heard a completeness of thought Miguelito had heretofore failed to exhibit. She thought with deceived reassurance that her brother was growing more mature.

The Unicorn could not fathom motives for lying, but he perceived the aura of mistrust growing within the ship. He was surprised to see that it emanated from the men Santiago was patronizing. The magic beast tried to ignore the intrigue hatching within the captain's quarters. Unsuccessfully: whenever the Lady's brother broke away from the circle of the Apostle Saint's interest and came into his sister's presence, the Unicorn was assaulted by the falsehood.

And he could not help. This was an affair between humans.

It was strange, the Unicorn felt, this new perception of verity. Always *he* had been the victim of deceit: sought for by men, he was lured by virgin women. The scent of betrayal struck his nerve endings always at the moment before a trap was sprung. That was what had saved him, this forewarning of the lie. Why could not the Lady smell her brother's lie?

But she could not, would not doubt her brother's words: the Unicorn observed with unexpected concern as Doña Aline smiled at Miguel's trap and stepped into it:

"Aline, the smallpox has broken out on this side of Cuba. We cannot go ashore here."

"But we are anchored?"

"The men Guzman is recruiting have all had the pox, or been quarantined. But if we go ashore here, we will be exposed as we travel overland to father's estates. Captain Guzman assures me we can be dropped off down the coast, close to the estates. The pox has not spread there."

Aline did not have time to doubt Miguel's invented story about the pox—for within hours she was confined to quarters with illness herself. It was the *cow*pox, however, picked up from fresh beef eaten at the small island the caravel had stopped at earlier for provisions. The Unicorn could have cured her, of course, but he did not: instinct told him that this sickness would not be fatal to the Lady—and would protect her from the deadly smallpox should he not be there to shield her.

The illness altered Miguel's plans, however, sending him into a paroxysm of panic.

"I can't desert her here, sick, even though we planned it!" he cried to the commander of his newly hired troops. "I will have to stay. Or we will have to wait until she is well!"

"She's not very sick," Captain Guzman noted coolly. "The friar can nurse her at a house on shore."

"I'm not going to abandon my sister!" Don Miguel answered loudly, showing more resolve in front of Guzman on this matter than he had on any other issue. At the back of the young Don's mind, too, was the fact that—without Aline—Miguel *needed* Fra Benedicto to read and write for him. No! Miguel had agreed to leaving Aline in Cuba, when she was healthy, but *he* was not going *totally* alone to face down Hernando Cortés with the Encomienda demand. Oh, no, not alone!

"If we wait for her to become well—another week, maybe ten days—the others will have left without us."

Guzman's observation was accurate: Conde Rodrigo's plan for his family to be the first to join Cortés with soldiers and land claims was not unique. The captain—and every freebooter in the Hispanic Indies—understood that what the King of Spain wanted, what he *really* wanted more than anything else, was his percentage of tribute from the reputed "Gold Cities of Meshico"—from *whoever* got there first and held on to it. These men would not wait for Doña Aline to regain her health.

Miguelito was at a loss. He did not, of course, consult Fra Benedicto with his dilemma.

"How long to Meshico, Captain Guzman?"

"The navigator says another two weeks, more-less, depending on the wind."

"And another three days here, provisioning . . ." The teenager forced his callow brain to calculate. "We can drop Aline off along the coast near our estates in six days—she will be better in six days!"

"That was the story for your sister," Guzman reminded his short-memoried patron. "The reality has your estates in the wrong direction. We must leave her here, Don Miguel—in three days—if we are not to lag behind."

"No, that is not acceptable!" Miguelito cried, starting to pout. He began to rationalize that perhaps, now with soldiers coming aboard, this Guzman—pardon, *Captain* Guzman—did not want Miguel along, either. A clever thought entered his head.

"Cortés has conquered the capital?" he asked slyly.

"This is the report you yourself bring from the Royal Court," Guzman answered with equally sly calculation. "Hernando

Cortés did not send messengers back to Cuba: he burned all but the one ship returning to the King. Or so it says in the report you showed me."

Miguel took Guzman on his word and shrugged: if that was what his captain said was written, fine—the young Don had never bothered to have Fra Benedicto read it to him. "So . . . the Conquest . . . is complete?"

"So it was written."

"Then we shall take Aline with us to Meshico—to be the first Spanish noblewoman of New Spain!"

✦✦✦✦✦✦✦✦✦✦✦✦✦✦✦

They had travelled too far.

Annunciata had no idea how many miles they logged that afternoon; Karus assured her that the number was small—mountain miles were tedious, not numerous—but some time after twelve noon the bearded man was seized by a fear that he had outdistanced the Unicorn. The girl had no thoughts on the matter either way. This was Karus' show. Annunciata found it hard to keep from nodding off, though, as he backtracked—down from Mount Baldy, where they had hiked past a nearly dried-out waterfall under a hot sun up to a cold peak under the same sun—returning to the white panel truck and a series of half-hour forays from the Foothill Freeway into the raw, gravelly mountains. Their general direction, she knew, was a return west, toward Los Angeles.

They were in Los Angeles *County* again; that much Annunciata knew for certain. Looking at a road map, she learned that this last turnoff into the mountains put them halfway back to Downtown, in a long, deep gash between the crags called San Gabriel Canyon. They were sitting now at the bottom of the canyon. The pink outline of the peak behind them gave clear indication that on the other side daylight still had twenty or so minutes to go. Night hit pretty squarely here, though. It was a hard, mountain dark, with stars Annunciata could never hope to see in the city beginning to fill the sky.

"Do you think we'll find him?" she asked Karus: he seemed to be less nervous in this canyon than at their previous five stops.

"He's got to come by here," Karus answered, his voice perhaps a bit too insistent. "We got a little ahead of him, I think, that's all."

"But we came so far?"

"He's fast."

Karus had driven the truck down a difficult but wide dirt road cut in the cliffside that overhung the lower regions of the canyon. A shallow, drought-starved river ran along the bottom, flanked on both sides by wide stretches of sand and gravel. The panel truck parked next to the cliff, the man and girl stood at the edge of the shallow river.

Karus tried to stare through the darkness and failed—until the moon came up, the mountain night was impenetrable beyond a few short yards' distance. The bearded man gave up the effort and headed for an outcropping of rock, a large boulder which pushed up from the dry river bed, then leaned precariously to one side as if it would fall back under the sand at any moment.

This was where Karus had set up a waiting spot in the last moments of strong daylight: he and the girl positioned themselves behind the rock and passed a bottle of orange juice back and forth between them.

"What do we do when we find him?" Annunciata asked, hugging the skirt Karus had given her a little closer around her legs in response to the increasingly chilly night air.

"It'll work itself out then," Karus answered, his tone more confident than a few moments earlier. The girl noticed that the small streaks of grey in his beard caught what little light there was, giving his jawline a faint, luminous glow. Her own face was almost obscured by the thick, dark hair falling across her cheeks from the center part. Annunciata shook her head and tossed it back to throw her hair behind her shoulders.

A small sound.

Karus continued his attempt to scan the horizon across the width of the dry-bed canyon. Annunciata's hazel-green eyes flashed with the delight of unexpected discovery: she picked up a hand-sized rock at her feet to find its smooth, river-worn roundness jewelled with delicate striations of color.

"They have gold here," Karus said over his shoulder, guessing from the girl's mild gasp what she had probably found. "Used to be tons of it washed down by the river every spring, hundred years ago."

Almost a tinkling of glass, but deeper (not as fragile, though).

"Karus?"

"Um."

"What do you do?"

"I'm a Rider now."

This was no answer, although Annunciata suspected she knew what Karus meant. She wanted better.

"And what'll you do with the Unicorn? Why do you have to find him?"

Karus turned to look at the girl, unsure of himself.

"It'll work itself out then. It has to: he knows somebody's got to find him . . . He's just got to make sure it's the right one."

"Ah-yiiii!" Annunciata's startled cry was almost-soundless air rushing past her vocal cords. Her eyes widened to embrace the darkness—

The Unicorn was outlined on the ledge above them!

Karus slapped his hand over the girl's mouth. "No, please, no!" he whispered; then the two of them stood gawking up at the ledge, motionless.

The Unicorn reared his head slightly, pawed at the ground, seeking the feel of a familiar path useful only to himself and the deer.

It was the man who recovered his wits first: hand still across Annunciata's mouth, he pulled her down behind the boulder, crouching to join her.

"We've got to wait!" he whispered.

"I—want to see!"

"Let'm get near enough, down to the water . . ."

The Unicorn's hooves found the deer trail—a flutter of shallow gouges in the cliff wall—and he began his descent to the riverbed. Barely breathing, Annunciata and Karus did not even chance raising their heads to follow the Unicorn's progress, judging his approach by the minor clattering of dislodged pebbles trickling down the rock wall.

A distant noise.

A buzz. A growl.

An engine.

Karus turned his head toward the far end of the canyon. Annunicata did not hear yet.

The Unicorn lifted his head.

A mile away, maybe further, a small light beam pierced the darkness at the floor of the canyon: the growl of the engine grew hungrily louder. Then, joining the first in sound and light, a second set of beams appeared.

Off-road vehicles, drag racing across the sand flats.

Annunciata, crouched low next to Karus, saw the intense, bitter look cross his face. "Blast!" he cried, jumping to his feet and running out to the edge of the shallow river, whirling desperately around to see if—

The Unicorn was gone.

"Karus, look out!"

The girl's cry caused Karus to jump back just as two off-road vehicles sheared close by the outcropping of rock, to continue on into the black distance. They almost disappeared; then the light beams could be seen crisscrossing as they turned back and made a second pass by the boulder, this time skidding across the shallow-bottomed river to send a shower of spray cascading in their wake. Against the harsh contrasts of mountain darkness and high-beam headlights it was impossible to see the vehicles' occupants. Karus ran out into the middle of the river, hurling insults at the departing cars.

"Get out, you— Get out! Idiots!"

The drivers' derisive laughter at his futile words joined the roar of their cars.

Of a sudden, Karus turned to Annunciata:

"Quick! Tell me a direction!"

"I don't know a 'direction'!" she cried, bewildered. "I'm not a Girl Scout!?!"

"Tell me a direction!" he shouted.

"East!" It was the first thing that came to her mind, nothing more.

Suddenly Karus was pulling her by the hand—"That's where he went! Come on!"—across the canyon floor toward his panel truck.

"But . . ." They passed the invisible path the Unicorn had taken.

"We'll get the truck," Karus muttered anxiously, noting the path—and the impossibility of their being able to follow it in the dark. "We'll find him—it wasn't here, that's all . . ." It was a voiced hope as much as a belief. Karus could not be certain; that fear was what squeezed at his emotions. He stopped pulling on Annunciata's hand, to turn and face her with a plea for understanding and agreement.

"It wasn't supposed to be *here*—that's all. This isn't the Place."

They heard the roaring engines make their distant preparation to return, amplified by numbers now, joined by more unseen off-road vehicles. The harvest moon finally made its appearance over the rim of the canyon, but its warm glow did not give solace, serving only to illuminate the skeletal frames of the dirt-roving cars gunning down the dry riverbed toward the disappointed man and girl.

"Come on," Karus said quietly, fishing in his pockets for the key to open the panel truck's doors. The encroaching buzzsaw of unmuffled engines made him edgy. Annunciata stopped his hand at the first lock:

"Karus—he was beautiful!" Her excited eyes still envisioned the moment she first saw the golden-horned beast standing on the ledge. "What does he look like up close?"

"I don't know." The words were a mumble.

"What?" Annunciata let one of Abalita's demanding tones creep into her question: she had trusted this man to here, he owed her a better explanation.

"I said, 'I don't know'—I never saw him before."

Karus quickly inserted the key into the lock, clicked open the passenger-side door, and avoided the girl's eyes by stepping around the panel truck over to the driver's door: Annunciata unlocked and opened it from the inside. Her face was framed by the doorway, barring his entrance.

"I . . . couldn't see him before . . . This was the first time." He did not tell the Lady Fair that he could not even be sure of having seen the Unicorn this time, so weak was his eyesight in the poor light. He was only sure of having seen Annunciata's face seeing the Unicorn. It was that moment only that he held on to.

The roar of the approaching off-road vehicles cut short further reflection. Annunciata let Karus slide in behind the steering wheel; he had the unwieldy panel truck straining up the pockmarked dirt road before the intrusive cars arrived. Just barely: in the passenger-side mirror Annunciata could see the dark canyon floor behind them crossed with the clashing beams of off-road vehicles, dozens of them, racing back and forth with the frenzy of a school of piranha. It was easy to turn away from this noisome, somehow threatening, sight and focus again on the Unicorn's ledge.

The ledge was just a faint outline against the rock wall now, lit by the moon but soon to disappear into shadow.

"He *was* beautiful, wasn't he?" Karus said by way of reaffirming the expression he had seen on Annunciata's face. He let his peripheral vision take in the girl's face again: the Lady Fair was nodding in silent agreement with him.

The panel truck exchanged dirt road for the paved mountain highway.

"Come on!" the Rider cried, changing subjects. "I need a drink and you need some food." He guided the truck deeper into the San Gabriel Canyon, toward the promise of food, drink and overnight camping offered by a well-worn road sign advertising "The Fort."

◆◆◆◆◆◆◆◆◆◆◆◆◆◆◆◆◆

Once upon a time—as the saying goes—The Fort might have been exactly what its name implied: lodged into a hillside above a tight bend in one of the San Gabriel River's tributary streams, the building's thick mortar-and-stone walls could have withstood the fiercest Indian attack or the most hostile forces of nature crashing down on the canyon in the Gold Rush winter of 1849. As it happened, there had never been hostile relations with the Native Americans in the region. And when Ma Nature played her games, it wasn't any namby-pamby effort that walls could hold off: every quarter-century or so heavy rains combined with a spring thaw to raise the water level half a hundred feet and wash out whatever inhabitants were foolish enough not to skedaddle up to high ground. A gold miners' boom town sank from sight that way, as did a more permanently intended community just after the turn of the century. Hence, anything to sight along the river and its feeder streams was not more than seventy years old. The Fort, for all its traditional, heavy lines, was even younger.

It was built by a Rolls-Royce car dealer from the ritzy neighborhood of Newport Beach. His name was Joe.

Nobody ever asked Joe his last name—it was there, written on his liquor license and posted above the bar for all to see—it was unnecessary to know. Joe told you his first name right off if you were a stranger; he expected you to call him by his name if you stayed longer than a five-minute beer-and-bathroom stop along the way from there to where.

"I got in the habit of telling people my name selling cars," said Joe, "only, the people who buy Rollses don't have any fun knowing a name. You've got to have fun."

So Joe gave up the "un-fun" business of selling cars at a fortune a pop, bought himself the wrecked-up foundation of an old general store, and had the "pleasure" of spending the next two years of his life slogging through mud, carrying lumber and moving earth in his efforts to create the castle-walled fort and its "backyard" of meandering campground. Twice in the years since the stream had boiled up into an angry spring-flooding river, threatening The Fort's existence: Joe fought back with heavy railroad ties bulldozed into a retaining dike and a small suspension cable strung out over the roiling, icy waters, across which provisions were ferried to The Fort's besieged defenders. During dry summers, Joe tried to dig a deeper channel in the stream, to give Ma Nature a reason to leave him alone. So far only those couple of spring thaws had battered at The Fort's portals—heavy rains had not coordinated their efforts with the melting snow yet. Joe wasn't certain how The Fort would fare when they did. For now, the battle was a lot more fun than selling Rolls-Royces.

All of which Joe told Karus and Annunciata out on the wide, picnic-table-strewn patio, where he stood in front of The Fort before they had a chance to enter. He was listening with displeasure to the far-off sounds of the off-road vehicles buzzing around the dry canyon floor on the other side of a wide ridge of hills. These Off-Roaders did not please him because they had been drinking: Joe did not disapprove of drinking—he sold beer proudly and drank it with enjoyment—but The Fort's owner held a rather poor opinion of breaking one's neck while driving drunk behind the wheel. The mountains and canyons were greedy; they took their victims however they could. Only mean bastards survived. Joe had nothing against bastards. He hated mean. Where was the fun in being mean?

He invited Karus and Annunciata inside The Fort to have some food and fun.

Annunciata felt a stomach-churning chill run through her shoulders: this was a redneck bar. A live band was playing country music. Adding another prick of apprehension to her dark-skinned fear was the huge Confederate flag tagged proudly on the wall behind them. It was safe to say the band would know no salsa tunes. They were twenty-five miles from Downtown L.A., fifty minutes by fast car from Alvarado Street, and Annunciata felt as if she had stumbled into an exotic, dangerous country.

Karus was in an up mood.

"Whatever you want, my Lady Fair," he declared over the music, expansively gesturing toward the long bar counter dominating a wall, "as long as it can be fried and hamburger!" He led the Latina tourist down the length of the counter to a pair of unoccupied bar stools. Perhaps it was the odd mixture of skirt and shirt the girl wore—every other woman in the place poured herself into hip-hugging jeans—or maybe it was the hazel-dark eyes peering out at the noisy scene nervously. Karus thought it was because, despite her young age, Annunciata was the most beautiful woman in the place—whatever: they began to be noticed.

And here, waiting for the sole waitress who commanded the bar with admirable division of attention, Annunciata began to actually *see* the people inside The Fort, rather than simply fear them.

"Redneck" was too narrow a word to describe the customers this night, except maybe in deference to the specific physical condition of those with hair short enough to show some neck, male and female alike. More than half the men wore long, sun-bleached ponytails to match the even longer braids hanging down the backs of the women with whom they sat (albeit the male contingent showing more than a couple of polished pates). Annunciata had seen a lot of men in the city wearing stylish ponytails; these men in The Fort did not look as if they knew (or cared) about the latest dance look or L.A. Exec Buzz. Pale blue eyes abounded, as well as freckled faces that would never tan despite years of exposure to the sun. Heavy boots suitable for construction work or slogging up mountainsides—again an increasingly *de rigueur* accessory at fashionable Valley Junior High—abounded here. The band, Annunciata noted, played its anthems with a rock backbeat: it wasn't salsa, but the girl didn't feel any of the usual cornpone false nostalgia she heard when a search through the L.A. radio frequencies brought her into brief collisions with country stations. At The Fort's large, round tables, several children, some of them a little ragged at the edges, sat near their parents, who nodded to the music or talked with heads close together.

Maybe it was just the effect of being tired, hungry and slightly cold: despite the strangeness of these Anglo faces, Annunciata felt an odd familiarity about the place. It reminded her of the Mexican village Abalita had taken her to visit one winter just after her parents died.

"What'cha want, folks?" Annunciata was brought back to the gnawing reality of her stomach by the waitress' polite but hurried question.

Karus was in a mood to be gracious:

"Something that tastes good."

"Something that tastes *good*!" the waitress barked a short, self-directed sarcastic laugh. "That's not often a restriction we get here! You very hungry?"

"I think I can speak for the company when I say that we are on the verge of starvation," Karus announced grandly, including the interested onlookers in his brief address to the waitress. He pecked the bar with a forefinger for emphasis, using the same index finger to point out a table of quiet revelers near The Fort's huge, roaring fireplace: "They seem to be enjoying their meal: two of the same. And then conversation with you, if you please."

The waitress scribbled the orders with a self-invented shorthand. "I'm busy," she said, starting to reenter the rush of her job.

"I'm not. I can wait. Find a moment, find me here." The smile that cracked through the grey-tinged beard matched the invitation in Karus' eyes. The waitress nodded an unexpectedly shy, tentative "yes," then hurried away to file their order with the cook.

"I feel tired!" Karus yawned elaborately, opening his mouth in a wide stretch, followed by his standing up from the bar stool, straightening his legs—then bending at the waist and touching his elbows to the wood floor with ease. Annunciata was surprised; the three boys sitting at the table behind her were astonished. Karus straightened up to face the pop-eyed stares and smile at the boys' parents.

"Kinks," he explained. The band had begun a new song. Karus turned to Annunciata. "I need a dance partner."

Annunciata did not hesitate to accept the invitation: at almost the age of thirteen, practicing dance steps with her girlfriends was a regular social activity.

They made a strange dancing pair. Annunciata realized at once that her skills were for a different music: she quickly adapted her movements to the more staid rhythms of the moment. Karus, too, understood that there were actually *steps* to go with the song being played. He made a half-hearted attempt to dance like the people crowded around him. The first chorus found the man and girl unsuccessfully clomping together in bad parody of the country two-step.

When the second chorus hit its stride, Karus pushed away from Annunciata. With the shaking movement of a wet dog coming in from the rain, Karus came to a complete standstill for a moment, let the music hit him anew, then tore into a frenetic series of gyrations from a generation earlier and a milieu unrelated to the song about Louisiana nights and a bayou fight.

And, because the rhythm inside him was true, Karus' dance made sense. Annunciata watched him bounce from foot to foot, her own inner sense of beat keeping the half-steps and small sways she made "proper"; her judgement of Karus' performance alternated between embarrassment and admiration.

The band, however, was unabashed in its enthusiasm for the bearded man's dancing. Picking up on the dancer's energy level, the lead guitar player launched into a tempo-building solo that the bass and drums had no choice but to follow and—once challenged—attempt to surpass. The polite two-steps of the crowd broke into spontaneous foot-clomps and bouncing that left the weak breathlessly behind. Karus could not let his Lady Fair falter: he grabbed both Annunciata's hands and began swinging his partner in leaping, exuberant strides across the dance floor.

With the grace borne of her Latin American blood, Annunciata followed suit at once. Urged on by the band and the crowd, the Rider and his Lady Fair invented their own dance steps to the ever faster, louder madness of the song. The lead singer repeated the chorus again and again: this was no time to stop! The crowd sang the chorus— Annunciata didn't know the words—she sang the chorus anyway. Karus bellowed something loudly, striking his feet against the scarred wood floor to seemingly fly above it for seconds at a time. The chorus again—Annunciata needed to scream something—the music would soon end—it wasn't enough—

"Ah-yiiii!!!" she cried, making the cry a part of the song.

"AH-YIIII!!!" the crowd echoed—in Mexico—in the mountains—in The Fort: the glint of eyes, sweep of bodies, louder, fast, to the end, TO THE END!

The break was sudden, abrupt, and proper: everyone froze at once—then broke into applause with the spontaneity of unforced appreciation. No one paid any attention to anyone else: they were congratulating one another. Karus and Annunciata swooped down upon their Hickory Burgers With The Works, ravenous self-absorption displacing interest in all else. Karus consumed the first half of his plate's contents in only sixty seconds; Annunciata's progress was only milliseconds slower.

It was at this juncture that a palm-sized, battery-operated toy truck raced across the counter to an inglorious crash with Annunciata's chili fries, followed a moment later by a ten-year-old boy's face staring down at the gory mess.

"Steve! I told you not to run your car on the counter," reprimanded the possessor of the ten-year-old face as he turned his gaze from the glop of chili-and-plastic to a boy half his size, presumably the incautious Steve. A third boy, again twice as large as Steve, joined the other two at Annunciata's plate. Behind them all, the exhausted band began to play a slow, stately, Texas waltz. Annunciata gingerly plucked the toy from her chili fries, wrapped it in a paper napkin and handed it over to the small boy. "Here." Steve looked maliciously at the first boy, accusing:

"Josh didn't tell me not to do it. He told me to do it."

Josh, his face flushed pink to the ears, appealed to the third boy: "Ryan, you tell your brother to stop lyin'!"

Apparently blood was thicker than water: there was no solidarity between the ten-year-olds. Ryan denounced his best friend: "Josh, my brother's not lyin'." Both of the older boys instantly froze in embarrassment as Annunciata laughed.

Steve was not embarrassed. "We have puppies," he announced.

Annunciata brushed her long hair back behind her shoulders to lean down to the small boy and ask: "What kind?"

"With tails."

Josh could not stand by and let this go on. "Very good, Steve," he intervened, "real smart. Of course they got tails— all dogs got tails."

"Boxers don't," Ryan said smugly.

Annunciata saw that Josh's pride was about to do a tailspin drop again. "But they start out with tails," she noted. "People cut 'em off."

Josh hopped onto this chance to reclaim his ego.

"Yeah! I seen 'em do it. It's real gory!"

"Blood!" Ryan chimed in with ten-year-old relish.

Karus leaned across the counter. "Beautiful conversation, gentlemen. Do you mind doing it somewhere away from the ketchup?"

Irretrievably embarrassed again, the two older boys began to back away from the counter—stopped by the small Steve throwing his arms wide in a demand for attention.

"I just want to say something!" he called out.

"Steve!" Josh whispered furiously under his breath.

"Do you want to see my puppies?" Steve asked Annunciata, his demanding tone leaving no doubt that he considered the question rhetorical.

"They're in our trailer about two hundred yards upstream," Ryan added.

After a brief look to Karus, who nodded his assent, Annunciata rose from her stool to follow the three boys. "What's your name?" Josh asked as they reached the heavy entrance door.

Annunciata felt an unexpected pang of self-consciousness. "Annunciata Cym— You're not gonna remember it anyway, so call me Nancy."

"Gentlemen!" Karus' voice boomed across the crowded room, stopping the small group in mid-escape. "Her name's Annunciata: call her that."

A rock plopped into the slow-running stream, shallow and narrow, gleaming under the moonlight.

"Annunciata Cymbelina de las Flores del Rio." The girl heard her name repeated by Steve.

"That's a long name." Josh's voice echoed hollowly in the empty canyon air.

Ahead of them, parked campers and small mobile homes were strung out under the thick clumps of trees that lined the stream.

Josh made a near-perfect pitch of a flat rock to send it skipping one—two—three—four!—times across the water. He straightened his body from the contorted position required by the effort to demand: "Watch this now!" He doubled his body in a headlong race toward the stream. There was no doubt in Annunciata's mind that Josh was aiming for a straight-ahead splash into the icy water—until at the last moment he slammed his foot onto a large rock at the water's edge, pushed off and leaped *over* the stream!

"Yah!" Josh cried from the opposite bank, triumphantly unscathed by water.

Inspired, Ryan shouted, "Let's go!" to the others, charging at the stream himself to attempt the feat, Annunciata and Steve galloping in his wake. He hit the rock with his right foot, pushed into the air, leaping the long leap wildly—

Then Annunciata—

Then—no one.

Annunciata crashed into Josh and Ryan, safely on the other bank, laughing at the wide jump she had made. Steve stood alone at the launching rock, on the other side.

"I'm a-scared!" he whined.

Josh was too pumped up to care. "C'mon, Ryan, make your brother jump."

"Come on, Steve, jump!" Ryan urged.

Annunciata was not so enthusiastic. "He can't make it. He's too small."

"Yeah, but he's afraid of jumping anyway," Josh said, dismissing her observation—and Steve: "Come on, Steve!" He turned away from the stream with cruel nonchalance.

Ryan joined him. "Come on!" he called over his shoulder.

When his brother did not budge, Ryan let out a slow "O-kay" and both boys started to walk away from the stream.

This ticked off Annunciata.

"Wait!" she demanded.

"If he wants to come on, he can jump," Josh answered, continuing to walk. "Let's go, Nancy."

Annunciata turned back to face the small boy across the stream.

"Okay, wait there." She backed up three steps, ran forward and jumped.

Annunciata's left foot hit the cold water with a splash. She ignored the unpleasant shock and swung her right foot around to leapfrog to the dry bank next to Steve.

"You didn't make it," the small boy observed with surprised concern: he thought big people could do everything.

"I don't care," Annunciata said angrily, directing the emotion across the stream—where Josh and Ryan hooted derisively at her failure. "Let's go see the puppies." An inspiration hit her fancy, and Annunciata grabbed at Steve's hand, pulling him along at a fast pace.

"You didn't make it!" Josh called out.

"I bet you can't, either!" she shouted back, pulling the little boy harder to up the pace, adding a taunt to the older boys: "And I bet you can't catch Steve, either!" Challenge thrown, Annunciata scooped up Steve, ducked her head, and began a full-blown race down the streambank, away from the campsites. With a whoop, Josh and Ryan launched themselves into the chase.

Neither one made the return jump, apropos—but, then, neither one let concern over the failure slow them down, either.

Annunciata could carry the five-year-old only so far before his weight seemed designed to make her lungs burst. With the older boys fast approaching, she dropped Steve down and let him set the pace: to her surprise, Annunciata had difficulty keeping up with the kid's short-legged scramble. Wet sneakers and over-rambunctious breathing slowed down the efforts of all three older runners: the young fireball led the pack past the last trailer and around a tree-shrouded bend in the stream. Josh and Ryan pulled even with Annunciata as she slipped on the slick bank and nearly slid into the water again while rounding the blind corner.

Where the Unicorn stood.

He was clearly visible to Annunciata this time. No shadows obscured his face; the strong moonlight made it possible to see every detail at that moment. Annunciata read a curious message in the Unicorn's eyes and turned her face away in disbelief—to which the Unicorn shook his head slightly, then bowed to drink from the stream.

The three boys stared at the Unicorn with awe, the two older ones frozen with a confusion of thoughts, small Steve rooted stock-still in delighted wonder.

Almost without conscious decision, Annunciata found herself stepping away from Josh and Ryan to approach the Unicorn. Brushing past Steve to do so, she felt the small boy's hand grasp hers, and led him with her to the magic beast.

The Unicorn raised his eyes from the water, looking at her. He felt a calm distrust of the older boys, but was unafraid.

Annunciata had to step into the mountain-chilled stream to reach the Unicorn. At the water's edge she hesitated, not wanting to lead Steve into the cold. The boy would not let go his hold on her hand. Annunciata had no choice but to step into the stream with him. Her first step sent an icy pain into her skin. The Unicorn dipped his horn into the water. Annunciata's next step felt the warm caress of the stream. The Unicorn raised his head fully to watch the young woman and small boy approach.

It was a tentative hand that touched his flank, too delicate for the Unicorn's skin to react to. He saw the boy release the Lady Fair's hand and pull back. Annunciata stepped next to the Unicorn's body, her leg next to his, drawing close to his head, her hand running along his graceful neck now.

"Can I touch him?" Steve asked in a tiny, whispered voice.

Annunciata turned her head away from the Unicorn's reluctantly.

"Of course not," she admonished the small boy gently. "You're scared! Stop being scared and then you can touch him."

Steve took a step forward, then stopped.

"I'm still scared!"

The Unicorn's answer to that filled Annunciata's thoughts:

"Then stop it," she said strongly. "Come on, now, stop it: you don't have to be brave—just not too scared." Steve took a step closer; the Unicorn let his silken tail whisk the boy's hand with a comforting tickle. "See?"

"I touched it!"

"Of course you did!" This all seemed so matter-of-fact to Annunciata, as if she had known these things all along. "But you've got to *really* touch him, like *this* . . ." She embraced the Unicorn with a full-armed wrap around his neck.

At her waist, the small boy hugged a foreleg.

"Yeah," he smiled.

The older boys' confused awe of the Unicorn turned into pangs of envious loss. They stepped forward, ready to join Annunciata and Steve.

The Unicorn shied away, pulling loose from the Lady Fair and her young vassal.

"W-what's the matter?" Ryan asked, distressed at the Unicorn's rejection.

Annunciata's thoughts were unclear on this, as were the Unicorn's:

"I . . . guess it's too late for you: you're too old. Now you're men—only the Rider can touch him now."

"The Rider?" asked Josh, starting to feel incredibly sad.

The answer to this question both the Unicorn and his Lady Fair knew without hesitation.

"That's Karus," Annunciata explained, adding proudly: "That's why we're here—to find the Unicorn." The final reality waiting at the end of their Quest hurt her to say aloud. "He's gonna die . . ."

The Unicorn felt the doubts and jealousies grow inside the older boys. With a gentle sigh he stepped away from the Lady Fair.

—*Not tonight. This isn't The Place.*

—*Karus still has to see you?*

—*Not here. At the Last Mountain.*

The Unicorn walked away from the stream.

He did not run away swiftly, though: the small child, the Lady Fair and the two "men" could watch him disappear into the moonlight. The moon glistened intensely along the water's surface where the stream began to turn chill again. A faint, almost tinkling sound lingered longer than the soft footfall of the Unicorn, then faded as well.

"What direction is that?" Annunciata asked when finally the Unicorn had left her sight.

"East," Josh answered, already beginning to doubt.

◆◆◆◆◆◆◆◆◆◆◆◆◆◆◆

"I knew east was the right direction. I knew it."

The white blur of an oncoming headlight glanced across the windshield, causing Annunciata to close her tired eyes against the harsh glare. She found it difficult to reopen them.

"How?" she asked, trying to keep up her end of the conversation. Karus, flushed with excitement and a degree of alcohol, did not notice.

"Because you said east, it had to be it!"

"What if I'd been wrong?"

Karus paused briefly before answering, taking his eyes from the road to do so, to see if Annunciata had been serious. Did she know of his doubts back in the canyon? He decided that the Lady Fair needed confidence more than candor. "Question doesn't make any sense," he blustered. "You know you weren't."

Karus had been too excited by the story Annunciata whispered in his ear at the bar to spend the night at The Fort's campground as planned. The map showed a ridge road crossing east through the mountains: he wanted to be headed in the right direction at once.

Annunciata woke up from an uncomfortable sitting sleep to remember something of importance:

"I don't think they'll tell anybody—I made 'em promise."

"Even the little guy?"

"Uh-huh." Annunciata felt satisfied in having conveyed the reassurance to Karus; she closed her eyes again.

"Doesn't matter, he'll tell—"

The girl's eyes popped open.

"—nobody'll believe him."

"But—why?" Annunciata demanded.

"The older ones will be the first to call him a liar," Karus explained, a tinge of regret to his words.

"They saw him, too!"

Karus shrugged. "You said it yourself: they're too old now. They can't believe it. . . ." He thought of how easy it was to not believe. "Not even their fault, everything's against them."

Annunciata would not accept what Karus was saying.

"But *I* believe in it," she challenged.

"So do I . . . so will the little one . . ." And then, because he knew what would probably happen, the Rider added: "Maybe for a while."

"It happened!" Annunciata yelled, angered by the man's pessimism.

"Only because you believe in the Unicorn!" Karus yelled

back, swerving the truck across the painted road divider with the tense reflex of his hands. "But who the hell else does anymore?! It's not just the Unicorn: you saw it, great! You see a movie, too—you think all that's real? It's not just believing in what you see, it's believing in what you *don't* see: I'm not talking mumbo-jumbo, I'm talking Honor, God, Choice— a whole lot of things! Once, people believed in those kinds of things, and believing in a Unicorn was easy. But if you don't believe—I mean *believe*, not just say it out loud—that you've got to be good, do the right thing, for no other reason than, just, because it's *right*—well, then, how do you expect to believe in a Unicorn?!

"Ah, Lady Fair!" Karus cried, shaking his head from side to side. "Ah—!" He let out a huge sigh. His next words were low-key, mumbled together:

"I know you're a virgin and I told you that purity is what the Unicorn sought—but I don't even know what 'pure' is anymore. I really don't. I can't believe that some of the bitches and bastards I know are pure—even if they're so proper a disinfectant couldn't get them any cleaner. Meanwhile, you're out here with me . . . and, if you haven't figured it out yet, half the world's going to figure you're a teenage whore and I'm a lip-smacking pervert. So there you are: the world is screwed up—

"Which, of course, doesn't mean anything, but makes me feel satisfied in the saying of it."

"I saw the Unicorn, Karus. I believe in it."

"That's what I needed to hear, Lady Fair."

They did not speak another word to each other until Karus realized that—heading east or not—the road he had chosen was not suited for overnight travel by a driver unfamiliar with its twists and turns: he would make twice the distance in half the time during daylight hours. A small grove of pine trees beckoned by the side of a passing turnoff. Karus pulled the white panel truck to a stop there.

"W-why are we stopping?" Annunciata asked, once more awakened from a neck-aching upright sleep.

Karus disappeared into the rear of his truck to prepare his cot for the Lady Fair. "Because the Unicorn is heading for his Place"—the Rider's voice echoed up to the front seats—"and we've got the time to let him get there." The bearded man reappeared next to the girl, holding a rolled-up sleeping bag.

"You go in back and sleep in my bed; I'll find a tree with dry ground and a good view of the stars."

"I—"

"I don't want to hear a protest," he cut her off, adding a gentle shove to aim Annunciata sleepily toward the invitation of the well-padded cot. "Good night, my Lady Fair!"

But the Lady Fair did not go straight to sleep: the blast of cold mountain air that punched into the truck when Karus opened the door to leave revived her slightly. Annunciata crept back to the driver's seat to look out the front windshield and see where Karus would set camp.

And he was not preparing a place to sleep, as he had told the girl. Instead, Karus stood at the edge of the cliff, into which the turnoff they were on had been cut. Annunciata could see the Rider's silhouette clearly against the star-speckled sky and the near mountain outlines.

Karus shivered, not from the cold. "Please—don't doubt," he whispered. But, of course, Annunciata could not hear his words.

AVENIDA
DOLOROSA

The Conquest of the Meshica Empire was *not* complete—and Cortés greeted the reinforcements with open arms.

And a sword to the throat.

The Unicorn could see this all directly from the caravel, standing invisible by his Lady as she watched her brother row ashore in the long boats at the head of his newly recruited hundred soldiers. Doña Aline stayed behind with Captain Guzman and the provisions. The Lady was nervous at the separation; had her human eyes been as sharp as the Unicorn's, she would have been more so.

Doña Aline was recovered by the time the *Santiago Matamoros* reached the small coastal village Cortés had dubbed Veracruz, reconciled to Miguel's betrayal as the price to be paid for her own lack of diligence. She would be diligent now, she promised herself and Fra Benedicto: her father would be heartbroken if anything were to happen to his teenage son.

Which almost did immediately upon landing ashore.

Hernando Cortés, the Conquistador of New Spain, greeted the arrivals with a smile and a wave of his arms, embracing Don Miguel in a huge hug, kissing Fra Benedicto's feet with the humility of a reverent Christian. Then he drew his sword and placed the tip to Miguel's neck!

"Your choice," the Conquistador said with the same look of hearty passion as when he had first embraced the new arrivals, "is to abandon all other claims and swear allegiance to me—and the King of Spain—or to die."

It is most improbable that any consideration of his family's Encomienda land claim entered Miguel's thoughts as he swore immediate fealty to Hernando Cortés.

It *is* probable that Captain Guzman conspired with the other ships' commanders to send his inexperienced patron with the first wave to confront the upstart Cortés. No doubt they expected a skirmish that would leave Cortés and his original mercenaries weakened. Arriving to find Hernando Cortés leading an army increased by a hundred, however, Guzman did not show surprise at the new development. Pragmatically turning over Conde Rodrigo's provisions to the Conquistador, the captain assumed a public attitude of "this is what was expected"—privately drawing Cortés aside to warn him of the intriguers from the other ships who would soon be following. Freshly armed, Cortés' army greeted the arriving contingents with smiles and gun barrels. The other captains proved as pragmatic as Guzman.

It was only on the road to Tenochtitlán, the Meshica's highland capital, that the reinforcements learned Cortés' troops had awaited their arrival in Veracruz virtually unarmed. This was not an act of courage or extreme self-confidence: Hernando Cortés had no other choice. Only a few months earlier, after sending his overly optimistic "I-Have-Conquered" dispatch to Spain, the Conquistador had been forced to abandon Tenochtitlán in a midnight retreat, a disaster that cost his small army all of its firearms, most of the crossbows and half of their number. Cortés' forces, until the newcomers' arrival, numbered scarcely four hundred men—facing the Meshica Empire's thousands.

And the "conquistadores" had lost a fortune in gold plunder during their flight, sucked under the bloody waters of the lake surrounding Tenochtitlán, over which their retreat had been forced.

Fra Benedicto learned all of this with the dismay of an ex-soldier's realization that they had arrived in the middle of a war. Where Don Miguel looked at the situation with unabashed, childish excitement, and Guzman viewed the crisis with scorn at Cortés's failure to ensure the safety of his gold, the hidalgo-turned-friar saw the ugliness and danger that inevitably must ensue in the months to come—and in which the Lady Aline was now caught up!

Doña Aline was oddly serene about the deepening abyss of crisis toward which they travelled. It was a long journey from Veracruz to Tenochtitlán: the seacoast was surrounded by steamy jungle above which rose the *meseta*, an expansive plateau, where the Meshica Empire centered in a temperate highland climate. Doña Aline was not the only Spanish woman in the expedition: at least a few Cuban hidalgos, also thinking the Conquest complete, had brought their wives with them to establish the new estates they planned on ruling. Cortés' old hands, moreover, were encouraged to marry native Indios—

the Conquistador believed in family—and the leader himself was accompanied by a curious Indio woman his men called Doña Marina. This woman translated for Cortés—and more.

Doña Marina was not Meshica. Called *Malintzin* before Cortés had her convert to Christianity, she was the daughter of a *Náhua* lord, vassal to the Meshica. This sanguine noblewoman laid claim to a kinship with Doña Aline as the two highest-ranking women in the Spanish contingent. The Lady Aline was expected to join Doña Marina at meals—often shared with Cortés and his commanding officers.

And the Indio allies.

Doña Marina was indispensable to Cortés in his negotiations with an alliance of former subjects of the Meshica, a confederation held together primarily by the force of the Conquistador's will and the vassals' hatred for their *meseta* overlords. It was these allies, in fact, who had sheltered the frail Spanish army these past few months since its ruinous expulsion from Tenochtitlán.

Aline felt comfortable with the Indios. After her first few days' initial shock at the constant, overwhelming presence of so many bronze, half-naked figures trotting on foot next to the Spaniards' horses, surrounding the large newcomer army with numbers too vast to count, Aline grew to accept them as a part of the country. They were certainly more comely than the Iberians in many ways. She admired the multicolored, plumed shields and headdresses the men wore.

Aline appreciated, too, how in this climate the Indios' minimal clothing was a logical improvement over her own people's heavy blouses and pantaloons, soaked and smelling after a few minutes' exertion. Aline quickly grew envious of Doña Marina's terse apparel, a thin cotton shift of draped material. She was not attracted by the turquoise stone ring plunging through Doña Marina's nose, even though the *Náhua* noblewoman assured Aline she would be only more beautiful by the wearing of one—and obviously designated as a Lady of High Birth.

"But—Doña—Marina," Aline spoke slowly, Spanish being still new to the *Náhua* translator's ear, "without fine jewelry you would yet be of noble birth."

Cortés' woman remembered when she was *Malintzin*. "To be a noblewoman and a slave does not carry distinction."

"You were a slave?"

"I was a slave when Don Hernando rescued me. I would have been better a bride of the Hummingbird: when my father gave me up in tribute to the Meshica, that is what he expected. But I was not." Her jet-black eyes narrowed into slits of painful memory. "I cried to be taken to the Hummingbird, but my new lords wanted only slaves to make their lives easier. They deserve to die by the hand of the Plumed Serpent." She smiled at this promise of justice made right. "My Don Hernando Cortés is *Quetzalcoatl*—the Plumed Serpent."

Fra Benedicto had spoken with some natives, too, and explained to Doña Aline that the Indios thought Cortés to be one of their gods, the Plumed Serpent, returned to the Empire of the Meshica to wreak his vengeance on the other gods of the *meseta* plateau.

"But who is the Hummingbird to whom you would be bride?" Aline asked, wondering how the romantic ideals of an Indio woman compared to her own.

"*Huitzilopochtli*," was the reply. Doña Marina was silent a moment before adding under her breath: "Another god—ruling god of the Meshica."

Aline smiled to herself at Doña Marina's unwitting confession of libidinous desire: if Cortés was a "Plumed Serpent god" to the Indios, then this ruling "Hummingbird god" was no mystery, either—the *Náhua* noblewoman had wanted to become a concubine to the Meshica emperor!

The Unicorn met *Huitzilopochtli* at the road's entrance to the high *meseta* plateau; the Hummingbird's frame was stripped of flesh and his eyes cried for blood.

—*I will have ten thousand sacrifices by the next moon!* he cried ferociously, eyeing the Unicorn with suspicion. —*Tell the Plumed Serpent I will drink from his heart!*

—*I do not talk to humans,* the Unicorn replied, careful to maintain his distance from the gleaming jade sword the Hummingbird swung in violent circles.

—*Tell them! You come with them!*

—*I do not speak* for *them, I do not speak* to *them: tell them yourself.*

—*They do not hear my voice!*

There was as much distressed amazement as outrage in the Hummingbird's speech. *Huitzilopochtli* disappeared from the road. A stain of crimson marked where his presence had been.

The Unicorn feared for the safety of his Lady.

The Spaniards' progress had been slow up the steep road from the jungle: Cortés' men were exhausted, the newcomers unprepared for the wearing journey. A tenth of the men had already died from lowland fevers. The Conquistador himself might not have survived the return to the *meseta* high plain had he not ridden one of Don Miguel's horses. Nightly the increasingly exhausted beasts pleaded with their cousin the Unicorn to aid them.

—This is humans' endeavor: I cannot help.

His slow-witted cousins could not understand the difference but, being horses, resigned themselves to their servitude.

Nor did he reveal himself to the Lady. She was too caught up in some great human event; he could not contact her without violating his code of interference. To do that would take more love—or hatred—than the Unicorn possessed. He was not human.

But he could not abandon the Lady, either, nor her old confessor, the Unicorn's one-time enemy/one-time ally, Fra Benedicto. The woman attracted him, the friar consoled him: around these two the Unicorn found an aura of purity and peace that none of the other conquistadores shared. His nightly visits to the sleeping Lady Fair were almost regular now, made easier by the wild and open nature of the land—as compared to the sea: after the close-quartered-with-humans experience of the ocean voyage, the Unicorn was undaunted by the prospect of entering the Spaniards' camp at night. There he would slip between the humans, feeling their thoughts and dreams as he stepped closer to wherever the Lady slept that evening. He calmed her troubled dreams with the touch of his horn to her brow.

Once—just once, and it was almost a disaster when it happened—the Lady Fair grasped his golden horn while she slept. The Unicorn felt his pulse race: had she been singing, or cast her dark eyes open to look in his, the magic beast would have revealed himself to the surrounding camp with a bray of ecstasy.

As it was, the Lady began to smile: her anxious nightmare shifted to a dream of pounding heartbeat and a face flushed with excitement. Aline woke with a sudden surprise, found nothing in the dark night to calm her overwhelming feeling of happiness, and sat awake until dawn letting the emotion drain from her in pleasant enervation. There was a hoofprint on the hem of her night dress, revealed when dawn finally broke: Doña Aline looked at it with disbelief and promised to be more careful about dragging her skirt.

The Unicorn found himself attracted by Fra Benedicto's increasing piety. It was not a simple religiosity the old friar practiced—the Unicorn was not so blinded by a growing affection for the man as to see him as naive. Perhaps, had the Unicorn been a reflective being, he might have realized that a large portion of his initial attraction to Fra Benedicto was as a silent rebuke to Santiago Matamoros: yes, the Apostle Saint was still with them. Santiago did not stand by the Franciscan, however, preferring instead the company of officers.

But that was only the first reason for avoiding one side of the invading army's camp in favor of the other; the Unicorn drifted into Fra Benedicto's company frequently for other reasons. The Lady being there often was one cause; the friar's uneasy balance between flesh and soul was another. In this Benedicto was similar to the Unicorn: man and magical beast both sought an ideal of purity, both felt a need to *touch* that purity. It was the Lady Aline, of course, that they shared in common—and the Unicorn, incapable of jealousy, respected Fra Benedicto's love for her.

Plus—it annoyed Santiago Matamoros to see the Unicorn in company with Fra Benedicto and Doña Aline, even if they were not aware of the mystic creature's pacing alongside their wagon. Santiago, unlike the Unicorn, possessed a human soul: he *was* capable of envy, despite centuries of closeness to the Creator's Son. Envy and disapproval: in this campaign into the Meshican Empire to displace their Gods, the Spanish army should have been reverently devoted to the Son. Of course—and Santiago knew this with the sad disappointment of experience—the common soldiers would also have illusions of power and booty driving them forward. But he expected more of the leaders. In this the Conquistador, Hernando Cortés, let the Apostle Saint down.

Cortés did not disown the civilization of the *meseta* Indios. Indeed, he *allied* his army with theirs—challenging the Meshica Empire only as an enemy, not as the citadel of different Gods that deserved to be destroyed as thoroughly as the Moorish kingdoms had been. Santiago Matamoros reported this failing to the Son with disapproval. The Son reported this to the

Creator, tempering the Apostle Saint's human belligerence with a compassionate call for a persuasive resolution to the problem. The Creator, as was the Creator's way, said nothing in response.

The Unicorn, of course, knew nothing of these discourses on the higher plane. But, then, Santiago Matamoros knew nothing of the Hummingbird's threat: the *Meseta* God had spoken only to the magical beast, not the messenger human spirit. *Huitzilopochtli*'s threat caused the Unicorn deep feelings of concern for his Lady, which led him to abandon his reservations and approach the haughty Santiago: he could not interfere in the humans' endeavor, but he *could* pass along the Hummingbird's message to the Apostle Saint, strained though their relationship was. Santiago smiled grimly at the information, disappearing immediately to bear the news to the Son.

The Unicorn touched both the Lady and the old friar that night: his contact brought only more trouble to their dreams, not solace.

◆◆◆◆◆◆◆◆◆◆◆◆◆◆◆◆

A mountain dawn—like sunrise everywhere—is always preceded by a period of twilight. It is a long moment of grey emotions in the swing of nature, unrelieved by a horizon offering little more than a weak, pink promise of sunlight. Night sounds have faded away; the day's noises have yet to begin.

Some people hate this period, feeling in its cold stillness a threat to their dreams. They're right: the religious of every faith in the world know this, too, and respect it accordingly. This is the time to confront your beliefs with reality, uninfluenced by midnight fears and sunshine illusions. Great plans have been worked out at this time of day, grand designs abandoned—as have an infinity of small ones. This grey hour is a better canvas on which to paint one's true decisions than are the white of day and black of night.

Lope stood alone in the colorless mountain dawn, idly tracing the outline of an Aztec phoenix on the dew-wet dust of his car's hood. Finishing the crude drawing, he stepped back to see how it fit into the overall design line of the white Barracuda.

The Barracuda is one of the best of the "ugly" beautiful cars. For it *is* ugly: looked at from the front, there is a distinct homeliness to the grill and "face" design; from the rear there is an almost-comical "squat" to the low-slung car. These warts are the result of the Barracuda's bastard conception: it was designed and built by Plymouth in the mid-1960s as the Chrysler Corporation answer to Ford's newly introduced, wildly successful sports car, the Mustang. Publicly the Plymouth advertising machine denied the mimicry, but everyone knew. Everyone *knew*. And this flawed imitation, rather than gaining immediate classic status like its Mustang inspiration, disappeared within a few years, the better aspects of its sweep-backed design absorbed into heavier, more upscale vehicles in the Chrysler inventory.

The part of its design that continued to live, that salvages the Barracuda from total aesthetic dismissal, is its profile. Seen from the side, it is very easy to fall in love with a Barracuda: images of the grimacing grillwork and dumpy rear end are overwhelmed by the sight of the sleek, fastback vehicle cutting through space. Then you begin to see beyond ugliness and prettiness into the soul of this car: under the paint there is metal. Real metal. Heavy and solid and bulletlike strong against the wind. This is important, because the engine inside the Barracuda—eight cylinders that bestow reality on the word "big"—give this car the power to fly. The speedometer reads up to 240. It is not an idle boast: the Barracuda can do it.

Without danger.

Whatever else Chrysler's designers did not know about sports vehicles, the creators of the Barracuda understood the secret of rooting a car to the road. On a trip into the Mojave Desert once, Lope had checked the sky for police surveillance helicopters, than pushed the gas petal of his Barracuda—*La Blanca*, "The White"—to feel its surging adrenal challenge to the resisting wind. Never once had his White wavered on the hot asphalt. It was an unbending stretch of empty highway, however.

Last night's dive into the mountains had seen the White—and the two Reds and three Blacks—corner the twisting roads with similar earth-hugging serenity. Separate from Lope's insistent concern for his cousin Nancy's safety, he was pleased by Los Barracudas' performance.

The trip into the mountains—where the six Barracudas had ended the night at a "Scenic View" parking area carved into a cliffside road—had been more a matter of flailing inspiration than plan: Lope remembered a campsite uphill from the San Gabriel Canyon where his father sometimes brought the family on Sunday afternoons. They never actually entered the campgrounds on those excursions, joining instead the hundreds of other Mexican families who parked by the side of the mountain highway and walked into the rocky arroyos a few dozen yards, there to dip their feet in the feeble streams which fed the almost-dry San Gabriel River further down. Everyone would talk quietly, like they did in the villages, and the kids could run around and come home with scrapes from rocks and cactuses—instead of from the metal cans and broken glass of the L.A. streets.

Maybe Nancy—who the wino Orson said went away with the bearded man on her own—maybe she went this way . . .

Or maybe not—but Lope felt the need to turn off the freeway when he realized that he was leading Los Barracudas fast into the night with no sense of where to start looking. He knew he had to do something, although it was easier to feel that way in front of the cliqua than when sitting alone with Blond Annie, charging along the highway into nothingness. Annie read the expression of bewilderment betrayed in tiny etchings at the corners of Lope's almost-impassive Indian eyes. Her clawed fingers snapped their flashing question in front of his face:

"If there is a better way—and I don't know that there could be—would you do this any different?"

Lope saw the White's reflection suddenly loom up on the freeway before him: a gasoline transport truck, its metal trailer polished to a sheen, mirrored the parade of Los Barracudas fast approaching behind with a clarity free of distortion. *It is beautiful!* Lope thought, making his mind up then and there to leave the pointless speed of the freeway behind.

"Ah, who the hell knows or cares?" he laughed at the sudden liberation of the idea. He took his right hand from the steering wheel to Sign his thoughts over to Blond Annie:

"Who the hell knows or cares? I don't—that's for certain."

Nor did Los Barracudas following him: the Reds and Blacks followed their jefe into the mountains willingly.

Of course there was no sign of the white panel truck parked along the narrow highway leading up to the campsite. Lope knew even as he guided the others past the canyon, up the mountain to a dead end, and back again, that he had not expected to find Nancita so easily. But, somehow, he did not yet feel defeated when he led Los Barracudas into the Scenic View parking spot, there to sleep away the remainder of the night.

Lope did not yet feel defeated now, either, facing the implications of his quixotic search in the grey pre-dawn. Behind him, curled up in her passenger's seat with only the vague assistance of comfort, Blond Annie slept quietly, her face visible through the slit of window she'd cracked open earlier. Lope knew that the chill air must have invaded her bones as it did his; he also knew that his deaf Angla *wanted* the fresh air more than she disliked the cold—just as he did. The Reds and the Blacks all had their windows sealed tightly shut, fighting off the mountain chill with their own, captured, warm breaths. The thick windows did not prevent a low bass line of music oozing from two of the cars; Lope smiled wryly and figured that his jumper cables would be put to good use before Los Barracudas were underway again this new day.

He threw his arms wide and stretched ambitiously: tired but unable to sleep. The intended exercise ended in a half-gesture that, at least, served to loosen his shoulder muscles, if nothing more. Lope looked down at the flat-bottomed canyon stretched out below the Scenic View and noted the criss-crossing tracks of dozens of tires, fresh, bisecting the thin ribbon of the shallow San Gabriel River at a hundred points. Lope turned away from the sight without a thought, intending to reenter the White as quietly as possible and let Annie sleep undisturbed.

It was only then that he noticed the hoofprint.

Lope squatted to examine the faint outline of the hoof on the parking area's gravel: there may have been more such prints before Los Barracudas' arrival, this was all that remained now. Although he knew nothing about animal tracks, one characteristic of this print was apparent even to the untrained eye: the horse was unshod. Beyond that observation, Lope could say nothing more about the meaning of the hoofprint—

Except that he had seen the same print on Abalita's windowsill the morning after Nancy disappeared through it.

•••••••••••••••

"Cortés is either a madman or a genius," Captain Guzman explained to his trembling patron, Don Miguel. "Either way, we are not returning to Veracruz." Guzman did not bother to add that he did not *want* to return to the coastal town, and, hence, to the safety of Cuba: the smell of gold masturbated the Captain's senses beyond the point of drawing back. "Besides," he added, "their emperor Motecuhzoma is dead, the pox rages in their city . . ."

"They are thousands strong, we are only nine hundred!"

"Our allies are *ten* thousands strong."

Guzman looked about the vast plaza of central Texcoco, the city across the lake from Tenochtitlán, where the confederation of anti-Meshica Indio nations had gathered under Cortés' command. There was another smell in the air that the captain recognized, a charged atmosphere as strong among the Indios as the scent of fortune was to the Spaniards. "And they *hate* the Meshica," Guzman added.

Miguelito returned to "console" his sister with this information, facts she already knew from long conversations with Doña Marina.

There really was no other choice: Aline was as perceptive as Cortés in realizing that—should the Spaniards not appear solidly united against the Meshica; should Miguel's hundred troops, or any others, attempt to desert—their Indio allies' confederation would fall apart—and turn on the Spaniards. It was human nature, really. Aline was not happy to be a part of this venture, but there was little option for alternative decision at this juncture. The best to be hoped for was survival—and survival depended upon Cortés' success. A very specific example of the extremity of their situation presented itself to all of the newcomers that afternoon.

There was a Flower War.

The Meshica capital of Tenochtitlán was, in fact, a city surrounded by a lake. The city where the conquistadores set up their headquarters with the Indio alliance stood across the lake where the water's edge met a flat plain.

The Unicorn waited with Santiago Matamoros at the edge of this plain and watched in uncomfortable partnership as the Meshica paddled their war canoes across the great lake to assemble in battle lines along the shore. The Hummingbird rode the lead canoe. This was the first time the Apostle Saint saw his adversary. Instead of the skeletal wraith who had accosted the Unicorn along the road, the Hummingbird appeared now seemingly re-fleshed and fully armed: shield and spear filled his hands, a green-plumed helmet adorned his brow, a serpent girdle of precious jewels wound round his tight-muscled waist. He was happy, and—the Unicorn's sharp eyes perceived across the distance—his teeth gnawed at the air hungrily.

By prearrangement with Cortés, the Tlaxcala nation's warriors were chosen from the confederation to oppose the Meshica. They assembled opposite the Meshica—accompanied by a *Meseta* God new to the Unicorn. At Santiago's bidding (and his own curiosity), the Unicorn galloped across the flat earth to inquire of the new deity his identity.

Drawing close to the Tlaxcala battle lines, the Unicorn saw that this God was reptilian—yet possessed of only an ephemeral body. Unlike the aggressive hysteria of the Hummingbird's greeting, the new *Meseta* God calmly identified himself as *Mixcoatl*, the Cloud Snake, and welcomed the Unicorn as an ally. Mistaken though the assumption was, the Unicorn did not dispute the Cloud Snake's belief that he would mix in human affairs. Without comment he returned to Santiago with the information that the Plumed Serpent—that is, Hernando Cortés—had condoned the Tlaxcala's engaging the Meshica in a ceremonial Flower War prior to the resumption of his own army's hostilities.

—*And the Cloud Snake recognizes the "Plumed Serpent" as a God?* Santiago Matamoros asked, incredulity and disgust blending with equal measure in his tone.

—*He does.* The Unicorn had never played messenger among beings of the Higher Plane before, although he knew that his ancestors had often done so in the millennium of the Olympians.

—*Then this is not a being that deserves to exist under the protection of the Son, either, if he so mistakes a man for God!*

The Unicorn was surprised by this sudden outburst of emotion from the normally staid Apostle Saint. He looked at Santiago's face for a sign of what that passion meant—and then he realized that Don Santiago Matamoros, so worshipped among the Spaniards almost on the level of a deity, *was himself a worshipper*! Saint James the Apostle the Moor-slayer worshipped the Creator's Son; Santiago Matamoros' entire existence was based upon his human love for the beneficent Son, his friend: he had died a martyr's death for this belief. In his eyes it was the utmost betrayal of trust for any divinity to mistake the humble, corrupted person of a human being for God! The Unicorn watched this violent play of emotions rush through the Apostle Saint and let the somber empathy he felt for other humans touch his own spirit: Santiago's soul was, after all, a *human* soul—elevated above the Unicorn's Plane of Being, true—but fallible with the taint of human heart nevertheless.

And that heart hardened faster than the Unicorn's at what happened on the battlefield before them. Santiago Matamoros saw beyond the immediate clash of bodies and rending of flesh—which agonized the Unicorn to watch, as it always did—saw to the ultimately unclean purpose behind the screaming, painted faces powering the flailing, weapon-filled arms. The Hummingbird was seemingly everywhere, cawing pleasure at one personal struggle, screeching his disappointment when exhaustion allowed capture in another quarter. The Unicorn saw, too, how the Cloud Snake encouraged the Tlaxcala warriors against the more ferocious Meshica: he was less effective than the Hummingbird, but just as strong-willed in his desire that few of his worshippers allow themselves to be captured. This puzzled the Unicorn: while not given to calculated thought, he reasoned instinctively that a living reverent could continue to worship a God, rather than become simply a dead body on the battlefield. Not until the fighting ended—it was a short encounter, with no apparent victory for either side—did the magical beast see just how jealous the *Meseta* Gods were.

For there was no purpose to this Flower War other than to take prisoners.

The Unicorn did not follow the Hummingbird back across the lake to view the Meshica capital up close, their war canoes filled with Tlaxcala prisoners taken in battle. It was natural, instead, for the Unicorn to accompany Santiago to where the Spaniards waited for their Tlaxcala allies. A hideous beat of deep, sullen drums greeted the warriors' return.

Santiago, perhaps naively, hurried to the central temple dominating the city, expecting to witness the Cloud Snake's priests consoling the Tlaxcala warriors—and the populace in general—on their losses in battle. This is how it would be in Spain. This is how it would be throughout the Son's realm: warriors were respected, but the loss of a life was still tragic, the failure of humans to exercise their Free Choice wisely. This was not how it would be for the *Meseta* Gods.

The Unicorn did not intend to stay with the Apostle Saint: his chosen destination was the Lady Fair, and *her* place was at the side of Doña Marina at the central temple. Both were witness with Don Hernando Cortés, the "Plumed Serpent," of the Tlaxcala tribute to the Cloud Snake, their nation's patron God. Cortés' face was shaded an ashen grey, as were those of his veteran lieutenants, who stood rigidly beside him. Doña Marina's eyes were wide with pride. Behind her the newly arrived officers and nobility of the Spanish forces—among them Captain Guzman, Don Miguel, Dõna Aline—sat arrayed in their finest to witness their allies' prayers of thanksgiving. Their faces were not discolored like the veterans', although the oppressive drums echoing through the city's stone streetways made them uneasy. Fra Benedicto was afforded a place of less honor standing behind the Lady Aline. It was he who caught her when the first sacrifice sent her swooning in horror. Guzman was too busy keeping his own head from filling with black dizziness at the sight to catch Miguel, who crashed to the ground limply, groaning in horror.

To awaken to a close-up view of the next sacrifice, and the next, as the Meshica captives were led in parallel lines up to the top of the temple, where the Snake Cloud's priests uttered cries of praise—then plunged obsidian-edged knives into the captive warriors' chests, pushing their clawing hands past the spurting blood to grasp at the victims' hearts and wrench the organs, still beating, from chests, still heaving, to raise the prize of the sacrifice high overhead.

—*This is how they love me,* said the Snake Cloud quietly from behind Santiago Matamoros and the Unicorn. Flecks of blood oozed from the corners of his nebulous mouth. The Unicorn stepped over to the Lady and touched her with his horn, sending her into a faint again: the Tlaxcala chieftains proudly insisted their Spanish confederates remain in attendance at least for the first hour of ceremony.

—*The Son sacrificed* himself *for us!* Santiago said between clenched teeth to the *Meseta* God.

—*It's all blood,* the Cloud Snake answered, drifting back to his priests to receive the next pair of sacrifices.

"Even if I don't understand the Creator's designs, some things are wrong," Fra Benedicto vowed to himself, holding the Lady Aline's head in his lap. He was grateful, at least, that she was not regaining consciousness, although the smell of hot blood flooding down the temple steps made even her unconscious senses twitch at the stench.

◆◆◆◆◆◆◆◆◆◆◆◆◆◆◆◆

Annunciata poked her head through the side window and leaned far out to see Karus at the rear of the truck, pumping gas.

"Can I get a snack?"

The bearded man felt a shiver run through his body. *Getting low on carbohydrates,* he thought. "Why don't we eat lunch instead?" he countered.

"I'm not very hungry."

"You're not used to the mountain air yet." Actually, although they were six thousand some-odd feet up into the San Bernardino Mountains, the atmosphere of this particular self-service station smelled like spilled gasoline. "Wait an hour and you'll be telling me you're starved."

Annunciata hopped out of the truck, her long hair flying, and ran back to Karus to begin the negotiation process: he was no match for a girl who had convinced a strict grandmother to purchase an indecent amount of junk food over the past dozen years.

In the four-wheel-drive Jeep Cherokee two pump stalls over—*not* pumping gas—Bill Peyton, Forest Service, U.S. Department of Agriculture, listened to the lopsided debate and flipped through a stack of bulletins on his clipboard. Technically, the two-lane highway the service station perched next to, just northeast of Big Bear Lake, was patrolled by the San Bernardino County Sheriff's Department. One hundred feet on either side of the road, however, the National Forest crept down to the edge of highway civilization—and people like Ranger Bill Peyton had their hands full maintaining some sense of coherent balance between the purveyors of that "civilization" and Nature.

Like distinguishing an unprepared tourist from the experienced hiker.

Or the fugitive from a visitor.

"Okay, here's the compromise: I eat a snack now *and* lunch in an hour."

Ranger Peyton did not recognize the man with sprinkles of grey in his beard who was pumping gas into the white panel truck. According to the photographs faxed around the region, there should have been an old woman. There wasn't. Bill Peyton took another inconspicuous look over at the bantering twosome and compared them once again to the INS bulletin snapped into his clipboard: "Annunciata del Rio" was definitely standing twenty yards away from the Ranger, clear as daylight in the warm October morning.

Peyton eased the Cherokee into drive and drifted out of the service station, steering left-handed. His right hand was occupied by a radio microphone, calling in to his post station.

"Hey, guys, get me the Soop—"

Annunciata's choice of nutritious late-morning snacks ran to candy bars.

"You have any frozen Snickers?" she asked the cash register attendant, who was simultaneously taking Karus' money for the gas, giving change, drinking coffee, reading a tabloid newspaper and watching a small portable TV.

Out on Highway 18, Peyton brought the Cherokee back past the service station for a confirming look at the white panel truck, jotting down the license plate number, before pulling over to the shoulder to wait. He listened to his superintendent's voice crackling questions over the radio, then offered:

"I'll follow 'em, Soop, no problem. I could pick 'em up if you want."

In his office at the Ranger Station overlooking Big Bear Lake, on the other side of Gold Mountain from where Peyton sat watching the white panel truck, Superintendent Don Taylor let his finger idly trace the same facsimile photograph of

Annunciata del Rio that his Ranger possessed. Unlike Bill Peyton, his "Soop" was not pleased with the discovery of the fugitive girl in his jurisdiction.

"No, Bill, just follow—at a big distance: I'll let Immigration come up here on this. Give me a make on the guy again, okay, 'cause I can't figure out why INS'd go after two women all the way up here."

"If they're running they're probably guilty of something, Don."

Taylor let the comment pass, cautioning:

"It's National Forest, so it's our responsibility, Bill, but remember: we're supposed to be Stumpies, not Cops."

"Tell that to the poachers and their guns."

"Yeah, well, if we're lucky those two will head into a town and stay out of the woods. I'm passing this on to the Sheriff's Department: let it be their business, pure and simple."

It wasn't. The panel truck pulled out of the service station back on to Highway 18, then almost immediately turned off it onto a dirt road leading into the National Forest.

Victoria Reynaga looked nervously at The Dreambreaker.

"Nancy's in El Paso with her grandmother," she said after a moment.

INS agent N. D. Charny gave a cursory glance at his notes.

"That's not what you said yesterday when I first came."

"We took them to the bus station . . ."

She stood in the doorway of her apartment. For some fortunate reason the little kids were quiet behind her. For some unfortunate reason, Sylvia del Rio's bus to El Paso had been delayed somewhere en route through Arizona: Victoria was unable to reach her mother to tell her what was happening and, maybe, find some papers to make The Dreambreaker go away.

Charny had no intention of entering the woman's apartment. He took a friendly but firm stance an unthreatening distance away—in front of Sylvia del Rio's closed door— and offered a dangerous smile that was not overtly "oppressive."

"Annunciata del Rio is near Big Bear with an unidentified man. Who is that man?"

Victoria's confusion was honest.

"I . . . don't know," she stuttered.

"She called you yesterday, didn't she?" It was not a question, really. "You answered the phone and said 'Nancy.' " Charny did not wait for her to lie. "Where is your son?"

"Lope is . . . with his club."

The unoppressive smile remained faintly traced on the corners of The Dreambreaker's mouth: he knew where Lope Reynaga and Los Barracudas were.

"Who is the man?"

◆◆◆◆◆◆◆◆◆◆◆◆◆◆◆◆

T o assault Tenochtitlán was—as Guzman had observed earlier—the conception of either a madman or a genius. In either event, there was no denying the slow success of Cortés' plan to destroy the Meshica capital.

Within days of the reinforcements' arrival a new caravan arrived from Veracruz—a ten-thousand-man army of Indio warriors escorting a small band of Spanish craftsmen, veterans of Cortés' original force—and carrying thirteen brigantines crafted from the wreckage of Spanish ships: Cortés had ordered the new arrivals' oceanworthy caravels to be stripped, broken down, then converted into shallow-draft warships manned by oar and sail. Under the craftsmen's guidance the Indios had accomplished this task with skill, carrying the small fleet—along with the ships' cannon—across the hundred leagues' cruel distance from beach to *meseta* to be reassembled on the shores of the lake surrounding Tenochtitlán.

Leaving the Spaniards one less hope of escaping with their lives at anything short of total victory.

Miguel, the horror of the previous week's sacrifices still filling his imagination, turned to religion for consolation: twice daily he forced Fra Benedicto to hear his confession, pouring out such an incessant stream of heartfelt pleas for forgiveness and salvation from this hell that the old friar had to restrain himself from becoming brusque.

"Stay with Guzman," Fra Benedicto advised Miguel. "I notice that this captain of your soldiers is careful of his own safety, no matter how fearless his actions appear."

Indeed, had the teenaged Don been able to look past his own fear, he would have seen how fear*less* Captain Guzman was under his volunteered command: as leader of the brigantines—and their cannon. The individual Meshica war canoes proved to be no match for the Spanish warships which Cortés unleashed upon their waters.

Day after day Captain Guzman led the small fleet in a wide circle around Tenochtitlán.

There was deadly purpose to this circling of Tenochtitlán: to cut off Meshica supply lines. Until now the rulers of this magnificent capital had been able to ignore the surviving Spaniards and growing alliance of ex-vassal Indio nations. The lake surrounding Tenochtitlán had a shoreline impossible to guard on foot. Every night Meshica canoes would race to a different subject village, where the frightened people would bow to their imperial overlords and supply food to the besieged inhabitants of Tenochtitlán—until the swift-moving brigantine patrol began to strangle the Meshica canoe lifeline. The city began to starve. They could not ignore their enemies any longer.

Miguel was persuaded to accompany Captain Guzman ("You cannot hide, my lord, and it is as safe as possible—in these circumstances," Fra Benedicto berated the young man). It was, unfortunately, the day the Meshica chose to do desperate battle with the white-winged ships, paddling out in full force to destroy their enemies on the very lake itself.

It was an impressive sight: at least twenty thousand warriors crammed into canoes, armed and painted for battle.

By contrast, the thirteen brigantines could carry less than a tenth that number. Miguelito stood next to Guzman at the helm of the captain's brigantine and watched the lake between Tenochtitlán and the Spanish ships evolve into a solid mass of small boats. He heard the beating of the Hummingbird's massive drums echoing through the morning: the *Meseta* God's priests expected nothing less than the sacrifice of every armor-skinned Spaniard by this evening. On their own shore, the Tlaxcala chieftains and their allies watched their Spanish leaders await the approaching Meshica wave and shook their heads at the foolishness. Only a few Indios joined the Spanish this morning, crazy men, converted to the Plumed Serpent's "Christianity" and anxious to please this new God with proof of their courage. The Cloud Snake, too, thought the Plumed Serpent a fool— but a strange uneasiness made him frightened as well. No good would come of this battle, he told the Unicorn, whom he had sought, frantically, expecting the messenger-beast to bring this information to his ally-Gods, Santiago Matamoros and the Plumed Serpent. The Unicorn unwillingly conveyed the feeling to the Apostle Saint.

Santiago agreed with a grim smile: the Cloud Snake was right—this would be his last battle.

There was no reason for the brigantines to engage the Meshica war canoes under such apparently uneven conditions. No reason save that it was Hernando Cortés' order. And Cortés was a madman and a genius, willing to stake his all on a strategy he believed correct. Thus, while Don Miguel fingered a rosary on his belt and prayed for a quick death, Captain Guzman followed Cortés' specific directive to line up the brigantines bow to stern.

The Meshicans' lust for battle grew shrill with anticipation as their canoes pushed nearer, so crowded that the warriors could literally walk from one vessel to another. They were close enough to clearly see the white faces of the Spanish invaders now, if not their eyes.

They would never draw closer.

"Slaughter," not "battle," would be the better word to describe the ensuing day: the brigantines greeted the attacking war canoes with broadside volleys of grapeshot—scrap metal and rock—blasts that shredded through the Meshica warriors with the force of volcanoes. The Spanish did not waste gunpowder on firearms: crossbowmen shot clouds of arrows into the sky, iron-tipped death descending on the packed hordes of canoes in devastating torrents. The waters of the lake turned red, but neither the Cloud Snake nor the Hummingbird were pleased.

Santiago was.

And on the shore, proudly showing his Indio allies the power of Spanish arms, the Plumed Serpent declared that no prisoners would be taken on this day. In fact, Cortés demanded, this day *proved* the superiority of the God even he, the Plumed Serpent, worshipped: all members of the Indio confederation must swear allegiance to the Christian God!

The logic of the Plumed Serpent's argument unfolding on the lake below them, the Indio leaders caved in to the demand. A mass baptism was convened. Fra Benedicto, despite reservations about the sincerity of this sudden turnabout in beliefs, blessed and dispensed holy water by the barrel: the warriors were eager to convert to the Plumed Serpent's God and join in the massacre of their former oppressors. Santiago Matamoros sped to the Son with the glad tidings.

Abandoned, betrayed, forgotten in a day, the Cloud Snake ceased to exist.

The Unicorn guessed at once that Santiago had taken a hand in the victory—and he saw the grimly smiling Apostle Saint standing next to Cortés when the Conquistador returned to the temple with a quickly fashioned wood cross, erected in place of the Cloud Snake's sacrificial altars. Then the Plumed Serpent led the new warrior-converts down to the lakeshore, where they waded into the red-scummed water and awaited the return of the shallow-draft Spanish boats to pick them up.

For the day's battle was not ended with the decimation of the Meshica flotilla. As the surviving canoes scattered, the brigantines pursued them, sounding Spanish trumpets and now— at Cortés' command—the *Christian* war drums of the Indio allies.

Panic swept through the streets of Tenochtitlán: in one quarter the demoralized Meshica warriors turned on their own leaders, murdering them before abandoning the lake-ringed quarter to hide behind the safety of a thick wall. Captain Guzman, smelling fear the way a terrier sniffs out rats, drew his brigantine alongside, reloaded the cannon with regular shot, and blew the wall into memories of stone, scattering the frightened Meshica without a second's endangerment to his own life.

Such security was not a part of Miguel's lot: emboldened by the pounding cannon and trumpeting horns, the teenager felt his blood race with the false courage of overwhelming victory. As the Meshica wall was reduced to dust, a second and third brigantine drew next to Guzman's, each filled with new-born Christian warriors. There was a rush over the sides, slipping and sliding in the shallow water, then to the solid land and over the ruined wall. Somewhere in that mad attack Don Miguel found himself leading a party from his own ship, screaming at the top of his lungs as they charged after the panicked Meshica. It was easy, he thought, wildly exhilarated, this hacking with a sword at naked backs! He swung left and right, striking stone walls more often than flesh. A paint-masked Meshican turned to face him, swinging a heavy, stone-encrusted club. Without conscious thought Miguel ducked the unaimed blow, the meaning of a thousand fencing lessons driven into his muscles, then brought his lighter, more controlled sword forward in a thrust to the man's chest. A boy warrior the age of the young Don was skewered by the blade and fell dead into his killer's arms.

"Good, mi hidalgo!" the bearded soldier behind Miguel laughed, his Catalonian accents rushing past the teenager as he ran around his "commander" in pursuit of the routing Meshicans. Miguel felt a thrill of pride at the veteran's compliment, pulled his wet sword from the dead boy's chest, and rejoined his troops. Across the waterway, they could hear Guzman's heavy cannon pounding away at Eagle Gate, which guarded a main causeway into the heart of Tenochtitlán. Don Miguel liked this taste of conquest and looked around for more victims.

The Meshica returned in a deluge.

Decimated and routed as the canoe warriors were, the military population of Tenochtitlán was too large to be destroyed by the loss of only ten thousand: under the leadership of Cuauhtémoc, the new emperor, the forces within the city began to regroup and strike back at the pursuing invaders. The Spanish and their Indio allies had the advantage of cannon and attacking momentum—but, once on land, winding through the streets of vast Tenochtitlán, the power of the brigantines was neutralized. Plus, the Meshica—so fierce in their conquests of other Indio nations—were doubly ferocious in defense of their own city. The Hummingbird was a demanding God: his appetite for conquest had been voracious, his hunger when deprived of Empire was insatiable. He saw the Plumed Serpent at Eagle Gate and would not let his people retreat further.

Don Miguel and his three hundred men saw themselves cut off from the lake by a thousand warriors.

Then another thousand.

And another.

Eagle Gate stood an island—and a causeway—away. Thousands of Meshica streamed from the heart of the city toward this battlefield—but it was the only way possibly open for the handful of Spaniards and disorganized mass of Indio allies with whom Miguel found himself. Ostensibly their leader, the teenage Don had no need to make pretense of his skills: everyone saw the same vague pipeline of hope and ran toward the causeway as one. That Miguel was among the first to reach the short bridge leading to the island on which Eagle Gate rested was a tribute to his youthful muscles. That he was among those to fall into the scummy canal was an attribute of inexperience: he did not have a veteran's understanding that momentum in breaching the enemy's line is what carries a man through, not skill or force or fancy footwork. A handful of Meshica blocked the causeway, far outnumbered by the three hundred charging invaders, but soon to be reinforced by Cuauhtémoc's swift-arriving troops. Miguel, remembering the success of his duck-and-thrust technique with the club-wielding Meshican, stopped just out of reach of the defender's battle line, prepared to jab in as soon as one of the three warriors in front of him committed to a blow.

The veterans behind the novice hidalgo did not wait upon such ceremony: they rushed forward, crushing the defenders underfoot by the sheer weight of their numbers—suffering barely a wound in return—pushing Miguel aside and off the causeway in the process.

Miguel could not swim, but the murky canal was refuse-clogged and shallow at that point anyway. It was to his benefit, in fact, that his fall into the muck left the young Don slime-covered and scarcely recognizable: rising to the surface, sputtering and retching from the foul water in his lungs, Miguel saw at once that the causeway was now filled not with Spaniards and Indio allies but with Meshica reinforcements the causeway defenders had so desperately needed moments earlier. A man's length above Miguel, running across the bridge to defend Eagle Gate, the warriors did not bother to look down in the water for Spanish prisoners. Instinct or exhaustion prevented the boy from rising to his full height; his muddy face was indistinguishable from the brown water to a battle-hurried glance, his white eyes were closed for fear of seeing the Meshica swoop down to capture him.

Eventually, cramped muscles forced the fugitive to move from his position of petrified rabbit fear. Miguel slid along the sludge-greased canal bed to embrace a stone pillar under the causeway, hidden now even more from overhead view. The cannon roared at Eagle Gate for an hour—Miguel could not hear their cries of success as the men he had tried escaping with broke back onto the Spanish ranks—then a silence ensued. A short silence only, while Hernando Cortés directed an orderly retreat to prevent entrapment of his forces, followed by the enraged monotony of the Meshica drums. Many prisoners were taken—but not enough to satisfy the Hummingbird's humiliation. The blood that had stained the lake red from the ruined war canoes began to seep into the canal. Miguel found himself surrounded by red. His throat was sore with dryness and fear.

◆◆◆◆◆◆◆◆◆◆◆◆◆◆◆◆

The Unicorn's Lady could not be consoled at the disappearance of her brother. Fra Benedicto tried. Guzman proclaimed words of praise "for the Don's bravery"—pointedly ignoring the fact that it was his brigantine that led the other ships' withdrawal from shore, leaving Miguel stranded. There was no one else casting blame: this was a night of victory. Even the Plumed Serpent's woman, Doña Marina, could not find a reason for her fellow noblewoman to be sad.

"If he died, Doña Aline, he died for our Christian God. If he is captured, he will marry the Hummingbird God, and that is an honor, too."

It was at that moment that Aline finally understood what the *Náhua* noblewoman's earlier ambition to be a "bride of the Hummingbird, rather than a slave" really meant. Her throat clenched in horror. She ran to Cortés himself to demand he rescue Miguel.

The Plumed Serpent would not entertain the idea: suicide was not among his strategic priorities.

"Besides, mi Doña," he whispered with true sympathy, "the Indio spies I have assure me there are no Spanish prisoners. Don Miguel is dead—fortunately."

But Miguel's death without a body to bury was as unacceptable to Aline as the thought of her brother's capture and torture at the hands of the Hummingbird's priests. While the victors' celebration wound into the night, she retreated to her chamber in the stone palace of the Tlaxcala king. She had no immediate plan in mind, only to be away from the company of others, but in her solitude the Spanish noblewoman grasped at a course of action.

It was an impossible idea, doomed to failure—or worse.

Which was why Doña Aline made full confession to Fra Benedicto that night, both cleansing her soul and soliciting his advice before setting out. And sealing his lips to secrecy, since her plan was revealed under the sacred protection of the confessional.

"I am going to go into Tenochtitlán to find Miguel."

Fra Benedicto's arms were still weary from the barrels of holy water he had carried that afternoon, his palms blistered from the rough wood dipper chafing his fingers as he baptized thousands of Indios on their way to attack the Meshica capital. Hearing Aline's words, however, Benedicto raised those cracked hands with the speed of a young man and shook her by the shoulders furiously.

"Do not even think of such stupidity!" he cried, breaking the spiritual wall between penitent and confessor with his violence.

"Thought is past, my confessor; it *is* to be done." Doña Aline's directness of purpose left no thought in his mind that this was to be the act of a foolish young woman. His hands stayed grasping her shoulders.

"How—tell me: *how* do you intend to enter the city without dying in the attempt, much less find Miguelito?"

The answer, truly, was the only part of her plan that Aline had thought out to the end.

"Dressed as a Meshica warrior."

And Fra Benedicto dropped his hands from her shoulders at the simple logic of this idea.

For disguising Doña Aline as a Meshica was no difficult task, made even less so by the addition of warrior paint across her face. There were Meshica nobles as pale-skinned as the Spanish, and the family of Conde Rodrigo was as dark-eyed as an Indio. With soot from a fire, Aline's hair could be made to look as black as needed—no one would look twice at a Meshica dirty from smoke after today's battle. Loosened, her long hair would be as a Meshica youth's. As for the fact that warriors were bare-chested under their plumed armor . . . It was a cold night; the "warrior" Aline would wrap an Indio cloak around her upper body and avoid that issue altogether.

Three months' acquaintance with the translator Doña Marina had given Aline command of several phrases in the dialect of the *meseta* Indios. There was no question of carrying on a conversation, but to come into so close contact with a Meshica would be the mission's failure anyway.

She would have to go alone: Benedicto's blue eyes and short, tonsured hair would betray him as a Spaniard instantly. Aline's confessor did not beg her to stay, though: the former hidalgo knew how important it was for the noblewoman to do all that she could for her family. The best he could offer was to distract the Spanish sentries as she slipped one of the captured Meshica canoes from the shore and paddled across the lake toward Tenochtitlán.

The Unicorn watched these machinations with horrified fascination: his Lady was heading into the claws of the Hummingbird! Without the power to alter human affairs, the magical beast was unable to stop her—but was the will of a *Meseta* God restrained by such a code?

The Unicorn knew that this was not so.

Against the drag of his own disgust, the Unicorn threw himself into the crimson-stained lake and swam after—then ahead of—the Lady Fair. This was no great accomplishment: she was unskilled in handling a canoe. Moreover, despite her determination, Doña Aline had to overcome every reasoning sense in her brain in order to approach Tenochtitlán's dangerous shore: once grounded where Miguel had breached the Meshica wall, there would be no return to safety until his body was found— or she herself captured. Aline hesitated.

The Unicorn did not wait to see if the Lady Fair overcame her fears: he knew that she would. Clambering ashore, he shook the tainted water from his coat and began to gallop with long, earnest strides through Eagle Gate, down the main causeway leading to the central island upon which the original village of Tenochtitlán had been built. There, the Unicorn knew, he would find the Temple of the Hummingbird.

The Meshica capital, destroyed now on the outskirts by Spanish cannon, was still vast and magnificent: the Unicorn did not pass through its streets to the heart quickly. Past Eagle Gate, the merchant classes lived, still Meshica overlords by the Empire's standards, but much lower on the hierarchy of the Hummingbird's concerns than warriors and nobility. The Unicorn raced past the merchants' lava stone dwellings, sturdy buildings of pale red color. Here the Meshicans who had born the brunt of this day's assault whimpered in terror and dug out from under the rubble of homes smashed by cannonballs.

Beyond them, closer to the center, the same red lava was now whitewashed. Life-sized friezes of men and deities were carved into the walls, jumping out at the Unicorn whenever his eyes caught a flicker of torchlight coming from a thin-slit window. Warriors resided here, the Unicorn realized, the moans of wounded men sounding clearly to his sensitive ears.

The Hummingbird's drums beat their monotone deeply into the night air.

At last the Unicorn reached the nobility's quarter—and the *Meseta* Gods' temples. Huge gardens separated Meshica aristocracy from the rest of the populace. Had the Unicorn time, he would have paused to gaze at the multicolored birds of brilliant plumage dancing about in huge public aviaries, their shrieks and songs filling the gardens so thoroughly that, for a moment, the Unicorn forgot that humans resided nearby. Jaguars and panthers were caged here, too: the Unicorn had met these swift, fierce animals in the jungle, on the road from Veracruz. The Temple of *Huitzilopochtli* loomed ahead, overshadowing that of the other *Meseta* Gods whose powers had dimmed under the Hummingbird's dominance. The Unicorn left the gardens behind, leaping across wide boulevards separating the Meshica palaces, running under the oversized murals of History: Four Suns had died on the *Meseta* Gods; the Fifth Sun would do so too, one day. Emperor Cuauhtémoc consulted with his advisors on the bottom step of the Hummingbird's temple, his hands bloodied from the prisoners he personally sacrificed to his hungry God. Above, on the highest platform, the Hummingbird raged.

The Unicorn allowed himself to become visible as he mounted the towering stairs. Self-sacrifice did *not* violate his code: if the humans wanted to pursue him—instead of the Lady—then he would lead them now on a chase to the opposite side of the city. But the Meshica lords did not have attention to spare for the golden-horned beast appearing on the temple steps. If any saw him, they were still in too much shock at the Godlike power displayed by the Spanish brigantines that morning to express more than quiet awe at yet another miraculous sign. The Unicorn had not counted on distracting the humans' attention anyway, at least not so simply: had that been his intent, he would have let the Meshica see him on first arrival. It was to the Hummingbird that the Unicorn planned to make his appeal.

Or, rather, to the Hummingbird's conceit. In the past weeks, since reaching the high plateau, the Unicorn had come to know other *Meseta* Gods—and from them to learn more of the Hummingbird. He knew, for instance, that *Huitzilopochtli* favored the Meshica—but they were not his sole worshippers.

—*The Plumed Serpent is not a God! He worships* another *God!* the Hummingbird cried on seeing the Unicorn, echoing Santiago Matamoros' scandalized outrage of earlier weeks.

—*The Plumed Serpent's God is now god of the Tlaxcala.*

—*The Cloud Snake is!*

—*No more.*

Which the Hummingbird knew, for if the Cloud Snake were still God of the Tlaxcala, his taunts would have echoed across the lake to the Hummingbird by now, after such a day of victory and bloodshed. For the first time since the Unicorn had first seen him, the Hummingbird ceased to rage, staring instead at the wide city spread out below.

—*How did the Plumed Serpent defeat him?*

The Unicorn would not lie to a God.

—*By subterfuge: he pretended acceptance, then allied himself with Santiago Matamoros.*

—*The Plumed Serpent's God?*

—*No, only a messenger, once a human.*

While the Hummingbird spoke with the Unicorn, his fiery anger slipped from the hearts of the Meshica: as before his dominance, they became afraid of the Night. The Meshica withdrew into their homes, fearful of the dark. Doña Aline beached her canoe at the shattered wall to find a city of deserted streets.

The Hummingbird roused himself with the pride of a conqueror.

—*I have fought Gods before.*

—*You will die faster.*

And now knowledge flooded the Unicorn as it always did: when expedient, at the moment of necessity. He had not reasoned it out, that was beyond a Unicorn's power, but the thoughts seemed right, the knowledge overwhelmingly correct.

—*You are like the Old Ones who preceded the Olympians: hungry for blood beyond your need.*

—*It was necessary to forge a world with fire and blood.*

—*Not beyond your needs! Not—beyond life!*

—*I created life! A civilization is life!*

—*And you took it, too much! Just like the Old Ones! And like them, your time is over: whatever you created, good or bad, beauty or horror, it is over.*

—*And this new God, he is better?*

—*He is on His second millennium, the child of yet a third. And you?*

—*Not yet one millennium, but soon.*

—*Maybe one millennium is all the time we have . . .*

Doña Aline, the cloaked Meshica "warrior," traced the route of Don Miguel's soldiers, following the stains of gore down moonlit, empty streets.

—*. . . maybe it is all the chance we are given.*

—*Were you given a second millennium?*

—*No—yes—no: there were my kind before . . . but . . . we changed.*

—*I will not change.*

The Unicorn saw the stern ferocity burning in the Hummingbird's eyes: the magical beast feared for his Lady's safety should this ferocity arouse the Meshica.

—*You made a wondrous creation,* the Unicorn noted, with honest admiration for the Hummingbird's city.

—*I could not give this up.*

The hidden Spaniard knew that he would drown before morning. His hands were exhausted from clutching at the stone pillar under the causeway. He knew that he would, finally, close his eyes and slip under the death-smelling water. A Meshica warrior was approaching the canal bridge, the first that Miguel had seen in an hour.

—*Perhaps they are unworthy for you.*

The Unicorn did not suggest more, waiting to see how the Hummingbird reacted to this seed of thought. He felt conceit gnaw through the *Meseta* God's resolve.

—*I am strong,* the Hummingbird thought to himself.

—*I am stronger than the Four-Eyed Rain, and the Wind, and the others!* he said aloud.

—*When your worshippers are worthy.*

The Hummingbird was not a contemplative God; his stomach when hungry required action to fill it: the Meshica had failed to fill his stomach with invaders' blood.

—*When they are worthy of me,* he agreed with the Unicorn, looking down with scorn now upon the pitiful Meshica who had been so weak as to let a handful of white-skins destroy the Empire the Hummingbird himself had inspired them to build.

—I will go north to the Tarasca nation. I have always thought them worthier than the Meshica. Their mountains smell better than this foul lake. Pah!

"Miguelito?" Aline whispered to the white eyes staring up from the canal at her.

FORTUNE

It was an old and silly child's singsong.

"Here's a to do to do—"

"—to do—"

"Wrong. Stop giggling, girl! Again: Here's a to do to do—"

"—today—"

"(Yes!)—at a minute or two—"

"—to two!" Giggle, snort, bitten tongue. "Ow!" Annunciata cried.

"You gotta stop *laughing*!" Karus cried back, giving up on this important attempt to impart culture to his passenger (between gulps of his own yowlping laughter). He saw what he was looking for on the crest of a small rise, almost hidden behind the pines. "Hang on, hangin' left!" He pulled hard on the steering wheel with both hands—sending the slow-moving panel truck into a dust-churning turn off the "main" dirt road and onto a tributary leading up to a green-painted cabin.

A mouthful of dust found its way to the laughing Annunciata through the open windows. "Where is this?" she spat the grime from her tongue, still giggling.

"I don't know," Karus answered, stopping the truck with a small jolt.

"I mean: *whose* is it?"

"Don't know that, either."

A half-mile down the mountain, following the truck's slow climb into the National Forest easily, Ranger Bill Peyton knew whose cabin it was, though: Old Hubert's. Only, Hubert wasn't old now, Peyton remembered, Hubert was dead—and the cabin belonged to Hubert's daughter, some doctor over nearby in Running Springs. Hubert had taken a lease on the plot from the government, paid it in advance, and as long as Doctor What's-Her-Name kept the cabin from falling apart the Forest Service was happy to have the place there.

Especially now that it looked pretty certain that the bearded guy and the wetback girl, Annunciata del Rio, had decided to spend the night in Hubert's cabin: there was only one road in and the same road out, not counting footpaths. Peyton eased his four-wheel-drive Jeep Cherokee into reverse, pulled off a tight three-point turn, and headed back toward the highway. Better not to be seen—just as easy to settle down at the end of the road and wait for the cavalry to arrive once he called up the Soop. They'd probably have to wait for somebody from Immigration to show, and maybe call in the volunteer Auxiliary Deputies from the Sheriff's Department: those guys usually got stuck with traffic control duties during ski season, that and foul-weather searches for lost hikers. They'd think *this* was a blast! So did Bill Peyton, for that matter—everybody likes a chase—except for the fact that he sort of thought the bearded guy sounded OK when he heard him talking to the girl over at the gas station. Seemed almost like you could just walk up to him and ask "Hey, fella, what the hell's this business all about?"

Couldn't do that, though: man could be a serial killer—*they* all looked normal, too. Seemed like everybody looked normal who did something bad if you looked at the pictures in the newspapers and TV, which didn't improve Peyton's faith in humanity terribly much, but reminded him once again why he preferred facing the occupational hazards of insomniac winter bears and love-starved coyote romancing the tourists' dogs. No man is an island, but some—like Ranger Bill Peyton— had happy little peninsular lives in relation to the rest of civilization.

The ill-fitting door burst open with only a little pressure from Karus' boot.

"There!" he pointed to the welcoming doorway. "Didn't even need to kick it. Go bring the sleeping bags."

Karus made the first survey of their intended night's abode: although in need of some repair and several amenities, the square-framed clapboard structure was in solid shape and not particularly dirty. This was better than he had expected from such an obviously unoccupied cabin.

"C'mon, Karus! Whose is it?" Annunciata demanded from the porch, struggling to enter the narrow doorway from behind a bundle of sleeping bags and blankets heaped on her arms.

"I don't know," he admitted.

Annunciata dropped the mass of bedding supplies and absorbed the information. "Then we can't stay here."

"We have to: if we've come too far for the Unicorn, we'll head back if we need to—but there's no time anymore to be choosy about where we wait."

Annunciata knew that: the Unicorn himself had passed on the urgency of his mission to her at the stream last night, not revealing the final destination then only because he, too, did not know the exact location of the Last Mountain. When Annunciata passed this feeling along to Karus, the greying Rider looked at maps, compared the Unicorn's direction of travel with the possibilities, and headed for what was, literally, the *last mountain* before the mountain range dropped off into foothills and the Mojave Desert.

In *this* direction: if the Unicorn shifted direction five degrees south, his Place could be somewhere twenty miles away.

Or *his* Last Mountain might be three mountains back from where Annunciata and Karus sat now.

The key was in the waiting: The Unicorn had the smell of Annunciata, his Lady Fair, in his senses now—and he would find them, lead them (if need be) to his Place. Or at least leave a sign to follow—for those looking to follow.

Still . . .

"It's not honest," Annunciata said, then repeated: "We can't stay here."

"Oh, *that* we can—" Karus answered with the same dismissive shrug he had given to so many of the girl's reasonable objections so far on their trip. This time, however, he graced her with an explanation:

"I'm not being crooked, Annunciata, I'm being 'traditional.' Did you know in some countries, in the mountains, they *expect* you to stay in the shelters built there—even when the owners aren't around? It's not just hospitality, it's practical. We sort of forget that here in the U. S. of A., what with our rugged individualism and 'respect' for personal property."

"If it doesn't belong—"

Karus cut her protest short with a smile. "Practical. The mountains aren't very idealistic, you know: they're cold fact at nighttime."

In response, Annunciata walked over to a dead, wood-burning stove in the middle of the cabin's single room—reserving a skeptical expression for Karus all the while. Despite his sincerity of conviction, the Rider wilted a little under the Lady Fair's concentrated stare.

"You can stay in the truck if you want to!" he protested defensively. "But I don't see the owners here, and I intend to leave this place in better shape than I'm finding it . . ."

"Besides"—Karus' subdued tone wiped the skepticism from Annunciata's thoughts—"it's tonight or tomorrow night. This might be the last night."

"You mean . . . it'll be over?"

"It had to end."

"I just saw him yesterday!?!" the girl cried.

The Rider covered his sympathy for Annunciata's feeling of dismay with an attempted joke:

"And what? We were supposed to go on looking forever? I hope we're not *that* incompetent!"

The joke worked its own feeble magic: the Lady Fair smiled.

"No, we're pretty competent."

"Of course we are! So—you going to stay in here with me at least till nightfall?"

Annunciata shook her head—for a different reason:

"No: it's warmer outside right now than it is in here!"

Karus stepped next to Annunciata and picked up a heavy ax lying by the cold wood stove. "*That* is why God made forests: to work!"

Finding the right wood to stoke a fire is not as simple as it first may appear: after discovering a saw to fit into Annunciata's hands, Karus headed deep into the forest.

"Don't even consider any of the stuff around the cabin," he advised. "We need *wood* for that old stove, not scrub brush."

Annunciata, whose experience with campfires extended to weekend excursions with charcoal briquets—plus a dose of the now-despised scrub brush—asked the obvious:

"Why don't we cut down one of the trees near the cabin?"

"Three reasons: One, it could fall down on the cabin. Two, do I look like Paul Bunyan? Those buggers are two feet thick, girl! And three, we need dead *dry* wood, not green *wet* stuff, or we'll never get a fire going."

"Oh."

"Thought you'd want to know."

She didn't, in fact: Annunciata's mind had already wandered to another thought.

"Karus?"

"Um-hmm." The Rider had hoped to find some dead wood

scattered on the ground, but after a summer of tourist campers the autumn supply was nil.

The girl's thoughts were on his earlier comment:

"You were joking about God . . . You believe in God?"

" 'Course."

"Why?" Annunciata had spent countless Sunday mornings at Mass with her grandmother: she could not imagine seeing the bearded Rider kneeling in a church.

Karus, for his part, stopped his mouth from firing off an easy sardonic quip and tried to answer with some degree of sincerity. "Well . . . when I see the forest, I know there's a God." It came out as sappy-sounding as he feared it would.

The almost-teenage girl did not notice. "How?" she asked simply.

But the Rider could no longer keep a touch of wry humor from flavoring his responses:

"Oh . . . the trees," he said, waving grandly at the majestic pines towering above them. "They have souls, each and every one."

"What kind of souls?"

"Souls like . . . like you and me! Why, I have one tree"—and here Karus slightly forgot that he was pulling the girl's leg— "one tree, back where I was born, that I'm sure has my soul— and I'm sure that somewhere there's a tree with your soul."

It was a mesquite tree, ugly and splayed, stuck out on the Texas flatlands like a lost hand reaching up from the hard earth. The more Karus thought about it, the more the idea pleased his fancy.

"That means that everywhere there's a tree, there's a soul."

Put like that, and knowing his mesquite like he did, it made sense. "That's right," Karus agreed.

Unlike the grey-bearded Rider, Annunciata was inclined to think ahead. "What happens to the soul when we cut down a tree?"

"Well . . ." He had not yet travelled that far on the thought. "What do *you* think?"

Annunciata recognized the implication for what it was: "If that tree . . . is somebody's soul . . . and we cut it down—then somebody dies."

It was a good enough answer for the Rider. "Of course!" he shrugged. "Has to be: that's life—like eating beef." He spotted a likely source of firewood. "Here's what we want!" Dropping the heavy ax, he began to strip off his jacket.

Annunciata walked a tight circle around the thin, leafless juniper Karus had selected.

"Look out a bit—" he cautioned, retrieving the ax.

She stood between him and the tree.

"Is it still alive?"

"A little, maybe, right in the center. Stay back, okay?" Karus gave the girl a gentle push out of his way and pulled back the ax to aim his first strike. Annunciata felt that she was witnessing an execution.

The ax bit deeply into the thin trunk just above ground level; the girl flinched with the blow, unconsciously wincing with each succeeding bite of metal into wood. The gash began to widen. Annunciata could not prevent her eyes from focussing on the deepening wound—

"Don't cut it down!" she cried, grabbing at the ax handle.

"What?!" Karus shouted with surprise, dragged from the hypnotic rhythm of chopping.

Annunciata's face flushed with sudden embarrassment.

"We . . . can find some logs on the ground. We don't need this one."

"Fine, fine," Karus muttered, trying to rediscover the right tempo of swing to the ax. "You go find some of that wood— ha! wherever *that* is—and start gathering it up." He swung the ax back.

"But we don't need to cut down this one, then, do we?"

Beads of sweat had already broken out under the Rider's thick beard. "Lady Fair, it's gonna die anyway—we might as well use it."

"We . . . don't have to be the ones to kill it, do we?"

But these last words Annunciata said almost to herself: they went unheard as Karus resumed chopping away at the dying tree. She dropped her saw near his feet and started to wander away, mumbling: "I'll go back and clean things up."

"What?" Karus asked between the thudding blows.

"I said I'll go back and start cleaning up the cabin."

"Good." Chop. "Good." Chop. The blade stuck in the damp center core of the thin juniper, snagged in a sticky artery of sap. "I won't be too long," Karus called over his shoulder, putting his back muscles into the effort of drawing out the ax. Annunciata did not watch him succeed in the effort. Behind her she could hear his renewed whacks crack through the last inch of the tree's life.

This is stupid, the hazel-eyed girl berated herself. *Who cares about a stupid, dead tree?* Annunciata started to turn back to the Rider, stopped, knowing that she did not want to watch, then angrily resumed walking through the forest to the square-framed cabin.

With something of a vengeance Annunciata attacked the problem of cleaning out a cabin whose every seam and porous surface appeared to be filled with dust. Despite a vicious assault on the floor, Annunciata immediately recognized the ultimate futility of her efforts—the drought-dominated weather of the past decade had made dust an omnipresent factor in the region. A thin layer of thirsty dirt particles clung to everything—until churned up into small clouds, as Annunciata was doing with the cabin's ragged broom. She conscientiously ushered the cloudlets from one side of the room to the other. After fifteen minutes of mainly cosmetic effort, feeling that an acceptable space had been cleared for the sleeping bags, Annunciata directed her attention to the dusty wooden table and chairs sitting beneath the cabin's only window.

"Ow!" she complained to the walls, stubbing her foot against the heavy chair nearest the stove. "Gracioso, Annunciata, very graceful," she complimented herself sarcastically, shoving at the chair to get it out of her way.

The chair did not move.

"C'mon!" she urged the inanimate object, pushing at it with both hands—only to have the chair stay rooted to its spot. Annunciata looked down at the chair's legs: they were caught on some unevenness in the floorboards.

By this time the girl was carrying on a full-fledged conversation for the benefit of the unhearing cabin walls.

"Probably nails sticking out—just what I'd need to step on . . ."

But, kneeling down to unhook the chair legs, Annunciata saw that there were no nails sticking out: in fact, the floorboard she was examining had no nails at all, which accounted for the uneven surface. All she had to do, really, was lift on it to unhook the chair legs and—

The entire board lifted out, revealing a large—planned—space beneath the cabin floor. Annunciata took a close look at the next floorboard and discovered that it, too, was not nailed down. And a third.

There was even a *fourth* nailless board, but it went untested:

Annunciata had already found the space created by three displaced boards wide enough to crawl through.

Which she did. Excited at the imaginary possibilities offered by this hiding place, Annunciata crawled down into the shallow hole, remembering only as an afterthought that rattlesnakes and rabies-carrying rodents might share a similar ideology vis-à-vis utilizing the potential of this discovery. Too late to worry about that. Stretching out her arms and legs to test the size of the space, the girl encountered no territorial beings feeling possessive, although in the dim light anything could have been hiding inches away and she would not have seen it. However, what her hand *did* touch caused Annunciata to draw it back with a scared hiss—before recognizing the object as nonliving (albeit with a soft and skinlike texture). She groped into the darkness again, rediscovered the unknown thing, and pulled it back into the pool of light cast through the hole.

A leather pouch.

Kneeling on the hard earth floor of the hiding space, Annunciata raised her body above the level of the floor and plopped the leather pouch on the boards in front of her face. It was heavy for its size. With nervous fingers the girl undid the thongs tying the top of the pouch together, loosened them, reached into the pouch—

And pulled out a handful of gold nuggets.

With almost embarrassed self-consciousness, Annunciata rose upright before the pouch, a smile frozen on her face. Holding the gold in one hand, grasping the pouch in the other, she stepped out of the shallow hole and began aimlessly walking about the room. Uncertain of the reality of this moment, she needed to open her hand and look at the nuggets for reassurance.

"It *is*," Annunciata said soundlessly, lest the walls overhear and prove her wrong. "It *is*!" She began to imagine the wonderful escapes this gold would buy for her family!

"Abalita! I will fly to El Paso! . . . A car—no! A house— near the ocean . . . or the desert! . . . I . . . Meat! Aunt Vicky, we will have meat for a week and no beans!"

The clatter of wood hitting the cabin porch beat a drumlike announcement of Karus' return; Annunciata turned toward the sound with a startled movement.

"Try to find some old paper and get a fire started in the stove," he said from outside, his voice growing distant. "I'm going down to the stream to wash off. Be right back."

"Kar—" Annunciata started to call, then hesitated.

The implications of where the gold came from made its full entrance into the girl's thoughts now, past her moneyed dreams and future plans. In the light of reason, that gold belonged to the owner of this cabin. In the light of the same reason, that gold would buy happiness for Annunciata's hard-lived Abalita and family. Guiltily the girl made her decisive action: she let Karus walk away, then hurriedly put the handful of gold back into its pouch, the pouch back into its hiding space and, frantically, the floorboards over the space.

"What? No fire yet?"

Karus stood in the doorway, on the porch, scraping a clod of dirt from his boot sole.

Annunciata turned away from the loose floorboards—surely Karus would see they were not nailed down!—and rapidly began shredding an old magazine, wadding the pieces into small balls of paper. She did this kneeling on the floor, her body between the loose boards and Karus. Her eyes were downcast: she could not bring them up to meet his.

"No . . . I couldn't keep it going."

"No problem." Karus sighed at the city girl's lack of camping skills, shutting the door behind him as he stepped into the cabin. "We'll get it going in a minute. Got to: it'll be dark soon."

It was good for Bill Peyton that the bearded guy in Old Hubert's cabin shut the door: the Ranger had wandered a bit too close trying to see how the fugitives were set up, and he could easily be seen by anyone *expecting* to be followed. He wasn't, though. By the time Annunciata del Rio stepped out onto the porch to bring in the wood piled there, Peyton was already gone from sight, heading down the trail to where his supervisor, Don Taylor, waited with an Immigration officer named N. D. Charny, two Deputy Sergeants and a dozen Auxiliary Deputies.

◆◆◆◆◆◆◆◆◆◆◆◆◆◆◆◆◆

Deserted by the Hummingbird, the Meshica did not survive the siege of Tenochtitlán.

It lasted eighty days from the destruction of the warriors' canoes.

The Unicorn himself did not stay to watch the siege: his Lady took her brother Miguel down to Veracruz, and the golden-horned beast accompanied them. As yet he had not revealed himself to her. Never was the moment right: her heart untroubled enough—or his, unconcerned. The Unicorn's last encounter with the Hummingbird left the magical animal ill at ease. Perhaps his action had been too close to an interference in human affairs. Perhaps he was disappointed in the weakness of Gods. Santiago Matamoros had greeted the Unicorn warmly upon his return from Tenochtitlán with the Lady; the Unicorn had not felt comfortable with the Apostle Saint's praise.

As for Doña Aline, her disguise as a Meshica warrior soon became a well-respected legend among the Spaniards and their allies. A curious transformation occurred, though: in the first retellings, Don Miguel's role expanded to one equal to Aline's—he became known as the conquistador who *intentionally* infiltrated the Meshica lines. As later accounts evolved, the young hidalgo's true heroism grew proportionally: it was *he* who disguised himself as a Meshican warrior—to rescue his sister, the Spanish noblewoman who was captured and dragged into Tenochtitlán, a victim of foul treachery by those among the Indio allies still blind enough to follow the discredited *Meseta* Gods.

However, before these stories caught hold, Don Miguel fell into a fever from the foul water he swallowed during hours spent hiding under the causeway. Tremendous stomach cramps racked Miguel's body—a convenience for Hernando Cortés, who decided it was necessary to send another supply train down to Veracruz in case more reinforcements were unexpectedly arriving. Don Miguel was taken with the supply train: if he recovered, he could greet newcomers—if he died, it would be out of sight. Doña Aline, of course, accompanied her brother. After their departure, on Captain Guzman's advice, Cortés encouraged the stories about them to grow and spread.

Fra Benedicto stayed at the siege, attending to the spiritual needs of the new converts, promising a letter to Aline with each courier to Veracruz.

His letters wrote of the costly price of victory.

Entrenched in Tenochtitlán, Emperor Cuauhtémoc countered the besiegers' daily assaults with a street-by-street resistance. He personally sacrificed three prisoners a day to the Hummingbird, unaware that the Meshica had been abandoned by their God. Hernando Cortés, the Plumed Serpent, responded by destroying the aqueduct bringing fresh water into Tenochtitlán: within days the inhabitants were drinking the same tainted water that had sickened Don Miguel, writhing with the same sickness as the young Spaniard.

Cuauhtémoc upped the sacrificial offering to a hundred prisoners each day, praying for victory; the Hummingbird did not return to listen.

A truce was called for Cortés and his staff to meet with Meshican envoys and discuss a peace.

Fra Benedicto attended, accompanying the chieftains of the Indio allies as their "priest-advisor," a result of his growing fluency in their tongue.

The negotiation was a failure. The Spaniards, having conquered two-thirds of the city by now and found none of the fortune greed had led them to believe existed (Empire, architecture and civilization could not be shipped back to Spain, or put in one's pocket!), convinced themselves that the Meshica were carrying their gold hoard with them.

The Indio allies, so long cruelly enslaved to the Meshica, wanted nothing less than the debilitating humiliation of their former overlords.

Cortés' woman, Doña Marina, summed up the cruel realities of both parties as she openly "translated" for the besiegers at the parley:

"Come forward," she demanded. "The Plumed Serpent wants to know what the chief men of the Meshica can be thinking about: is Cuauhtémoc a foolish boy? Ha! See here the lords allied behind us?" Fra Benedicto's head grew pained at the repetition of Indio names, each sounded with a threatening finality. All had once been vassal nations of the Meshica: unlike the Romans, who came to face the loss of their Empire over a decline of two hundred years, the Meshica saw this thrown in their faces after less than two. The pride of a ruler does not bend so willfully, even against overwhelming odds. The Meshica left without answering Doña Marina's tirade.

This was something of a surprise to Captain Guzman, the other Spanish officers and the Indio allies. For all of them the

logic of bowing to a stronger force was a natural expedient—
at least in terms of surface appearance. To these players the
heaping on of threat and insult they encouraged Doña Marina
to translate was a necessary part of convincing the Meshica
to capitulate. None of *them* would have resisted in the face of
such an inevitable end to the siege.

Only Hernando Cortés understood. He knew in advance of
this day's negotiations that the Meshica would reject any offer
of peace based on threats and humiliation.

He had nothing else to offer.

There *was* nothing else to offer: an appetite was let loose in
the belly of the conquistadores and their Indio allies that—had
they worshipped the Hummingbird—the *Meseta* God would
have been proud to encourage. At this point, no man could
totally control it. The best the Plumed Serpent might hope for
was to keep their hunger directed at the Meshica.

Fra Benedicto's June letter did not elaborate on the details
of the Meshica's last moment of minor triumph. The brief
outline of the event was grim enough: after the intentionally "failed" negotiation—growing drunk with continued victory—the Spaniards marched through the plaza of a Meshica-
occupied market square, advancing to the beat of drum and
screech of flute. There was virtually no resistance, until they
blundered all the way to the lakeshore opposite to become
bogged down in the mud. The Meshica at once reappeared,
literally "harvesting" their enemies in great swaths of blood—
capturing over fifty Spaniards and their horses. While Captain
Guzman and the others watched from the safety of the
brigantines and cannon-protected causeways, the prisoners were
stripped, dressed in feathered battle gear, and made to dance in
the plaza. Then they were sacrificed, one by one, to great cheers
from the besieged defenders of Tenochtitlán, to great screams
from the diminishing number of remaining prisoners. Their
heads were mounted on spears, facing the sun. After them,
the horses were slaughtered, heads set on poles to join their
masters'.

It was at the mention of the horses that the Unicorn felt himself startled and drawn away from the Lady. It was nothing new
to him, horses dying in battle, participants in human debacles.
He had often berated his lowly cousins for their subservience
to such causes. But the Unicorn knew also that horses had little

control over their destinies: their trust of humans was implicit. Why, then, *this* betrayal? To his own surprise, the Unicorn found himself trodding the road back to Tenochtitlán.

He could have been there in mere days; the Unicorn allowed his feet to drag and let it take weeks.

The siege was nearly over when he arrived: all but a small corner of Tenochtitlán was destroyed; those dwellings still standing were occupied by Cortés and his officers. The Unicorn found Fra Benedicto offering a Mass for a thousand Indio converts atop the ruined Temple of the Hummingbird. He did not climb the steps to see the old friar up close, for fear Santiago Matamoros might be nearby. A contrasting desire to be both near to—and far from—the human pageant arose within the Unicorn. There was no interest in the other Spaniards: he was less and less attracted to familiar faces and voices. The Indios were nothing to the magical beast yet—neither threat, nor lure. His three weeks' journey to Tenochtitlán had been solitary but not lonely.

Every *Meseta* God's temple was ruined: this had been a deliberate act on behalf of the Plumed Serpent's God. Nothing remained of Tenochtitlán's luxurious gardens and immense zoos. Jaguars roamed the ruined city at night, wreaking an individual vengeance on hidden survivors much as the Indio nations did on the Meshica Empire. In a cruel reversal, the trampled garden flowers let their pollen float into the fouled canals, discovering sustenance there where humans found only disease. Flowers thrived and clogged the dank waterways with color and scent. Their perfume could not disguise the stench of death permeating Tenochtitlán. When the Unicorn discovered *Tlaloc*, Four-Eyed Rain, squatting at the foot of his shattered temple, the magical beast asked why the *Meseta* God did not wash away the smell.

—*Because he's afraid!* a chorus of small voices cried in unison.

Four-Eyed Rain still sat in his miserable squat, saying nothing; the Unicorn looked around for the source of this comment. There was a tweak at his mane, then a pull on his tail. Kicking instinctively, the Unicorn whirled about to find the source of these irritations and saw a pair of tiny imps scurrying under the temple steps.

—*Pichilingis*, Four-Eyed Rain explained dully. When he saw that the Unicorn did not respond to the word, he repeated:

—*They are "pichilingis." Annoying.*

The Unicorn could not disagree. But the *pichilingis* imps did not reappear and he forgot them shortly.

—*Why do you sit here?* he asked again, wrinkling his nose to clearly convey the reasoning behind his question.

—*Because they still pray to the Hummingbird, or the Plumed Serpent's God,* Four-Eyed Rain answered bitterly.

A memory of his last conversation on temple steps returned to the Unicorn with sudden clarity:

Maybe one millennium is all the time we have . . .
maybe it is all the chance we are given, he had
shared with the Hummingbird, keeping to himself
the thought: *Or maybe we become too human.*

The Unicorn saw the human emotion in *Tlaloc*'s eyes; he left the *Meseta* God's ruined temple to search for the horses.

The Unicorn found the horses and calmed them: bone-thin from hunger and exertion, they were dispirited, performing the most heinous tasks meekly. They displayed none of the spirit that had brought terror into the eyes of the Indios upon beholding horses for the first time. The magic beast touched the horses' sores with his horn, healing the most wicked, leaving a few of the superficial ones for the humans to see and not give Santiago credit for yet another miracle. Nightly the Unicorn purified his lowly cousins' drinking water.

About food he could do nothing: it was an easy endeavor to desert the city and forage in the green, forested mountains on the horizon—the mountains were pulling the Unicorn more and more to their embrace—but he was unable to bring back proper feed for the domesticated animals. The Spaniards' supply of grain was exhausted. Their horses were forced to graze upon the former gardens of Tenochtitlán—flowers and strange plants—with unsatisfied stomachs and, sometimes, wild dreams springing from the mushrooms and seeds they ingested. It was one such mad dream, babbled by a stallion noted for his strength and endurance, that first inspired the Unicorn with his Idea—which the magic beast rejected at once as being too human.

There was no great battle to mark the death of the Meshica Empire. The young Emperor Cuauhtémoc, finally, forbade their women from fighting, ordering them to take what children still survived and flee the city, to seek refuge across the lake among whatever former allies remained neutral. Hernando

Cortés ordered the causeway bridges rebuilt and let these refugees escape under his soldiers' watchful eyes: each woman was stripped, searched for hidden gold. Enough trinkets were found among the defeated noblewomen to whet the greed of the conquistadores. Captain Guzman's brigantines were kept busy intercepting the steady stream of refugee canoes, in pursuit of the same goal. Occasionally warriors were discovered among the refugees: they were put under guard, branded on the cheek as slaves, then herded into work details.

There was no strength left to resist. Abandoned by the Hummingbird, thirst-weakened by the delay of the embittered Four-Eyed Rain, the last Meshica warriors were too weak and dazed to fight. Even their victorious Indio enemies were subdued by the final, catatonic demise of the Empire. An uncomfortable impression of foreboding infected what should have been a wildly celebratory moment of release from Meshica tyranny.

Attempting to escape and establish a resistance in the mountains, Cuauhtémoc was captured on the lake. Surrounded by Spanish brigantines, the last Meshica Emperor threw down his weapons and asked the Plumed Serpent for death. With eerie condescension, Cortés ordered a chair to be brought for the Emperor's comfort, then patted Cuauhtémoc on the head.

Thirty thousand Meshica dropped their clubs and shields and walked across the final causeway into slavery that afternoon. Captain Guzman led the brigantines in firing every cannon aboard ship a dozen times in celebration. Nothing remained of Tenochtitlán but flowers and sad songs.

◆◆◆◆◆◆◆◆◆◆◆◆◆◆◆

Authority and responsibility are two different animals, with many people demanding the former while evading the latter. Superintendent Don Taylor figured that, since the fugitives were in National Forest jurisdiction and he was stuck with the responsibility, he certainly wasn't going to let anybody else steal away his authority. The Deputy Sergeants and their Auxiliaries seemed to take this in stride—it was a well-established form of cooperation anyway, up here in the San Bernardino National Forest, where federal land predominated and the Rangers often acted as de facto marshals. The INS Border Patrol officer, who made the long L.A.-to-Big Bear trip in just under three hours, was less comfortable with the situation. N. D. Charny did not like it when the Forest Ranger jogged down the dirt road, past the roadblock of low-speaking Auxiliaries, and answered to the Superintendent—instead of to him.

"Don, they're settled into Hubert's place quarter-mile up the road," Bill Peyton reported.

This fit into Charny's outline for an illegal alien transport operation. "Someone's working with them." The Dreambreaker nodded to confirm the Ranger's information.

"Hubert's been dead a year," the Superintendent corrected, allowing a note of peevishness to cloy his words.

"An abandoned cabin, then"—this did not alter Charny's hypothesis unfavorably—"a meeting place."

Superintendent Taylor handed a cup of coffee over to Peyton. "Here, Bill, warm up." He tried to keep annoyance from his voice as he explained to Charny:

"Didn't say 'abandoned.' Irena Brandon still uses it. Polish woman, a doctor—Hubert's *daughter*: she's legal!" Another concern popped into Taylor's mind: Hubert's dog. A *wolf*-dog, to be more precise; fifty percent wolf, fifty percent malamute (which was practically the same thing to begin with). *Hell,* thought the Superintendent, *that thing's still roaming around here, crazy ol' Hubert taught it to run wild!* And Irena Brandon, just like her father, had this persnickety streak of cussedness that *encouraged* the damn wolf-dog. Beautiful animal, but dangerous. Just what he needed on top of everything else to worry about.

A few of the Auxiliary Deputies cracked a joke over at the roadblock. Taylor turned his annoyance at the situation on them, saying in a voice low-toned to carry only a few feet:

"Quiet! Think you guys have never been hunting. How far do you think your voices will carry, eh?"

A couple of feet stamped the dirt road. "It's cold!"

"We-ell!" Taylor drawled in mock sympathy, turning away from them—and Charny—and walking off the road toward a stand of junipers.

"Why you so ticked off, Don?" Bill Peyton said under his breath, following his Superintendent.

"Nothing. Gotta piss."

"Me, too," Peyton agreed, knowing that Taylor had more on his mind than a full bladder. They disappeared behind the junipers and relieved themselves. Taylor began talking before they were finished.

" 'Cause I think this guy sees some sort of conspiracy, and all I see is some kid. And if he's right, I don't want it happening in my forest anyway."

"What if he's not right?"

"What?!" Taylor smiled. "A federal official makes a mistake?! Why, you work for the government, Bill, what do you think would happen if Mr. Charny turns out to be wrong? Barring the obvious like a couple of wrecked lives."

Peyton did not have to mull hard on that one: the last two national Administrations had seen his branch of government headed by men who opposed most everything a Forest Ranger stood for, either on purpose or by incompetence.

"They'd either fry his tail or promote him, Don."

"You're talking bureaucratic politics, aren't you?"

Charny was beside them, leaning against a juniper, smiling comfortably.

"You had a good idea, coming up here before we get down to business, Superintendent: thought I'd do the same." He did not move. "I appreciate how you called out the troops. Especially since we still don't know how the man fits in."

"And the girl?"

The Dreambreaker's posture of leaning grew more relaxed.

"Hold the man on suspicion of Conspiracy; I'll take the girl down to L.A. for processing, then send her safely back to Mexico. She'll be home by morning."

Taylor let his eyes stare at the ground, then over at Peyton. "You can have the Sheriff's office hold the man."

"Illegal alien transport is a *federal* offense, Superintendent. You have a holding cell in one of your stations, keep him overnight, then we'll bring him down to the city. Easier to keep this between federal branches, 'in-family,' yes?"

"You still haven't said enough about the girl."

"And I don't have to," Charny answered, pulling away from the tree to stand up straight. "INS has its established procedures, it's all legal—which is more than she probably is."

"Due process—"

"Due process doesn't apply to Immigration enforcement or to illegals caught on the border: we're within a hundred miles of Mexico as the crow flies, probably closer, and it's a deluge, Superintendent, a deluge that we just have to try to keep holding back until the dam is strong enough to keep them on their side."

That was the speech. Once said, Charny decided to share the insight behind his actions:

"The girl's disappearance has caused a little shakeup in the Hispanic community. You have a lot of Mexicans up here, Superintendent?"

"No."

"Keep your eyes open: they'll be up here in the next few days." Sooner, actually, thought Charny, knowing that the gang of Low Riders was already gunning around the foothills. "Something is happening, the girl's a part of it—maybe only a small part . . ." He smiled directly at the Superintendent. "They don't belong here, do they?"

Don Taylor had never given it much thought. From deep in his gut, then, the answer came as an instinct:

"I don't agree."

The Dreambreaker's smile never wavered.

"It's the law, Superintendent: I obey the law, I ask them to do the same. I don't have to agree. You don't, either. You ever been posted upstate?"

Taylor nodded.

"You think the Old Growth forests should be logged?"

"No."

"Why?"

"They can't be replaced."

"Is it legal?"

"For now."

The Dreambreaker let his smile drop. "I will do what the law says, the way the law says to do it. Just like you do."

"What if you're wrong?" Bill Peyton asked from within the lengthening juniper shadows over to the side.

Charny's smile was renewed.

"I can't be wrong if I follow the law: maybe the law's wrong, but I'm not."

Taylor turned away from Charny to look up the dirt road: Hubert's cabin was over the next ridge; he could see smoke rising from the unseen chimney. "I already talked it out with the Sheriff's men before you got here, Mr. Charny: we'll wait until dark. No one goes into the cabin, we'll make them come out. In case there are any guns."

"That's sounds fine," Charny said. Then, seeing that the Superintendent gave no indication of moving, he started walking back toward the roadblock. "I'm going to go down and talk with the troops."

Bill Peyton watched the Immigration man head across to the Deputy Sergeants and their Auxiliaries. He looked over at Don Taylor.

"The land of opportunity . . ." he heard his Superintendent say, still not moving.

The cabin's single window opened on a now-dark world: the sun had set with a mountain finality that allowed no pink horizon. Inside the clapboard structure it was dark, too. A weak glow trickled from the fuel door of the wood stove, by the light of which Karus squatted, trying to coax a Coleman lantern into life.

". . . according to the directions, which rarely work"—he pumped furiously on the kerosine lantern's plunger, set the catch, struck a match—"no."

The sweating Rider began to pump the plunger again. "This time we'll succeed," he panted—this was harder than chopping wood.

"How do you know?" Annunciata asked, breaking a long silence that had begun to make Karus uncomfortable.

"Feel success in my bones," he answered, setting the catch.

"That doesn't mean anything."

"Sure it does." He struck a match, thrusting its flame under the lamp's glass hood. "It means this better work now or I'll go crazy. And—" A spark. "There!" The combination of kerosine and pumped air ignited, catching afire the small muslin shroud that served as the lamp's wick. It faltered discouragingly, then glowed into a full-flowered brilliance that cast shadows of the Rider and his Lady Fair into grotesque silhouette against the cabin walls. Karus handed the lantern over to Annunciata to hang from a hook in the ceiling and stood up to review the pot of bubbling victuals simmering on the stove top.

"Now for food," he grinned with the delight of a mountain-fed hunger soon to be satisfied. "Thank God for hot food!"

Karus ladled the pot's contents (a canned stew that tasted considerably better than its price would have indicated) into a pair
of mugs, then settled on the floor next to where Annunciata
sat cross-legged in front of the warm stove. The girl lapsed
into an awkward silence again. They ate the first half of their
meal wordlessly.

It was Annunciata, however, who spoke first.

"Karus?"

"Yo—Hot!" he cried, fanning his mouth in overacted pain
at the hidden well of blistering heat discovered inside a chunk
of stewed potato.

Annunciata waited for him to finish his pantomime show
before continuing. "You ever think about money?"

"Many times," he muttered, nursing his sore tongue.

"What about this cabin? You feel bad that we're not paying
for it?"

"I already explained that."

Annunciata had thought about it, too: "Then maybe it's the
same with money sometimes?"

Karus was about to nod in agreement, then stopped himself,
suddenly aware of the meaning under her comment. After a
moment of thought, the Rider decided:

"No."

But Annunciata had thought beyond his expected first
response.

"Even when there's a good reason?" she prodded.

"No . . ."

The awkward silence threatened to return.

"And now you're thinking of asking 'Why not?'" Karus
said rapidly to fend off the end of conversation. "And I'll
answer you now: because this house is real. Money is not."

"Money's real!" Annunciata disagreed hotly.

"No: money exists in people's minds—that's the whole reason money exists—and you can't take it, you can't 'use' it and
give it back—because you would have to go into their minds
and take its value. And you can't know what's in their minds.
There's an invisible line: you just don't cross it on people without their permission."

Annunciata could not let this statement go unchallenged:

"Money is real! People need it. My family needs it!"

"Is that all going to be solved by money?" Karus looked at
the dark-haired girl as at a stranger: she was his Lady Fair, he

needed to know no more than that. But he owed his Lady Fair the courtesy of a Rider's candor:

"Look around you, little one! The world is going to pot and it can't be put back together again by just a few good ol' Yankee dollars, or pesos, or pounds or yen."

Annunciata shook her head against this thought, sending her long hair flying across her face. "Why, then?" she demanded.

"Why is it going to pot?"

"Yes!"

"Because evil is winning, Lady Fair! Because . . . because everywhere you look no one remembers why they're supposed to be good: gentlemen no longer tip their hats at ladies and ladies now speak from the gutter. Industries come that build up a town, then poison the town with their product, then desert the town to boot. TV preachers and politicians have spoiled religion, no one goes to church and the Devil has his own way. So what do you expect to happen when the Devil has his own way? You expect to tell wrong from right? One person says it's all right to live together, another says it's a sin. One president says a war is good and not murder—but only for our side. Boys don't play baseball anymore, girls do. Cars aren't made to last anymore and gasoline costs an arm and a leg. Men marry men and women marry women and maybe that's even all right—who cares! It's their bed, not mine—but poor kids are growing up bastards while rich people make their babies in test tubes *and a candy bar costs more than half a buck!*"

For all her own inner turbulence, Annunciata had been unprepared for this outburst—which, somehow, did not feel as insane as it sounded.

"Why does God allow the Devil to win?" she asked at last.

Karus sighed.

"Ah, that is the problem. You see, God is getting old . . ."

There was nothing more the girl could ask. Silence reasserted its presence, a calm and unoppressive silence this time, broken gently by Karus smiling:

"Do you understand it all, Lady Fair?"

"No . . ."

The smile broadened.

"Well, the Irish call it 'malarkey' "—the Rider drawled his Texas accents through the words—"and I wouldn't take it too literally. But it's true, too: it's all a mess and money is only a part of it. So are you. So am I. You've got to make a decision and know that it's yours—don't look for excuses."

Annunciata began to notice that the Coleman lantern had grown very dim: air needed to be pumped in again.

"Karus?"

"Yes?"

She made her decision.

"I—"

The room was flooded by the beam of a searchlight crashing through the cabin window!

"Karus!"

The Rider grabbed at the Lady Fair's waist and pulled her to a crouching position against the wall, under the window, knocking the table aside. The air inside the cabin was charged with a paling glow, the huge beams of light cutting through the darkness like knives. A loudspeaker voice echoed in from the mountainside:

"This is the Immigration and Naturalization Service."

Charny spoke clearly and confidently through the portable megaphone: the road down to the highway was securely blocked, Auxiliary Deputies surrounded the cabin. "We are looking for Annunciata del Rio and all associates who have assisted in her flight. You will have three minutes to leave the cabin." He began to repeat the announcement in Spanish.

Karus' face was only inches from the girl's.

"What's he talking about?!" he whispered urgently.

Only one of Annunciata's eyes was visible through her dishevelled hair, and that eye was wild with bewilderment. "I don't know!?"

Karus was thinking furiously, out loud: "You're legal! Of course you're legal, you're not a wetback, I saw the papers!"

"We can explain it to them," Annunciata proposed.

Karus raised his eyes cautiously to the lower edge of the window and peered through the glass: the dark night was dotted with flashlights, bobbing in erratic waves around the static beam of the spotlight focussed on the cabin.

"We can talk, but something tells me they won't be listening."

"This is the Immigration and Naturalization Service." Charny repeated the announcement, reducing the surrender time to two minutes and including instructions on how to leave the cabin: single file, hands high, wide and empty.

Karus slid back down to the floor, squatting disconsolately. "Blast it! We were close!" His eyes took on a mad glaze. The Rider twisted his face into Annunciata's.

"You've got to make a run for it!"

"I didn't *do* anything!"

"I know that—and they'll know it, too! But that's the government out there: it could take them a week to clear up whatever mess they made. A week! Hell, it could take a year! And the Unicorn is coming tonight or tomorrow!" He hit the wall a thumping whack with his fist, seizing upon the desperate idea. "You've got to stay free!"

"But—*you're* supposed to find him!" Annunciata protested. Karus wasn't paying attention.

"Let's see: if I *run* out, they'll try to follow me. You wait here a minute, and no one'll be looking, maybe, and you can . . ." He looked to the Lady Fair now for approval of his plan.

"You're supposed to find him," Annunciata repeated.

"Annunciata Cymbelina de las Flores del Rio, I haven't got a chance in heaven without you there. And you have more than a chance without me. You've done it already. I've never found him yet, alone: what makes you think I could do it without you now?" Karus looked at the girl's feet and not her eyes while saying this. "Lace your shoes tighter, Lady Fair, helps you run better in the mountains."

"I've got a place to hide." The words were spoken low and quietly.

"What?" Karus could not be certain of what he had heard: Charny's third repetition of the demand to surrender was louder than the previous ones—the circle was drawing tighter.

"I've got a place to hide." Annunciata leaned forward and withdrew the first floorboard covering the hiding space.

Without another word passing between them, Karus moved away from the wall and helped her pull up the other two boards. Annunciata slid under the floor without difficulty. The Rider began replacing the boards.

Without warning, the searchlight was extinguished, plunging the cabin into darkness.

A still silence surrounded the structure, inside and out. Annunciata, her face framed by the opening of the last unreplaced floorboard, could not see Karus' face only a foot away.

"Was it all a dream?" she asked the darkness.

Karus listened for a moment—still silence, still dark—then smiled back at the pale outline of the Lady Fair's face that was beginning to emerge from the swimming emptiness.

"Ask me that when we meet again. Find him for me!"

He dropped the last board into place.

◆◆◆◆◆◆◆◆◆◆◆◆◆◆◆◆

The Unicorn's world had reached that point of chaos. He returned now to Tenochtitlán in hopes of finding the Lady and reestablishing a sense of order.

The magical beast had not been in the city when the Lady returned: the mountains, finally, drew him to their comforting distance and gave him a refuge from human contact. It was only a brief respite. Just as refugees streamed from Tenochtitlán for a harder future with a diminishing hope of life, so the *Meseta* Gods fled the fallen Empire for vassal nations to the west and north, accompanying the returning Indio warriors to their homelands. Much reduced in numbers, the *Meseta* Gods clung to the outskirts of the victorious armies, armies now sworn in allegiance to the Plumed Serpent's God. There was hope among the *Meseta* Gods that the Plumed Serpent would forget them and be content with Tenochtitlán, a hope that the Indio allies shared. It is said that hope is the last refuge of belief against reason.

And so the Unicorn, disturbed from the mountains by the passing spectacle, sought to explore the high plateau and the lowland jungle. Everything was weakened: Gods and humans. Because the Indios had no knowledge of the Unicorn, they posed no threat to him. But without knowledge, there was also no belief. The Unicorn was unable to use his healing powers to save them when the smallpox disease swept off the Spanish ships in Veracruz harbor, up to Tenochtitlán, past the city and into the mountains. One of ten Spaniards died—although the Unicorn did not know this since he was not with them—two of every three Indios perished: this he saw firsthand. In human affairs, the Unicorn did not interfere; against sickness, he often aided. This was the first time the Unicorn sensed his magic's utter failure. The Indios did not believe in him: he was powerless to help them. He retreated to Tenochtitlán to find solace in the Lady.

He had not yet arrived when Doña Aline received the letter from Spain. It was from her father, personally, and Aline was surprised to see the sealed envelope addressed so. Who could have written a private correspondence for the Count? she wondered—then remembered an old servant woman to whom Fra Benedicto had always shown an unusual respect. Shara—was that the name? It most certainly was an aged and unsteady hand that scribed the private letter from her father.

Conde Rodrigo was dying.

Shara wrote—and she identified herself as the correspondent—that the Count lay in a fever even as the letter was being dictated: the words were his, uttered in moments of clarity. There was no sense to the dying man's words, other than a father's blessing on his children, but the writer herself added that the fever was mortal—not so much painful as weakening, not so much illness as age. The letter closed with old Shara's bewildered worry that Conde Rodrigo's creditors were waiting outside the door, and when she left the room at his death, would the new owners of his properties in Castile keep her on?

That was it, then: beside a daughter's natural grief for a parent, Aline had to weigh the reality of her and Miguel's situation—whatever their position would be in the future, it must be decided in New Spain.

The Unicorn returned to Tenochtitlán with a vague sense of homecoming, even pleasure. He knew the ruined temples and boulevards by heart. The *Meseta* Gods were driven from them for months now and the pallor of blood hanging over the city last summer had lifted. And the Lady was here.

Conversely, for the first time in months, the Unicorn was in danger of discovery. A Spanish lady—there were many Spanish ladies now—cried out in the evening at the sight of the beautiful golden-horned beast trotting along the lakeshore: she was too stupid to know that Unicorns were not supposed to be in New Spain and so, believing in the magical creatures with the faith of a lifetime, she saw the Unicorn in a moment of unguarded approach. Her squealed delight set tongues to wagging. Within the hour another dozen Spaniards found yet one more object of nostalgia for their homeland upon which to reminisce. They carried it to the wedding ceremony at which most of the hidalgos planned to be in attendance that night. Two hundred more heard the news, discounting the doubters, adding to the odds favoring the Unicorn's discovery were he foolish enough to enter the city without caution.

As it was, the Unicorn's sensitive ears heard the first woman's unrestrained cry of discovery, even across the wide lake, and by the time he made his way into Tenochtitlán via a causeway the magic beast had dissolved his appearance into pure invisibility. An unsuspecting hidalgo and his lady might still catch a glimpse of the horned creature, such was the loose-fabriced nature of happenstance and magic. Still, the Unicorn's entry into the city was, finally, more cautious than originally planned. The slight aura of discovery enhanced his enjoyment of the return.

He sought out Fra Benedicto first. The old friar had been settled in the city before the Unicorn left it; if he was still in Tenochtitlán, the Unicorn could use him as a starting point for finding the Lady. This night he would finally reveal himself to her, the magic beast decided, casting aside his earlier reservations about opportune times and troubled thoughts. It was precisely because of his troubled thoughts—or were they dreams? He could not tell—the Unicorn needed the Lady Fair now.

And she would need him. She must—after so much . . . that had happened.

Fra Benedicto was not at the ruined palace he had set up as a temporary church: Cortés, Guzman, Miguel and a handful of Spanish officers were.

Torturing Cuauhtémoc.

The officers, directed by Captain Guzman, held the captive Emperor's feet above a brazier of glowing coals.

"Is this the proper way, my Governor?" Guzman addressed Cortés.

The Plumed Serpent pushed the officers back, forcing Cuauhtémoc's blistered feet away from the fire. "I told you to rub his feet with oil to prevent permanent injury!" he snarled at the calm-voiced hidalgo.

"If he, or his princes, will tell us where the Empire's gold is hidden, there will not *be* any injury!" Miguel answered for the other officers, rushing forward to be with Governor Cortés, rather than have to hold the stoic Emperor. The Plumed Serpent shook off the young man's hand and bent low to Cuauhtémoc's ear:

"Tell them where your gold is hidden: they will protect you from our soldiers, who grow close to rebellion at your stubbornness."

The last Meshica Emperor bit his teeth firmly together to keep from screaming. "Why do you not tell them what you know?" he whispered back to Cortés. "Tell them *what you know*: that we gave you everything when you first came and that you *lost it in the lake* when you ran from the city. That you preferred your lives to gold. Why do you not tell them that?"

The Plumed Serpent's eyes turned dull.

"Because I prefer my life."

A Meshica prince screamed in pain as Guzman directed the Spanish officers to thrust his feet into the coals. Cuauhtémoc unclenched his teeth to spit at the prince for his weakness.

"Am I myself in a pleasant bath?" he asked bitingly.

Don Miguel fainted as they pressed Cuauhtémoc's feet back into the fire.

The Unicorn stood rooted at his vantage point, watching with . . . a void in his heart . . .

Cortés let his officers destroy the Meshicans' feet.

In the end, even the bland-eyed Guzman was convinced that they knew of no other gold to be found. One officer laughed that this was a fine preparation for a wedding feast, and Guzman answered that it was only appropriate to be frying the Devil's children. He repeated the joke several times for Miguel's benefit, then helped the young Don out of the torture chamber and onto his horse.

"Come, mi *caballero*," the captain cried, "to your house, then a wedding!"

Cortés was nowhere to be seen, gone already, pleading a Pilate's disinterest in the senseless torture. His officers seemed to forget their released, crippled captives in the ensuing rush to follow Guzman and Miguel.

The Unicorn stepped into the chamber, shedding his invisibility. There was no reaction form the Meshica. They did not believe. They could not see him.

He touched his horn to Cuauhtémoc's charred feet. They were not healed.

The Unicorn turned and left the chamber. Following the sound of hooves on stone, he trailed the brave *caballeros* to the home of his Lady.

There were, perhaps, all of the original conquistadores in attendance at the wedding—plus at least half of the following wave of hidalgos, albeit conquerors who conquered without the necessity of battle. Almost all brought their wives, if not from Spain, then from among the Indio nobility: Governor Cortés preferred his men to be married. Fra Benedicto had performed over two hundred such ceremonies, frequently doubling as translator between the Spanish groom and his Indio bride (often met only the same morning). Tonight's marriage, however, would be the first celebrated between an hidalgo and a Spanish lady in New Spain. As such it drew a special crowd. Don Miguel offered his spacious courtyard for the ceremony in substitution for the cathedral, which was too cramped by ongoing construction to contain the expected crowd.

The Unicorn approached the courtyard walls uneasily: already he heard whisperings of his sighting that afternoon. Despite his determination, the golden-horned animal knew that to reveal himself to the Lady in such circumstances would be impossible. He had all night, however. And the next day, too, if necessary. Or the week or the month. Time was always on the Unicorn's side. One of Tenochtitlán's ruined gardens ran along the back courtyard wall of the newly constructed house: the Unicorn entered the garden and sought a stand of trees in which to seclude himself.

The Lady was already in the garden, speaking in quiet tones with Fra Benedicto.

"—will ally my family—Miguel—for the future."

"As you wish."

"So I wish."

In deference to the Creator's Son, the Unicorn did not interrupt the Lady's confession. She uttered prayers and supposed sins to the old friar and was forgiven her trespasses accordingly. The Unicorn stood near and smelled her quiet purity. His eyes glowed with the imagined comfort of her touch this evening.

And of the comfort he could give: there was luck to be found in a Unicorn's magic, shared only rarely. He would share it with the Lady tonight, her future assured.

The Lady's brother, Don Miguel, entered the garden decked in a ceremonial array of silk finery that could not disguise the drunken slackness of his face. It was only then the Unicorn noticed that the Lady, too, was attired in special raiment. All in white.

Doña Aline took her brother's hand and pretended to let his unsteady arm lead her into their house, under the approving gaze of the assembled guests. Ahead of them, a disapproving Fra Benedicto proceeded to join Captain Guzman at the private altar, where the actual wedding ceremony would be performed.

The Unicorn did not move a muscle for the next several hours. The invisible animal did not remain in the garden because he wanted to witness the marriage of his Lady to the hidalgo. He had no interest at all in her future after this hour, nor of the alliance Doña Aline made ensuring her family's position in New Spain under the *written* authority of the King's Encomienda land trust and the *practical* authority of Captain Guzman's protection. The Unicorn waited only for Fra Benedicto to finish this human business and come out of the house.

However long—he could wait.

Then the magical beast would enlist the old friar's assistance in the execution of his Idea.

It was an Idea couched in human emotions.

The Unicorn doubted whether the Creator would extend his being another millennium after this. With the bitterness of another human emotion, the Unicorn did not care.

◆◆◆◆◆◆◆◆◆◆◆◆◆◆◆

Don Taylor wasn't overly enthused by the prospect of the half-trained Auxiliary Deputies rushing the cabin, and he told Charny so. In response, The Dreambreaker suggested they cut out all lights for thirty seconds.

"It will paralyze the people inside; their eyes won't have time to adjust to the dark: when the lights go back on, you can rush in close—they won't have time to react."

"You expect violence, Mr. Charny?"

"No—these people don't fight back."

But when the order to switch on lights was given, the grey-bearded man was already standing on the porch outside the cabin, his arms stretched wide and empty.

He looked down at the Auxiliary Deputies charging up the slope. "Y'all can stop rushing the place, boys! I'm out!" he shouted.

As if commanded, the flashlight beams stopped bobbing closer.

"Where is the girl?" Charny's voice crackled through the loudspeaker.

Karus stepped to the edge of the porch, answering with a smile in his voice: "Only me!"

Charny looked over at Superintendent Taylor: there was a glint of challenge in the Ranger's eyes. The Dreambreaker simply gritted his teeth, nodded toward the man on the cabin porch. "Suspicion of conspiracy," he said tersely.

An hour later, comparing notes in the Blue Elk cocktail bar, the dismissed volunteers of the Auxiliary Deputy force remembered mainly a lot of hustle and bustle about the affair, little else. They all agreed that the man on the porch was friendly enough, smiling and squinting against the glare of the searchlight which the Immigration guy Charny continued to point at the cabin. The bearded man kept saying, "I think you've made a mistake," and even though he was not supposed to be in Old Hubert's cabin, nobody could say it didn't look better for him being there. Still, y'know, they wouldn't have been after the man if he hadn't done something. Nice truck, though, parked over in the Sheriff's impound yard—got the guy over at the Ranger Station for some reason.

It was also pretty interesting having the television crews up in the mountains outside of ski season, even if it was only a pretty-faced lady reporter, red-cheeked by the cold night, facing a pair of grumbling technicians, one holding a camera, another controlling the transmission feed back to Los Angeles.

"Brenda, Mark"—the woman journalist smiled at the camera, sending her greetings to the equally pretty-faced news anchors sitting comfortably warm down in Burbank—"while there are no further details on the search, we have a report—"

A white Barracuda whizzed by on the street behind the reporter, drowning out her voice.

"—Authorities have not yet identified the male sus—"

Two red Barracudas, riding low to the ground, cruised behind the White.

In Los Angeles, the producer of the eleven o'clock Action Eye News drew a line across his throat with his index finger. "Kill it."

The reporter's superimposed image disappeared from the screen behind the two anchors.

"Mark, I'm afraid we have transmission problems," Brenda explained to her partner, smiling brightly and drawing her eyebrows together in rueful disappointment at this untimely termination of the report.

Too bad: they missed the procession of the three Blacks joining the rest of Los Barracudas arriving in the village of Big Bear.

Across the lake, inside the Ranger Station, a Deputy Sergeant was taking improvised "mug shot" photos of the suspect in the Supervisor's office.

"We could do this easier over at our place," he complained to Don Taylor.

"I know you can," the Supervisor agreed, "but, as Mr. Charny here *insists*, this is a *federal* problem, and Mr. 'Karus' here"—he called across the room to where the bearded suspect stood against the white office wall, blinking from the flashbulb just popped in his face—"you want to give us a whole name, Mr. Karus?"

"Peas 'n."

Taylor wrinkled his forehead into a frown even as his mouth broadened into a smile. "Thank you, sir. I'll just write 'Mr. Karus.' "

"You can drop the 'Mister.' "

"You can help us out, 'Mister-Karus-Drop-The-*Mister*,' " Charny said from a corner of the room, where he was on the telephone speaking with his office in Los Angeles.

"I haven't done anything," Karus answered. "It seems to me anything more I do would be just getting in deeper into something I don't want to be a part of."

Charny shrugged, then turned back to talk into the receiver: "I'll do some prelims here, bring him down to L.A. for the formal questioning tomorrow—" He looked over at the Superintendent for confirmation. "Tomorrow okay?"

Don Taylor ran his fingers through his hair in tired annoyance. "If you don't have anything by tomorrow, why not just let the guy go?"

Charny flashed a tight little smile. "Local weather storms on the horizon. Back at eight with an update," he said quietly into the receiver before placing it down on the cradle. There was no memory of a smile when he crossed the office to lean on the Supervisor's desk. "I've got judicial discretionary rights and the power to back them up—what do you have?" It was time to show the locals some muscle.

◆◆◆◆◆◆◆◆◆◆◆◆◆◆◆

The sarcastic moon illuminated the room almost as clearly as the searchlight had two hours earlier. Even in the recess of the hiding spot, a shaft of light spilled through a crack in the floorboards, dropping a beam onto the gold-filled leather pouch to taunt Annunciata: *You wanted this, it's yours now.*

It was too late to tell the Rider.

"I wanted to, Karus. I wanted . . ."

Were intentions equal to action?

Finally, her muscles aching from the still coldness of the packed earth under the floor, the girl emerged from her hiding spot.

What was left of the fire in the wood stove was a single glowing ember now: Annunciata could not feel its warmth without thrusting her hand inside the metal box. The stove itself was long since cold. She was afraid to rebuild the fire.

Still, Annunciata crouched next to the wood stove with its dying ember until even that fragile light disappeared.

CABALLOS

The sun was already creeping up on the horizon when Fra Benedicto escaped the wedding celebration: he had not wanted to linger so late, but to leave before the long round of toasts and tributes were completely offered would have been an insult to Governor Cortés and the newly married Captain Guzman. The friar had wearied of their company hours before; he wanted to return to his Indios, who did not seem to understand the merciful love of God, but trusted the humble messenger who carried it. Benedicto himself was not so certain that their trust was warranted: he could make no promises that he could be certain the conquistadores would honor. He could not even protect the rights of his patron's family, as evidenced by the Lady Aline's need to ally herself with the increasingly influential Guzman.

The Unicorn nuzzled Fra Benedicto's shoulder as the old friar crossed under the rubbled remains of the Hummingbird's temple.

—*I had heard the rumors* . . . the friar sighed, feeling an unexpected surge of happiness at the golden-horned beast's appearance.

The Unicorn bent his knees to let the former hidalgo slide onto his back.

—*Did you believe rumors?*

—*I had only the hope. Doña Aline will be pleased.*

—*No.*

There were no *Meseta* Gods left to threaten their walk through the dawning city. An Indio worker or two, returning early to Tenochtitlán to begin the next day's forced labor, noticed the Christian God's priest astride the magical beast and thought it only natural. There was no need to be surprised: it was only to be expected that the new rulers' God would bless His kingdoms likewise.

But Benedicto knew what an honor the golden-horned animal was bestowing upon him—and felt disappointment at knowing the Lady Aline would be denied the Unicorn's presence.

—*Why?*

—*She is not innocent enough,* the Unicorn replied, falling back upon the easy cliché of all mystical creatures to explain their decision not to communicate with people.

—*She is . . . a very good person,* the friar insisted. *The sacrifice she is making for her family today . . .*

—*Perhaps a family is not big enough to sacrifice for. Perhaps a bigger sacrifice is needed. Or no sacrifice at all.*

—*You give me riddles.*

—*We live in riddles.*

They had arrived at the Unicorn's destination: the conquistadores' main corral. A hundred horses were herded together here, war veterans and sleek new blood. Among the Conquest's survivors a minor furor was raised at the Unicorn's appearance, their weak brains vaguely recalling how their powerful cousin had helped them, somehow, fed them once when they were very hungry.

The Unicorn's Idea—his *human* Idea—needed the friar's assistance now.

—*I am taking some of my cousins from the city. I will need you to lead them past the guardians at the causeway.*

—*Why do you do this?* Fra Benedicto inquired.

—*Ask me when we are ready to part.*

And so, at the Unicorn's bidding, Benedicto opened the corral and allowed sixteen horses, the most strong of the veteran caballos, four stallions and twelve mares, to walk free of the fenced enclosure. The Unicorn became invisible to the friar's eyes. Fra Benedicto mounted a stallion. To all appearances he was guiding the small herd, although, in fact, they followed their magical cousin as he led them quietly through the morning streets and to the causeway crossing over to the mainland.

As the Unicorn anticipated, Indio guards posted by their foreign overlords considered blocking the way—but relented upon being faced with the practical consideration that the friar was Spanish and therefore not to be questioned. Benedicto "led" his herd of sturdy caballos to the lakeshore and past the nearby Indio towns, toward the northern mountains.

At noon "he" halted his procession at a dirty spring, where the Unicorn reappeared, stuck his horn into the cloudy water, and immediately it was pure and tasteful to the tongue. The horses greedily attacked the spring, drinking their fill of the sweet liquid while the Unicorn bid his farewell to the human.

—*It will be a longer walk for you to return than to come this far. I am sorry. I cannot desert the herd to take you back into the city.*

—*Why do you do this?*

The Unicorn reared his head, allowing the friar to see the cold anger in his eyes.

—*Revenge.*

Fra Benedicto had seen too much anger in his own soul to doubt the Unicorn's thoughts.

—*On who?*

—*I don't know,* the golden-horned creature admitted, tossing his mane haughtily. *This is a human emotion, it is new to me. I know that I will do this to even the sides. I know that.*

Grazing on a cornucopia of pine nuts and wild oats, the horses looked over at the human and the Unicorn. Neither the friar nor their magical cousin moved for long moments.

—*I am sorry.* Fra Benedicto's thoughts broke into the Unicorn's at last.

—*For what?*

—*For doing this to you.*

Benedicto turned away from the Unicorn then and began his long walk back into Tenochtitlán.

It took him three months to make the journey, stopping as he did at every Indio farm, town and city ringing the lake. Later accounts, written by other hands, stated that the friar was preaching to the former vassals of the Meshica Empire, freed now from bloodthirsty tyranny. Perhaps he was. Or maybe, like the Unicorn, Fra Benedicto no longer knew which side was deserving, and he was apologizing to the subjects of New Spain.

The journey north from Tenochtitlán took longer than the Unicorn anticipated. A year longer. The distance itself was not one to hamper the magic beast, but the landscape north of the forested mountains ringing the lake was harsh. Too harsh to push the horses through quickly if the Unicorn wanted his Idea to unfold properly: to give the Indio the gift of horses, his herd would have to be strong.

Away from the influence of human masters, the horses grew wilder—and stronger. The stallions mated with every mare: the herd almost doubled in size. The Unicorn decided to take them further north, but was slowed by the colts' unformed legs and skittish youth.

And by the desert.

Here, indeed, it was only the Unicorn's speed and endurance that enabled the herd to survive. Nightly the golden-horned animal would leave his cousins grazing on scraggly brush at a shallow water hole, while he raced in wide circles to find the next oasis in this parched land—to lead them there in the day-light, crossing long stretches of hard ground between havens. Often, desert predators attacked the exhausted horses while he was absent trailblazing.

The horses grew warier, though, less dependent on the pro-tection of the Unicorn—and humans—as their journey length-ened into enough months to produce a second season's foals. These newest birthlings were at once wilder and stronger than their older kin, born with the instincts of survival in their blood: they *must* survive. *Mustang* instinct blended with the caballo breeding of their parents to give the herd a new spirit, one it had not possessed when starting out from Tenochtitlán. By the time the Unicorn finally led the herd to the long river, his protection was no longer required.

This was not a part of the Unicorn's Idea, but it was good: he left them there.

The land was still harsh north of the long river, but plains of grass reached down to some of its banks in the winter, and the horses could now fend for themselves. The Unicorn expected them to. He expected them to grow wilder and stronger and free-roaming. And breed to a thousand mustangs.

And then be captured by the humans, Apache and Comanche, who lived along the banks of the long river. Or travel further north and be tamed by others. This time the Indios would not be so unprepared. The conquerors deserved that.

SACRIFICE

"Is this the Place, Karus?"

Annunciata had never been alone in the night before. Never in the mountains. She was not afraid, but there was no sense of security to her emotions. She was frightened by what had happened to Karus, frightened by the understanding that it was *she* who was sought by The Dreambreaker of La Migra. But she was not afraid of being where she was that night. Abalita had told her about the mountains of Mexico too many times for Annunciata to be afraid.

She was cold, though, and surprised that her muscles would not stop quivering with the chill. The air had been so warm during the day. Then the fire in the cabin stove—until The Dreambreaker himself drowned it with water. The cold air seeped into Annunciata's body then, slowly, as she hid under the floorboards, and the hazel-dark-eyed girl was already shaking when she emerged from her haven.

Later, before venturing from the cabin, Annunciata found one of Karus' rolled-up sleeping bags which the Polices had left behind. Throwing it across her shoulders serape-style, she set out into the forest with the moon as her guide.

It was not a full moon yet, as Karus had explained, but it was close to full, flooding the crisp night with a bright light that made Annunciata squint her eyes when first stepping into it. She had only the vaguest notion of where to go: downhill was the highway leading back to town, the direction the Polices and La Migra had taken Karus; uphill was deeper into the mountains—

And where the Unicorn might be waiting.

"Is this the Place?" she asked again, no longer addressing her question to the absent Rider, but feeling comfortable with the familiar Night. The cabin was far below Annunciata, still easily visible, though hovering on the edge of shadows cast by the ridge upon which she now travelled. There was a thin ribbon of pale dirt winding through the shadows, the road that had led Karus' truck up to the cabin—and brought him down the mountain in the back of a Polices' car. And on the ridge?

Annunciata stopped walking to look past the immediate trail: there was another ridge beyond this one, and another ridge beyond that one—and she could go higher—or give up and go down to the lights of the town miles below.

She was cold. Annunciata pulled the sleeping bag tightly around her shoulders, trying to stop her teeth from clicking together. She had seen the distances, now she would look at her near surroundings: the high-altitude piñón pines stood far apart, there was no undergrowth, the sky overhead was easy to touch—if she could just stretch far enough. In the moonlight everything appeared so very clear and close.

The moon stood near the horizon.

"Is this the time?"

The moon climbed an hour higher into the sky.

Annunciata had long since staked out a pattern of movement to keep warm: still on the first ridge, the girl walked constantly between two dying pines, weaving among the young saplings sprinkled between them. Small patches of warm air clung to the saplings' branches, islands of momentary comfort for the bare legs underneath her skirt.

Though she no longer asked her questions of Karus or the Night, there was more uncertainty in her eyes now. Annunciata could not stop herself from doubting. Had she done something wrong? Where was the Unicorn? She was not a Rider, Karus was; what if—?

And she was very tired.

In the higher-angled moonlight, the cabin below looked much clearer now than it had earlier.

Annunciata realized that her nose and ears were numb with cold. She tried to move the muscles of her face: her skin felt hard, plastic. This almost made Annunciata laugh, thinking of her face as some huge rubber doll's face—which was good, taking the girl's mind from her discomfort for a moment. But the hard-won smile quickly transformed itself into a yawn. Followed by another. Followed by another which, shaking still from the cold, caused the girl to close her eyes even as she shuffled her feet, directing her body from tree to tree . . .

Absently, Annunciata worked her hand from under the sleeping bag serape, reached up and pulled off the rubber band that held back her hair in a loose ponytail. The small tugs hurt her neck at the hairline, and then she felt the soft darkness slide free of the rubber band, spilling over her neck, covering, warming her ears, drifting across her cheeks. With the same rapidly chilling hand, Annunciata stroked her hair flat against her face, to hold it like a sheet around her head, bringing the blood back into her skin.

At some point she would never remember, Annunciata sank to a sitting position atop a deep pile of pine needles, her back propped against the larger of the two trees she had set as her beacons. Wrapped tightly in the sleeping bag, weariness finally overcame her. Annunciata slept, her head leaning forward on drawn-up knees.

As the hours passed, the shadows changed. The moon had shrunk small now. The miracle was that, even in her unfullness, she still cast such brilliant light.

A small sound.

Almost a tinkling of glass, but deeper (just as fragile, though).

The Lady Fair opened her eyes without effort. She raised her head.

The Unicorn stood quietly above her.

The confession came simply; Annunciata did not need to move.

—He's not here. He is in trouble—because of me.

The Unicorn's eyes, as they had been for centuries, were unfathomable in their moonwarm beauty. He moved his head slightly, catching his horn on a shaft of moonlight broken through the branches overhead. Annunciata heard clearly the ringing to his sound now, resolve deepening from the fragility of glass to the strength of metal. The Lady Fair stood up, understanding.

—He has to be with you, doesn't he?! Annunciata felt herself shaking, filled with a growing excitement that replaced the cold chill.

—He has to—just as I have to help him find you!

The Unicorn stamped his hooves nervously; after a thousand years' freedom, his time was now boxed in with limits. Annunciata felt his fear.

—?! . . . he could be . . . days . . .

And the Unicorn sensed a failure: the Lady Fair had been touched by a greed. Time and human avarice. The Unicorn had no reassurance that they could be overcome.

—I—

To the Lady's thoughts the Unicorn turned his head brusquely away: the pathetically few town lights left on overnight sparkled in his eyes.

—*It* . . . Annunciata realized that her explanation was only that: an explanation, not a solution. Not an excuse. She made her decision without further need for consideration.

—*I hope it is not too late for you. I am sorry. I'll try.*

It hurt to leave the warmth surrounding the Unicorn, but the girl turned away from him to head down the ridge, toward the dirt road. Toward the town of Big Bear, where the Unicorn's Rider was held captive because of her.

Annunciata would have preferred a graceful exit from the presence of the Unicorn. Instead, she slid awkwardly down the dew-soaked incline. Progress was rapid, though, and Annunciata made the first hundred yards faster than an experienced night-hiker would have deemed prudent. Fortunately, there were few patches of pine needles blanketing the ground on this incline—the chill-hardened earth gave her a solid footing.

The sound of galloping hooves thudded forcefully on the hard ground behind her. Annunciata's balance at this point was too precarious to allow the luxury of a backward glance. She felt, rather than saw, the Unicorn lope down the hill, his pace assured, unslipping, as he passed to the side and entered her sightline. He stood at the bottom of the incline, at the edge of the dirt road, waiting for his Lady Fair.

Doña Sylvia would have respected her granddaughter's proud heart spurning the obvious offer of help: Annunciata stepped past the magical beast to make her own way, unaided.

The Unicorn had no need for Latin pride: he had given that to his Spanish Lady almost half a lifetime earlier. Annunciata heard him gallop rapidly over the next ridge—to see him appear on the road ahead of her several hundred yards further down.

Instincts of pride aside, Annunciata could not understand why she rejected his offer. But she turned away from the Unicorn again nonetheless.

He moved to stop her.

Another direction—the Unicorn stepped there as well.

Annunciata turned away from him, facing uphill now, away from the town.

The Unicorn touched her back.

—I will help you alone! she hissed, spinning on her heel to face him angrily.

There it was: the need for personal worth. The need, Annunciata knew, to be *indispensable* to Karus and the Unicorn, to be a part of their magic. Karus said he needed her—but he only needed a "Lady Fair": no mention of an "Annunciata"—or a "Nancy." The Unicorn needed Karus the Rider, not her. Not the go-between. They were magic—Karus, crazy magic; the Unicorn, golden magic. But where was *her* magic? It was not enough to be a spectator. She could live like that in L.A., watching the street show of tiredness and destiny take her over as it did everyone in her life, in her city.

But not here in the mountains. Not here. She would not be a spectator! Annunciata cried her thoughts into words screamed at the Unicorn:

—They are following me! *Not you. Not Karus. I am the one who can help him ride you! I have to do something! I have to!*

The moonlight glistened fiercely along the Unicorn's close form, glinting on his white mane and golden horn, beckoning . . .

Her hand was around the horn for only an instant. Whether she had reached out to grasp it—or he had lowered his head to her hand—she would never remember who had submitted. Without further invitation, Annunciata thrust her free hand deeply into his mane and pulled herself astride the Unicorn.

There was no resistance.

No difficulty from the Unicorn.

Between her legs the beast's muscles touched the Lady Fair with warm and glowing strength.

The cabin stood across the dirt road opposite them. Very simply and with the Lady Fair upon his back, the Unicorn began walking down the road and away from the place where his Rider had been captured.

Within a few dozen paces the Unicorn abandoned the road and proceeded across-country, favoring his own instincts over the man-made windings of the horse trails trampled down through the junipers and piñon. Climbing the next ridge, and the next, disappearing over each successive obstacle with steady ease, he and the girl drew clear and pale figures in the moonlight.

At first Annunciata was able to sit upright, excitement carrying her along for the first hour, a sense of dutiful purpose tugging her straight through the wearying second. The steepness of the slope the Unicorn chose to descend helped, forcing her to balance in opposition to the sharp direction his precise hooves stepped down. They passed many "new" places along the way, inaccessible places, unexplored except by the stray hunter and the foolish hiker, inhospitable to large predators and, thus, havens for smaller prey. Had Annunciata not been so close to the verge of sleep, she might have felt uneasy at the sight of so many small, ferret-red eyes staring with alarm at the two trespassers. The frightened animals did not know the Unicorn any better than they trusted the human girl. It was better to be afraid.

The Unicorn's self-made path through the mountains gradually flattened out as they approached the furthest border of the town, still some several miles from the center where houses clumped together along the lake-bordered main street of Big Bear. The moon was many hours higher in the sky now. Annunciata lay stretched along the Unicorn's back, asleep, her hands unconsciously clinging to his mane. The Unicorn slowed his steps. His few weeks of waning magic and the accompanying visibility had taught him a new form of caution: he would not stride boldly into the town.

An hour later the pre-dawn twilight killed the moon's bright illumination and replaced it with a grey, fog-dulled closeness. The Unicorn passed through the outskirts of the town, past isolated houses with barking dogs occasionally yelping to themselves—through a silent world, the sleeping girl upon his back.

Past a line of cars parked along the side of the road. Long cars. Sleek automobiles from an age as bygone as the magical beast's. The Unicorn did not know about the nature of cars, but they reminded him always of Dragons, beautifully powerful creatures who had carried their own destruction within, shortening their Time before the appointed end. These cars were shiny with dew, their metal hulls glistening like the Dragons' scales—glistening even in the dull light. Up close, the Lady Fair upon his back, these cars looked somehow more familiar than the always-distant Dragons . . .

Horses. Yes.

Strong.

The Unicorn allowed his steps to pass near the line of steel horses, his steps nearly silent on the soft gravel of the road's shoulder. Annunciata's face, resting along the Unicorn's neck, glided past the side windows of Los Barracudas. She did not see the snoring Manolo and red-mouth Chita crunched into the back seat of their low rider. Ernesto and Rosa and Tomas and the new girlfriend of Tomas (and the tag-along Bato)—the parade of Reds and Blacks lined up behind Lope's proud White—all slept uncomfortably deep while the object of their leader's search passed by.

Blond Annie did not sleep, although her eyes were only half-open. She rested her bleached head upon Lope's shoulder, his shallow breath caressing her cheek, and watched the green lights of the car stereo blink mildly to the beat of the quiet song playing somewhere in a radio station sixty miles away, in the valley below the mountains, in L.A. Somewhere near home. The stereo was Lope's one concession to the modern: the leather interior of his white Barracuda was stretched across original seat frames; the steering wheel, dashboard, knob handles—all were originals, rebuilt by Lope or salvaged from dead hulks of other Barracudas. The stereo was new. Blond Annie knew that was Lope's need: he loved the music, even in his sleep. She looked at the blinking green light and wondered what it sounded like—did he hear it?—the volume too low for the pulse to enter her skin. What did Lope's breathing sound like? It felt gentle, smelled slightly stale—that was from too long without water, Blond Annie did not hold it against him. They had lived a long, cold night. The heat from their bodies caused the windows to steam up. She was only half-awake now, and the figures passing the window were indistinct.

But Blond Annie bolted out of the car without waiting for thought, soundlessly opening her mouth at the sight of the Unicorn and the girl. She began to run in pursuit.

The Unicorn stopped at her approach.

Blond Annie suddenly felt ruffled, unready to see—or be seen. She felt her tired, mascara-ringed eyes grow wide with wonder.

The Unicorn stood patiently, waiting for the woman to finish her gaping and come close.

And, even though the Unicorn was fantastic, Blond Annie found her attention drawn first to the sleeping Nancy—No, not "Nancy," she corrected herself for no reason she could imagine: "Annunciata." Fear could not overcome Blond Annie's instinct to draw near to the girl. With careful hands, Annie used her long fingernails to brush back the hair from Annunciata's face, pulled the sleeping bag serape more securely around the girl's shoulders—only then did she turn her whole attention to the wondrous creature she was inadvertently touching.

A small sound.

Almost a tinkling of glass—

Blond Annie ran back to the car, to Lope's side: he had to know Annunciata was safe! He had to see! He had to *hear*! She raised her hand, ready to knock on Lope's window, but she needed to see the Unicorn and Annunciata again, to hear the sound. With fisted hand raised above the window, Annie stopped and turned for another look—

The Unicorn and Annunciata had disappeared.

Blond Annie straightened up, looking at the scuffled earth where the Unicorn and Lope's cousin had been. She did not know what was happening, but she was unafraid of its mystery.

◆◆◆◆◆◆◆◆◆◆◆◆◆◆◆◆

 S ome nights are screwed up from the start; others are the sole domain of human creation. Superintendent Don Taylor liked to consider himself a "nice guy"—or so he explained to his wife over the telephone. Like a "nice guy," he let the rest of his staff go to their own homes and warm beds this night while sacking out himself on a portable cot in the Communications Room. The Ranger Station's temporary prisoner *à la* INS suspect, the single-named "Karus," was ensconced in the holding cell usually reserved for drunk tourists found trying to start "campfires" the size of a school bus. For protocol's sake, and to save a little of his overtime budget (Don Taylor was, after all, responsible for the fiscal management of the post), the Superintendent had acceded to Charny's demand that a Deputy from the Sheriff's Department remain at the Ranger Station to "help" guard the prisoner.

Charny did not trust the Ranger Superintendent not to release the suspect. In the Border Patrol agent's opinion, Don Taylor did not seem to fully accept the fact that the Immigration and Naturalization Service *was* a branch of the Department of Justice and *was* exempted from the rules of evidence that bound the rest of the U.S. legal system. Logic pointed to this special status—if a suspect was an illegal, then the suspect was not a citizen; if the suspect was not a citizen, then there could be no *rights* of a citizen. And so forth. Charny had cited a handful of examples to convince the stubborn Superintendent. Even the Supreme Court supported the INS's point of view that most of these illegals were in this country for the money and no other legitimate reason. Take the so-called "refugees" (and here was where the highest court in the land used its discretionary judgement to the finest ends): except for Mexicans, who at least had the decency to be straightforward about what they wanted in the U.S., the illegals from the south weren't fleeing any *political* persecution when they came here, no matter what they said.

"If a Nazi regime persecutes Jews, it is not, within the ordinary meaning of language, engaging in persecution on account of political opinion; and if a fundamentalist Moslem regime persecutes democrats, it is not engaging in persecution on account of religion." Hell, that's what *the Supreme Court* wrote! So what's a Guatemalan supposed to be meaning when he says he came here because a couple of thugs with guns told him to join their cause or they'd blow him away? There's nothing political there—it's just like street gangs in L.A.—and the Supreme Court Justices backed up the Immigration and Naturalization Service on this one and a score of like cases, sending the Guatemalan back home where he belonged.

Charny hit Don Taylor with enough legal expertise to bowl over an elephant; the Superintendent had no choice but to agree with the Immigration official. Still, Charny felt, keeping a Deputy on duty would dampen any recidivist tendencies on the Ranger's part.

·And, for his part, Don Taylor wanted to stay close to the prisoner in case INS agent N. D. Charny decided to pull a fast one and spirit away Karus into the night.

That was how the Superintendent found himself awakened from an uneasy sleep by a Deputy he hardly knew.

"They want to know if you want an escort," the Deputy, stationed at the radio, called from across the Communications Room, undeterred by the syncopated snoring noises that had emanated from the Superintendent's mouth only moments before.

"Wh-what time is it?" Don Taylor snorted, trying to pry open his eyelids.

"What time is it?" the Deputy asked into the radio microphone.

"I didn't mean you to ask *them*—" Taylor sat upright, rubbing his face. "Just: what time is it?"

The Deputy uttered a dumbfounded "Oh" at the logic of the proposition and looked at his wristwatch.

"It's about five-thirty, five-thirty-five," a voice buzzed over the radio speaker.

"I have five-twenty-five, actually," the Deputy corrected.

"I have five-thirty-three," the radio voice disagreed.

The Deputy was not to be outdone.

"I got it from the telephone time this morning," he said petulantly. He turned to the Superintendent to insist: "I got it from the telephone time. You know, you call in to the phone company and they tell—"

The radio voice was not to be outdone: "We have a tie-in with—"

"Thank you!" the Superintendent cried. "I—just—wanted—to know—*why* they were calling so *early*!" Taylor stood up from the shaky structure of the portable cot, walking about the Communications Room with the restless, aimless movements of the just-awakened. ". . . He's not even—the guy in there, y'know—he's not even a—" Taylor rubbed his face briskly in a scrubbing motion, then looked severely down at the Deputy seated before the station radio. "Why're you in my Communications Room on this? Why aren't you out watching the prisoner or drinking coffee or—"

"Do we send an escort?" the radio voice interrupted.

Taylor grabbed the microphone from the Deputy. "Where did you get the idea that we needed an escort?"

"Saw it on the news last night and figured . . . Anyway, it's federal, isn't it?"

"It's not anything, yet, except suspicion of conspiracy to waste my time! NO! We don't need an escort! Thank you!" Taylor clicked off the receiver switch before there could be any continuation of the conversation.

"You're supposed to sign off 'Ten-Four,' " the Deputy said, a mild note of reproof in his voice at the unprofessional behavior exhibited by the Ranger Service.

Don Taylor did not answer immediately, counting silently to ten. "You don't work for me, do you?" he asked at last. "You're not Civil Service or anything like that? I don't *ever* get the honor of working with you again, do I?" He slowly stretched out his arm and handed the microphone back to the waiting hands of this interloper from the Sheriff's Department.

"Superintendent?" The Deputy looked up, innocent emptiness filling his eyes.

"*You* can take him down the mountain!" the Ranger muttered, stalking out of the Communications Room.

The Deputy stared at the departing Superintendent's back, initially a little bewildered by the abrupt flux in the man's method of command, finally deciding that he felt honored by the position of trust just given him. He suddenly remembered the microphone in his hand; the Deputy clicked it back on and hurriedly said:

"Ten-Four."

Annunciata woke up curled inside a cardboard carton with the words "This Side Up" stencilled along the visible side. She knew how she got there: the Unicorn had stopped at the point where streetlights began to fully illuminate the town. Annunciata wakened then, slid off the magic animal's back, and continued into Big Bear on her own. She did not look back to see how long he stood there, afraid she would run back to him if she saw the Unicorn again. An hour's walk past the deserted shopping plazas and a long stretch of chain-linked fence workyards had found the girl approaching what she imagined was the central part of town: at one point, she remembered from Karus' map yesterday, all of Big Bear's streets would converge back onto the road leading down to Los Angeles, Highway 18. If Karus was not already down in the city yet, the basic outline of the girl's thinking went, then they would be bringing him past that intersection point.

Probably.

Annunciata walked through the empty business district, exploring, until the cold and dampness of the nearby lake imposed itself on her bones. Then she found the large carton behind a Sears catalogue outlet store, crouched comfortably inside it with the sleeping bag wrapping her head to toe, and fell asleep deliberately. She could do nothing more until full daylight.

It was well into the daylight hours now—9:07 by the electronic clock on the bank down at the corner. Annunciata scurried from her cardboard refuge before anyone discovered her. Immediately she faced the decision of what to do with the sleeping bag: Annunciata was still cold—Karus' flannel shirt and her long skirt did not match the penetrating abilities of the high-altitude atmosphere—but walking around wearing a sleeping bag seemed more than a little like waving a flag and saying, "Look at me!"

Then she remembered the money. Not the gold—that was left under the cabin floorboards. The pocketful of dollar bills Karus had entrusted to the girl's flannel shirt the day before. A hundred yards down the street a diner offered opportunities for "$2.99 Breakfast Specials—Only Here!": Annunciata bunched up the sleeping bag, shoved it down into the cardboard carton, and hurried toward the promised warmth of the feast.

To stop half a block away at the sight of a Sheriff's patrol car heading toward her. Annunciata was unsure what to do. She had not been sighted yet, but there were only three pedestrians on the entire block at this hour of a Friday morning, non-tourist season. Annunciata saw that the sporting goods store she stood paralyzed in front of was "Open for Business." She stepped inside.

"Just opening up, can I help you?" a man behind the front counter said without looking up from counting the cash in his register.

The patrol car was approaching this end of the block. Annunciata stepped away from the glass entrance door. "No, just looking," she said, adding as she spied a rack of ski apparel: "And a little cold."

The girl's hazel-green eyes glanced back at the entrance door: the patrol car was stopping just outside! Annunciata scurried rapidly to the far end of the store, burying her head in a rack of parkas as the Deputy entered.

"Morning, Jack!"

"Lyle," the man at the register said, nose still pointed at his cash.

"Won't be round for lunch today: they picked me to take the prisoner down to L.A."

"Why you?" Jack asked without interest: something was wrong with the cash count.

The Deputy smiled in self-effacing modesty. "Why me, Jack? Talent. Opportunity. I was the only one there." Lyle saw that his friend was paying less than full attention. "See you tonight, unless you wanta join me for breakfast right now."

"Gotta customer."

Annunciata, who had been spying through the hanging coats, turned her back and began "searching" through leather jackets. She needn't have bothered: the Deputy simply nodded a cursory "S'long" and left the store.

"S'long, Lyle." Jack returned the farewell, about two seconds too late: he had finally gotten the cash drawer to add up to the correct amount. He turned his attention to the lone customer, seeing her for the first time.

"Can I help you now? You said you were cold—looking for a leather coat?"

Annunciata nodded, then looked at the price tag on the bomber jacket in her hands—

Then settled on the cheapest hooded sweatshirt and pair of jeans the store sold.

The patrol car was still in front of the sporting goods store, but locked up and empty: the Deputy could be seen entering the diner for his Breakfast Special. Annunciata changed clothes in the store's dressing room, then stepped out onto the sidewalk, confident and hungry. Like a moth drawn to the flame, the girl walked next to the patrol car, staring down into it with a curious mixture of bravado and fear. She could see a nightstick and a heavy flashlight snapped into their holders on the dashboard. Radio controls. A clipboard—with her photograph filling the top page.

Annunciata jumped back from the patrol car.

She looked away from the car and saw her reflection in the sporting store's plate-glass window: it was identical to the face in the photograph.

Annunciata looked back into the car: she had to compare again. The same. Always the same: her eyes only half-seen in the picture, half-covered by a curtain of hair, her ears never seen, her neck, even, lost in proportion to the fall of long, dark hair flowing down her shoulders, past the border of the photograph.

Always the same: just as she looked now, reflected in the plate glass, standing on the sidewalk in the middle of a near-empty block of just-opening shops in the quiet town of Big Bear.

Annunciata turned away from the face staring out from both images: she felt exposed, vulnerable. Over at the diner, a couple were returning to their car. Both glanced down the street— the fugitive girl knew they were looking at her. Annunciata turned her back to the diner and began to walk with a deliberately even pace away from that center of observation.

"Hey, Lyle!"

Annunciata looked back quickly at the distant shout.

"I'm just putting your breakfast on the table, Lyle!"

"Gotta get something from the patrol car."

The Deputy was walking in her direction!

Annunciata tried to quicken her pace without seeming obvious. She forced herself to look like she was interested in the display windows she was passing:

> Prime Rate Financing—Zero Down.
> Rent Skis Here.
> Skis Rented Here.
> Best Skis HERE.
> Style Cuts Unisex.
> "Excuse me."

Annunciata neatly plowed into the old man without a second thought, so concentrated was she on appearing interested in the shop window. Fortunately, the old man was spry. The girl offered her nervous apology.

"Excuse me, sir—uh: Perdón, señora." The offended party was an elderly *woman*—wearing a mannish haircut just produced in the shop from which she had emerged. Annunciata did not think more about it, whirling her head back to see if the approaching Deputy had noticed the minor collision. When he got to his patrol car he would see her photo, then spot the fugitive herself standing only yards away—

"You *should* excuse yourself, young lady," the old woman huffed in a loud voice. Annunciata turned back to the offended woman to apologize again and, hopefully, keep her from talking any louder. But the elderly lady had already shown her back to Annunciata, springing down the sidewalk with an energy that belied her seventy-year-old appearance. Still, Annunciata could not help but notice how, from the rear, in her pants and sweater and mannish haircut, she still resembled an old man.

The Deputy was almost to his car: Annunciata could not walk away now without reencountering the woman. She turned her face toward the front window of the beauty shop, pretending to look at the pictures of hollow-cheeked anorexics promoting the virtues of Nexxus Hair.

The reflection facing her looked very much like a girl, even if her clothes did not.

Annunciata could hear the Deputy open his car door behind her. In a moment he would pick up the clipboard from the seat, see the photograph of Annunciata del Rio, look out his windshield, see the fugitive girl, and . . . It took only a moment for Annunciata to make the decision. The Deputy was grabbing his clipboard even as she stepped into the beauty shop.

It was an "Abalita" place: her grandmother used to go to a beauty shop just like this every month. Two nondescript women sat under hair dryers, their heads wrapped in plastic and curlers, while a middle-aged, curly-blonde beautician wearing a pink smock swept the floor around a swivel chair surrounded by mirrors. She looked up at the sound of the door opening.

"Hi, honey! What can we do for you?"

Annunciata looked out the tinted glass door: the Deputy had not seen her; he was taking a folded newspaper from the patrol car and returning to the diner for his waiting breakfast. But the problem remained; the girl could not walk through town without fear of instant recognition.

Annunciata stepped toward the beautician, away from the door and possible sighting from the street.

"I want a haircut."

"No, no, no, no, no!" The beautician, who stood in high heels (and she always wore high heels) barely as tall as the young customer, puffed out her ample chest with proprietary ego. "We don't do haircuts here, we do hair *styles*." Her words punched the air with the pitch of a deep-voiced Munchkin. She deftly removed the bundle of old clothes from Annunciata's hands. "Been out campin', honey? These smell like a campfire!" Then she guided the girl into the depths of her domain. "Come on over here—you're early enough to get the personal attention of the owner. Call me 'De-*ni*.' "

She happily plopped Annunciata into the swivel chair, in front of a mirror over which hung a framed diploma with the words "Denise Moore" highlighted in colored marker. While "De-ni" began to busily attack the girl's long hair with a comb, Annunciata noticed that the beautician's name existed in various forms of lettering plastered throughout the shop: wooden cut-out letters were tacked around the door frame—"D-E-N-I-S-E"; a plaster mold, brightly painted, announced "Deni's Den" above the door to a back room; "DENI DENi DEni Deni deni" was painted across the wall behind the hair dryers, fighting for space with an omnipresent array of "Style Cut" posters, each with a model displaying a hairstyle outdated by at least five years.

"There, now"—Deni puffed a little from the effort of being energetic for a new client—"we'll just lean you back and shampoo and—"

"I just want it cut," Annunciata said stiffly, the towel Deni had pinned around her neck seeming to cut into her throat.

"Oh." Deni was disappointed: a shampoo was three dollars easy profit. "Well, we'll just trim the ends, then?" She let her fingers slide down a long strand of hair and grabbed it a short length from the end. "We don't need to wash for that—this much?"

Annunciata shook her head no.

"Oh, a little more." Deni slid her fingers an inch higher on the luxuriantly thick lock of hair.

"More," the girl croaked hoarsely.

The beautician's aesthetic spirit in Deni became a bit annoyed. "This is very beautiful hair," she said reprovingly, taking her fingers from the girl's hair and indicating a shoulder-length cut with a chopping gesture of her hands.

Annunciata looked at her mirrored reflection, remembered the Deputy's photograph: three years of her life would be cut off now if she gave the OK and it would still be too little to change anything.

"No."

Deni raised the chopping gesture to chin-length. "Here!?"

She had to save Karus. Somehow.

"No."

The beautician dropped her hands in dismay, turning to her unhearing, oblivious regular customers under the hair dryers as she appealed to the girl:

"What do you want, then? You don't want shorter than *that*!? Not with your hair!"

What Annunciata personally wanted did not matter now: next to her reflection in the mirror she could see the street outside through the front window, see the patrol car parked a block down at the diner, see—as clearly as if it was a reflection and not memory—the Deputy's bulletin with its photograph of a dark-haired fugitive, eyes barely visible, ears hidden behind the thick waves of hair, neck obscured by the cascade—the face of a person on the verge of adulthood, perhaps, very much the face of a girl.

Annunciata stared at the face in the beautician's mirror with that same strange failure to recognize it as she—and Abalita—sometimes felt at home. "Go look in a mirror," Abalita would say. "Maybe you don't know this face anymore. Maybe you have to meet it again." Annunciata pulled a hand from under the towel wrapped around her neck and grabbed a lock of hair at the crown of her head, an inch from the scalp.

"Like a boy . . ." she said with some embarrassment.

Charny knew he had won the small point: over the Superintendent's protests, the suspect Karus would be going down to Los Angeles in a half-hour or so. But Annunciata del Rio was still at large and the Rangers were making no moves to mount a search. Charny could not tell the Forest Service how to manage their jurisdiction. He *could* argue about the handling of the suspect, though:

"Why do you have only two men on it? And one of them not even a federal officer?" he complained, referring to the pending transfer of Karus.

Don Taylor leaned back from his desk and looked across the room at the INS man: he hoped to God that the guy wasn't too solidly connected into Washington, but if any manure came flying down, Taylor intended to argue Cost as his defense—which had the advantage of being half-true.

"Because," he explained for the fifth time, "*you* haven't proved a thing that warrants spending a thousand dollars from *my* budget just for security on the man."

"I don't need to prove anything: I need the show of force."

"Why? Just to show someone in L.A. or Washington"—
Taylor knew that his paranoia was showing through—"just
to show off that something's happening? Well, it's not."

Charny did not smile, but his voice contained a confident smirk of superiority. "I have reports of half a dozen
Mexicans low riding through the town: that usual for around
here?"

Don Taylor answered reluctantly, knowing also about the
Low Riders. "The town's not my responsibility."

"Neither's this whole business, Superintendent—I just need
your cooperation."

Karus was led in at that moment, providing Taylor with a
respite from Charny's relentless pressuring. The Ranger turned
his frustration on the suspect:

"Don't you have *any* statement to make?" The Superintendent's eyes bored into Karus', demanding: give me something,
man, *any*thing to let me say "screw off" to Charny!

The grey-bearded man shook his head helplessly.

"You've got my papers. You know who I am."

Taylor sagged back in his chair. "An international driver's
license: your photo, one name, no address. A visa, expired,
same one name, from . . ." He tried to remember. "Kenya?"

"Yep."

"No passport: how'd you get back, anyway?"

Karus smiled. "That wasn't the problem; this is my country.
It was getting *out*."

Charny snorted a laugh. "You really American?"

Karus' smile did not linger for the benefit of Charny. "Off
'n on."

Charny stepped over to the Superintendent's desk to stand
close to his suspect. "You've got to be a part of it, or not,"
he said sternly.

"I'll tell you what I'm not."

"What are you 'not'?" Charny asked pointedly.

"I'm not someone who does very good with orders:
'either/or.' Wiser and better men may prevail—but I can't
run up a beach, take a village, and kill somebody just
for the vague term 'national interest.' Give me an explanation, let me analyze the situation, and I may agree with
the action."

"You *may*?"

"That's right—I'm not afraid of doing it. Are you?"

Karus directed the question directly to Charny, whose failure to answer did not disguise the fact that he and the bearded suspect were at a common point.

"We understand one another, don't we?" Karus continued. "Only, I won't do it anymore if I don't think it's right."

Again there was no response from the Immigration official. Karus shrugged off the tension and gave the man an almost-smile of understanding. "So there's no room for me in the organization. I understand that: nothing could work with an organization full of people like me."

Charny finally broke his silence. "No, it couldn't," he quietly agreed.

Just as quietly, the Rider continued:

"But when you're talking about life and death, I can't accept the consolations of patriotic slogans. Like I said: they may be right, but *I* have to come to that conclusion, too . . . not give up my right to decide by joining the organization."

"They need me," Charny said very simply.

"I don't think they need anybody . . . Do you know what they call you in Mexico?"

"Yes," The Dreambreaker answered.

◆◆◆◆◆◆◆◆◆◆◆◆◆◆◆

Deni was angry: the beautiful-haired girl wanted to look "like a *boy*"—Stupid! She took out her anger on a hank of hair in front of the girl's face and snapped the scissors shut violently, pulling the severed lock away to leave a line of bangs roughly cut across the forehead—the rest of the girl's hair was just as crudely cut to shoulder-length.

"There!" the beautician cried, stepping back to let Annunciata see herself in the mirror. "You see? Halfway there." The expression of shock that crossed the Latino girl's face softened Deni's aggression at once: she had refused to attack Annunciata's hair to the short length directed exactly because she *knew* the girl would have second thoughts.

"I can still keep it nice-looking, honey," Deni assured the girl, taking delicate snips at the bangs—they still masked the forehead—to even them out, smoothing down the back hair to show that it was still long. "I can stop now and shape it up real pretty? . . ." Deni waited for the inevitable concession.

Annunciata looked at her half-altered features with numb surprise. Her resolve was being gnawed at.

"I . . . don't want to look bad, but . . ." The reflected image was still that of the girl in the fugitive bulletin. "Like a boy . . ." she whispered, ". . . like a boy."

The beautician imitated the girl's earlier gesture and grabbed a section of hair just behind the bangs and held it steady only an inch above the scalp. This would frighten the girl into being reasonable. "Sure?"

"Uh-huh."

Stupid girl! Deni clicked her scissors shut and let the lock of silken darkness drop into the girl's lap. Annunciata saw the two-foot length of hair float past her eyes and tried not to let her eyes water up.

"You want to look nice, heh? Look nice . . ." Deni muttered, grasping section after section flat between her fingers, biting the scissors through the soft waves, dropping long strands in an unattached cascade onto the girl's towel-covered shoulders. "You looked nice before, you don't have to do this . . . but—"

Inspiration is an unpredictable Muse. In the twenty-three years since graduating the National Beauty Academy, Denise Moore's major creative achievement had been exemplified by an ability to recreate celebrity hairdos on inappropriate heads with a minimum of ridiculous aftershock. Despite the front window's proclamation of "Style Cuts Unisex," Deni's shop hours were dominated by decade-old perm styles and low-maintenance, boring cuts. But she read the professional stylists' magazines—and Deni, like anyone else, sometimes dreamed she had a creative imagination greater than the place in which she existed. That unexercised imagination kicked the Muse into a jump-start now.

She lowered the scissors from Annunciata's partially hacked hair and looked at the girl's reflection in the mirror. A spark of dream began to flit through Deni's mind. She dropped the scissors into her smock pocket and stepped slowly behind the dark-haired girl, gently placing the palms of her hands against Annunciata's temples and drawing her hands back, pulling the girl's hair back from her face and holding it there.

"You . . . you . . ." Deni began to feel excitement enter her imagination now. "You can look beautiful still, honey . . . You can . . ."

Annunciata had no choice but to see her face in the mirror, too, framed by the beautician's hands. It is doubtful, though, that she saw the same, abstract vision as Deni: a young face almost sculpted of smooth, dark stone. A girl's face and a woman's face.

Annunciata's plan of disguise was a failure.

Technically, perhaps, the results of Deni's "creation" produced the desired effect: no one casually looking at the sweatshirt-clad, blue-jeaned, short-haired teenager would at first glance think that this was a girl. Nor would a lingering attention draw the conclusion that this youth was the Annunciata del Rio of the fugitive photo.

But the lingering gaze would also discard any thought that this was a boy. And the eyes would probably pause even longer in admiration.

After the beautician's enigmatic placing of her hands against the girl's face, Annunciata had let her eyes go out of focus: she did not want to see what was being done. She heard the clever snips of the scissors next to her ears, felt the last of her long hair fall onto her shoulders, and knew that what had been her identity for as long as she could remember was no more. Still, when she heard the buzz of the electric clippers in the curly-headed beautician's hand, Annunciata closed her eyes even more tightly.

"Relax your face, honey," Deni cooed. "This is gonna be precise and you're wrinkling your skin." She began to run the electric clippers over the girl's head. Annunciata heard the unfamiliar noise closely brush past her temple—there was a hesitation as Deni carefully avoided catching the motor-powered blades on the pierced earring the Latino girl had worn since birth. Since birth. Abalita had run a needle through her crying granddaughter's earlobe right after delivery, leaving a sterile thread there—red, "to keep away jealous eyes"—a simple operation that left Annunciata's skin ready to accept the small earring placed there at her baptism. Annunciata had forgotten that it was there, hidden as her ears usually were by her hair . . .

Were. Annunciata did not open her eyes until the beautician said that she was finished. The warm electric blades buzzed close haloes around her head, and Annunciata fought the temptation to pull her hands from under the plastic towel and touch her hair. What there was of it. *I will look like from a concentration camp,* she thought, and consoled herself at this image of shorn disaster with the reconciliation that, at least, she would no longer be recognized as a girl.

Annunciata's plan of disguise was a failure: she did not look like a boy—the image facing her in the mirror belonged to a woman.

More specifically, to Deni's awareness of her own creative success: "You look like an African princess!" she sighed in triumphant awe.

And she was right: Despite—or, rather, *enhanced* by—Annunciata's facial structure that was a classical combination of Spanish noblesse touched with a hint of Indio blood, the close-cropped profile of the dark-skinned Latina bore a striking resemblance to that of a blackamoor queen. Her head now could be see in its full, comely attractiveness, perched in fragile, excellently held balance atop a long, fine-stroked neck. Even the collar of the sweatshirt's cowl hood contributed to the impression, lending a timeless ritual quality to the seated figure, her hands draped over the swivel chair's arm rests as if in repose upon a throne. The tiny earring seemed to sparkle in its new, exposed setting with a value exceeding its monetary worth, setting off Annunciata's hazel-dark eyes, now seen with doelike fullness as the central focus of her delicate features. A subtle strength underrode that delicacy, waiting to assert itself in the woman that would be fully emerging in the coming years.

"Do you like it, honey?" Deni thrust her face between Annunciata's and the mirror, teeth fully exposed in beaming pride. "You *have* to like it!"

In truth, Annunciata did not see herself clearly enough to be pleased or displeased. "Like" was a word without meaning to her at this moment of recognition. An answer was unnecessary for the beautician anyway; Deni stroked her hand over Annunciata's head with an overwhelming, suddenly maternal pride and pronounced her creation perfect. If her "princess" could not express open joy, this was decorum: the creator-servant was free to cry with happiness for the two of them.

And she did.

Annunciata stepped out of the beauty shop in a straight-forward manner, still wary. The sudden exposure to the chill mountain air caused her to put her hand to her neck uncon-sciously, unused to the sensation of coolness there. Unavoid-ably, she glanced at her reflection in the shop window: the different person she saw standing there assured Annunciata that she would not be easily discovered. It was a few min-utes past ten o'clock—Annunciata ignored the emptiness in her stomach to hurry past the diner's $2.99 Breakfast Spe-cial, on her way to the intersection of Highway 18 with the town streets. The vague outlines of a plan to rescue the Rider were starting to assume a definite, if desperate, shape. The Dreambreaker would be taking Karus down to Los Angeles this morning—she had gleaned that fact from Deni's excited gossip in the beauty shop: Annunciata intended to intercept them. Somehow.

The convergence of highway and streets was not far away, almost in sight. Annunciata began to feel lightheaded from walking so fast in the thin mountain air. And warm. That was natural, too; the oxygen-thin atmosphere at this altitude did not encourage heavy exertion from visiting flatlanders. Without thinking about it, she peeled off the sweatshirt—then put it back on at once.

Her breasts were showing through her T-shirt.

Annunciata experienced a moment of ridiculous surprise at the sight: the two little round protrusions had always seemed so . . . *flat* . . . especially when compared to Maria's at school, or Gloria's big boobs when she went parading around the neighborhood. Now, suddenly and inconveniently, Annunciata saw the curved swellings make their presence known—in a rather pronounced manner for a supposed *boy*. Abalita would tease her and make jokes about "The Conversation" (which Annunciata had heard three years earlier and her grandmother always threatened to repeat).

The Polices would catch her.

Too late Annunciata remembered the bundled clothes sitting in a corner of the beauty shop: Karus' flannel shirt would have been the perfect compromise between wearing lighter apparel than a sweatshirt and the need to disguise her increasingly apparent womanhood. Reluctantly Annunciata slid back into the perspiration-damp sweatshirt; at least she had had the sense to take the money from the flannel shirt and put it into her jeans pocket. A gas station sat at the corner of her intended destination: Annunciata decided that she would have to buy something like a Snickers, or some other candy bar, to fight off the chilly-hot feeling crawling around her skin as a side product of the lightheadedness. Maybe that would help.

Los Barracudas were parked there: the two Reds at the gas pumps, the Blacks over to the side—Annunciata could see Manolo and Rosa inside buying snacks. The others in the cliqua were standing around their cars, talking idly.

Although uncertain exactly what to do beyond this moment, Annunciata's first instinct on seeing Los Barracudas was to quickly turn away from the gas station and step into the first of a pair of telephone booths at the corner of the lot. No one would recognize her from the rear. She did not expect to be facing Lope's back as he spoke on the pay phone—with Blond Annie standing in the tiny booth beside him, facing Annunciata. Her eyes were on Lope, though.

Until he hung up the telephone and spun on his heel to leave.

There was never really a second when Annunciata was unrecognized by her cousin and his Anglo girlfriend. It was a long moment, however, before the three of them understood that this chance encounter was *real*. The thoughts that raced through Lope's and Blond Annie's minds were probably a thousand miles apart—which was still not as far removed as Annunciata's thoughts were from theirs. The two cousins spoke at once in a jumble of excitement:

"LOPE! ANNIE!"

"NANCY!"

It was the wrong word—Annunciata's first reaction was to push away. "Lope! I can't!—You won't understand, but I gotta go!"

He grabbed her tightly by the arms. "Wha' happen to you! Why you look—!? *Go?*" He raised his head to call Los Barracudas.

"No!" Annunciata cried. With unexpected strength, she pulled Lope close, rushing through the words: "I can't have anyone know me! I don't have time!"

"Wha'!"

Blond Annie saved the situation from total incoherence by pushing between them—and shielding Annunciata from the view of the other Low Riders. She put a long-nailed hand over Lope's mouth, gesturing with the other and insisting with her thick-voiced accents: "Listen! Listen!"

Annunciata hugged Blond Annie tightly.

"I've got to help him! I've got to stop them from taking him away—"

And now her vaguely outlined plan came into focus.

Annunciata released Blond Annie and addressed the two of them with conviction. "I know how. Then he'll get free. He can!"

Lope struggled hard to follow this sudden flipflop of situation. Annunciata's cousin knew who the "he" was: it was the man in the truck, the one they talked about capturing on the local radio last night—that same capture that had brought Los Barracudas up to Big Bear searching for Nancy del Rio. This wasn't "Nancy del Rio" standing in front of him, though, this was . . .

Blond Annie had heard none of Annunciata's words, did not need to. In the silence of Lope's hesitation, she began to stroke the young woman's short hair, at her cheekbones.

"Who is—" Lope began. To be cut off again by Blond Annie, whose clicking fingernails signed the word "Listen" furiously in the air.

"He's good," the hazel-eyed "princess" said with quiet confidence to her cousin. "You saw him. He helped me. And I have to help him."

Lope let only his eyes move, shifting his attention from his cousin to Blond Annie. "May I talk now?" they asked.

The reply was a nod.

The impassive Aztec eyes went back to the stranger once called Nancy. "I suppose' a go 'way now 'n leave you?"

"If I go with you, La Migra will get me."

"Yeah." Lope recognized the truth in that: down in L.A. or up here in the mountains, The Dreambreaker was looking. "And—?"

"I know how to get him away from them. Alone." Annunciata's large doe eyes bored into the eyes of Los Barracudas' jefe as she laid down the challenge: "Or maybe with help . . ."

Lope was familiar with this type of stare: it reminded him of Abalita's expectations—and he had not lived up to her standards, certainly not!, except maybe in restoring the cars for Los

Barracudas, of which she seemed to approve. He walked back and forth in front of the two women, agitated.

" 'S loco!" he spat. "You wan' me to act crazy!" He pointed at Blond Annie: "Two hour ago she wake me up and sayss you all right. No reason." He spoke now directly to Blond Annie, with his hands, the only person he would trust without a reason. "I believed you before—with no reason given, no reason asked. Should I listen to Annunciata now?"

Blond Annie let her listening eyes swing from Lope to Annunciata: the young woman had stepped back from the two of them, smiling confidently, no longer a vulnerable girl lost for two days. Annie shook her tangled mane of bleached hair and let her thoughts display themselves through the parting of her blood-red lips into a smile—Annunciata had never been "lost," she realized, remembering the beautiful twilight morning dream. She shared her smile with Lope until he, too, finally broke into a smile of acquiescence to the Lady Fair's command.

◆◆◆◆◆◆◆◆◆◆◆◆◆◆◆◆

Bill Peyton could not help it: he liked the guy. Sitting in the sun next to the handcuffed Karus, waiting outside the Ranger Station for Lyle to come back with the patrol car on "cooperative loan" from the Sheriff's Department for the day, the Ranger and the grey-bearded suspect began talking about mutual places known. They found one. Beirut.

". . . used to be a beautiful city . . ." Karus mused tiredly, enjoying the warm sunshine despite the nervous tension in his stomach.

"Yeah," the Ranger nodded, "I liked the Mediterranean, it's . . ."

"No other color like it."

"—no other color like it," Peyton agreed. "Saw it from an old Crusader's castle one morning . . ."—the Ranger lost himself in the recollection—"before the place blew up . . . Stupid!" The flare of emotion caught Bill Peyton unprepared. He was spared the need to explain by the arrival of the patrol car.

"Thanks a lot, Lyle: said you were going for breakfast, and it's an hour and a half!"

"I just—" the Deputy started to explain, then remembered: "Where's the Superintendent? He's supposed to be going with me."

"Going down with the Immigration guy: logistics problem, something about two cars and too many chiefs."

"Y'know," Karus smiled, "I could save y'all the trouble: just buy me a bus ticket and—"

"In the back!" Lyle barked at the suspect.

"Careful," Peyton said to the Deputy, aiming a mock-serious look at Karus. "It took three of us to cuff him last night." He helped the handcuffed suspect into the rear seat of the patrol car, then started to load himself in as well when the Deputy stopped him.

"Don't you think you need a gun, Bill?"

"Yeah, probably," Peyton grudgingly admitted, making no move to go back into the station and requisition one: all they had in there anyway were hunting rifles issued for the purpose of destroying the occasional rabid animal. After a moment of looking uncertainly at one another over the roof of the patrol car, the Deputy offered:

"Why don't you drive, then: I'll sit with the suspect."

"Thanks." The Ranger smiled ruefully, seeing his chance for two hours' interesting conversation with Karus exchanged for the dubious honor of driving a patrol car—and watching in the rear-view mirror as the Deputy cast nervous glances at the bearded man.

After enduring a flurry of backseat driving instructions notable only for their redundancy, Bill Peyton began to pilot the patrol car and its passengers from the Ranger Station to Big Bear. Traffic was light; they were quickly almost through the town to where the main street converged with Highway 18. Taylor and Charny had not yet come out to the transportation pool when the patrol car rolled out of the station: Peyton assumed they would meet together down at the INS office in L.A.

Karus watched the town of Big Bear roll past his window with a blank expression on his face. Despite an apparent calm, a deep sadness lodged within the Rider at his failure. He hardly noticed the white Barracuda halted at the stoplight where the main street turned into highway, even though the low-riding vehicle appeared there only a second ahead of the patrol car, causing Bill Peyton to curse gently and step on his brake pedal harder than intended.

The jerking motion of the abrupt stop shook Karus slightly from his indifference: his eyes refocussed through the side window to see a Mexican kid emerge from the white Barracuda and stand on the corner under the stoplight, waiting to cross the street.

The "kid" was Annunciata!

The stoplight changed to green. The white Barracuda did not move. Peyton pushed down on his car horn, annoyed, producing a short, blaring honk. "Move it! No one's coming!"

Suddenly the Barracuda accelerated with a roar—

"Hey! We gotta ticket that guy!" Lyle shouted from the rear seat. Peyton turned his annoyance at Delay and Deputy into a heavy stomp on the accelerator and lurched forward— just as the Mexican teenager darted out into the middle of the street!

"Jeez!" Bill Peyton cried, jamming on the brakes. The patrol car jarred to a stop.

Too late—the teenage boy seemed to fall under the car.

"You hit him, Bill!"

"I didn't!"

The boy's howl of pain was all too clear.

Peyton did not think twice after hearing that cry: he snapped off the ignition and jumped out of the patrol car. Behind him, fumbling with his keys to unlock the handleless back door, Lyle was only seconds slower in starting to exit the vehicle.

The concerned Ranger was already on his knees when the "kid" jumped up and ran to the opposite side of the street, screaming in a female voice: "KARUS!"

Peyton understood immediately: they had been had.

"Lyle! Don't—" he started to warn the Deputy.

But the rear door was already half-open: Lyle had only time to cast a frightened look back at the prisoner—to see Karus rushing at him shoulder-first! With a flying crash the Deputy was shoved out of the car and onto the pavement.

Karus burst through the door with his victim, stopping just for a moment to catch sight of—

"Annunciata!"

Then, with a dash that would have done a linebacker proud, Karus charged across the street to his Lady Fair.

Bill Peyton did not stand idly by: during the brief seconds of Karus' sprinting escape, the Ranger jumped to his feet and ran over to help the fallen Deputy. "Lyle, get your gun!" he called, seeing that the Deputy was uninjured and feeling free to turn his attention to the fleeing prisoner. He started to race across the asphalt himself—

To be cut off from the fugitives by a red Barracuda speeding down the street.

Then a second.

The bearded man and his young female accomplice were starting to run back into the town. Lyle pulled his service revolver and fired a warning shot into the air.

The fugitives hesitated a second, then began running again.

"I don't have a choice, Bill!" the Deputy shouted over to the Ranger, bringing his revolver down to aim at the fleeing couple.

"I know, Lyle!" Peyton called back, the excited adrenal surge in his blood fighting with a defeated reluctance in his heart. Damn Karus!

The Deputy aimed at the man; there was still a decent chance of hitting him.

The three black Barracudas roaring past obscured his vision of the running pair. One—two—three! There were no fugitives on the street a second later.

Bill Peyton was not upset that the Deputy had been unable to shoot; the chase lust in him did not want the fugitives to escape, however. "C'mon, Lyle!" he bawled, pumping his legs in tight sprint form after the pair. The Deputy was not far behind in joining the pursuit.

Annunciata led Karus through the zigzagging alleyways she had explored in the twilight morning, buying the fugitives time: their pursuers were forced to hesitate at each corner. But the main street of Big Bear is only a short length. Soon, very soon, the fugitives would have to emerge from the alley. Karus, who did not know the town as well as Annunciata, recognized that fact before she did. When they could hear the Ranger and the Deputy shouting a safe half-block distance around two corners, the Rider stopped running and sat down on the ground. Before Annunciata could question his action, Karus pushed his knees up into his chest and forced his handcuffed hands from behind his back, under his feet, and to the front of his body. The metal cuffs bit into his wrists. It hurt wickedly. There was nothing to be done for it. Karus stood then and leaned his back against the brick wall of a one-story hardware shop.

"Up!" he commanded, panting heavily. The Rider cupped his hands together and nodded his head toward the sky. Understanding at once, Annunciata put a foot into the handmade elevator. Springing at the knee with the other leg, she let him lift her until she could reach the edge of the low-slung roof. Annunciata pulled herself over the top, scratching the palms of her hands on the rough surface.

"Only here or here, Bill. Let's go!" The pursuers' voices were dangerously close.

Karus stepped back from the wall several paces, then launched himself at it, kicking down against the bricks and jumping up: the momentum sent him ten feet into the air, although it was a scramble to catch the roof's edge with his cuffed hands. He did, though, and with his Lady Fair's help the Rider hoisted himself onto the roof beside her.

"Lie down flat!" he wheezed urgently.

Ten feet below, the Ranger and the Deputy turned into the alley behind the hardware store. Bill Peyton stopped running toward the building before his partner did.

"Not that way, Lyle, it dead-ends." He was panting heavily from the fast-running pursuit—which kept him from hearing Karus' loud gasps overhead.

"We saw 'em go this way!?" Lyle protested, joining in on the forced-breath chorus.

"Doesn't mean they're here. Get back to the radio, I'll hit the street." The trample of their departing footsteps sounded slower than the arrival. Karus swallowed a mouthful of air and turned his gravel-covered face toward Annunciata to berate her in hushed, angry tones:

"I told you to find the Unicorn!"

Annunciata, just as scratched and dirty, responded with equally passionate fervor. "I already did! I thought I was supposed to help *you* find him!"

"Yeah, well, you were!"

"Yeah, so I'm doing it!"

"Yeah."

"Yeah."

Karus felt his eyesight going black from lack of oxygen; he bit at another mouthful of the thin mountain air and rolled onto his back. Lying beside him, Annunciata felt her chest heave from similar cause. It was the Rider who broke the anger first, seized by a sudden realization of how changed Annunciata looked, a transformation that made him almost ashamed of his age and poor appearance, embarrassed. He struggled with the words.

"You look a lot different, beautiful Lady Fair—with the emphasis on the 'beautiful,' thank you." His face flushed a dark color under his deep tan, not from exertion.

Annunciata suddenly remembered who she was now and smiled. The wail of an approaching patrol car siren wiped it away at once. Karus was still catching his breath; Annunciata rolled onto her knees and raised her body slightly to look down on the man she had just rescued.

"Where will he be?" the Rider asked the Unicorn's Lady Fair.

"Up on the mountain. Near the cabin."

Karus raised his head and looked across the flat plain of adjacent roofs to see the mountains looming nearby. "Yeah . . . well, we can't go there straight," he said quietly, thinking aloud, trying to recall details from the maps of the area he had stared at in the Ranger Station all night. "They're gonna cut off the roads down to the city and back to where they found us— maybe we'll have to guess a direction they'll never think of looking."

The grey-bearded man rose to his feet, the handcuffs restricting his movement and making it an unsteady transition. Annunciata stepped up beside him and gave Karus her shoulders to hold onto until his whirling head cleared and he was able to stand steadily.

"I hope we feel like walking," the Rider muttered, embarrassed by his momentary weakness, as he started to head across the rooftops and away from the sounds of converging law enforcement vehicles. "Have you ever been to the desert, Lady Fair?"

Charny was angry. He appealed to the commanding Deputy Sergeant at the Big Bear Sheriff's Station for support.

"They're both here, in this town, and I don't want to depend on the Rangers' half-hearted efforts in closing down the roads through the forest. Can you put your men at every road leading out of town, and how fast can your Deputies be there?"

Bob Thompson looked sympathetically over at Don Taylor and let the Superintendent of Rangers know that he commiserated with the man's situation: after all, his own Deputy, Lyle, was fifty percent responsible for the escape—Thompson appreciated the unfair fact that Charny was taking only the Forest Rangers to task. He smiled reassuringly at the INS man. Besides, he intended to lie.

"Of course: Auxiliaries are already on their way (in a half-hour at best). What are your priorities, though, and I'll double-team there (I'll make sure at least *those* roads are closed)."

Charny stabbed a finger at the primary routes leading from the town: the Sheriff's Station in Big Bear didn't *begin* to have enough manpower to satisfy the federal officer's demands on such short notice. Deputy Sergeant Bob Thompson decided to have his men on duty cover the exits west and south—those would lead to L.A. and a million refuges for the fugitives. There was only one northern route, Highway 18, which went back to the cabin where the man was arrested, then wound down past it to the edges of the high desert country. They'd be fools to head back that way. Thompson never doubted that criminals were fools, but given the amount of territory to cover, he'd let the Auxiliaries block that route out of town as soon as they arrived in response to his emergency call.

He looked over at Don Taylor, standing hot and miserable next to the Border Patrol official's car. "You'll put some men up at the cabin?" he asked the Superintendent.

"I'll have 'em on the highway," the Ranger agreed. "Hubert's daughter's up at the cabin: she'll holler if the vandals show up there, tho' I doubt they will." He saw Bill Peyton walk disconsolately down the street toward him: Rangers were out of their jurisdiction in town. The Deputies were patrolling the streets in force, but finding their efforts constantly interrupted by the Mexican Low Riders charging around Big Bear. Taylor shook his head, confused. Maybe Charny was right—just an illegal alien transport ring trying to cover its tracks. Peyton walked up to his Soop and leaned against the INS car.

"Why'd he do it, Don?" the Ranger asked.

Don Taylor did not have an answer. When they caught the fugitives, they'd find out.

PLACE

As Deputy Sergeant Bob Thompson and INS agent N. D. Charny—and, now, Karus—noted, there were essentially only three escape routes from the area once out of the town proper. Big Bear, like all towns bigger than a one-corner way station, was prickled with myriad small streets, roads, alleys and extended driveways leading to those three exits, however. Escaping Big Bear during the first few minutes of law enforcement disorganization, then, was not a problem. Especially on foot, over the rooftops.

The Rider had played this game as a child in Dallas, during the war when his Dad had been flying a wondrously named airplane called the Thunderbolt somewhere over Europe, and small Texas city kids pretended that they were Davy Crockett running both brave and scared from Redstick and his hordes of bloodthirsty Injuns. Not a lot of forests in the middle of Dallas, but this never stopped the heroes from making their own wilderness out of the factory roofs. Karus Crockett and his Injun buddies (who, he noted jealously, were almost all *real* redskins from the Cherokee Nation over in Oklahoma) would silently stalk one another, battle, then form an alliance at the last building on the block—which would miraculously transform itself into The Alamo. There Cowboy and Indian would become blood brothers and fight to the death in valiant resistance to the cruel tyrant Generalissimo Santa Anna. Unfortunately, Juan Martinez usually drew the short straw of playing the general due to his being the only Mexican on the block who did not speak English. Juan wanted to be a priest and so he kept forgiving the brave Texicans defending the Alamo, sparing their lives. At this point, then, it was important for *all* Texans—Crockett, Redstick, Santa Anna—to unite in vigilant effort to watch the skies in case of surprise attack by The Enemy. Everybody knew who The Enemy was—it was a cleaner time then—and the United Rooftop Army of Texas, Dallas Division, was frightened enough by the newsreels to take this particular duty seriously. Twenty-five years later, stuck on a rooftop in the middle of Da Nang during the

Tet holiday explosion—when it was impossible to figure out *who* The Enemy was with such simple clarity—Karus stayed alive for hours replaying the game.

It wasn't much different now. Easier again, like childhood: you could tell who was after you. The Rider led his Lady Fair across the block of stores, down an alley and back up to the roofs again, and over the next line of low buildings before the first wave of roadblocks was decided upon.

After that, the intrusive foliage of the San Bernardino National Forest thrust into Big Bear, allowing the two fugitives to escape the rooftops and streets. They headed north, the last end of town to be blocked off: like the officials, Karus understood it would be foolish to head straight back to the cabin—even though that must be their ultimate destination if they were to find the Unicorn's Place. Unlike the officials, though, Karus knew that the cabin was his *first* priority. This priority allowed him and the Lady Fair the opportunity to escape beyond the northern roadblock before it was established.

The next part of their flight required a more patient approach.

Crouched only scant yards from the highway, Annunciata and Karus could see clearly that pickup trucks filled with locals wearing "Auxiliary Deputy" patches on their caps were being dispatched to patrol the highway. It was a safe bet that a hitchhiking couple would be stopped for questioning, particularly when the male contingent wore handcuffs.

Karus decided to use Annunciata's new persona to advantage again. Stripping off her sweatshirt—"You can *look* like a woman," Karus reasoned. "They're going to be looking for a kid in a sweatshirt with *me*."—he helped Annunciata clean her face and hands; then she abandoned their forest cover to "stroll" into the parking lot of the small shopping plaza dominated by a Brady Brothers supermarket. It was that store in particular that drew the fugitives' interest: the short-haired, T-shirted young woman—attracting a number of admiring (but unsuspecting) glances—sidled around to the side of the huge market and surveyed the produce delivery operations in progress. On Karus' instructions, Annunciata noted the home base stencilled along the driver's door on each of the three trucks in various stages of unloading: two of the three were from Victorville, a straight drive northwest from the mountains— along Highway 18. One truck hauled a refrigerated trailer, its rear doors secured by bolt and lock. The second carried fresh produce from Apple Valley farms nestled around Victorville. It hauled an open-top trailer, exposed to the sky—and to furtive passengers.

Annunciata returned to the forest, joining Karus in a long, roundabout trek through the woods until they came as close behind the Brady Brothers market as possible without risking exposure. Then they waited.

It would not do to climb into the produce truck before it finished unloading. They needed to wait until certain that no one would be coming back to the trailer again before it departed. Apparently a coffee break was one of the perks of the job, for the near-empty truck stood unattended an additional forty minutes, trailer gate hanging open. Finally, a team of box boys emerged from the store's back door to ferry in the remaining boxes of lettuce on two-wheeled hand lorries. Before the last load was inside the driver slammed the back gate shut, popped into his cab, and had the engine warming up.

A panic-fuelled fear of discovery and imminent failure clutched at the fugitives' shared observation: a produce-carrying box boy was still outside the store—and the truck was beginning to leave!

"Try it!" Karus whispered encouragingly, more to himself than to the Lady Fair, charging out from their cover of undergrowth to rush at the slow-moving produce truck from its blind corner. His young rescuer was climbing over the side before him, her lithe muscles springing to the task with an ease the grey-bearded man envied.

"I hate youth," he panted, smiling: since the driver had not jammed on his brakes yet, they were probably undiscovered.

Annunciata forgot to think that Karus was old and smiled back confidently, unavoidably breaking the Rider's heart without knowing it.

The empty produce truck wound north through the San Bernardino Mountains toward Victorville, slowed by sharp turns and steep curves that had the driver praying a bookful of curses at his air brakes to hold. Through the wide slats of the trailer walls Annunciata and Karus could see the occasional Auxiliary Deputy car patrolling the highway between Big Bear and the cabin turnoff. They threw themselves flat on the trailer bed at those times. The patrols ended once the produce truck was past the turnoff—and then the highway began to descend the mountains.

Forest cover grew sparse almost immediately, as the piñón pines and junipers refused to abandon the high altitudes, giving sway over the lowlands to Joshua trees and desert foliage. Karus watched the road closely now. The truck reduced its speed to twenty miles at the curve. Without warning, the Rider cried "C'mon!" and jumped over the side. Annunciata had no time to consider the rashness of his act: she followed immediately, taking a hard but undamaging spill onto the highway's dirt shoulder just as Karus had.

Inside the produce truck the driver saw a figure leaping from his trailer in the distorted reflection of his side-view mirror, but left it at that: no way was he stopping on the mountain. Later that evening, safely sitting at home in Victorville watching the eleven-o'clock news and waiting to see the next day's weather, the driver understood who the hitchhikers had to be: he called the California Highway Patrol with the information. When the television crew arrived at one A.M. waking him up, he had the pleasure of embellishing his role in the story dramatically for the early morning news report. He looked good on camera. His wife told him so. They made video copies and sent them to the relatives; expensive, but worth it.

Karus' memory of the terrain had been correct. They landed on the side of the highway where it now overlooked Cactus Flat, facing the shadow of Blackhawk Mountain looming across the desert landscape. Steep above the Rider and his Lady Fair towered the very mountain they had set sentinel in the afternoon before. The southern slope, yesterday. Today they were on the *northern* face of the mountain, facing a short, but difficult, climb.

Hampered by the restrictive nature of the handcuffs and the eroded nature of the terrain, Karus and Annunciata could do nothing about either. The hazel-eyed Lady Fair tried hammering with a rock at the links bonding his cuffs: the quartz-striated stone she found available was too soft for forge-hardened metal, crumbling in her hands as she struck. The ground here had a covering of loose pebbles, remnants of the sluice-sifting operations of the abandoned gold mines which dotted the slopes. Paths existed, but were exposed to the clear sky. The fugitives felt extremely vulnerable moving across the open spaces from tree to distant tree up the mountain. Once, for a tense fifteen minutes, a single-engine airplane was heard buzzing through the range. Impossible to place, its echoes doubled back on themselves to give the impression of coming from several directions at once. Annunciata and Karus crouched under a Joshua tree until the sound faded away.

Annunciata's calves and thighs ached: climbing the mountain this way was like taking a flight of stairs three at a time without benefit of handrails and seemingly without end. The Rider did not appeared to be faring better, although his leather work boots bit into the soil more securely than the Lady Fair's rubber-soled sneakers. They reached the forest cover of piñón and juniper at last and were saved from exhaustion by the opportunity to walk along established hiking trails hidden from aerial surveillance.

There was no water, though. Annunciata had never gone so long feeling thirsty, a pale weakness seeming to emanate from her mouth, down the throat and into her stomach. Her leg muscles quaked mildly from exertion, but this was overshadowed by the enervation of thirst. She could see that the Rider struggled equally: his face was white from effort underneath the grey-speckled beard.

Upon sighting the cabin at last, Annunciata and Karus sank to their knees on a cushion of pine needles, falling next to the stream that trickled downhill to it. They had "come through the back door," just as Karus had extemporaneously planned—nobody had stopped them. The exhausted fugitives drank greedily from the stream and did not care about their success. Again and again they returned to the quenching waters, resting on their sides, satiated, drifting into sleep like dogs within safe, distant sight of their quest.

It was Karus who woke first, the chill of impending twilight choosing the Rider's older muscles before those of the young Lady Fair. He felt refreshed by his brief rest and the excitement of impending success. The Rider decided not to awaken his Lady Fair, but scooped Annunciata up in his thick arms and carried her toward the cabin, its green-painted clapboard frame glowing blue now in the gathering dusk. Its window thrown open wide and gaping, the door still ajar, it looked almost wounded, mourning the Questers' abrupt departure.

A woman was inside.

She appeared at the door as Karus, following the bank downhill to the cabin, started to cross the stream, stepping cautiously on a flat stone in the middle of the current. Her footsteps were muffled by the same carpet of pine needles this entire section of forest shared. Silently, head bent in thought, the woman leaned a broom against the door frame, picked up a bucket from the porch, and trudged the few short paces necessary to reach the stream. Karus did not notice her approach, so concentrated was he on maintaining his precarious stance on the wet stone while balancing Annunciata in his arms. They met, then, totally unprepared for the sight of one another.

The woman froze in mid-step, separated from the two fugitives by only a few scant feet of running stream.

"I . . ."—Karus' voice cracked—"won't hurt you." He was speaking for the first time in over an hour. He tried to put a note of reassurance into the hoarse sounds coming from his mouth. "I left my things here."

The woman looked first at Karus, then at the sleeping Annunciata. Karus could not tell if she was deciding whether to run—or what?

"You are the man they arrested yesterday." The woman said it as a simple statement of fact, her words rolling in European accents. "The one in my father's cabin . . ." She slowly lowered the empty bucket to the ground, then straightened up again.

"Tell your father that I am sorry: I needed shelter for the girl." Annunciata began to waken at the sound of voices. "We're here," the Rider whispered to her.

"We—uh?" Annunciata had not been carried for years—more than that, the woman standing across the stream was a stranger! Awkwardly, the Lady Fair slid from Karus' arms and joined him on the narrow stone in midstream: she stared at the stranger with the same noncommittal intensity the woman bore on the two fugitives.

"It's her father's cabin," the Rider explained. He remembered a name overheard at the Ranger Station: "Hubert?"

The woman nodded. "My father died a year ago." Her voice softened even as her eyes remained unfathomable. "I don't think he would have minded."

Impulsively Annunciata started to blurt, "Then it's your go—" before stopping herself abruptly.

"What?" Karus inquired, turning his attention from the woman to his companion.

"Nothing . . ." Annunciata said in a small voice; she could not go through with her confession. To the woman: "It's your cabin?"

"Now, yes . . ." Her eyes grew clear, a memory visible in them, "and some others' . . . who need it sometimes." That memory sharpened into a thought of the present circumstance: "It's not safe here: officials came by today, and they will be back."

It was time now for the Rider to state his case.

"You don't have to be afraid of us: I'll stay on this rock while Annunciata gets our things, then we'll go."

The woman smiled. "I am not afraid of you: I am fearful for you." Whatever fears she had were immediately disguised behind a sudden switch to a businesslike tone. "Her name is Annunciata, yes? My name is Irena. Yours?"

"Karus." The grey-bearded Rider nodded his head in formal greeting.

"Why did you come back here?"

"For our belongings."

"No, not just to this cabin—" The woman's eyes stared into the private memory again, as clearly as at the two fugitives across from her. "*Here*. This mountain . . . ?"

"For—our business. What we came for before they caught me." Annunciata looked at Karus, surprised by the Rider's reticence about their urgent mission.

The woman, however, was not put off by the man's lack of full candor. Contemplating Karus' and Annunciata's situation with an ironic smile, she noted:

"So you cannot really hide—having to be in the only place they know where to look for you."

Except for the constant gurgle of water running through the stream, there was no other sound to be heard when the woman turned back to the cabin, leaving the two fugitives standing on their stone perch. Until she called over her shoulder:

"I have a hatchet and a screwdriver—which one do you want to try first?"

The hatchet: it severed the chain between the handcuffs in short order of a dozen sharp blows. Karus tucked the screwdriver into his belt for later use in trying to pick open the cuff locks. His wrists were swollen and aching, but at least his arms were allowed free movement again.

"Thank you, Irena," he said to the deep-eyed woman wielding the hatchet; they left Annunciata to gather Karus' things from inside the cabin while the assault on his handcuffs was managed.

"You are thanking me for breaking your chains or for not cutting off your hands?" The gentle sarcasm was self-directed and filled with humor.

"Both."

"You should not have worried, then: I am a doctor and could have stitched you together again."

"What's your specialty?"

The eyes flashed another smile. "Not surgery—but I sew very beautiful quilts as a hobby."

Inside the cabin, Annunciata nervously listened to the chopping hatchet and uncovered the gold-filled leather pouch under the floorboards: it had not been disturbed. She understood at once that Irena had not looked to see if the gold was safe. She probably did not even know that it was there. And if Irena did not know of the gold's existence, could it be called stealing . . . ?

"I found one sleeping bag," Annunciata announced as she emerged from the cabin. The leather pouch was also securely on her troubled person; she did not share that fact. "I forgot I left the other sleeping bag down in town; that's why it took me so long," she nervously explained, adding a number of quick gestures and unnecessary grimaces of concern.

"You can take mine, too," Irena offered, adding: "I know of two places you can camp at tonight. Both have some shelter. I will bring you food."

"Why are you helping us?" Karus asked.

The European woman quickly rose and left his side.

"You have your reasons for being on this mountain, I have mine. We will tell each other later."

Annunciata began to close the cabin door behind.

"Don't bother!" Irena laughed. "That door was always open for twenty years!"

With that comment, followed by a quick retrieval of her sleeping bag from a backpack on the porch, Irena led Karus and Annunciata into the forest.

By evening it was apparent that the roadblocks around Big Bear had failed to contain the two fugitives. Charny gave instructions to detain the Low Riders buzzing about the streets for questioning on their immigration status, but by then Los Barracudas had left the confines of Big Bear and were speeding over the San Bernardino Mountains in a circular flight designed to return them to the area via the same back-door entrance Annunciata and Karus had used in their escape to the cabin.

Charny's position was improved vis-à-vis evidence of illegal activity.

"The acts committed today are indicative of the kind of criminals we are dealing with in Immigration. I am confident, however, that our cooperative efforts with the Sheriff's Department and the Forest Service will once more return security to the area." He had honed this statement to a twelve-second sound bite that went over well with the media. In Los Angeles, Charny's superiors thought he presented the Immigration and Naturalization Service position with clarity and dignity. Momentum was on The Dreambreaker's side.

Later, at midnight, when the Brady Brothers truck driver gave his information about the fugitives to the Highway Patrol, N. D. Charny understood that events were breaking to his credit even more favorably.

◆◆◆◆◆◆◆◆◆◆◆◆◆◆◆◆

Through the cover of trees in the nighttime forest several clouds could be seen dotting the sky overhead. Bundled up in their sleeping bags, Annunciata and Karus crouched over a low campfire next to one another, the Rider explaining in hushed tones:

"It's overcast tonight, so I'm not afraid about airplanes seeing us . . ." He let his voice drift off the sentence lazily. Beside him, the Lady Fair leaned her face in very close to the fire, staring into its intricate flames.

"You don't think he'll come tonight, then?" she asked in a similar dreamy, hushed voice.

"I don't know . . . I just don't think so. Anyway, *this* isn't the Place for him to die—that I know. It's just not right . . . something's not right . . ."

Annunciata felt the leather pouch weigh heavily into her stomach.

". . . If we don't have to run tomorrow, we'll find the Place." Karus stood up, shaking off the sleeping bag, buoyed by the night air and nearness of his Quest's end. "Tomorrow we'll know!"

He began to whistle a Confederate anthem.

"What—are you—*doing*?" Annunciata asked incredulously, a note of disapproval in her question.

"Whistling 'Dixie.' I like it."

"But—they were terrible!?" The reproof was complete. "Slaves and war . . . !"

"Most likely," the Rider agreed, whistling a few more bars in quick delight before adding: "But they also had romance, too. It's the legend. Sometimes you don't care about the truth."

"Why not?" a European voice demanded; Irena appeared behind Karus at the edge of the campfire's dim circle of light.

The Rider turned to face his challenger with a smile.

"Because the legend tells you what the people wanted to believe about themselves: Yankees are hard-working and industrious, Southerners fight for lost causes and bow to ladies."

He bent deeply at the waist to Irena, then to his Lady Fair. "It's a lot easier to believe in a lady than a factory."

"Tfooey!" the deep-eyed woman laughed. "Lies and a mess—like you are in!"

All three found themselves laughing—at nothing in particular.

"Here, I have more blankets for you." Irena dropped a small bundle next to the campfire.

"You'll be cold," Annunciata protested.

"*I* am in the cabin." She pulled a small black bag from under her arm and turned to Karus. "Did you get the handcuffs off? Let me see your wrists." She grabbed his forearms firmly and pulled the Rider down near the fire.

"Ow! What do you think you're doing?" Karus complained. He had grown accustomed to the dull, throbbing pain: this was reviving its pulsing anger.

"Trying to keep you from getting gangrene. I'm a doctor."

"So you said."

"I am." Her voice was businesslike. "And if you look at the welts and broken skin around your wrists, you will understand why I am going to give you this." She pulled a needle and syringe from the small black bag.

Without waiting for protest, Irena jabbed the needle into Karus' arm.

"Aaach!"

"You are too late in pain: I am finished." A glint of relished revenge lit Irena's eyes. "Now you will believe me I am a doctor?"

Karus rubbed his shoulder, a childlike pout on his lips. "I believe you." A deeper thought took over from his immediate discomfort. "Question is: why do you believe us?"

"There is nothing to believe, yet."

Annunciata saw a more complex answer in the woman's eyes.

"Why do you trust us?" she asked, feeling the betrayal of the leather pouch against her skin.

Irena avoided looking at both Karus and Annunciata as she attempted to dismiss their queries: "I only keep the cabin for a memory—nothing to lose."

The Rider had more experience to draw upon than the Lady Fair in observing: "You could lose the memory."

Annunciata saw a clear thought pierce the memories reflected in the older woman's eyes.

"Maybe . . . I don't think so." Irena addressed the young Latina: "You needed the cabin, didn't you?"

Annunciata nodded agreement.

"Then if I did not trust you I would lose it."

And Irena saw the flash of conscience light in Annunciata's troubled eyes. Another million words of meaning passed between the women. Karus felt left out of their wordless conversation. He did not know why his Lady Fair stood and walked behind Irena, now kneeling before the campfire.

Annunciata reached into her sweatshirt and pulled out the leather pouch. She dropped it to the ground next to Irena, spilling a fistful of gold nuggets. The precious metal glinted in the dancing firelight.

"I'm sorry."

The deep-eyed woman's expression was lost to Annunciata as she looked down at the leather pouch for a moment, then picked it up, dangling the pouch by its leather thongs.

"Were you looking for this when you found it?"

"No . . . it was an accident."

Irena raised her eyes toward Annunciata now, smiling, not seeing her. "He was right, Hubert was: 'You can never find it by looking.' It's been there for years, you know."

"You knew it was there?" Annunciata was ashamed.

"My father spent years up here. He did not die poor."

Irena scooped up the fallen nuggets and held them out to Annunciata. "Here—I am not poor, either."

But Sylvia del Rio's granddaughter had made her decision. "I . . ." The decision hurt. ". . . gave it back."

"Oh." The European woman turned to Karus, offering the handful of fortune to the Rider. "Then, for you."

He did not move to take them.

"Buy me a lot of things I like," he mused, admiring the soft metal's reflection of firelight. "No, thanks: I owe you."

Irena looked back and forth between the two of them, between grey-bearded escapee and crop-haired fugitive, between Rider and Lady Fair . . .

"Then—here!" she laughed, snatching the nuggets into her fist and throwing the gold-filled leather pouch up to the surprised Annunciata. "Take it—and don't say a word! I do not get to play God often."

"I—"

"There is more!" Irena said with a furious passion, rising to her feet. "I said: I am not poor!"

Annunciata and Karus could say nothing in the face of this gesture and its accompanying emotion. An awkward silence ensued. Irena stepped away from the campfire, hiding her face in the dark night.

"I will be back in the morning with more food. There will be search parties, but . . . it is a big mountain."

Karus did not forget his Quest. "Any special places?" he asked to the retreating form in the shadows.

Irena stopped walking away. "How special?—To hide?"

"We're not hiding. A special place."

Irena turned now to face the fugitives, closing her eyes as she did so, letting the memory come alive again. . . .

Nothing in her medical training had prepared her to fight for her father's life—against her father. She silently appealed to the wolf-dog crouched at the old man's feet: his heart is sick, Mara, make him leave with me and come to a hospital! The half-wild animal's sympathies were with Irena's father, who had taught her to live wild, planning ahead for his own death.

"Irena—" Hubert began. "I'm not coming down from here."

"Why?!"

"Because I've got a spot." Hubert saw the look of dis-illusionment in his daughter's eyes and hastened to add: "It's not home. it's not this place, Irena: I could leave this place in a minute. But there's one . . . place in there . . . and I like it. It's my place. It's got nothing spectacular to look at, but it's got a stupid tree, growing crooked and all out of proportion to symmetry and when I see it . . . I'm all the places I've ever liked being."

Irena looked at the father she had not known for the first twenty years of her life and asked the question she already knew the answer to.

"Are you angry?"

"Always."

Irena opened her eyes, turned away from them again, and plunged into the dark forest.

"I know a place, but I must get some help. What are you looking for?"

"A Unicorn."

Irena hesitated—a moment only—before disappearing into the shadows. If they were crazy, so was she.

"I will find help for you tonight."

Irena knew the path back to the cabin by heart, even with-out the pinpoint glow of the lantern she had left hanging on the porch to guide her through the forest. She extinguished the lantern on the pass, bringing it with her through the door and into the cabin, where she stirred the glowing embers in the stove firebox into small dancing flames with an iron poker. She returned to the door and opened it a foot-wide crack. Then she laid down a series of horse blankets upon the rough floor in front of the stove and crawled in among the middle layers. Irena moved her lips in soundless repetition of the bedtime prayers she had recited since childhood and closed her eyes.

It was like this always when she returned to the cabin: Hubert's daughter added a wordless prayer that nothing would change tonight.

It didn't: when Irena opened her eyes an hour later—the

cabin dark and the stove cold—she raised herself on an elbow expectantly and sensed, rather than saw, the familiar presence. A moment later the large, powerful form padded silently through the open door and lay down next to her. Irena buried a hand in the thick fur. Smiling, she lowered her head on the animal's soft back and closed her eyes, falling asleep almost immediately.

◆◆◆◆◆◆◆◆◆◆◆◆◆◆◆◆◆

The animal's fangs were two inches long, its face a Kabuki mask of rapacious threat.

"Don't move . . ." the Rider cautioned.

Annunciata had no intention of moving: the animal hovered only inches from her throat.

"Her name is Mara. She is half-wolf."

Annunciata's eyes refocussed beyond the threatening teeth to the reassuring figure of Irena standing in the dim twilight behind the wolf-dog. At her back, she could hear Karus begin to chuckle with amusement.

"You sure she's not going to eat us?"

"Almost positive," Irena answered with a straight face, bending down to put her cheek against Mara's thick fur. "Touch," she suggested to Annunciata.

The animal's fur was surprisingly soft. Behind the perfect mask of white and grey, Mara's eyes did not indicate any response—but she gently stepped forward and laid her head across Annunciata's throat, a low growl of acceptance emanating from her own thick neck.

"Positive," Irena smiled.

Mara began nosing Annunciata's face: initial surprise over, the Lady Fair calmly enjoyed the sensation. She closed her eyes to the wide tongue's gentle licks. She could hear Karus rise from his sleeping bag and shuffle over to the dead campfire, stamping his feet against the morning cold.

"What is she here for?" Annunciata struggled to ask Irena between Mara's sweeping "kisses."

"She knows where your Place is—she's the guide."

"A wolf?"

"We're looking for a Unicorn," the Rider interrupted with this matter-of-fact observation, helping his Lady Fair to her feet while making a cautious introduction of his hand to the wolf-dog. As Annunciata rubbed herself against the morning cold—her newly exposed neck and ears, especially, reacted to the temperature—Mara padded away from the humans. Noting this, Karus shot a hurried glance to Irena for confirmation. He asked Annunciata: "You hungry?"

"Starved."

"Good, then I won't be alone—let's go." The Rider's attention was fully on the wolf-dog now: Mara melted into the forest, Karus close behind, leaving Irena and Annunciata to follow.

"Leave your things here, I'll come back for them," the deep-eyed European woman said quickly, abandoning the campsite to dive into the woods after the other two. Annunciata slipped her feet into her sneakers; without bothering to lace them, she sprang to the chase and was even with the wolf-dog in a matter of seconds. She looked back over her shoulder at Karus and Irena with the slightly haughty triumph of youth and speed. Karus' focus, however, was only on the Quest:

"We're *her* passengers now," he said, with a nod to Mara, "and I don't think she guarantees us a straight trip." The distant sound of a growling engine scarcely interested the Rider.

The sound was loud enough for The Dreambreaker's ears, coming as it did from the unmuffled engine of the all-terrain vehicle he plowed up the mountainside toward the cabin. His ears were filled with the harsh noise—which coincided with the grating anger pulsing through his body. Charny pushed the ATV to accelerate up the last steep incline leading to the cabin and jumped from the three-wheeler onto the porch without touching ground. He carried a single-bolt hunting rifle slung over his shoulder; this he brought into the cabin, too.

The cabin was empty—it was no surprise to The Dreambreaker. The Immigration agent cursed the Superintendent of Rangers, whose quiet resistance had held back a return to the mountain until first light: Well, here it was, first light!, and of course the fugitives were gone! And—of course!—the Rangers were working their way methodically up the mountain from all sides—*instead* of joining in with Charny to rush the cabin, where everybody *knew* the escapees were headed! The damn wood stove had been used this morning; there was still a jar of instant coffee and a wet spoon on the table!

Charny's anger at the "cooperative efforts" of the local officials did not prevent him from recognizing the significance of these finds. He stepped out of the cabin, past the growling ATV, and began a methodical circling of the structure. His career had begun with Border Patrol searches through the underbrush for illegals making "The Rush" across the border on foot into the wild canyons south of San Diego. Most of the time that was a simple procedure, like flushing rabbits out of the bushes—usually Mexicans who would try and try again until they made it. The more desperate Hispanics—Guatemalans, Salvadorans, even Mexicanos, all with some supposed "political" reason for seeking sanctuary in the U.S.—these people would often hire an experienced "coyote" to guide them through the tortured arroyos and on to hope. The coyotes were clever: The Dreambreaker had made his reputation tracking them.

A paper wrapper at the side of a footpath indicated that Charny's fugitives had probably gone into the forest at that point. He returned to the ATV, revved the motor into ear-splitting revolutions, and set off to find his quarry.

"Take the first path you can find. I have Bill Peyton going in with his group a mile up. Dave'll be working from the top down." Don Taylor traced his finger over the map coordinates and double-checked the search parties' positions.

"Bill here, Don: we're in about a mile from Joshua Tree Creek and found a campfire, coordinates G-7." Peyton's voice hissed across the radio waves now. Taylor hated the crappy reception on walkie-talkie communication. "See some ATV tracks here, too. Fresh."

"Charny's ahead of you," the Superintendent snorted.

"Thought so—following."

Don Taylor was glad that at least one of his Rangers was close to the scene: the INS official had charged in ahead of the organized parties, inspiring half the Auxiliary Deputies to break rank and set off in groups of three and four without a Ranger assigned to guide them. Not that they didn't know the area, the Auxiliaries were all local volunteers, but this *was* National Forest jurisdiction and Don Taylor did not want the search parties getting out of hand.

Not that it wasn't happening already. This was a Saturday morning—free day for all the weekend warriors who started buzzing up to the mountains in their off-road vehicles to "help" search for the escapees. There were only a few so far, but bright, dry Saturdays like this usually brought up the Off-Roaders in hordes. The Superintendent knew that if the fugitives were not captured by noon then the unwanted "volunteers" would be swarming. Loose-disciplined Auxiliaries were one thing, out-of-control Off-Roaders an undesirable other.

But it did not look to be a problem: despite Charny's impatience, the Rangers' familiarity with the area around Hubert's cabin—and the advantages of a *daylight* search—appeared to be paying off. Don Taylor expected Karus and Annunciata del Rio to be picked up shortly.

"We're heading Bill's way, Don," the Superintendent heard crackle over the radio.

"Fine, Dave, glad to hear you're paying attention," Taylor acknowledged, shifting his own four-wheel drive vehicle into gear and aiming toward the coordinates of the campfire.

Annunciata, Karus and Irena heard the entire conversation clearly.

The small posse led by Bill Peyton trooped away from the deserted campsite. Anxious seconds later, Irena's head popped up from behind a fallen log, her eyes searching the small clearing for signs that it was safe to emerge from hiding. A moment later, the Rider and his Lady Fair followed her lead. Mara crouched with elaborate ennui at their feet; the wolf-dog had led them a rambling circle back to their starting point and was not interested in how the campsite looked, having heard and smelled indications of the pursuers' closeness without need to rely upon her eyesight.

"They found the campfire," Irena whispered.

"And the wrong direction," Karus noted with mild satisfaction. "All we have to do is go the other way—"

Mara rose from her indolent crouch and headed off in the general direction of the departing search party.

"Then again," the Rider said with a shrug, starting to follow, "it looks like we follow wolf-logic."

"This is the way we just came!" Annunciata whispered, jogging past Karus to catch up with Mara.

"I know!" he whispered back, vaguely wild-eyed at their

guide's apparent indifference to their plight.

But "general direction" in a forest terrain can be deceptive: within a hundred yards the wolf-dog's new path led them down a ridge and into a gorge missed entirely by the search party. Back at the campsite, Annunciata could hear, a second search party was converging on the scene.

"Don, I can follow Bill and join up in a few minutes!" the Ranger heading the small party of Auxiliaries was calling loudly into his walkie-talkie, trying to overwhelm the radio wave interference of a mountainside with the strength of his lungs.

He didn't succeed: Don Taylor had to ask Dave to repeat his coordinates twice before advising:

"Bill's group is following their trail, Dave: you parallel them about twenty yards south—that'll take you down one of the gullies."

And in direct pursuit of the fugitives.

Annunciata stood with Mara, whose bored demeanor was a stolid contrast to the Lady Fair's nervous impatience as they waited for Karus and Irena to catch up with them. Before the Rider and the European woman were fully drawn even, the wolf-dog rose again, Annunciata at her heels, and led the Questers through the winding corners of the gorge—past a thick stand of junipers—down into a beautiful, steep-sided, narrow arroyo. A clear stream sprang from the ground here: once again the guide waited with animal stoicism while the less agile humans picked their way among the rocks and waters.

A half-mile further uphill, where the stream disappeared into its underground channel, The Dreambreaker sipped from the same clear liquid, then spread a topographic map out on the ATV's saddle seat. Charny traced his finger along the coordinates called in to the Superintendent: of the three potential spots he expected to intercept the fugitives at, two search parties were headed toward one, three others toward the second. The INS agent folded the map and remounted the three-wheeler, splashing the ATV across the stream and up the hill overlooking it. He had to ride high off the seat to execute the steep maneuver, but Charny's bent-kneed skill allowed him to steer successfully to the top and on to his planned destination.

Blond Annie would have felt a deep fear at the sharp curves racing toward them—the rock sides violently inclined and red-brown, looking out from a mile-high over bottomless valleys below—had not Lope been at the wheel and the white Barracuda vibrating in such sweet strength around her body. Still, as the formation of Los Barracudas returned to the mountains, racing uphill in defiance of gravity, at each corner it appeared as if they would fly off the edge, plunging into space. The obvious danger of the curves did not trouble Lope, did not fill his chest with the same excited thrill it shot into the others. He worked his hands in concentrated syncopation, enjoying only the sensation of constant motion: he had led the Reds and Blacks a three-hundred-mile circle around the San Bernardino Mountains overnight, down them, through the desert, up again—"the back door" now—to where he and his young cousin had agreed to rendezvous. Blackhawk Mountain pulled into stationary view on Lope's left; Blond Annie could look down on her right into Cushenbury Canyon; Los Barracudas drove up, up! Highway 18 to where Annunciata del Rio had told their jefe to be. There was a spot near Cactus Flat, under her mountain, where the shoulder was wide and Los Barracudas could wait. Blond Annie looked at the map and touched Lope with a long, lacquered fingernail: this was the spot. He led his cliqua to a grinding halt along the shoulder. A cloud of red dust stirred up from the gravel and settled over the just-stopped noses of the cars.

The Dreambreaker felt his vehicle soar over the top of the small rise, fly weightless for a beautiful instant, then bounce back onto the ground under his firm control. He swerved the front wheel slightly to avoid pitching the machine over an outcropping of rock, then buzzed on—to a quick stop at the edge of a sharp drop.

He had reached the arroyo marked on the topographic map— and the end of his progress via the three-wheeler: there was no way his all-terrain vehicle could safely descend the sharp incline. With little internal debate, Charny snatched up his rifle and map, abandoning the ATV to set off down the arroyo on foot.

The fugitives were no longer confined by the steep-walled pass, however. Led by the surefooted Mara, they had reemerged at a part of the mountain characterized by widely spaced piñón and a needle-covered, gentle slope. This was a more beautiful passage through the forest than Annunciata had seen before— discounting the exquisite shadows of her overnight journey with the Unicorn—rich greens and browns carried an almost palpable scent of life in their color. Where yesterday's trek had been hot and beautiful in a rugged, struggling fashion, this section of the same mountainside was comfortable and inviting . . .

Mara passed through the sentinel pines, the wolf-dog walking with rapid purpose as she homed in on the Place.

Karus took up the rear, watching carefully behind, on the sides, where one could see—and be seen—for a hundred yards.

Irena paced herself ahead of the Rider, revelling in the remembered trail of the half-wolf, seeing the forest her father had loved, privately, shared only with his wolf-dog and, now, his daughter.

And Annunciata travelled with lively step before them both, at Mara's side. Forgetting her fears of pursuit, she felt strangely elated by the movement, fascinated by the sun sparkling through the trees above, the squirrel skittering nearby, the large, wind-sculpted boulders they passed. It was not difficult for her to imagine magic taking place here, to picture in her thoughts the Unicorn awaiting her appearance around the upcoming bend of eroded rock wall.

There was a search party there instead.

The search party, one of the Auxiliary Deputy posses set off on its own without benefit of a coordinating Ranger guide, was not close: perhaps a hundred yards distant, probably further. Close enough to recognize the escaped man and suspect Latina, though—the fugitives had turned onto the same trailway the search party was using—there was no escaping the posse's line of vision. Shouts of identification carried across the mountain air to Annunciata's ears with alarming clarity.

"We see 'em!" the Auxiliaries screamed into their walkie-talkie in elated chorus.

"Up!" Karus shouted desperately after a moment of shocked immobility. Without looking to see if the women understood him, the Rider began climbing the eroded and crumbling rock wall, hand over hand, grabbing at loose roots and (hopefully) solid stones, pulling himself up as on a ladder. Annunciata and Irena did not need further encouragement to follow, finding in the search party's rapid approach adequate incentive to disregard any qualms about falling.

"What—are—the—coordinates?" Don Taylor yelled into

his radio microphone. "The coordinates! Stop running long enough to—" The leaderless posse of Auxiliaries disregarded the Superintendent's repeated demand and raced up the trail.

"Mara!" Annunciata called down, scaling the fifteen-foot-high wall and throwing herself onto the small ridge above the trail. The wolf-dog looked at the rampaging charge of the Auxiliaries with bored disdain, then leapt up the wall in three scrambling bounds. Joining her humans, Mara raced with them over the heads of the impotent posse as the Auxiliaries tried vainly to match the speed of the fugitives' adrenaline-pushed climb.

But a moment's escape did not relieve the Rider and his Lady Fair from the obligation of their Quest: they outran the main body of the search party, but the demands of finding the Unicorn's Place forced them to slow down and consult the wolf-dog again.

"Where is she leading us?" Karus demanded of Irena.

"Where is the Place?" Annunciata demanded of Mara, holding the half-wolf's huge head between her hands, facing the impenetrable, feral eyes. She bent her long, delicate neck into the animal's broad chest, letting her increasingly hardening will filter into command of the wolf-dog's spirit. Mara looked at the young Lady Fair with an ageless stare of regal fealty: she would help them escape *and* find their Place; this was an accepted fact in the wolf-dog's character—could they have thought any *less* of her?

"How many are still behind us?" Karus asked Irena, who stood in lookout.

"I see only three."

Mara began to lead them at a sharp angle from their previous direction of flight.

"They can't be more than two hundred yards ahead of us," a tall Auxiliary, one of three able to scale the rock wall, spoke into his walkie-talkie.

"That's northeast," Don Taylor decided from a mile away after consulting his map: the fugitives were circling back again.

"Northeast," the tall Auxiliary agreed. "We're following."

Mara guided the fugitives across a wide stream, where they lost time, then to a grass field, where they gained distance on their pursuers. Stopping on the far side, ducking low to avoid being spotted, they could see the three Auxiliaries halt at the edge of the grass field, searching the horizon for sight of their human prey.

"Karus! I could let them catch *me* this time," Annunciata suggested, seeing that the grey-bearded Rider was breathing heavily from the effort of escape. "It would slow them up!"

"I could, too!" Irena agreed, not understanding the full significance of Annunciata's offer, but realizing that she was the most expendable of the three: Mara could guide Annunciata and Karus to the Place without her, she would sacrifice the chance to honor her father's memory for them.

"No! Nobody!" Karus panted. "We make it!"

Mara left ahead of them, alone this time, crawling stealthily away from the hiding spot: when almost out of sight, she paused and waited for the humans to follow—at a distance. Anyone who spotted the wolf-dog would not necessarily see the fugitives.

"We got a eye on the wolf," the tall Auxiliary explained over his walkie-talkie. "We could pop him from here." The small posse had three decent rifles and at least two good hunting eyes among them.

"There's no wolves up here," Don Taylor answered. "That's ol' Hubert's wolf-dog and *you* don't shoot her. Bill—" he called over the radio to his Ranger's search party. "Bill!"

"Yeah?"

"You far away?"

"Nope."

"Get your group fanned out and over to I-7. Dave, move your party to—"

"Heard the coordinates, Don. Got a dropoff here gonna hold us up, though—and a growing problem."

"What problem?"

"Buncha Off-Roaders runnin' down just below the treeline and over the Cactus Flat. 'Volunteers for the hunt.' Tried to talk to 'em, but they don't listen."

"They ever listen?" Don Taylor asked sarcastically.

"We still see the fugitives running sometimes in the distance," the tall Auxiliary called in, afraid of losing the spotlight of attention.

"Well, I expect you to follow them, don't I? Just don't go shooting at anything unless it's a situation of Extreme Danger to Officer. Got that, only Extreme Danger to Officer."

"Sure," the tall Auxiliary agreed, nodding to his posse

companions: sure enough to them, that bearded guy looked *extremely* dangerous. "This way."

The wolf-dog and fugitives had disappeared again, but the three Auxiliaries had a bead on their direction and would head them off.

Annunciata saw the blades of grass in front of her face closer than she had ever looked at anything on the ground before. Her ear was pressed hard to the earth; her earring dug into the side of her neck, but Annunciata would not raise her head to ease the sharp prick, fearing to rustle the bushes overhead. Next to her face the wolf-dog crouched in similar fashion low to the ground: behind them, Karus and Irena.

Three pairs of thick, waffle-soled boots trampled the blades of grass only inches from Annunciata's nose. She did not consciously hold her breath, but after a moment the hazel-eyed Lady Fair became aware that she was not breathing. Mara's shallow, patient breath tickled at her jaw. Then the three Auxiliaries had passed.

Where do we go now? the Lady Fair's eyes demanded of the wolf-dog. Mara raised herself to full height and silently stepped out of the undergrowth, followed with an attempt at similar stealth by the humans.

The Dreambreaker lowered his binoculars and cursed the blind Auxiliaries who had passed right by the fugitives. He tried to see if he could located them with his naked eyes; success was minimal. Charny raised the binoculars again and judged the distance: by the time he arrived, they would be gone.

"Let's go!"

Annunciata felt her heart triple-beat at the loud voices coming from behind.

"They doubled back!" Karus yelled wildly, grabbing at the two women and charging after Mara, not allowing them to look back at the returning search party, who saw the fugitives clearly now that they had abandoned their hiding spot.

Mara loped ahead to an outcropping of exposed boulders; Annunciata quickly outpaced the Rider and Irena to join her there, waiting for them to draw even, then racing with their half-wolf guide as a group through a small maze of boulders—

To emerge at the Place.

There was no doubt about the location. Not to Irena: the same homely tree, same ugly stump nearby. Not to Karus: nothing special, and at the same time reminiscent of some ancient meeting place. Not to Annunciata: she felt it at once.

Karus, Irena and Mara had stopped walking, watching the Lady Fair walk about the Place, testing its rightness with arms hung down limply at her sides . . . waiting . . . to touch . . .

". . . He's not here, Karus."

❖❖❖❖❖❖❖❖❖❖❖❖❖❖❖❖

"The Unicorn . . ."

"No . . ." The Rider's disappointment made his voice crack. "This is the Place, Karus. This *is* the Place!"

"HERE!"

The search party was only fifty yards away.

Karus turned to the women and shouted with a fury:

"RUN!"

"But this is the Pl—"

"If we're free, we still have a chance!"

The fifty-yard distance between pursuers and pursued was separated by a handful of obstacles: the three fugitives broke their lungs striving to make that distance and number of obstructions greater, blindly plunging through a break in the rocks—

Down the next hillside—

Through a narrow gorge—

To a steep hillside leading down to the dry Flats. Karus stopped abruptly at the edge, panting heavily.

"We can try it," Irena urged, misunderstanding the reason for the Rider's hesitation.

"It's too open." Karus shook his head, bent over at the waist, hands on knees. "They'll catch us on the Flats—or be able to shoot us . . ."

The search posse could be heard approaching through the gorge.

". . . unless we can stop them." Karus made the decision, turned to Irena, and commanded: "Take care of her! You two go!"

"You can't stay here!" Annunciata cried.

Karus mustered enough labored breath to smile broadly without panting. "Of course I can—that's what I'm hired to do!"

The Lady Fair would not see their Quest fail.

"We can't split up: it takes both of us!"

"Then I'll make it across after you. But you get across first!" The Rider grabbed his Lady Fair by the wrist and flung her over the edge.

Annunciata had no time for protest after that, her stumbling run down the severe incline being at best a controlled fall. All other considerations aside, it was a struggle not to lose balance and break her neck. Even with a more careful approach to the dirt hillside, Irena followed Annunciata down with scarcely better command of the situation. The sole virtue of their rapid descent was its speed. Karus watched the two women for a moment, watched his chance of finding the Unicorn grow slimmer, and he was able to dredge up a small solace at their increased likelihood of escape.

The Rider turned away from the edge and looked back at the narrow gorge the fugitives came through: the search posse had not appeared yet. He recalled once again the lessons of Redstick and Davy Crockett and Da Nang and made himself ready.

The three Auxiliaries were as tired as the fugitives at this point in the chase. They jostled one another nervously, crowding together as they pushed through the narrow passage. So nervous and tired, in fact, that the first man in line was practically unaware of the act when Karus appeared before him at the mouth of the gorge, pulled the rifle from his sweaty hands, and hurled the weapon in a wide arc down the hill.

The second Auxiliary started to raise his rifle—but it was too late: the Rider grabbed the gun by its barrel and pulled hard, wrenching it out of the man's hands. Only the tall Auxiliary had a weapon now. The grey-bearded fugitive swung his captured rifle like a baseball bat down on the tall Auxiliary's gun, cracking it in half at the stock and caving in the barrel. The three-man search posse was now weaponless, facing an armed fugitive.

Karus saw that the barrel of the rifle he held was also dangerously bent; he dropped it to the ground.

"I don't know what you think I did," he began, "but let me explain—"

Words fallen on deaf ears: the three Auxiliaries rushed at Karus!

They did not notice the wolf-dog until almost on top of the Rider—and then, at the sudden recognition of the long-toothed animal's presence, they momentarily halted their attack. This prudent, if untimely, hesitation proved disastrous to their efforts. Then again, after Karus downed the tall Auxiliary with a football block to the solar plexus, then raised a second pursuer high enough to drop him in a breath-crushing body slam to the ground, perhaps Mara's grip on the third man's calf was unnecessary. Mere show.

"I told you I want to explain!" the Rider shouted between wheezing breaths.

In either event, the ensuing melee was quickly a one-sided affair.

Annunciata and Irena knew nothing of Karus' failed attempt at diplomacy. Just as tired as the Rider—although forty years and twenty years younger, respectively—the two women may have escaped the search parties in the forest, but they were keenly aware of their exposed situation now, crossing the Flats. Almost a mile of open space stood between them and the next possible cover. The sun, which had seemed so warm and comforting in the mountains when filtered through an awning of pine branches, was a noxious presence out here on the edge of the desert's domain. There was no ground covering to hold down the topsoil; every scuffed footstep (and their hurried flight allowed no time for careful placing of feet) kicked a small cloud of dust into the air—to be picked up by the slight breeze that fluttered constantly across the Flats in a faint, keening moan. Soon the women's mouths and nostrils choked with dust, their throats scratched, eyes red-rimmed with irritation. There was no time to stop, take the necessary slow, controlled breath, to let the dust settle and proceed in calm and orderly fashion across the Flats. Annunciata and Irena found themselves holding each other's hand, jogging, stumbling toward the haven of the next mountain's forest.

The Unicorn had not come to the Place.

Annunciata's heart was dragged by the thought. The Unicorn had not come. The Lady Fair knew they had found the

Place. Against consideration of practical thoughts, she turned her head back and looked across the Flats at the mountain they had just deserted: it *was* the Unicorn's Last Mountain. It was! Annunciata's left foot caught in a ground squirrel hole and she nearly pitched headlong to the ground; only the European woman's balancing hand saved her. The Lady Fair nodded her beautiful head in thanks and returned her eyes to the forefront, her thoughts behind her: I *will* return to the Last Mountain; the Unicorn will be there.

She did not hear the distant buzz at first, then, her thoughts so severely concentrated upon the future; it was Irena who noticed the low, grinding sound approaching. She pulled at Annunciata's hand, and when the young woman finally listened to the sound and recognized it, the two of them tried to increase their speed to a long-paced run.

The sound grew into an angry roar. Echoing off the mountains surrounding the Flats, the battering noise hit the women from all directions, confusing them as to its source. There was no choice but to slow down, stop, wait.

Find the source, and then run from it.

By then, of course, it was too late: a dozen off-road vehicles made their appearance at the far end of the Flats, churning a tornado of dust behind them, thundering toward the two women at speeds it was impossible to contest on foot. Annunciata felt the same restless anger in her heart she had known when the Off-Roaders chased away the Unicorn three nights earlier with their monster-eyed headlights and cutting motors. Now she saw the vehicles behind the sharp beams: big-wheeled, odd-shaped machines, covered in their own dust, the drivers faceless behind goggles and masks, many of the machines without a skin—just powerful engines and exposed, muscular springs bolted into skeletal frames. From their point of standstill, Annunciata gripped the older woman's hand tighter and they began running again, fleeing faster and faster, trying to reach the other side of the Flats before—

Their escape was cut off by a mass of Off-Roaders screaming across the Flats, forcing the women to stop in the choking dust.

The Lady Fair turned her body around to look for escape back to the Last Mountain: Off-Roaders whirled in skidding half-circles to cut off that venue of retreat.

The lust of the hunt and scent of cornered prey began to

intoxicate the Off-Roaders. A green-framed Dirt Master skid-
ded by within a yard of the women, accelerating as he drew
close.

A dark yellow Hill Lord bounced over a small ramp of clay
only feet away, causing Irena to fall back into Annunciata, her
face scratched by a spray of wheel-thrown dirt.

The Off-Roaders—faceless, dust-rousing, dangerous—
slammed past the two fugitives, creating a prison whose walls
were ever shrinking together.

The Dirt Master and the Hill Lord challenged one another,
brushing in so closely by the women that Annunciata and Irena
were forced to release one another's hands, stumbling to the
ground. Angrily, Annunciata grabbed up a hand-sized rock and
hurled it at the departing vehicles.

Whether she hit anything or not was unimportant: the Lady
Fair knew at once that this was what she had to do, futile
or not. With a look of wildness Annunciata bent down and
grabbed another rock, looking over at Irena as she did so:
the European woman rose from the ground with a rock in her
hand as well, hurling it at a passing cloud of Off-Roader dust.

The two began throwing whatever they could pick up—
rocks, handfuls of pebbles, clods of earth—flinging their puny
missiles through the blind clouds of dirt churned up by the Off-
Roaders. The deafening roar of motors served only to inspire
the women's reckless defense, retreating sometimes, pursuing
sometimes—gestures not of desperation, but of defiance.

A rock struck a windshield, networking it into a spider's
web of cracks.

The Hill Lord drove in between Annunciata and Irena, causing them to separate.

Somehow one of Irena's larger hurled stones hit an Off-
Roader's front wheel at a vulnerable angle, forcing it to twist,
causing the steering wheel to rip from its driver's hand and
sending the vehicle into a tire-blowing skid.

Neither woman saw the success: they were too busy throwing furiously. The Off-Roaders, exhilarated by the dangerous
game, spun out in deliriously tight circles around their quarry.
The Dirt Master played payback: the green-skeleton'd vehicle
bent in tight on Irena, lashing her arm with its whipping radio
aerial. The European woman was knocked to the ground. Tears
of pain welled up in her deep-set eyes, but Irena immediately
rolled back onto her feet to avoid the charging wheels of

another Off-Roader. Her arm was useless for throwing now, numb.

Annunciata looked across the twenty yards separating her from the injured Irena and felt the hopelessness of their situation penetrate her anger: to continue resisting the vigilante posse of Off-Roaders would only incite them further, would only invite further injury to the innocent. Or maybe it was too late: the violence-lust of the Off-Roaders would not be satiated by submission. Oddly, the Lady Fair did not think of her own safety at this moment. With the same realization of failure that filled the Rider watching helplessly from above, Annunciata began running away from the European woman, hoping to draw the hunt-crazed Off-Roaders after their true prey.

She did not expect to go far.

Lope had been watching the cycloning clouds of dust roar distantly on the Flats below for minutes, his eyes drawn to the miniature portrait of chaos without comprehending the reason why. Los Barracudas had seen the Off-Roaders pass on their way down to the Flats earlier, an unspoken tension between the sleek-vehicled Low Riders and the skeleton-riding power drivers charging the mountain atmosphere. When Los Barracudas' jefe heard the Off-Roaders making pass after pass across the Flats, he stepped over to the highway's edge to look down on the foreign spectacle: the skeletal vehicles were circling something, something lost in the fog of dust raised by their churning, oversized wheels. Lope snorted contemptuously at the Off-Roaders' lack of mastery on the Flats: over such terrain, he knew, even the smaller-wheeled Los Barracudas could ride their cars easily, fly with skill across the hard-packed, sand-and-clay surface.

Blond Annie grabbed Lope's arm and wrenched his attention away from the mesmerizing tableau. She shook her bleached mane violently, trying to form the urgent words with her darkly red mouth:

"Tha Oo-ni-cor!" she cried with muffled accents, the word unfamiliar to her lips' muscle memory. "U-N-I-C-O-R-N!" her clawed fingers spelled out, not remembering the Sign for the golden-horned animal's existence.

Lope did not know the word in either instance. He stared at Blond Annie, uncomprehending.

"Annunciata!" Annie screamed without sound, pointing at the center of the chaos of dust on the Flats, then sweeping her arm to a small cliff midway between the highway's edge and the scene below. Lope saw nothing at first—

"Oo-ni-cor-*nah*!" Annie repeated.

And then—the thought pushed into his imagination—Lope recognized the magic beast:

A Unicorn!

Lope looked in belief, raised his fist, and slammed it down onto his car horn!

The loud, triumphant horn—joined by one—two—five others!—echoed into the mountain range and bounced down on the Flats redoubled, tripled in volume!

Irena, holding her numb arm, raised her head, searching the sky for the source of the incongruent fanfare.

Annunciata, racing desperate from the pursuing threat of the Dirt Master, ceased running abruptly and let her eyes scan the horizon—

The Off-Roaders, too, heard the choral horns. The Dirt Master bypassed the motionless Annunciata, regrouping with the Hill Lord and others, understanding the challenge—

And each one saw what was meant to be seen.

For the expectant Lady Fair—and the wondrously shocked Irena—the Unicorn's white, magnificent form appeared on the crest of a far hill—pawing at the earth, impatient—then leapt out impossibly through space to land on the Flats and gallop toward the women.

For the Off-Roaders—to the rough eyes of the Dirt Master and callous Hill Lord—there was the punk threat of the wetback Low Riders lining the rim above the Flats, sounding their ancient car horns in personal challenge to the Off-Roaders' domain.

Lope kept his hand pressed down hard on the horn as he stepped around the wide car door and into the driver's seat, seeing now both the Unicorn and Annunciata. He did not care if the other Los Barracudas saw the golden-horned beast—*he* did, that was enough—and he understood, finally, the service he must give to his cousin. Lope strapped his seatbelt tight with his free hand, then adjusted his mirrors: he could see the women passengers of Los Barracudas getting out of their boyfriends' cars, running to the safety of the nearby rocks.

"Go, please," he looked at Blond Annie and traced the words with delicate plea in the air.

Her half-smile was decisive: Blond Annie shook her head no, leaned over, and touched the tip of her tongue to his. Lope removed his hand from the car horn to help his woman lock her seatbelt into place. The White's engine purred with anticipation as he led the two Reds and three Blacks along the dirt road leading from the highway down onto the Flats.

But it was the Unicorn that guided Lope's Barracuda, loping across the Flats in long, glorious strides, displaying such speed and power as he pounded across the dry, hard ground, racing through the unseeing, self-concerned Off-Roaders, that dust rose in his wake like a bronze fog.

Or perhaps some of the drivers did see: there was never a straight report about it afterwards and, as Karus had observed about the boys at the stream, none of the Off-Roaders had any reason *not* to lie. In either event, because of the Unicorn or because of the advancing Low Riders, the Off-Roaders drew back from the two women as the Unicorn raced toward his Lady Fair.

He drew next to Annunciata first. But the young woman did not mount her magic beast, leading him over to Irena: it was only after helping the injured woman onto his back that the Lady Fair climbed up herself, sitting behind. She guided the other's hands to grasp the Unicorn's long, white mane. Without need for direction, the golden-horned animal turned toward the Last Mountain, where his Rider waited at the Place.

With the instinctive perception of a leader, Lope noticed the direction the Unicorn intended to head and guided Los Barracudas toward it. Driving across the broad Flats, not yet in high gear, the vehicles drifted into their parade formation: their jefe's White—*La Blanca*; the two Reds in a pair behind—*Los Rojos*; the three Blacks fanned out in rear guard—*Los Negros*! They followed Lope's Barracuda in a wide, sweeping arc that put the Unicorn's Last Mountain behind them all, drifting to a slow stop to face the threatening Off-Roaders.

Lope had no time now to pay attention to the Unicorn, other than to peripherally notice the beast's careful progress across the Flats toward the Low Riders, his pace increasing to the speed of a canter, the canter lengthening into long, stretching strides over the hard earth. It was Blond Annie's eyes that were free from concentration upon the Off-Roaders beginning to muster their force in dust-raising circles behind the loping Unicorn, seeing Annunciata and another woman bent low on the magic animal's back. A wildness filled Annunciata's eyes; a reckless madness informed her every gesture in response to the Unicorn's movement, as if she, too, could race over the ground like her steed.

The Off-Roaders began to charge forward.

Lope shifted his Barracuda into gear.

The Dirt Master and the Hill Lord jumped out in advance of the pack, spewing their threatening cloud of dust and exhaust into the sky.

Los Barracudas followed their jefe's lead, hard pyramid formation, widely spaced, their highway tires spinning across the sandy earth grabbing for traction, accelerating rapidly.

The Unicorn's magnificent speed could not outrace the Off-Roaders, Blond Annie saw: the Dirt Master and the Hill Lord were gaining distance.

A blowout behind the White—Manolo's Red swerved uncontrollably to the side, spinning into obscurity within a cloud of dust.

The Dirt Master's driver flipped an obscene finger high overhead to taunt the Low Riders.

Tomas' Black hit a shelf of wind-eroded clay and launched off it as if from a ramp, soaring through the air a dozen yards before landing with a muffler-crushing jolt and regaining control.

The Hill Lord's driver could not believe that the white Barracuda charging at him would not fly off its wheels from a similar clay ramp lying between them. He surged forward, confident that the Low Rider would have to lose courage or crash.

The Unicorn reached the first Low Rider—Lope's White—flashing by Blond Annie's face and through the following ranks of Los Barracudas. Annunciata's piercing eyes met the Aztec gleam in Lope's, a cry of triumph on his lips, Blond Annie's long-nailed fingers flashing in rage—

The White hit the clay shelf at accelerated speed—

The Hill Lord saw the Barracuda hurtling through the air toward him: he jammed on his brakes, dragged the steering wheel with all his strength!

The Dirt Master felt the side-plowing smash of the Hill Lord shatter its skeletal frame without benefit of warning:

his attention was on the red Barracuda sliding forward in a long, screaming skid of dust and burning brakes. Behind them both, the White came to earth solidly and disappeared in the next cloud of dirt, sending two Off-Roaders splitting off from their forward charge, jerking into their companions. The unformed mass of Off-Roaders lost sight of one another as the remaining ranks of Low Riders drove into their midst, a confusing clench of dust and noise, abrupt, thudding collisions and the emptily revving motors of overturning vehicles whose wheels, freed from traction with the earth, clawed emptily at the clouded air.

The Unicorn did not slow his pace to witness the apocalypse: his time to die was fast approaching, he had neither the leisure nor the inclination to see the humans harm one another. His powerful legs crested the steep hill Annunciata and Irena had descended so recently, driving up through the loose earth to arrive at the edge where Karus had stood his ground.

The Rider, in fact, was preparing to join his Lady Fair in her desperate battle down on the Flats: his back to the scene below, he had just finished tying the three defeated Auxiliary Deputies to a tree, using their shoelaces and belts, preparatory to descending the hill himself. He was surprised, then, to step away from his task and turn toward the edge—and see the Unicorn standing there, only feet away, with Annunciata and Irena on his back.

Karus had never seen the Unicorn before.

And yet—he had always known. Gently, the Rider stepped toward the Unicorn, helping the women off his back. As he set down the Lady Fair:

"Thank you . . . for bringing him to me."

Mara watched the humans pay respect to the Unicorn and turned away from the clearing: the Unicorn's magic was not attractive to the wolf-dog, the forest was. She would let the others share in the Unicorn's presence.

Karus began currying the magical beast with his hands, his fingers clawlike, yet loving. Sad.

". . . Are you tired? . . . A thousand years . . . What was it like the first years? . . ." The words were unimportant and, perhaps, the Rider only thought of them as comforting sounds as he ran his hands over the Unicorn's skin.

Until the crack of a rifle shattered their peace: the Unicorn reared on his hind legs, Karus whirled about to face the violence's source.

The Dreambreaker stood at the hill's edge, his back to the steep incline, calmly reloading the single-shot rifle he had just fired into the air. He lowered the weapon toward Karus' chest.

"Hold your hands high," Charny said with matter-of-fact confidence, "and *do not* make any sudden gestures."

Karus raised his arms over his head.

"Stop it!" Annunciata cried out suddenly. "Stop coming after us! Can't you see what we've got? We've got the Unicorn!"

Maintaining the rifle's aim on Karus' chest, The Dreambreaker looked on her as he would at an hysterical child.

"You gave us quite a chase, Miss del Rio. Don't worry, Mexico's not as bad as you remember."

Charny swept the rifle in a half-circle across the clearing to indicate to the fugitives that he had them all covered. "I'm sorry, ladies"—he gave a stern, tight-mouthed smile to Irena—"I don't even know who *you* are—but all of you have given too much trouble to let you keep your arms down." He made a very clear motion with the rifle. "Up, please . . ."

"You can't stop us now!" the Lady Fair demanded, refusing to raise her arms. "Go away! We're here, we made it! This is—"

The Rider cut her off: "He can't see it."

"Of course he can, you're . . ." She, too, suddenly understood The Dreambreaker's limitation.

Karus stood before the Unicorn, the magic beast still invisible to Charny's doubt-filled eyes, and asked rhetorically: "You can't see anything, can you?"

"I can see what's necessary," the Immigration official replied, adding sarcastically: "Please—don't cop an insanity plea on me, I would like to respect you." He turned his attention on Annunciata again. "That was not a request I made: Hands—up!"

Reluctantly, the Lady Fair lifted her hands and clasped them across the back of her crewcut head sullenly: *What good had been* that *sacrifice?* she thought angrily, feeling the cropped hairs that replaced the silken tresses of her life before, *What use has* all *of this been?!*

—For me.

Annunciata heard the Unicorn's thoughts and saw him paw the ground impatiently with a forehoof.

—*And for what I shared with you.*

The Lady Fair decided to distract The Dreambreaker's attention, give the Unicorn and his Rider a chance to escape. Another sacrifice could be endured—

But the Rider, too, had listened to the Unicorn.

"It's time, isn't it?" he asked, not knowing how to think the thoughts, turning his back on The Dreambreaker. The provocation irked.

"Turn around!" Charny commanded. Catching his annoyance before it escalated into anger, he continued in a calmer, still superior tone: "And you're right about the time—it's time to leave."

The Rider turned halfway back around, facing his Lady Fair to ask: "You *are* legal, aren't you? You can handle it?"

Wrenched from her own thoughts of action, Annunciata was uncertain where his questions were leading. "Uh-huh," she answered vaguely. Irena stepped next to the young woman to assure the Rider: "I will help her."

"Get back! Don't stand together!" Charny ordered.

"Sorry, can't go with you," the Rider turned to face The Dreambreaker, offering a reasonable smile.

Charny returned the same expression. "We can wait, then. I'll untie our friends here"—the three Auxiliaries were still dazed and staring stupidly at the ground from exhaustion—"when they're feeling more awake. *They* can escort you down."

"Sorry, can't wait."

The Dreambreaker laughed. "Can't go, can't wait, you're—"

Karus dived suddenly to the ground, rolling sideways; Charny instinctively fired at where the captive had stood—

Striking the Unicorn in the shoulder!

For a flashing second, The Dreambreaker saw the image of a magnificent beast rearing up in pain, a bright streak of red running down its side. Then the disillusioned memory that all things die and mean nothing erased the image, and Charny was left with only the thought that he had missed his target. He began to hurriedly eject the hot, empty shell casing from his rifle and reload. His unexpected nervousness made his fingers stumble and he lost a precious second, then another.

Annunciata stared at the wounded Unicorn in shock, then rushed to his side.

Lying in the dirt, Karus understood the situation at once and continued with his original strategy: raising himself from the ground, the Rider charged at The Dreambreaker, trying to reach the man before—

Charny pushed the shell in, firing from the hip.

Karus reeled from the glancing blow, his ribs pushed so hard by the grazing slam of the bullet that he practically spun around, the wind knocked from his lungs. But only for a second: he continued to charge.

Surprised, Charny did not start to reload immediately. But when he finally did, his fingers did not fumble this time: he snapped out the empty shell, pushed in a new one, raised the barrel—

Karus grabbed the weapon by its barrel, feeling the flash of the discharge burn his palm as he ripped it from The Dreambreaker's hands and flung it aside.

Still charging forward, the Rider shoved his body into Charny's, driving The Dreambreaker back toward the edge of the hill, gripping the startled man under the arms and raising him over the edge—

Then stopped.

Thrown backwards, without a chance for balance, it was a fatal drop.

Karus smiled: in a single motion he let the INS agent slide down to a foothold, raised his right hand into a fist, and slammed a punch down on The Dreambreaker's jaw that sent the man sprawling across the ground, unconscious.

Then the Rider fainted from lack of oxygen in his rib-crushed lungs, a smile of triumph across his face as he tried to turn to the Unicorn.

Irena was at his side immediately.

Her medical skills were unnecessary.

The Unicorn snorted in approval at the Lady Fair and Rider he had chosen—and at the second, beautiful woman they had brought with them (*Too late!*) he thought with rueful pleasure. *Too late for that!*)—then walked over to the fallen Rider, touching his golden horn to the man's ribs and healing them instantly.

—*There is no more time.* His magic eyes smiled down into his Rider's. Grabbing at the long white mane, Karus pulled himself up to standing, then onto the Unicorn's back with difficulty. He looked over at Irena and confessed: "He forgot to touch my legs. I'm afraid the muscles are a little cramped"—the Rider added a tiny grin—"Doctor."

It earned a flash of smile in return.

Then the deep-eyed woman stepped close to the Rider and began massaging his leg muscles, letting her hands experience the Unicorn through him.

Annunciata walked near to the Unicorn's opposite flank, bringing her fingers close to his bleeding wound, stopping just short of doing so. The Unicorn's gentle muzzle brushed against her proud head.

—*Thank you, Lady Fair, for helping us.*

The Unicorn raised his eyes, alert: the coordinated search parties, led now by the Ranger Superintendent, Don Taylor, appeared at the far end of the clearing. The golden-horned beast shook his head.

The Lady Fair saw two drops of blood streak from her Unicorn's side onto the ground.

The Rider bent his head close to the Unicorn's: hands clenched in the white mane, he guided the magic beast backwards, away from the steep falling edge.

Next to the Superintendent, an Auxiliary Deputy raised his rifle and took aim at the strange horse and escaping fugitive. Don Taylor angrily knocked the barrel skyward.

The sound of the gunshot echoed through the treetops.

The Unicorn, Rider hugging close to his body, galloped forward to the edge and leapt into the air over the clifflike incline. He stretched his white legs out into the empty space—slowly—beautifully—and disappeared as if he had been a dream melting away . . .

Annunciata let her eyes linger on the empty space.

Then, as her shoulders straightened in simple, classic noblesse, she tilted her elegant profile down to review the fate of her rescuers.

The keening wind still persisted, appropriate now, more forceful, smothering all other sounds rising up from the Flats. It was justified now: several vehicles lay disabled, strewn about in smoking wrecks—all but two of them Off-Roaders. One Red and two Blacks could be seen reascending the dirt road to the highway. Lope's White was still below, the inarticulate jefe of Los Barracudas helping Tomas of the disabled Black out of the ruin, then setting fire to a rag stuffed into the car's gas cap. Doña Sylvia del Rio would understand her grandson: no prizes for the remaining Off-Roaders to scavenge. Manolo saw what they did and performed the same act on his shattered Red. He limped across the Flats to join the others at the White, where Blond Annie waited outside the car, her eyes first on Lope, then—attracted by Annunciata's straightforward gaze—to the Last Mountain.

"Dave, get them untied from the trees."

Annunciata heard the voice behind her—she watched Lope's White roar away with a confidence of motor and driving skill—then returned her attention to the clearing: her rescuers were unharmed, she would thank them later. A Forest Ranger was apparently in command of the situation for the moment. "See if anybody is hurt," he was saying.

Annunciata smiled gently at the expressions of indecision plastered across the men's faces surrounding her and Irena: obviously, unlike The Dreambreaker, they *had* seen. Only the Superintendent was keeping things moving, by quickly and quietly giving the men specific tasks.

"Bill, go and try to wake up Charny."

Peyton flashed a sour look at his Superintendent.

"Kick him if you want," Don Taylor added by way of placating his Ranger's displeasure in having to deal with the Immigration agent. He began to approach the European woman, who stepped over to the young Latina and embraced her in a protective hug.

"Dr. Brandon?" Don Taylor asked, recognizing the late Hubert's daughter.

Irena turned to face the Superintendent with a defiant set to her jaw.

"I thought it was you," he added, holding out his hand in greeting.

The Superintendent was at the edge of the steep hill, next to them now. He looked down at the wreckage-scarred Flats: two unidentifiable vehicles in a complete blaze and a half-dozen disabled Off-Roaders. A few photographs of this would convince the politicians to ban the Off-Roaders from his forest. He gave his attention back to the two women.

"Do you know her, Dr. Brandon?" he asked with a nod to the Latino woman.

Annunciata smiled into the Superintendent's eyes, prodding more than his conscience.

"Her name is Annunciata Cymbelina de las Flores del Rio," he heard Irena Brandon say. "I vouch for her."

Don Taylor ducked his head, surprised by the depths of meaning he had seen in the young woman's eyes. "That'll be enough for Mr. Charny's case, then," he said without second thought on the decision. "He can go back to L.A. empty-handed."

The Superintendent stepped over to where Bill Peyton was holding the groggy Immigration official in precarious balance leaning against a tree. He had a few choice thoughts he wanted to share. "I think we'll keep the report brief: there was no case. Don't go into details, Mr. Charny."

"I want—" Charny began to protest . . .

—To be cut off by a semi-long speech sternly explaining that "The details," as the Ranger and his men were already simultaneously forgetting and remembering them, involved "an eyewitness account of an INS agent—you, Mr. Charny—shooting with *unprovoked disregard for public safety at a local doctor* and a dark-skinned *American* woman of Mexican heritage." That sounded right to Don Taylor: he felt certain his wife, Carmelita, would appreciate this interpretation of events if Charny pushed for a hearing. (About the Unicorn, he would only whisper the story to Carmelita in the dark, when they were close together in bed. It had happened so quickly, there had been no time to savor the wonder of its presence through the temper of the moment. But the feeling . . .)

Annunciata returned Irena's warm hug now, feeling in the woman a need to share the day's experience longer than for just the moment. *Abalita will like Irena,* she thought. Over her shoulder, Annunciata saw the half-wolf's huge head peer down from a high outcropping of rock.

"Irena," she said quietly with a comforting voice, then let Hubert's daughter go over to Mara alone.

But the wolf-dog's eyes remained fixed in a piercing stare at the ground, even as Irena came and grasped her masklike face in an emotional embrace. Annunciata turned to where the animal's look was aimed—

Near the edge of the steep fall, where two drops of the Unicorn's blood had spilled on the hard ground—and still glistened in red wetness—two full-grown flowers now stood. Annunciata lowered her well-formed head to the blossoms, the worthless jewel in her newly exposed earring sparkling pricelessly, her hazel eyes dazzled by the rich colour, so close to her now.

There was a small sound.

Almost a tinkling of glass.

But deeper (just as fragile, though) . . .

PICHILINGIS

The Virgin Mother was unhappy: she did not like disagreements, and here was one facing her with steadfast refusal to go away.

The Creator could decide for punishment, of course. A Special Creation interfering with human affairs was never allowed; the Unicorn had known that five hundred years ago—but the Creator deferred to the Son.

The Son could decide easily enough for mercy, but His friend, the Apostle Saint James the Moor-Slayer, was offended by the Unicorn. The Son deferred to His Mother.

Fra Benedicto pleaded on the Unicorn's behalf: "He found a Rider!" the minor saint pointed out. ("He was your own descendant," Santiago snidely noted. "A Rider, nevertheless," Benedicto replied.) Did that outweigh the crime of having set loose the horses upon the humans?

What else could she weigh in the Unicorn's favor?

The Rider—

Karus sat astride the Unicorn and felt their debate in his soul, unprepared for the nether to which they had come—and unafraid.

—*I will not abandon you,* he let the golden-horned beast know. He refused to put forth any argument on his own behalf, lest he be raised higher than the Unicorn and separated from his steed.

The Lady Fair—

She was changed, that was obvious for all to see: materially, because of the gold (again Santiago brought up the conundrum: the girl's original impulse had been greed); personally, in her acceptance of a responsibility for herself that went beyond simple self-interest. She lived between the two older women now: her grandmother and the doctor who had helped. ("He found *another* human to help him!" Benedicto cried in the Unicorn's defense. "She helped the girl," Santiago answered. "A Lady Fair!" Benedicto protested, his ex-hidalgo's blood raging with pride at the Apostle-Saint's refusal to see that the Lady Fair-Rider-Unicorn were all of a same.)

The arguments were all too impassioned and—*human*—which was why the Virgin Mother was left to decide: the Creator could never understand; the Son was still too divine. The Virgin Mother could touch a human soul and understand.

Her understanding always led back to the Unicorn, who had abandoned his dispassion for human affairs. Why?

It would show in his eyes, but that story was too deep, never-ending. Maybe a moment would tell . . .

After the horses had been set loose, half the millennium before his Last Mountain . . .

The Unicorn turned away from the long river and headed south again. Against his own judgement, after three years of wandering, he returned to Tenochtitlán, full-blown capital of the thriving New Spain.

His Lady was dead.

She was killed by a fever sweeping through the city and given impetus by the polluted waters of the lake. Thirty thousand Indios died with her, but it was not enough to hinder the work of construction the Spanish conquerors demanded of their vassals.

Hernando Cortés was back in Castile, stripped of power, pleading with the King to restore him to his governorship, subtly stolen from him by the machinations of Guzman and his intrigues.

The Unicorn felt bitter pleasure at the Lady's death: she was not there to be shamed by the actions of her brother. The "respected" *caballero* Don Miguel had joined with her "noble" husband in a new territorial enterprise among the Indio nations to the northwest. It was an enterprise that expanded the wealth of the rapacious Guzman, if not the Crown and New Spain. Honor was not a consideration; Miguel had forsaken that long before.

The Unicorn could not find Fra Benedicto.

He did not know that the old friar, defeated, had travelled westward—so far west as to join the East, believing he had found in Nippon a land where one could offer simple testimony without interference of politics and empire. He was wrong. Fra Benedicto, as the Creator's Son had hinted to the Shadow of Death a half-century earlier, joined the ranks of the Saints by his martyrdom there, vaguely distressed in his old man's con-fusion at the unwarranted persecution of his converts, know-ing only that he would not take the preferred opportunity to flee given him. He would not desert the people who believed in him. Not this time. The Virgin Mother took an immediate liking to his devotion, and embraced his soul in hers, where Benedicto used every opportunity he could to convince the Virgin Mother to use her influence and help temper the Creator's displeasure with the Unicorn.

But the Unicorn was unaware of this tragedy and redemption on his behalf: broken now with the vow to avoid interference in human affairs, he was left alone to wander the streets of Tenochtitlán and face their constant reminders of the complex beauty and ugliness of human *souls*. He knew that his soul, too, had been infected.

Once again the Unicorn decided to leave the city, this time to explore the wilderness north of the long river, or maybe to the west. He would avoid the mustangs as long as possible. He set out at midnight, walking through the silent city in full view of the moon and stars.

A sudden irritation clutched at his skin as the Unicorn made his final cross by the plaza where the Hummingbird's temple once stood. Just as suddenly, the sensation was gone.

His mane was plucked at—

—and then his tail.

The Unicorn stamped with annoyance. A small chorus of voices cheered. The Unicorn kicked back with his hind legs and felt his hooves make contact.

A dozen tiny fingers pinched his skin.

The Unicorn snapped his teeth, then stopped moving entirely.

Pluck, pluck! His muzzle was touched.

The Unicorn did not move.

Pluck, pluck, pluck! The long hairs in his tail were painfully attacked.

The Unicorn remained motionless.

Pluck—

—*Please! Do something!*

The face of an imp popped up before the Unicorn's eyes, joined by a handful of pichilingi brothers pleading with the magical beast to display annoyed recognition of their irritating behavior.

—*Pinch away, pluck away, bite away, fly!* the Unicorn answered, the edges of a smile beginning to return to his heart.

They did.

He did nothing.

—*Pleeeeeeeease!!* the minuscule voices cried.

—*Bother others, not me.*

—*There are only humans here to bother. The Gods are gone.*

—*The Gods are dead.* The Unicorn shook his head slowly and let his mane be plucked. A row of dejected pichilingis sat down on the cobblestones at his feet.

—*The Gods are dead, we know.*

They did not even trouble themselves to bother the Unicorn as he knelt before them.

—*How did you survive? This was the Creator's doing.*

A tiny pichilingi, smaller than most, raised himself up to a full-blown speck before the Unicorn's eye to declaim:

—*I don't know. I guess we just were forgotten.*

ACKNOWLEDGMENTS

It is always a pleasure to thank those who have helped one create—some directly, some indirectly. All of the following played a part in the writing of *Last Mountain*, to me at least, whether aware of my existence or not: Witold Lesczynski's beautiful film *Konopielka*; Mikhail Bulgakov's tragi-comic satire *The Master and Margarita*; Steve Szpak-Fleet and my own film *Brothers of the Wilderness,* along with Bitsy Topper and her colleagues from the San Bernardino National Forest Ranger Station, plus Joe Davidson and his folks at Follow's Camp; Aftab, Shagufta, Umar and Tariq Hassan at Theo's Cafe; the historical writings of Fernando Benitez and T. R. Fehrenbach (among dozens of other reference authors); the recounters of myth Nancy Hathaway, Carleton Beals and Anthony John Campos (again, from dozens of excellent resource authors); my street Spanish translators Chrissy Cajas, David Pizano and David Quezada; Sharyn Lynne Sala, Esq., and Archie Lee Simpson for their insights into the L.A. "system"; Denny Dillon, Leslie Caron, Audrey Hepburn and Alina Szpak—beautiful inspirations all; and, very deeply, Messrs. William Shakespeare and Jean Giraudoux. I must also acknowledge—although *thanking* is inappropriate—the Immigration and Naturalization Service for so regularly demonstrating to me on a personal and public level the inherent tension between ideals, justice and law—and, of course, the United States Supreme Court, whom I have quoted verbatim in this novel. It-it-it's all *real*, folks!

RCF